Life Swap

For Tina

With best wishes ~ great to meet
you at last.

Carol x

Life Swap

CAROL WYER

Bookouture

Published by Bookouture

An imprint of StoryFire Ltd.
23 Sussex Road, Ickenham, UB10 8PN
United Kingdom

www.bookouture.com

ISBN: 978-1-910751-73-2
eBook ISBN: 978-1-910751-72-5

ACKNOWLEDGEMENTS

I have a few people to thank for helping me write *Life Swap,* starting with car salesman Andy Beach, who patiently put up with me wandering into the showroom at regular intervals. He explained selling techniques and revealed what goes on behind the scenes yet didn't once insist I purchase a new car.

Inspiration for the book came from a variety of sources including Nikki Bywater and her famous collection of outrageous socks. I really want those Minion socks, Nikki. Special thanks to my blogging pal Diane Croad who has been a terrific friend and fantastic support since I began writing in 2009. She gave me an insight into owning a French bulldog and introduced me to the totally adorable Alfred, who won my heart.

Some days I'm overwhelmed by the kindness of folk I have met online. Many have become true friends and one of the nicest is Kim Nash, who has encouraged me from the start of my blogging and writing career.

I want to thank the wonderful team at Bookouture, especially Lydia Vassar-Smith for editing *Life Swap* and for coming up with some excellent suggestions to make the book even better.

Last but definitely not least, my heartfelt thanks to you, the readers. Your comments, reviews, messages and emails about my books keep me writing. My thanks to each and every one of you.

CHAPTER ONE
Simon

Simon Green was drowning in a large vat of fluffy white marsh-mallows. He flailed beneath the killer's powerful hands, which were forcing him deeper into the gooey, vanilla depths, each marshmallow stifling his ragged breaths and blocking his respiratory passages. Some primeval instinct warned him this was no dream. He came to in an instant, heart thudding, aware he could neither open his eyes nor breathe. Simon attempted to thrash his head from side to side to no avail. He was pinned down by a leaden weight. One word sprang to mind: *Ivan.* Now fully conscious, Simon scrabbled to grip his attacker by the neck then tugged with all his strength. He felt a cool draught on his cheeks and gulped in a lungful of air, still clinging on to his assailant. The enormous tabby cat stared back defiantly, irritation visible in its chartreuse eyes. It was the second time in a week the damn cat had cut off his air supply while he was asleep. *Was it trying to bump him off?* Simon considered launching the animal through the bedroom window. Ivan hissed and instinctively unsheathed his claws.

'Is that my precious little bundle?' mumbled a voice from beside Simon. On cue, the cat withdrew its claws and let out a pitiful meow.

'Simon,' said his wife, Veronica, in a sharp tone. 'What are you doing? Put Ivan down at once!' Then in a grating little-girl voice she continued, 'Come to Mummy, Ivan. Daddy was going to try and push my furry baby off the bed, wasn't he? Naughty Daddy. Ignore him. He's just a big bad-tempered bully because he drank too much last night.'

Simon released the hefty animal. Ivan fell onto the bed with a *whoomp*. Veronica's plump arm emerged from under the duvet. She extended her hand towards Ivan and waggled her pasty fingers. Simon removed the cat fur from between his teeth and checked the clock display – it was only six o'clock. *Wretched animal.* He huffed in irritation then attempted to snuggle down under the duvet. The cat, now on its back and basking in its mistress's attention, surveyed him with disdain, a sneer almost visible on its face. Veronica cooed at Ivan. The Machiavellian moggy had taken a recent dislike to Simon – a feeling that was reciprocated. It had either taken offence because a few days earlier Simon had booted it from his favourite chair, or it felt some weird rivalry over Veronica. As far as Simon was concerned, Ivan was welcome to her. She was nothing but a right old nag.

'Poor baby,' continued Veronica in her irritating voice. 'You're pining for Georgie, aren't you?'

Simon glowered at the pampered cat. It didn't look too dismayed by the absence of its sulky mistress, their teenage daughter. Simon wasn't missing her or the sullen strops and general bad temper that Georgina now displayed. Whatever had happened to his little princess? Only last year, when she was a content twelve-year-old, they had been the best of friends. He had always been close to Georgie. They shared the same silly sense of humour and would often sit together on the sofa watching Lee Evans or Harry Hill, snorting with laughter while Veronica surveyed them with a po-faced expression. These days his daughter either ignored him or snapped at him almost as much as Veronica. Maybe she would be in a better mood when she returned from her trip. On reflection, that was as likely as him winning the EuroMillions. He sighed, heaved himself from the bed and pulled on his tortoiseshell-framed glasses. The room swam into clearer vision.

'Tea, dear?' he asked, as he did every morning. Veronica made some non-committal noise. Simon shrugged on his dressing gown. The cat stretched languorously, filling the space he had vacated.

'Don't forget to fix Georgie's wardrobe door before she gets back,' said Veronica, turning over onto her side.

'I still don't see why the school decided to take them to China,' he complained, pushing his feet into his slippers and noting that the sole on one was coming adrift. He examined them. The tops appeared to have been chewed. *Bloody cat!* He scowled at Ivan. 'When I was her age we considered ourselves fortunate if we went on the annual day trip to Boulogne.'

'Not again, Simon,' mumbled Veronica. 'It's cultural, for heaven's sake. Think of all the marvels she's visiting and experiences she's having. It'll open her eyes to the world.'

'Opened my wallet, more like – eight hundred pounds. Jesus! We can't even afford a week in Bognor—' He stopped ranting. Veronica had opened one eye and was giving him *that* look.

'Shut up, Simon. You're a miserable old skinflint. You couldn't refuse to send her. She'd have been the only one in the school year not to go. It'll do her good and, after all, we should make sacrifices for our kids. That's what parents do. You're in a bad mood – probably thanks to that second bottle of wine. I told you not to open it. Go and get a coffee and cheer up, for goodness sake. Georgie will be back at the weekend. Try and have the wardrobe mended by then.'

'Yes, dear.' Simon had learned a long time ago that the best way to handle Veronica was to do as she said. If crossed, Veronica could make life very difficult. He recalled one particular occasion he'd annoyed her – 3 March 2005 – when she'd lost it big time and threw his prized collection of classic-car magazines into the recycling bin, screamed obscenities at him while he was getting changed from work, then pushed him out the back door and locked him out of the house. Wearing only underpants and socks, he'd spent the night in his shed, sitting on an uncomfortable old deckchair under a smelly blanket. The fumes from his lawnmower had given him the headache of all headaches, which was compounded when he was finally allowed back into the house only to be treated to more yelling. In the following ten years, he'd never forgotten another wedding anniversary.

In his defence, he'd been under a lot of pressure at the time. He'd been trying to get the title of 'salesman of the month' to win the extra thousand pounds he desperately needed to help pay the mortgage and all the bills they had racked up by moving to a larger house – a house that Veronica had insisted on buying. 'It's in a gorgeous village, Simon. It's so picturesque there, Simon. It has a wonderful village school nearby – perfect for the children. There's even a pub up the road, Simon. I know it's a bit out of our price range, but I love it. Let's buy it, Simon. Please!' Funny: the pressure had never let up since.

Simon heaved a sigh. Ivan, still observing his movements, began to lick one leg. It was fine for him. He got oodles of attention and fuss from the female members of the household. He was fed on demand and had no worries. Apart from eating his way through mountains of food, Ivan's only other interest seemed to be sleeping. Simon lugged himself into the bathroom, ensuring he didn't disturb the now slumbering Veronica. He lifted his glasses and peered into the mirror. Mistake. The man with dark circles under his eyes who squinted back at him appeared to be in his late fifties, not late forties. He touched the balding patch on the top of his head and cursed. It appeared to have grown larger overnight. He braved a closer look in the mirror and recoiled.

The bloodshot eyes were too much to face at this hour of the day. He should not have drunk all that wine. He didn't normally drink that much and certainly not during the week. Something crashed in the kitchen below. The reason he'd been up drinking into the small hours had finally returned home. Simon headed downstairs to do battle.

His seventeen-year-old son Haydon stood by the open fridge door, drinking from a carton of milk.

'Do you have to do that?' grumbled Simon.

Haydon shrugged, wiped his mouth with the back of his hand and replied, 'Didn't want to cause you any unnecessary washing-up.'

'Rubbish. You're just lazy,' said Simon. He marched over to a cupboard, pulled out a glass and handed it to Haydon. 'Pour the milk into that. Others have to drink it too and we don't want your germs. Right. We need to talk.'

'If this is about me staying out all night…'

'You know damn well it is. We agreed you would be back by ten-thirty.'

'You agreed ten-thirty, not me. Ten-thirty is for kids. It's a stupid time to come home. No one my age goes home at ten.'

'You said you would be home by ten-thirty so don't try that line of attack with me. This isn't the first time you've ignored curfews, but it is the first time you've blatantly stayed out all night.'

'I couldn't get home at ten-thirty. The others wanted to go on to Galaxy nightclub and they'd have thought I was a right sissy if I'd insisted on coming home.'

Simon seriously doubted if anyone would think his six-foot-two-inch son was a sissy. Haydon completely dwarfed him and if he cared to admit it, Simon was somewhat jealous of his son's strength and height. No one would treat this boy like a doormat. He was always amazed at how his son could be so physically different from him. He decided that Haydon had inherited some throwback genes. Simon's grandfather had been a man-mountain too – not that Simon had ever met him. The man had keeled over and died one day at work. Simon hoped he himself hadn't inherited the weaker genes – the ones that led to heart attack and early death. If he took on any more stress he would almost certainly drop dead.

'If you'd phoned, I'd have come and got you.'

'Yeah, right. That would've looked well cool – my old man tipping up in his dressing gown and slippers to come and fetch me. You're normally in bed by ten anyway.'

Simon decided to change tack. Haydon was being defensive. He would never win an argument with the lad at this rate.

'Okay, let's look at this from a different angle,' argued Simon, running one hand through his hair. 'Think about how we felt. We knew you were going out with Ricky and Adam. When you didn't come home we started to worry.'

Haydon continued to glare. Simon decided to play his trump card.

'Your mum was frantic.' He paused. For one brief moment Haydon looked down at his feet. Haydon had always been a bit of a mummy's boy and didn't like to upset Veronica. Simon continued, 'You know how upset she can get. By eleven she wanted to phone all the hospitals in the area to make sure you hadn't been involved in an accident.'

This wasn't the case. In truth, Veronica, slumped in front of the television, hadn't been at all concerned. When Simon complained that Haydon wasn't home she told him to 'chill' and reminded him that Haydon wasn't a child. Simon had poured another glass of wine and fumed. It wasn't much to ask for his family to show him a little consideration; after all, he was their provider.

'I sent a text to let you know. I'm not an idiot,' muttered Haydon.

'Ah yes, the text that arrived at eleven-thirty. The one that said, "Wiv Adam. See you tomoz." '

'Well, at least I let you know, didn't I?'

'You did, but you were still irresponsible. Ten-thirty is ten-thirty, not eleven-thirty or six-thirty the following morning… you should have returned home when you were asked to. It's a matter of respect.'

Haydon muttered something under his breath and in a peeved tone added, 'For goodness sake, Dad. Take a chill pill. Adam's car broke down again and it was easier to stay at his place rather than get a lift back here. I'm seventeen not seven, so stop treating me like I'm some dumb kid.'

'Don't act like one then,' Simon retorted, feeling his hackles rising.

'Maybe if you let me take driving lessons, we wouldn't be having this conversation.'

Simon spluttered. 'And how am I supposed to afford lessons for you?'

'You managed to find money to send Georgie to China,' Haydon replied, crossing his arms and glowering at his father. Simon could see the marked resemblance to Veronica – the same strong chin and resolute attitude.

'That was different.'

'Yeah, of course it was. I'm not your blue-eyed little girl. That's what's different,' Haydon snapped and stomped off, leaving Simon open-mouthed.

'Haydon!' he yelled. He heard Haydon clomping upstairs.

'Haydon!'

A bedroom door slammed shut.

Simon admitted defeat. He filled the kettle and stared out of the kitchen window into the garden. The grass needed cutting again. He would have to find time this coming weekend – difficult since he was working Saturday and Sunday. The grass consisted largely of moss and weeds. It looked like he felt – past its best, tired and in need of replacing. He counted eight fresh mounds made by the resident mole. He bet he was the only person in the street with molehills.

The sound of a helicopter overhead made him grit his teeth; local multi-millionaire Tony Hedge was on his way to work. Simon bet there were no molehills in Tony's ten-acre garden. His mind drifted for a moment…

'Hi, I'm Tony Hedge. Nice to meet you,' says the man peering over the fence into Simon's garden. Simon wanders across and shakes the proffered hand. Tony has a hearty, strong handshake and a warm smile. He is wearing an outrageous Hawaiian shirt over blue shorts and flip-flops – not usual gardening attire, but somehow he carries it off with confidence. His thick, dark, wavy hair is damp with sweat. He rubs a meaty hand over his brow.

'Lousy country! We're either freezing our gonads off here or swelter-ing due to humidity. It's a rotten day to be gardening. I loathe it,' he complains, jerking a thumb in the direction of his lawnmower, abandoned in the middle of the lawn. 'I really ought to pack it all in and emigrate to somewhere like Spain, or Lanzarote – they don't have lawns there, only black volcanic sand and cacti.'

Simon agrees with him. His own T-shirt is stuck to his back thanks to the muggy day. He would prefer to be inside, but Veronica has gone out shopping and left him to sort out the tangle of weeds and neglected flowerbeds.

'Hope you're settled in okay. It's great to have neighbours again. The house has been empty for too long. Listen,' he adds after a moment's thought, 'why don't you dump that trowel and nip round here? My wife's out and I've got some cold cans of beer chilling in my man

shed. Come on round and I'll fill you in about the others here in "the hood",' he says, his grin widening. 'By the way, do you like golf?'

Simon nods enthusiastically. He knows he's going to get on just fine with his new neighbour.

Eighteen months later, Tony's business as a financial advisor had taken off. He began to attract some seriously wealthy clients; all of them eager to invest in schemes that would help preserve their earnings. Almost overnight Tony became rich. He and his wife split up, sold their house and Tony moved to a palatial property at the far end of the village. Thanks to work obligations Simon saw less and less of him. Tony started moving in very different social circles to Simon and their friendship waned. Simon sighed again. It was a pity. Tony and he had really bonded. Lucky old Tony. He had it all now – even a place in Spain for his holidays, a villa with a full-time gardener.

Simon heard the muffled thudding of rock music starting up in his son's bedroom. He finished his tea and rinsed the cup using hot water from the kettle, leaving it to drain beside the sink. Veronica hated dirty crockery lying about. He ought to get ready for work. He needed six sales this month to reach his target. He stared at the molehills. One was quivering. The little bastard was pushing up more earth.

Before he could race outside and stamp on the hill, Veronica marched into the kitchen followed by Ivan, who purred around her feet in a figure of eight, hoping for breakfast. Simon glared at the cat.

'What did you say to Haydon? He's been clumping about in his room ever since he came in. You didn't give him a hard time, did you? You did. I can tell. Why, Simon? He let us know where he was. He hasn't got any classes this week and he's a good lad. You ought to cut him some slack at the moment. He's worried sick about his A levels. He's been studying all hours this holiday. That's why I thought a night out would do him good. He doesn't need any extra pressure from you. Honestly, Simon. Don't you remember what it's like to be young? No, of course you don't. You've forgotten what fun is. You're turning into a grumpy old man,' she added, emphasising the word 'old'. She froze him with a look before opening the cupboard for food to placate the cat, whose plaintive meowing wasn't assisting the situation.

'Well there's not a great deal to be cheerful about, is there?' he replied.

The cat's bowl clattered to the floor. Veronica spun around, her face contorted with anger. 'It's no fun for me either, you know. Have you any idea what it's like living with someone who mopes about all the time grumbling about every little thing? You may go to work, but I deal with the children and their anxieties, the housework and all the other problems that crop up here and then, when you come home miserable about work, I have to maintain a positive attitude and spend every night trying to drag you out of the pit of misery you inhabit these days. It's becoming too repetitive. You're draining me with your complaints and moaning, Simon. You used to be much more... alive. That's what I loved about you – your good humour, your sense of the ridiculous and even your daft jokes. You used to be a laugh. Nowadays, you come home and slump in the chair and can hardly be bothered to talk to me or to the kids.'

'By the time I get home I'm—'

'Tired. I know, Simon. That's all you seem to say these days.' She rested against the kitchen counter and sighed, the fight drained out of her. Simon looked out of the window. The molehill quivered again. There was no point racing out to try and catch the mole. It would be long gone, burrowing deep underground in search of worms. The kitchen suddenly felt claustrophobic. He needed to get out and away from this hostile atmosphere.

'I'm going to get ready for work. I have an early start.' The words came out harsher than he intended. Veronica looked away. She'd hurt him. His mind refused to accept he was that bad to live with. Everything he did was for his family. It was a shame they didn't appreciate his efforts. He picked up the food bowl and hesitated before placing it on the worktop. Veronica continued to stare into space, ignoring him. Under the table, two large as-yellow-as-green eyes ringed with amber studied him. It was a pity the cat hadn't managed to suffocate him, he mused. There was little pleasure in living.

CHAPTER TWO
Polly

Polly MacGregor had been an angel for an entire week and hated every moment of it. It wasn't that she was a bad angel; she was simply not a very good one. At present she was trussed up in a heavy costume posing on a wall in front of Playa Meloneras, a vast sandy blanket of sunbathing space in Gran Canaria. She was one of the many living sculptures attempting to earn money from passing tourists. This was quite a change from her usual job as a sports therapist and at the moment she would much rather be back in the grey UK massaging someone's injured thigh or shoulders than standing there sweltering. She reminded herself of why she was there – it was for her best friend Kaitlin, who had sprained her ankle and couldn't bring in the much-needed cash. Polly had volunteered to replace her while she was visiting the island. Right now she regretted that choice.

'What ya s'posed to be then?' asked the small boy with a buzz cut and freckles who had been staring at her for a full five minutes. He sported a faded Bart Simpson T-shirt emblazoned with the message 'Eat My Shorts!' Polly ignored the child. She was going to be the perfect angel. She wished him joy and maintained what she considered to be a benevolent smile and pose. The child glared at her.

'You're a fairy. A fat fairy.'

Polly bristled with annoyance. 'I'm not a fairy. I'm an angel,' she hissed at the boy, who continued to stare with large, unblinking eyes. 'And,' she added against her better judgement, 'I'm not fat.'

'You're not an angel. Angels live on clouds in heaven. You're a fairy. Fat fairy, fat fairy, fat fairy,' the boy sang, pointing at her.

Polly looked about for the child's parents.

'You moved. You're not supposed to move. You're rubbish at being a fairy,' the child said.

'Go away,' she retorted.

'Why?' he asked.

'Because I'm a magic fairy and I'll turn you into a frog if you don't go away.'

'You can't do any magic.'

'I can.'

'No, you can't. You haven't got a wand. All magic fairies have wands. If you do magic, you need a wand like… Harry Potter.' He waved in the direction of the beach. 'There's a proper magic man down there. He's a wizard. He flies in the air. That's magic. Can you fly?' he asked.

'No,' she replied through gritted teeth. She wished she'd ignored the child altogether. He poked a grubby finger up his left nostril and regarded her coolly for several more minutes.

'If you can't fly like a proper fairy, then are you the tooth fairy? I've got a wobbly tooth. Want to see it? You can give me some money for it. I'll wobble it out for you.' He shoved the same finger into his mouth and pulled at his front tooth.

'No, don't do that. I'm not the tooth fairy. You'd better go. I think your parents are calling you.'

'No they're not. They're over there.' The child nodded towards a nearby café where a couple sat at a table drinking pints of lager and chatting. Polly groaned.

'Go away. Please.'

The boy continued, oblivious to her discomfort, 'And there's a pirate with no head. He had loads of birds sitting on him. I think there's some bird poop on him as well.' He giggled. 'He's cool. I like the magic tree best. It looks like a real tree. When you stop to look at it, it speaks. It has a mouth! It made my mum jump. My dad took a photo of me with it. The tree gave me a sweet.' He looked Polly up and down. 'If you can't float like the magic man and you can't fly, what can you do?'

'I mostly stand still, but I wave and give lollipops to kind people who drop coins in my pot,' she replied. 'And to nice little boys who go away and sit with their parents.'

'Give me one.'

'Only if you say "please".'

'Give me a lolly. I want one.'

'Not until you ask politely.'

The boy stared at her, a frown on his face. Without warning his lip trembled and he began to cry. The sobs turned into wails. Polly tried to calm him down by shushing at him. He was attracting looks from people passing by and from his hefty father who, concerned by the commotion, was now getting to his feet. Polly noted the bulging tattooed arms and gulped.

'Here,' she said, bending down and thrusting a small bucket at the boy. 'Take one.' A sudden ripping noise from her dress made her curse. The man was now stomping towards her. The boy grabbed a fistful of lollipops.

'Hey, only one. P-put them back,' she stuttered.

The boy wailed loudly again.

'Oy, oy, what's going on here? Are you all right, Tyson?' asked the father, placing a protective hand on the child's head.

'The fat fairy gave me all these lollies then shouted at me,' blubbed the child. 'She frightened me. And she said a bad word.

It's wrong to say bad words.' He wailed again. Polly rolled her eyes. The kid would make a great actor.

'Did she, indeed? A fine fairy you are. You should be ashamed of yourself. You don't want those, Tyson. They'll rot your teeth – nasty, cheap old lollies. Here, take 'em back and don't shout at my boy again or I'll bust your wings. Oh, and a word of advice… ease up on eating lollipops yourself. That costume's far too tight already. You seem to have split the seams on it. Good thing you're not the fairy on top of a Christmas tree. Poor tree would collapse.' He chuckled and rubbed his son's head with his large hand.

'Come on, little tiger, let's finish your lemonade and then we'll go play footie on the beach.'

The boy looked up at Polly, tossed the lollipops on the floor and stuck out his tongue. Without thinking, she thrust out her own tongue and blew a raspberry. The boy ignored her and strolled off back to his parents' table, hanging onto his father's hand. An elderly man caught her in the act and frowned at her. She sighed and slumped against the wall.

Polly was sick of being an angel. Most of the people who walked past her didn't even acknowledge her. Then there was the effort she took to get ready. No one appreciated that. And effort it was. Every morning, before they all came scuffing along the walkway, she had to paint her face and spray any exposed flesh with gold paint, struggle into a ready-made costume that allowed its owner to change position within its hooped frame yet sat firmly on Polly's ample hips, restricting her every movement. Then there were the ridiculously heavy wings that made her back ache. Finally, she had to stand completely still on a wall, sun blazing on her head, making her sticky and uncomfortable, with gold paint running down her face in little rivulets.

Mickey and Minnie Mouse wandered by and waved. Polly raised her hand in return. This part of Gran Canaria was a hotspot for tourists and, as such, attracted a variety of people all trying to earn a crust. There were the living sculptures and those like Mickey who dressed up and had photographs taken with tourists. Then there were the puppet masters and sand-sculpture artists. Meloneras beach was the smartest and most fashionable resort in Gran Canaria. Even so, Polly was still surprised to see just how packed it was with tourists. She felt exhausted observing the never-ending parade of people meandering to and from the sand dunes, cafés and hotels.

Polly dabbed at the sweat now pooling in the nape of her neck. She had never enjoyed sunbathing. Her pale complexion never went golden brown like her friend Kaitlin's. She only assumed various shades of red before her skin peeled. 'It's a sign of beauty,' her mother would say when she complained. 'Pale ladies were considered high class and beauties in the olden days. Those from poorer families or labourers would have darker, tanned faces. You are beautiful,' she said, ignoring her daughter's irritated expression.

Polly wasn't heartened by her mother's comments. She didn't live in the eighteenth century and her pasty face wasn't attractive. Kaitlin, on the other hand, glowed after only an hour in the sunshine and now, having lived here for a year, she looked like a perfect Mediterranean beauty.

This was the dumbest way to earn money she'd come across. How Kaitlin did it day after day she had no idea. Thank goodness her friend's ankle was on the mend. Polly couldn't face another moment of being an angel. Fortunately, she wouldn't have to. A Volkswagen van screeched into the car park not far from where she was standing. An athletic man wearing sunglasses and a white T-shirt that set off his deep-brown tan jumped out of the cab and sauntered towards her. A couple of young girls glanced in his direction, nudged each other and giggled as he flashed a white-toothed smile at them. Women often gawped at this raven-haired hunk with a steady gaze and the confident walk of a man comfortable with himself and life.

It was little wonder Kaitlin had fallen for him on sight. They had first met him in London when he was working in a bar …

'Oh God! Don't turn around, but I've just seen my future children's father,' gasps Kaitlin.

'If I can't turn around, you'll have to describe him to me,' replies Polly, knocking back the remainder of her drink.

'Think a brooding Joaquín Cortés with dark solemn brows and piercing eyes.'

'He's not stomping about the dance floor, is he, perspiration shining on his rugged face, as all the women watch in awe and swoon at his feet?' jokes Polly. Kaitlin ignores the comment, eyes focused on her man.

'Add to that luscious black hair I want to run my fingers through – preferably as he places his full lips on mine. And a fit body that will look amazing naked, especially his butt.' She wriggles in glee and closes her eyes, an ecstatic smile on her face as she plays out the fantasy. 'Polly, he's the one. I can see us now, naked after a lengthy session of unadulterated passion, bodies entwined, his muscular thighs draped over mine—'

'Hello. Can I get you something?' asks the young man. His honeyed voice denotes Spanish origin. 'Anything?' he adds, as Kaitlin's eyes fly open. She appears frozen in time, overcome by a debilitating inertia, eyes wide.

'Please,' says Polly, willing her friend to speak. 'Two glasses of dry white house wine,' she continues. 'Thank you, erm, what's your name?'

'Miguel.'

'Thank you, Miguel,' she repeats.

'My pleasure,' he purrs and turns back towards the bar.

Kaitlin comes to. 'Did he hear me?' she whispers.

'Judging by the smile on his face, he heard, understood and is quite keen to take you up on your offer,' replies Polly.

'Hello, angel,' Miguel said now. 'Are you ready to go?'

'Hi, Miguel. Am I glad to see you! I'm just about cooked in this outfit. Can you help me out?'

Miguel removed the cumbersome wings from her back with ease and laid them on the ground, then held her hand for support as she clambered out of the ready-made outfit. Standing now in only a swimming costume and conscious of her bulges, she grabbed a pair of denim shorts from a bag that had been propped against the wall beside her, wriggled into them and pulled on a baggy T-shirt. She scooped up her long hair and twisted it into a ponytail, securing it with a bright green band, and extracted a pot of cream to remove some of the make-up stuck to her face. Miguel ambled a little way off to give her space while she did this. He was certainly a considerate man, she mused. It had been a shock when Kaitlin had announced that she was leaving to start a life here with him, but Polly would never had prevented her best friend from doing it …

The Number One bar is jam-packed with people celebrating the start of the weekend. Polly squeezes past a group of city traders clad in designer suits and crisp shirts with ties now abandoned, stuffed in pockets or hanging loose around necks. Kaitlin is perched on a high stool by the bar, elegant in a black sleeveless dress and slingbacks. A chunky beaded necklace in vibrant orange sets off the outfit nicely and compliments her painted nails. She has two mojitos lined up in front of her and a grin stretches across her face when she spots Polly. She's flushed with excitement, pink patches on each cheek.

'Here,' she says before Polly, in jeans that are too tight, can wriggle her backside onto the barstool. Kaitlin passes a glass to her

friend and holds up two fingers to the guy behind the bar, who nods in acknowledgement. Polly swigs the mojito, savouring the taste of lime and the fresh mint that lingers on her tongue. She leans into Kaitlin. 'Come on, spill the beans,' she says. Excitement is bubbling out of Kaitlin like champagne overflowing from a glass poured too quickly.

Kaitlin's grin widens further, threatening to split her face in two. 'I've quit.'

Polly's mouth opens in a perfect 'O'.

'I've left Henderson's Bank,' she repeats, 'and all my boring colleagues. And Mr Smarmy,' she adds, referring to one of the senior members of staff who is always on her back. 'Cheers!' she shouts, clinking her glass against Polly's.

'So what next?' asks Polly.

'A bottle of champagne?' Kaitlin replies, reaching for the freshly prepared mojitos that have arrived.

'No, you ninny. What's next for you? Got another job lined up?'

Kaitlin does an impression of the Cheshire Cat but manages to look guilty at the same time.

'I'm going to Gran Canaria to live with Miguel. We've talked about it and he hates the climate here. And he doesn't want to be a barman all his life. It sounds wonderful in the Canary Islands. So much more relaxed than here. I hate the climate too and I despise my job. He has friends and family there so we'll easily find work.' The words tumble from her mouth at such speed even Polly struggles to make sense of it all.

'I'm going to write. I've always wanted to write. I'll do something simple, like waitressing and in my spare time I'll write novels. We don't need much to live on there. Oh, Polly! It'll be freedom. It'll be freedom from catching that blasted train every day; from standing underneath other people's stinking armpits in the Tube; from racing to the office in the pouring rain and from the rules, regulations,

*deadlines, targets – everything!' She stops and grabs Polly's hand.
'Not everything. I don't mean you. I'm being stupid, aren't I? Here
I am acting like a giddy schoolgirl and pretending it's perfect but
it isn't. I'll be leaving you. Come with us. Start your business in
Gran Canaria.'*

*Polly thinks for a moment. 'I really don't like too much sun and
besides, I've got Mike. I can't up and leave my boyfriend. The Canary
Islands aren't on Mars and we can Skype or email or chat on the
phone. I believe there are even those huge metal birds that fly in the
sky – what are they called? Aeroplanes?'*

Kaitlin giggles. 'Come on. Join us. It'll be a whole new adventure.'

*'No, I can't. I would really rather stay here. The business is going
well and besides, there's always Dignity to chill out with.'*

*Kaitlin nods. 'She's lovely. I'm glad she works in the treatment room
next to yours. She's always so serene. I'll miss her too. Not as much as
you though. We'll stay in touch, won't we? And you'll come to visit?'*

*Polly nods reassuringly at her friend, wanting to share in her
happiness, but inside she feels hollow. An important part of her is
about to be ripped away and Polly hopes she can survive without it.*

Miguel wandered back as she hoisted her bag onto her shoulder.
'That'll do until I get showered. I must stink to high heaven,'
she said.

Miguel sniffed the air and pulled a face, then grinned at her.
She smiled back and punched him lightly. He rubbed his arm,
still smirking.

'You're strong for an angel.'

His words reminded her of what had happened with the
little boy and his father, and for a second she felt the weight of
the world on her shoulders. Unaware of the mood shift, Miguel
peered into the pot still on the ground in front of her.

'At least forty euros,' he said. 'Not bad.'

'You're joking. I've been stood there since eight-thirty this morning. That works out at just over four euros an hour. I'll be glad to hang up my wings tomorrow.'

'Kaitlin too. She's desperate to come back to work.'

'She is? How can she do this day after day?'

'Enjoys it. She does a lot of meditation while she's in position. She also loves – what does she call it? – "people seeing".'

'People watching,' replied Polly. 'Yes, she's always liked that. She's been making notes on what she sees and hears on the promenade and is putting them together for a book – *Angel Eyes*.'

'Yes, she tells me this.'

'Told. She *told* me this.'

'Ah yes, thank you. Silly mistake.'

'You speak better English than some English people. I wish I could speak Spanish like you speak English.'

'If you stayed longer, you could learn.'

'All things must come to an end and I have to go back,' she said with a sigh. 'I really appreciate the lift, Miguel. What time do you have to meet up with the band?'

'Seven-thirty. I'll take you to the apartment first, and then go and collect them. We practised all day yesterday so we don't need to go through the routine again before the show. Jessica and Maria are very good now. They sing very well and look very beautiful – just like the girls in ABBA. Me, I am not so good,' he said with a smile. 'The outfit is uncomfortable. I feel very stupid. So does Matías. He hates his wig. It makes him scratch all the time.'

'You're one of the best tribute bands I've seen. An audience of holidaymakers won't mind if you go wrong or don't look like carbon copies of the original group. Keep singing, smiling and dancing and they'll be happy. I bet most of them will be singing along with you. Everyone loves an ABBA song. You'll be brilliant.'

Polly stretched her neck from one side to the other. She could do with a massage. She was stiff from holding her head in the one position all day and the wings had made her shoulders ache. Pity Dignity, who worked in the treatment room adjacent to hers, wasn't here with her. She would be able to magic away the tension. Polly smiled, remembering the first time she'd met Dignity …

A gentle tapping at the door announces the arrival of Polly's next appointment. She glances at her bright blue Swatch watch. He is early.

'Come in, Joe,' she calls, fully expecting to see the florid face of her sturdy, rugby-playing client, who was currently being treated for a groin strain.

The door opens a crack revealing a small, heart-shaped face instead of his. A woman in her twenties with delicate features but large, grey-blue, sincere eyes appears in his place. She gives a shy smile, displaying even white teeth. Her make-up-free face radiates health.

'Hi. It's not Joe. I'm Dignity. I've just rented the other treatment room. Hope you don't mind me interrupting. I thought I'd come and say hello.'

Polly beckons her in. She hesitates and then comes forward, bringing with her the aroma of incense. Her light-brown hair hangs over straight shoulders. She wears a long full skirt that swishes gently as she walks, teamed with a pretty beaded blouse, creating the impression of an exotic gypsy dancer; an image further enhanced by the way she bounces lightly on tiny feet clad in ballet pumps, a woven bracelet around one neat ankle.

'Nice to meet you, Dignity. I'm Polly. Are you a sports therapist too?'

'I'm more into holistic healing. I'd rather show you than explain. Why don't you pop in after you finish for a treatment?'

'I'll be available at four.'

'That's ideal. I need to finish setting up the room. I'll see you later,' she says and breezes out.

Polly would prefer to race home to Mike, her boyfriend. He's been complaining that she never has time for him. She knows the void between them is growing and it will be up to her to put their relationship back on track, but she's still hurt by a comment he made about her weight that morning. He can wait. She wants to find out more about Dignity.

The treatment is a revelation. Lying fully clothed upon a treatment bed Polly experiences a feeling of serenity she hasn't known for a long time. Dignity does little more than rest her hands near Polly's body, allowing heat to emanate from them. The warmth seeps into her flesh, relaxing her. As Dignity moves her hands, placing them above her throat, Polly feels as if sunrays are burning her flesh. She almost calls out but Dignity moves her hands away and the sensation departs.

After the session, Dignity pours her a glass of cold water and chats quietly, her words falling like gentle rain.

'You have a wonderfully strong aura,' she says, her head tilted to one side, her eyes fixed on Polly. 'But you are damaged and you need to heal. You may have experienced some heat here,' she continues, touching the base of her own throat lightly. Polly nods. 'This tells me you're afraid to open up and to voice your concerns. You are suffering, Polly. Something or someone is eating away at your aura. You must find out what and fix it before you're hurt too deeply.'

'You think so?' said Miguel, sweeping her costume under his arm as if it was weightless, and striding towards the old Volkswagen van parked behind the lighthouse.

Polly dragged herself back to the present and the conversation about Miguel's group.

'Yes, you will. Don't worry. The hotel will definitely want you to go back. You'll see. They'll love you.'

'Thank you. You are very kind. We could do with regular work at the Grande Vista. It's one of the best hotels on the island and the guests go back year after year because of the entertainment they offer. It would be wonderful to be one of their acts. It will help our reputation and maybe we'll be able to make enough money to give up our regular jobs.'

'Who knows? I'll keep my fingers crossed for you.'

'So, you are leaving tomorrow,' said Miguel as they drove back to Kaitlin's apartment. 'Are you looking forward to going home?'

Polly tore her gaze away from at the aquamarine sea, the late afternoon sun scattering diamonds across its surface. Ahead, the hills were ablaze with russets, apricots and marigold yellows.

'Yes and no. More "no" at present. I have a lot to do back home. I have to sort out a lot of… problems,' she said, unwilling to divulge too much. 'I came to help Kaitlin and… to escape. Some bad things happened and now I have to go back.' She chewed her bottom lip. Miguel focussed his attention on driving. A scooter driven by a man carrying a large box on his lap was weaving about in front of them.

'You will come back and see us again?' he asked.

'Of course. I don't know when I'll be able to return though,' she replied.

Satisfied with her response, Miguel drove to the apartment in silence, leaving Polly to her thoughts. She wished she could hide on Gran Canaria forever. However, that wasn't possible and, even if Kaitlin managed to survive on meagre earnings, Polly wouldn't be able to. Forty euros wouldn't last her five minutes, let alone a week.

Miguel pulled up to the apartment block and insisted on carrying the outfit upstairs to the flat. Good-looking and a gentleman – no wonder Kaitlin had dumped her job in the UK to come and live with this man. Polly thought about her own recent disastrous relationship, the latest in a line of truly bad character judgements. There was no chance she would ever be loved by a man like Miguel. Women like her never found their knight in shining armour and, if she were honest, she was no longer bothered by the prospect of being single. For now it would suit. Relationships weren't high priority for women facing prison...

CHAPTER THREE
Simon

Simon pulled up outside the small brick bungalow. A couple of roof tiles had blown off and rested in pieces on the path. He picked them up and propped them beside the front door, fumbled under a terracotta pot for a key and let himself in.

He visited Eric at least once a fortnight, if not more often. Colleagues at Tideswell car dealership for many years, the pair had struck up an unlikely friendship. Eric was a mechanic – one of the best, in Simon's opinion. Simon respected and liked the reserved man who always had time for him. Whenever Simon suffered a knock-back or a bad day, he'd always headed for the workshop to let off steam with Eric. His calm approach usually helped Simon regain his composure. Eric, a widower, and his sister-in-law, Jackie, had become an offshoot of Simon's family, dropping around for birthdays, Christmas and the like. He and Eric had spent many a lunchtime together putting the world to rights so when Eric retired, Simon took to visiting him at home and keeping him up to date with the gossip at the dealership.

'Eric, you up?' he called.

''Course I am. Been up since four-thirty. In here, Simon,' came the reply.

Simon stuck his head around the door to the lounge. 'Morning, Eric. I brought you some milk, bread, cheese… and a couple of your favourites,' he added, holding up a bag containing cans of Guinness.

'Oh, you know how to spoil me,' replied Eric. His large-knuckled hands, brown-spotted by the years, were gripped around a walking frame. His grin revealed a row of shiny, even white teeth that couldn't have been his own. He headed towards Simon, a difficult, shuffling gait.

'It's only a few bits and pieces. Stay there, I'll put the kettle on and make you a cup of tea. How are you?'

'You know, the usual. A few aches and pains. Can't grumble. It's old age. Can't do much about it.'

'Comes to us all, Eric.'

The old man chuckled. 'You're still a whippersnapper,' he said.

'Hmm, I'm not sure about that. It seems parts of me are wearing out faster than others – my eyes, for one thing. Can't see much without the old specs these days.'

Simon rummaged about in the cupboards, found the tea bags and made two strong mugs of tea. He added a few of the biscuits he'd purchased onto a plate and carried it all through to Eric.

'There you go. Bet you didn't have breakfast.'

'Nah. Those cornflakes you got me are okay, but they keep getting stuck in my plate,' said Eric. 'Devil to scrape off.'

'Eat them without your teeth in,' replied Simon. 'They'll go soggy and you can gum them to death.'

Eric chuckled once more, making his rheumy eyes run a little. He dabbed at them with a large checked handkerchief then took a noisy slurp of his tea.

'Good of you to drop by. I wasn't expecting you.'

'To be honest, I needed to get out of the house. That flaming cat woke me up at the crack of dawn and then I had an argument with Haydon, and then another with his mother.'

'Things not better between you and Haydon?'

'No. He never listens to a word I say. He rolls his eyes at everything in an irritating manner that makes me want to shake him. He seems to delight in doing the opposite of what I tell him.'

'It's just a phase. He's growing up and testing the boundaries. He's becoming a man. It's like stags when they rut.'

'Is it?'

'During the rutting period male stags will try to assert their dominance. An old stag has to stand his ground and fight a younger one if challenged – sometimes even to the death. Haydon is going through a human form of rutting. He's taking you on. He won't want to be told what to do by the old stag.'

'So I'm the old stag now, am I?'

'I'm afraid so. It's the circle of life, Simon.'

'Maybe that's why Ivan is out to murder me too? He's asserting his dominance. He wants to be the alpha male in the house.'

The old man spluttered with laughter. 'Your cat is trying to kill you?'

'Seems like it. Why else would he splatter himself across my face? He usually sleeps with Georgina. Since she's been away he insists on joining us. Twice this week he's smothered me. I wouldn't mind, but it's like sleeping with a tiny elephant. He's so heavy. I don't think I've seen a cat that size before.'

'He's a big 'un, that's a fact. Maybe you snore and it's his way of shutting you up,' said Eric, smiling at his own joke.

'If that were the case, he'd spend all night flat out on Veronica's face,' replied Simon.

There was a hiss and the room filled with the scent of lavender. Simon looked for the source of the noise and spotted a plug-in air freshener. Eric's sister-in-law had no doubt purchased it.

'So what have you been up to this week?'

'Oh the same as usual. Went skydiving last Thursday, then had a go at paintballing on Friday.' He cackled loudly. The laugh turned into a hacking cough. It took a while for him to regain his composure. 'That'll teach me to tell fibs,' he said, taking a sip of tea. A thought crossed his mind. His brow furrowed. He opened his mouth to speak, closed it immediately and took another sip of tea. An object caught his attention and he nodded towards it.

'By the way, you left your little black book of customer details last time you were here. It's on the bookcase. No good salesman should be without his black book. It takes a long time to build up connections like yours. I wouldn't know where to begin trying to get people to buy a car, let alone keep them coming back as you have.'

'I've been looking for that everywhere. Thank you. I thought I'd lost it for good. I'd be snookered without it. Not your usual little black book, eh? It's more valuable than that.'

'Good thing I spotted it.'

Simon collected the notebook. He thumbed through the first few pages and smiled.

'Oh yes. It was Rob Miller who taught me to keep a record. Best manager ever. I might have given up selling cars if it hadn't been for him – him and you, of course,' he said, looking at the putty-faced old man, skin hanging loose around his neck jowls. He smiled at Eric – a kindly smile. 'I'll never forget all those times I hung out in your workshop moaning about losing sales. The amount of time I spent there, I should have picked up some of your mechanic skills.' He stopped, lost in thought for a second, before resuming. 'Rob used to get all of us salesmen together every morning for a team talk that always ended with him rubbing his hands together and saying, "Smell the money and go sell, lads!" Kept us all motivated. I can't imagine what I'd do now if I didn't sell cars. I miss that man. I couldn't believe it when he said he was retiring to the sunshine to play golf. He never struck me as a golfer. He always used to send me to the golfing corporate events.'

'You were the only one who could actually hit a golf ball, as I recall.'

'I enjoyed it. Haven't played in a long time, though. There aren't the same opportunities. I'd like to take it up seriously then one day go and play Rob on his golf course in Portugal. I doubt it'll happen though. Whenever I get a day off, Veronica has a list of jobs for me to do.'

'How are you getting along with Rob's replacement?'

'Did you not hear about my faux pas? Surely Jackie told you?'

'No. She hasn't said anything.'

'Really? Oh well, I made a major gaff at Rob's leaving do. I drank too much. It loosened my tongue and you know me – don't know when to shut up at the best of times, let alone after a few pints. I was apparently blabbing away about women managers and made some glib remark along the lines of, "What do women know about cars? They can't even tell their left from their right." It must have got back to Her Highness because from day one she's been extra frosty with me.'

'Oh dear, that rapier wit of yours let you down, did it?'

'You could say that. I try to keep my head down when she's about. Hopefully, give it another month and she'll have forgotten about it.'

Eric dunked a Bourbon biscuit into his mug and sucked on it.

'I still look at that black book from time to time,' continued Simon. 'It's not just a list of clients – it's a historical document. Remember Charles Mountfield?'

'The scrap-metal dealer from Lichfield?'

'That's him. I sold him his very first Mercedes. It was an E300 diesel in palladium silver with cloth seats. It was when his business took off so he treated himself to a new car. I was flicking through the book and found out I've now sold cars to him, his wife, his father, his son and, a few weeks ago, to his granddaughter. In a strange way, I felt proud. Is that odd?'

'Not at all. You're a people person. It's not all about selling cars for you. That's why customers come back to you time and time again. You've got the patter, the charm – the knack.'

' "Come in a client, go out a friend" – that's my motto. I miss those early days, Eric. A customer would bowl up in his best bib and tucker to test drive a car he'd spotted in the showroom. We'd have a chat about life, sport, the economy or his family. Then we'd get around to discussing the car and seal the deal with a handshake. It's different today. I wasted most of last Thursday with a bloke who strolled into the showroom wearing an old ripped T-shirt and dirty trainers, spent hours test-driving six different models, discussed various finance options, ate all the free biscuits then announced he could get a better price at one of the larger car supermarkets.'

Simon removed his glasses and massaged the bridge of his nose before continuing.

'Nowadays, there are so many models of cars and engine types you need a degree in automotive history to begin to comprehend the various combinations available to today's punters. We don't sell premium products to people who aspire to a luxury vehicle – it's only about numbers and turnover. It's about selling finance and arranging loans. I spend hours sorting through paperwork rather than chatting to clients. Half of the time, I'm fiddling numbers so someone who really can't afford a car can get the funding to drive it away. Somehow that seems wrong. I'm encouraging debt and that's never good. I should know. I've been in debt for years. There's always some bill to deal with. I'm still paying off last Christmas's bills on my credit card. Our whole economy is probably built on debt and millions of men and women like me struggling to make ends meet each month. Still, that's the man's job, isn't it? Provide for his family?'

'Only if you don't work yourself into an early grave. Lots of women work nowadays. I'm sure Veronica would be happy to get a job to help out if you needed her to.'

'She's got a job – she looks after our kids. That's plenty. Besides, I'm on top of it, just about. I can't have that old bat Morag pointing her broomstick at me and claiming I can't look after my family.'

Eric gave a throaty chuckle. 'Glad my mother-in-law was never like her. Morag's a character.'

'That's one way of putting it.' He shook his head in dismay and drained his mug. 'I really do have a soft spot for my mother-in-law. It's out in the garden behind the garage.'

Eric guffawed, making Simon smile. He continued, 'I'm not sure what the future holds for me, Eric. I love the customers and working with the sales team, but I'm afraid of becoming the old dinosaur struggling to understand the new technology in cars and all the jargon that accompanies it. Who cares if it has Bluetooth or iDrive? I'm really more interested in the mechanics, the speed, the design of the car; not the fact I can play my iPod in it.'

'You have to – what do they call it? "Hang out with the kids", that's it. You need to keep up with all the new technology and jargon. The world is changing.'

'I know I should, but it's difficult for me. I'm one of the last of a dying breed of salesmen. Tideswell's transformed beyond recognition. Actually, I shouldn't call it "Tideswell", should I? It's part of Ernest-Deal now. We're all part of one huge corporation owned by bosses we've never met and run by faceless bigwigs who don't care about the people who work for them.'

Eric picked up another biscuit and dunked it into his tea. 'I wouldn't like that.'

'No, you wouldn't. No more sitting about for hour-long lunch breaks with a pile of potted-meat sandwiches and a flask of tea,' said Simon, wagging his finger at Eric. They sat lost in memories for a few minutes.

'You remember when we swapped Bob Haskitt's Scotch egg for a golf ball covered in breadcrumbs?'

'Crikey! That poor man. Good thing he didn't break his teeth on it.'

Eric chortled merrily. 'You always were such a joker. You still play the fool?'

'Jokes and laughter help make the day go quicker. Besides, life's too short to be miserable.'

'Maybe you should take your own advice – laugh more. You always kept our spirits up. Times haven't changed all that much, surely? I bet it's not as bad as you think,' said Eric, waving his biscuit at Simon. 'With your experience you're valuable to Ernest-Deal.'

'Not as valuable as I used to be. I'm not on target for sales this month and, between you and me, I'm getting anxious.'

'Pah! You've nothing to worry about. You've been there far too long and know too many customers for them to give you the chop.'

'I'm not so sure. Ever since Supercars opened up in the area, we've lost a few of our regular customers and we're all struggling with monthly sales targets. Top brass sent this new manager in for a reason. She's got a fearsome reputation. She doesn't think twice about sacking people. I think that's one of the reasons Rob was keen to leave. He preferred to jump before he was pushed and he certainly didn't want to make any decisions about who to fire.'

'Nah. They won't sack you. You're a team player.'

'Thanks for the vote of confidence. Talking of teams: do you remember that day trip we all took to Blackpool?'

Eric's eyes lit up. 'The one when you and I carried the coach driver back to the meeting point? We pretended we'd been drinking all day and he was too plastered to drive. You leapt in the driver's seat and started the engine to drive us back while singing some rude song.'

Simon chortled at the memory. 'We had them going, didn't we? Old Rob was horrified. I can still hear him telling us off for getting the driver drunk, then the look on his face when he discovered it was all play-acting.'

'Happy days,' said Eric, scratching his chin thoughtfully. 'Work outings were always entertaining.'

Simon checked his watch.

'Better get going. Don't want to be late. Besides, I have a couple of clients I need to reach before they go to work. I want to try and flog them a pricey motor before Patrick sells it.'

'Of course. Thanks for dropping by. I enjoy our chats. It's good of you to find time for me.'

'Always got time for my friends,' replied Simon, getting up and collecting the empty mugs. 'See you again next week.'

'Look forward to it. Good luck and don't worry. You'll be fine at work. You've still got it, you know – the knack.'

'Thanks, Eric. I only wish I knew where I'd hidden it,' Simon retorted.

Neither man was aware of the person who had been parked opposite the bungalow ever since Simon's arrival. Sat astride a BMW bike, he was dressed in full leathers with a jet-black helmet covering his face. He spoke into an earpiece.

'He's still inside with the old guy – Eric. Hang on a sec. He's got up. I think he's about to leave. Get ready.'

CHAPTER FOUR
Mission Imp-ossible Headquarters

'You know why I called this meeting. The top brass is concerned. They feel they've put their faith in you and you have yet to deliver. We're running out of time. The deadline is fast approaching and a lot is invested in this venture.'

'It took longer than we expected to get suitable candidates lined up and we had a setback when Ronald Wilson, who we had down as a definite, won the lottery and bought an island in the Caribbean. We're in the final stages with the shortlisted candidates and we've made all the necessary arrangements to reel them in. It'll be fine – a little tight, but fine. Besides, we thrive on adrenaline.'

'The boss thinks you should notch it up a gear. He wants you to go the whole hog, so to speak. Don't hold back. Be more demon-like. You have to convince these people that you are who you say you are. They'll initially refuse to believe you're from Hell. Pull out all the stops to make sure they are in no doubt of your credentials; after all, it's crucial they understand that you're demons.'

'It's all in hand, guv. There will be no doubt whatsoever.'

'Okay. However, if you can't get enough candidates to sign by the end of the month you know what will happen?'

'Yes. Heads will roll.'

'And rightly so. You approached us with this proposition and promised it would be a huge success. You said people would be falling over themselves to get involved with this. "*They'll be desperate to sign up*" was what you actually said. Look, lads – management need it to succeed.'

'I know. And we stand by our pitch. We've got some excellent candidates and I'm pretty confident we can swing it with all of them. In fact, two of them look especially promising. Simon Green is a definite runner. Lives near Birmingham, overworked and struggling to keep up with the usual repayments, approaching the big five-oh, fed up with his lot in life and appears to be having a mid-life crisis.'

'Yes, I was looking through the latest report on him earlier – according to our sources he's been researching male menopause on the web and looking at hair regrowth products. The poor man is clearly dreading getting older. His wife was overheard in the hairdressers complaining about their lack of sex life too. He's certainly frustrated with his lot in life. He'll be ideal if you can convince him – should prove most entertaining. The big boss is very keen to get hold of him. How far along are you with him?'

'He's in the latter stages. Had a dreadful week and according to sources is ready to throw in the towel and jet off to become a Buddhist monk. Can't stand much more. Would happily change places with anyone who hasn't got a hefty mortgage, a nagging wife, two truculent kids and a harpy of a mother-in-law.'

'Don't let him become a monk! Make sure you *encourage* him to swap. With only two weeks left—' The sentence hung in the air.

'We're onto it, aren't we, Nick?'

Nick nodded. The horns on his head waggled up and down. He scratched his beard.

'We'll have him signed up by the end of the week, guv. I'll eat my tail if we don't.'

CHAPTER FIVE
Polly

'Hi, Polly,' shouted Kaitlin from the kitchen. 'Hello, lover,' she added. In five paces Miguel had crossed the room to her. Flinging her arms around his neck she murmured words Polly couldn't hear. His lips pressed against hers in an embrace that made Polly's heart ache. She'd never been kissed like that in her life. She headed towards the bathroom.

'Sorry to race off. I really need a shower to feel human again. Thanks, Miguel. And good luck for tonight.'

'It was my pleasure,' he replied, flashing her a smile that made her stomach flutter.

'I've got a bottle of wine chilling,' said Kaitlin. 'That should make you feel better.'

'Great. I'll be out in a jiffy. See you later, Miguel. Break a leg.'

Miguel cocked a quizzical eyebrow. Kaitlin laughed. 'I'll explain it to him,' she said. 'Go get your shower.'

Twenty minutes later, Polly entered the kitchen dressed in a daffodil-yellow cotton dress with damp hair, smelling of lime shower gel.

'Ah, that's much better,' she said as she plopped onto a stylish bar stool and swivelled around. 'It's so hot out there. How do you cope with the temperature?'

Kaitlin shrugged. 'Get used to it, I suppose.'

Polly swivelled on her stool again.

'I'm really sorry about the angel dress. We both knew it was tight on me, but when I bent over to pick up the lollipop bucket, the side seam ripped. I'm more of a heifer than we thought. And I've lost weight. Obviously not enough weight.'

'Don't be daft. You're not fat. I'm just very, very skinny. It's fine. I'll sew it up again. It's really not a problem. I'm just grateful you stood in for me. I couldn't have managed it.'

'Did you see the doctor?'

'She was surprised at how quickly the ankle's healed. I told her I had an amazing sports therapist staying with me who'd made sure I got the best treatment. Those hot and cold packs and rubs have helped so much. Without you, I'd have still been hobbling about, shrieking every time I put my foot down. You're my heroine.'

'Ha! I wouldn't go that far.'

'Well, you've been a tremendous help then. You went beyond the call of duty being my stand in.'

'You needed the money and I couldn't loaf about here all day. After all, I came to help you out.'

'Not many friends would have given up their own business commitments to help an old friend.'

'You're not an old friend. You're my best friend.'

An amiable silence fell between them. Polly chewed on her lip. She ought to tell her best friend the real reason she'd come to Gran Canaria.

'That smells incredible,' she said, wandering over to the cooker to check the pot.

'It's a spicy chicken stew with chorizo sausage. A last Spanish treat before you abandon me.' She opened the fridge and waved a bottle of wine at Polly.

'You know me well.'

Kaitlin pulled out another bottle and waved it at Polly.

'You know me very well!'

'We have to enjoy our final night together. I'm off the painkillers and I'm not going to miss out on a girly night.'

'Too right. Bring it on.'

The balcony door was open, affording the women a view of the star-studded sky. Polly slumped in her chair, building up the courage to talk to Kaitlin about what was troubling her. Kaitlin was already trying to fathom out the reason behind Polly's unusual quiet behaviour.

'You miss Mike?' asked Kaitlin.

'Not as much as at first. After we broke up, I hurt so badly I wanted to stay in bed forever. What made it worse was that I don't know what I did wrong. I made every effort to be everything he wanted and it still wasn't enough. I tried so hard, Kaitlin.'

'It's his loss, Polly. You're a lovely, warm person. I don't know what he was looking for.'

Polly gazed at the stars, fighting tears that threatened to spill. Memories flooded back …

The heart-shaped tealights flicker, their flames dance and cast leaping shadows across the carefully laid table before spluttering and extinguishing, one by one. Rose petals are scattered liberally on the tablecloth, each releasing a delicate scent that perfumes the air like a warm summer's evening.

Adele sings about the wrenching experience of losing a great love, her words finding resonance with Polly, whose heart aches. She checks her watch again. It's twenty-five past ten. He isn't coming home. He's forgotten what day it is.

Polly scrapes back her chair as the song ends and silence falls again. She picks up a rose petal, holds it to her nose, breathing in its perfume and places it on the unopened card marked 'Mike' on the table.

She dials his number. It goes to answerphone. She doesn't leave another message. She's left five already.

Just when she's lost all hope, there's the sound of a key at the front door and rustling as Mike arrives. There's a momentary look of confusion followed by a frown as he takes in the elaborately decorated table. She'd expected guilt or remorse but not aggression.

'I suppose you're going to give me a hard time,' he huffs, eyes narrowing as they do when he's being mean. 'Well, don't start on me. I've had a pig of a day and had to cover for another bloke who didn't turn up for his shift. I've only just got away from work so I don't need you bleating on about forgetting Valentine's Day,' he continues, his ice-cold silver-grey eyes daring her to confront him. 'See,' he says triumphantly and thrusts a bunch of tired carnations at her. She's so pitifully grateful she doesn't say anything about the strong smell of alcohol on his breath as she hugs him or complain about the reduced price tag that reveal the flowers have come from the garage down the road. Nor does she comment on the perfume that emanates from his collar – a brand she doesn't use.

'Neither do I,' she says to Kaitlin at last. 'It seemed perfect. I'd found my ideal man – considerate, compassionate, loving and great in bed. It changed the moment he moved in with me and within days little things began to irritate him. He complained about the way I laughed – told me I sounded like a donkey braying. Then he began to comment on the way I dressed. He decided he didn't like me in trousers so I stopped wearing them. Then he claimed the skirts I bought especially to please him were too short and made me look like some sort of tart. Next, my heels were too high. Apparently, I deliberately wore them to make him look short and then when I wore flat shoes, he said I looked frumpy. He wanted me to work less and spend more time with him yet hated going out with me. He kept finding excuses not to go or to leave early.

He even moaned about the decor in the house – my house.' Polly chewed on her bottom lip before continuing. 'He became less interested in sex too. Our sex life turned into wham, bam and snore. It eroded my confidence little by little so I spent more time at work. At least I felt I was in control there. I suppose that was where I went wrong. I should have tried to sort it out – confront him, talk to him even. By the time he was ready to walk out, I'd transformed into a weak, gibbering buffoon. I actually went on my knees and begged him to stay. How sad was I?'

'Oh Polly! Why didn't you talk to me about this before? I'd have come over and hauled his arse out of there. Or punched his lights out.'

Polly smiled weakly at her friend. It was difficult to imagine delicate Kaitlin punching a balloon, let alone a grown man.

'I hoped it would improve. I thought it was a phase and he'd get over it.' She sighed deeply. 'I guess I'm just not the sort of woman men want to settle with.'

'What rot! You only need to find the right person. One day you will.'

'I'm not convinced. I'm hardly a great catch, am I? I'm a chunky woman with frizzy hair rapidly headed towards middle age. My eyes are the colour of old white knickers that have been washed too many times. My face is too round and my nose is crooked. If I look in the mirror and don't like what I see, how can I expect anyone else to like me?'

'Oh for goodness sake! You're always putting yourself down. I don't see you like that at all. You've got an attractive face. It's open and friendly. Your nose is cute – crooked but cute.' She winked at Polly before continuing. 'And your eyes are perfectly normal, in fact they are a very nice shade of grey. They're more the colour of a gentle lapping ocean a few seconds before dawn's first rays strike the water.'

Polly snorted into her drink. Kaitlin ignored her. 'And they always look so clear, even after a night on the booze. You're your own worst enemy sometimes.'

'You're my friend. Of course you're going to say nice things about me.'

'I give up. How many times do you have to be told you're lovely? No, you don't look like Jennifer Lawrence or Rihanna or Scarlett Johansson. It's your personality that makes you who you are and that is what counts; not how long your eyelashes are or how good your bone structure is or whether you have a phenomenal figure.'

Polly looked at her legs and glowered.

'You're right and still that doesn't help me. My brain refuses to accept the fact. I don't see myself the same way you do. I see a frumpy, boring woman who has lost her sparkle. Friends always see the best in each other.'

'You'll find a man who will become a friend and will love you for being you. It will happen. I can foresee the future. It's written in this magic orb.' She chuckled and, cupping her glass, swirled the contents. Peering at them she continued, 'Yes, I see a handsome man on a white horse. No, it's not a horse. It's a bicycle. A bicycle made for two. He is carrying a spare helmet for you.' Polly sniggered.

'Hope the bicycle has a large comfy saddle and he's fit. I'll get puffed out if I have to do too much pedalling.'

'Oh dear. The vision has gone. I see a computer. A man's face is on the screen.'

'I'm never trying online dating again,' Polly replied.

'You met some interesting guys through the internet,' said Kaitlin, swigging the contents of the glass. 'Mike, for one.'

'He was the exception. Before him, I met a bunch of time-wasting hopeless cases. I didn't want to admit to dating any of them so I never told you. There was Alex, a man who got trapped on an escalator because it stopped working and he didn't register you could walk down it!'

'No!' said Kaitlin leaning forward, a large smile spreading across her face. 'Tell me you just made that up!'

'No, Guide's honour. I only went out with him once. Once was more than enough. Then after him I went out with the original Mr Muscle – all seven stone and five foot of him. He'd posted his friend's photograph to impress the girls. You can imagine how that evening went. Then there was Thomas, who spent every date talking about his mum. He was the only 35-year-old I know whose mum tucked him into bed every night.'

'That's not true! Oh my!' Kaitlin exclaimed.

Polly nodded. 'All true. I could do with a handsome knight tipping up soon,' she mumbled. 'Preferably on a very large horse and wielding a sword.'

'I'm going to miss you when you go, Polly,' said Kaitlin, changing the subject.

'Me too.'

'Stay here then. You can stand by me on the wall at the beach.'

'Stand by me!' sang Polly.

'You're funny.'

'I can't stay here. I'll melt away in the heat – hang on, that wouldn't be a bad thing. Does fat melt away?' she asked, grabbing a small handful of blubber around her midriff and wobbling it dramatically. 'No, I can't stay. I don't think Miguel could put up with me any longer either. It's clear he wants to be alone with you again. I can't stand in the way of lust and love.' Kaitlin flushed. 'Anyway, I have to go back and face the music.'

'What music?'

Polly sat up straight and put her wine glass down on the table.

'It's about time I told you. I've wanted to say something ever since I arrived. I was too ashamed to tell you. I'm in trouble.'

'What trouble? Pregnant trouble?'

Polly laughed. 'Pregnant? No chance. Not unless it's the Immaculate Conception.'

Polly bit her lip again. This was going to be difficult. Kaitlin observed her friend squirming in her chair and decided to intervene.

'Dignity phoned me a couple of weeks ago. She normally emails me once a month or so, but she was worried about you. Ever since I left the UK she's been keeping an eye on you for me. She said you were distracted and she'd heard you crying in your office.'

'Dignity was concerned?'

'Of course she was. She likes you a lot and you've been sharing the same space over the hairdressing salon for some time now. I know she seems a bit flaky, what with her long scarves, peasant-girl lace skirts and her appetite for tofu... still, if your mum had named you after a Deacon Blue song, you'd probably be a bit odd.'

'Yeah,' mused Polly, the corners of her mouth lifting slightly. 'Fancy calling your child after a song about a ship. I used to think her mum was the one who'd slipped her moorings.'

Kaitlin smiled. 'Poor Dignity. She thought it would be a good idea if I got you to the island. She hoped you'd open up about what was happening. That's why I begged you to come and help me out. I've not been entirely honest. I actually did injure my ankle and I couldn't have worked, but I'd have coped. Miguel would have looked after me. Dignity phoned me the day after I twisted it, so I used it as an excuse to lure you here. I thought a break away would give you a chance to escape from your worries. We both assumed it was boyfriend trouble.'

'You both planned this? I guess that explains why Dignity insisted I came.'

'So are you ready to talk about it? I guess now it wasn't just because of Mike. How serious is it?'

'On a scale of one to ten it's a ten,' said Polly, staring at her hands. 'I'm being sued,' she blurted out. 'For thousands of pounds that I don't have. I'll lose everything – my business, my clients and, worst of all, my reputation.'

Kaitlin sat forward, her eyes darkened. 'Who's doing this to you?'

'Gabi Dawson.'

'Gabi who had an affair with your ex-husband, Callum, and then married him? Gob Off Gabi?'

'The very same.'

'Why? And how on earth did you get involved with her? She's a spiteful little minx. She always was a bitch, even at school.'

They both knew why Kaitlin despised Gabi even though the event had taken place fifteen years earlier, after they had finished their GCSE exams.

Robbie Williams is on full volume in the cramped lounge. Kaitlin, wearing a tight micro skirt revealing long coltish legs and a skimpy vest top that hangs fetchingly over her pert breasts and narrow waist, drags dramatically on her second cigarette. This time she doesn't splutter or gag.

'So do I look provocative?' she asks Polly, waving the cigarette in a casual manner.

'You sure Tommy smokes? If he doesn't, he's going to think it's rank,' replies Polly, her arms folded and nose wrinkled in disgust.

'Of course he smokes. Have you never smelt it on him when he comes into class after break?'

'Never got close enough,' says Polly. 'He's always surrounded by his female fan club.'

'After tonight, I'll be the only girl he notices,' says Kaitlin, renewing her lipgloss and pouting. She blows a kiss at her reflection.

Polly tugs at her own top. 'This feels too tight.'

'It's supposed to be snug. It shows off your fab tits. Wish mine were like yours. I had to nick my mum's chicken fillets to fill out my bra.'

'Chicken fillets?'

Kaitlin removes a pale pink gel bag and waves it at Polly before shoving it back in her bra.

'Gross!' Polly exclaims.

'As long as the effect catches Tommy's eye, I don't care what they look like. I'll have to watch he doesn't see them though. It'll put him off.'

'He'll probably try to cop a feel of them.'

'Tonight is about grabbing his attention,' says Kaitlin with confidence, 'not getting too involved. I'm going to play it cool. Boys love that. I read it in a magazine. I'm going to make him ask me out on a proper date. I'm not going to throw myself at him like some of the other girls do – that Gabi Dawson for one. Fancy shagging him in the science block, the tart! No wonder he didn't bother with her afterwards. Not that that put her off. She was full of herself.' *Kaitlin drags on the cigarette again and splutters, making a ghastly gagging noise.*

'He'll notice you all right if you put up displays like that. Drop the cigarette idea. It's awful. Are you positive your parents don't know about this party?' asks Polly, as Kaitlin stubs out the cigarette.

'They're miles away by now, headed to Uncle Ronnie's, and as far as they're concerned, it's you, me, a large bag of Pick 'n' Mix and a soppy DVD,' Kaitlin answers, checking she's not ruined her heavily applied eyeliner. 'You didn't blab to your folks, did you?' she asks, the thought making her turn her head in alarm.

'No way!' Polly responds, her eyebrows raised in horror. 'You know my dad. He'd have locked me in my room if he suspected I was going to a party. He lives in the Victorian era. He expects me to stay at home like my mum and take up embroidery or cross-stitching. He drives me crazy some days. He has no idea what it's like to be young. I wish he'd loosen up.'

Kaitlin passes her a bottle of cider. 'Drink up and forget the oldies. This is our night and we have the whole of summer to look forward to. They can't watch you twenty-four seven. Sandy's bringing wine,' Kaitlin says, her eyes sparkling. George Marriott, known as Sandy because of his sandy-coloured hair and eyebrows, is the youngest in their year. He is a slight boy who would ordinarily have been unpopular were it not for the fact that his parents own a shop and he brings in copious amounts of sherbet pips, cola bottles, pineapple chunks and every possible sweet treat to appease sixteen-year-olds. He also sneaks in the occasional packet of cigarettes for the older boys who hang about at the back of the science block. Polly wasn't keen on him for that reason alone and never accepted his gifts.

Kaitlin is still talking, 'Tommy's coming and Jack. They always go everywhere together. I think Jack fancies you.'

Polly shrugs. Jack isn't on her radar. None of the boys in her class interest her. They are too juvenile.

'Which girls did you invite? Did you invite Gabi?'

'It made no sense to invite a rival to my party. She's always hanging around Tommy and I don't want him distracted. I didn't invite Katie, her best mate, either. Or Slug, 'cos he's a tosser.'

Polly agrees. Slug is revolting. He always behaves like a kid and does stupid things like farting on the back of the school bus.

'Maddy, Saul, Darren and Kathleen can't come. I think Trudi is bringing her boyfriend even though he doesn't know any of us.'

Polly has an uneasy feeling. Gabi Dawson isn't someone to take such a snub lying down. She'll undoubtedly turn up and spoil Kaitlin's night. Kaitlin has been planning the party for ages and even saved up her pocket money to buy vodka and cider for the event. Polly hopes it all goes well for her. Kaitlin's been mad keen on Tommy Ranger for months and this may be the last opportunity she has to attract his attention.

Several ciders later, Kaitlin is no longer excited. She's slumped on the settee. 'Where is everyone?' she asks for the umpteenth time. 'They know where I live.'

'I'll call Jessie,' suggests Polly. Jessie is the most popular girl in the class and is friendly with most of the other girls. She and Polly did some coursework together and got on well. Polly dials Jessie's phone. It rings for a while before a hesitant voice answers.

'Hi, Jessie. It's Polly. Where are you? We're waiting for you.'

There is a silence during which Polly detects laughter and background music.

'Sorry,' says Jessie eventually. 'I forgot the party was tonight. Gabi's dad was given tickets to see the Foo Fighters so we couldn't miss out on that. You can't get tickets anywhere. We're grabbing some food and heading off to the gig.'

'Who's we?'

'Me, Gabi, Tommy and Jack. Hope you don't mind but it is the Foo Fighters. Have fun. Got to go.' The phone dies.

Polly scrolls through Kaitlin's contact list and dials Sandy. Surely he'll be coming. He's talked non-stop about the party all week.

'Sandy, it's Polly. Did you forget about Kaitlin's party tonight?'

'No, I was looking forward to it. I even had some booze I sneaked out of the stockroom. Gabi called me as I was leaving and said Kaitlin's parents had come home unexpectedly so the party was off. I'm at the bowling alley with a few of the others. We got together and came to Derby for a night out. I'm winning at the moment. We're going for a curry afterwards. Pity we're so far away. You could've joined us.'

Polly ends the call. Kaitlin's lip trembles. 'It's Gabi, isn't it? She's wrecked it.'

Polly hugs her friend as she sobs. A loud rat-ta-tat-tat at the door interrupts them. 'Tell them to go away,' begs Kaitlin and races off to her bedroom to carry on crying.

Polly opens the door. He stands nonchalantly as if he has somewhere better to be. He is tall and square-shouldered in jeans and a white shirt that shows off his tanned complexion. His hair is jet black, short and spiked with gel. His eyes, hazelnut brown with almond flecks, appraise her and lower to her chest where they linger. A smile plays across his full lips.

'I must have pressed the wrong doorbell,' he says. She hesitates, wants to speak but has lost her voice in front of this man in his early twenties who makes her nervous and excited in equal measure.

'I seem to have arrived at the gates of heaven,' he says, with a grin that dimples his cheeks. He laughs then adds, 'Heard there was a party kicking off here with some hot birds. Looks like I'm in the right place,' he continues, looking her up and down again, making her insides turn to liquid. He waves a large bottle of vodka at her. 'I'm Callum,' he says, 'and you're going to go out with me.'

'I know,' said Polly. 'I should have refused to have anything to do with Gabi, but I felt sorry for her. She was in tears and I'm the only sports therapist in the town. She arrived at my treatment room one evening, just as I was packing up to go home.' Polly drew a deep breath. 'I was in a hurry to meet up with Mike and I should have checked her over more carefully before I set to work on her. Gabi told me she had shoulder problems. She was clearly struggling to lift her arm so I checked for any obvious injuries and decided she had a torn rotator cuff. I gave her a massage and moved her arm into various positions to try and ease the pain. She couldn't think of any way she'd injured herself so I concluded she must have slept incorrectly. I worked on her neck and shoulders then I advised her to see a doctor if she had any more problems. She was perkier after the treatment and even thanked me.' Polly looked at Kaitlin and shrugged.

'I rather foolishly thought she might want to bury the hatchet. It was four years ago, after all. Part of me expected my marriage to

end. I was too young when I ran off with Callum. It was surprising
we lasted as long as we did. We shouldn't have got married. It was
better before we tied the knot. The seven-year itch got us – well,
him. But I'm over it and have been for some time,' she continued,
recalling the day her marriage ended ...

*The church bell chimes four o'clock. She trudges past the churchyard,
scarf wrapped around her neck, head down against the cold. Her
throat feels raw. She's caught the bug from Lorraine, a fellow receptionist. Lorraine has been coughing all week, long spells of phlegmy
hacking. It was inevitable. Lorraine didn't want to take time off from
work. She needs the money, what with three kids and Christmas only
twenty-seven days away. Polly needs the money too, although not for
children or Christmas presents. She needs it to pay the rent. Callum
hasn't found another job. Not that he's bothered. He collects his dole
money and beetles off to the pub with it as soon as it's in his pocket.*

*His last position was in a warehouse where he told a supervisor to
'screw himself' before quitting. Polly wanted to challenge the wisdom
of his actions, but she sensed the anger bubbling under the surface as
he ranted about the 'bloody dictator' who had tried to suggest Callum
work harder and held her tongue. Callum was quite volatile these
days. It didn't pay to question his decisions.*

*She works evening shifts at the local pub to bring in extra cash –
evenings of leering men and bawdy jokes. She has no choice. During
the day she works at the clinic checking in patients who are sick or
believe they are. Today it's her turn to feel lousy. Her head throbs
and her eyes stream. It's no wonder Dr Truman sent her home. He
probably didn't want another employee coughing and spluttering over
the patients. They are sick enough.*

*Polly heads home. It isn't really 'home'. It's a rented flat on an
estate. They cannot afford anywhere better so for the meantime she
has to put up with graffiti on walls, stairwells that smell of urine and*

clusters of youths that hang about in dark places. It's a far cry from the life she imagined. Kaitlin has told her time and time again to move out. Kaitlin earns ten times as much as her. She has offered to help, but Polly cannot take her money – she has her pride. Kaitlin's friendship is all she needs.

She reaches the door to her flat, fumbles for her key and goes in. She's met with silence. Callum is out. She's relieved he isn't sprawled on the settee as usual. He can be quite ugly when he has had a few drinks. She removes her coat and shoes and trudges to the bedroom. She needs some sleep. She'll feel better after some rest.

She knows before she turns the knob. She can sense it. Then everything turns into slow motion and she opens the bedroom door. She's hit by the smell of sweat, alcohol and sex. Callum is standing up, face red with exertion as he enters the woman from behind. His eyes are closed. His hair is damp with perspiration. Sprawled across the bed, her plump, white backside in the air is Gabi Dawson.

'As far as I'm concerned she did me a favour, taking him on. He was, and still is, an absolute loser. By the way, he was given the boot from his last job as a van driver and is now working shifts at the huge distribution warehouse on the outskirts of town. Ever downwards with Callum.' Polly paused and stared at the sky. It was sprinkled with stars, each one twinkling at her. She wished she could go and join them.

'A couple of weeks ago, I received a letter from a solicitor I've never heard of telling me Gabi's set up proceedings against me. She claims the treatment I gave her damaged nerve endings and as a consequence she has to undergo surgery. She also claims that I deliberately manipulated her to cause injury to her neck during a massage, saying it was vindictive revenge for her past misdemeanours with my ex-husband. She's currently unable to work due to the pain so she's suing me for injury, medical expenses to have private surgery and is also claiming for mental trauma. At the moment, I can fight it or agree to settle outside court for a ludicrous amount of money.'

'Oh, Polly, the utter cow! I'm speechless. Surely everyone who knows you understands that would never be the case?'

'It's amazing how fickle people can be. Gabi's been spotted wearing a surgical neck collar and being helped along by Callum. Callum is apparently worried sick about her and has been extracting sympathy from everyone who speaks to him. Word has spread that I've been waiting for this moment and have ruined her life. She's either acting superbly or she's in terrible pain. She looks ghastly – all pale and thin-faced. I keep going over that evening and wondering if I was too rough with her. My mind wasn't on the treatment. I was thinking about going out with Mike – we were having a rare date night – and I have firm fingers. I can really press hard when I want to.'

'Rubbish. You're far too professional to cause any injury. We both know how hard you worked to get those qualifications and you've helped hundreds of people get better. No, this is some sort of bizarre payback or scam to extract money from you. I can't believe you caused her any injuries.'

'She does look awful, Kaitlin. I might have been too quick with my assessment of her and missed something important.'

'Have you enlisted a solicitor yet?'

Polly looked at the sky. Tears sprang to her eyes. She blinked them away. 'I've not done anything yet. I'm such a coward. I hoped it would go away. I put the letter in my drawer and left it there.'

'Polly! You have to face up to the charges. You need to prove you're innocent. And don't worry about going to prison. It would be a civil action. You won't be tried. Get a solicitor. You're covered by personal insurance. They'll pay any costs if the worst happens.'

Polly avoided her gaze. A tear trickled down her cheek and plopped onto her hand.

'Polly, please tell me you have cover,' whispered Kaitlin.

In a voice barely audible, Polly replied, 'No. I let my insurance lapse. I wasn't covered for a week – the week she visited.'

Kaitlin's eyes opened in surprise. 'Oh no!'

'I'd intended renewing it on time,' Polly continued, suddenly feeling a lot more sober than she would like. 'Don't look at me like that. It was only a blip. I had other stuff on my mind – Mike and so on – and I would've paid up. I just needed—' She stopped, stood up and walked to the open window. A bright star suddenly flitted across the sky and dropped into the inky blackness. Polly drew in a breath of the warm air, perfumed with the menthol-lime aroma of Bentham's Mountain Thyme, a woody perennial herb that grew on the slopes beside the apartment block. She forced her mouth to smile, turned to face Kaitlin and in a cheerful tone said, 'Anyhow, I refuse to talk about it any more. This isn't the way to spend our last night. I'd rather get drunk with my best friend.' Kaitlin began to protest. Polly raised a hand to silence her. 'Kaitlin, you know me. I always bounce back. I'll deal with it tomorrow. I've had a couple of weeks away to think about it all and I'll sort it out.'

'How dare Gabi do this? Have you contacted her or Callum and asked him to talk to her?' continued Kaitlin, refusing to let the subject go. Polly groaned. When Kaitlin had the bit between her teeth she was difficult to calm down.

'He wouldn't pick up his mobile when I called him. I'm not surprised. We haven't been on speaking terms for some time. I'll engage a solicitor to deal with this as soon as I get home. I need to find one happy to do pro bono work or whatever it's called.'

Kaitlin took her friend's hand in hers. 'I'm so sorry, hon. I had no idea it was so serious. You should have told me. I should have been there for you. I haven't been a good friend.'

' 'Course you have. You've always been there for me. See, even now you've let me stay here and not hassled me once. Besides, I shouldn't keep running to you with my woes. I'm a grown woman. You have your own life to lead. You're still a terrific friend. No distance will change that. Dignity's been really kind too. She's not the sort of girl, however, to go out drinking shots and table dancing to help a friend get over her problems,' added Polly with a thin smile. 'She only drinks herbal tea or elderflower water. I've never met anyone who is so careful about what they eat and drink. I think the last party she went to was one when everyone sang or played an instrument.'

'She might surprise you. She told me she liked music festivals. They're usually lively, aren't they? Don't write her off. I've had quite a few enlightening chats with her when I was waiting for you to finish work. She's not as alternative as you might think. She's a bit of a dark horse, although you're right about her being teetotal. She doesn't drink alcohol and that's what you need right now! Drink up,' said Kaitlin, refilling Polly's glass. 'You're my best buddy and I won't let some stupid bitch assassinate your character.'

'I'm afraid it's already too late for help in that department. My appointment book is looking empty again. I'll have to wait for the outcome and hope I can prove my innocence.' Polly's eyes filled up once more. She wiped at the tears angrily with the back of her hand and stared ahead of her. 'It's such a damn mess though. I'd love someone to wave a magic wand and make it all right again. I've got to go and blow my nose. Back in a minute.'

Kaitlin stood up and hugged her. 'It'll be okay, Polly. Something will happen to fix it.' She stroked Polly's hair.

'I wish I had your confidence, Kaitlin,' Polly replied, squeezing her friend's hand. 'Still, who knows? Maybe miracles can happen. Now that's enough of this misery. It's my last night and we need to send me off in style. I'll bring that second bottle of wine through on my way back. I feel the need to numb my senses.'

CHAPTER SIX
Simon

Patrick called out a cheerful, 'Morning, Simon,' as he dropped his coat onto the back of his chair before rummaging through a pile of papers. Simon raised his hand in acknowledgement, noting the designer label protruding from the collar and deducing that the coat had cost significantly more than Georgina's trip to China.

His well-dressed work colleague was a ferociously competitive salesman. Before coming to the dealership he'd sold timeshares in Malta – a job he hadn't liked, but which had helped him hone his selling techniques. Simon christened him 'The Shark' because as soon as a client entered the showroom, Patrick would appear from nowhere, glide towards them soundlessly and circle around them, showing off his brilliant white teeth. Patrick had 'cool' written all over his face and had perfected the art of the flirtatious wink that melted any female buyer. It was difficult to dislike the cornflower-blue-eyed Patrick with his engaging Irish lilt and charm, even if he pounced on a customer before any other salesman could react. Patrick and his wife were expecting their first child, so he was working flat out to get extra sales and bonuses.

'Come on, then. Where's the regular comedy-routine start to the day? You feeling okay?' Patrick asked. He opened a drawer and removed a tin of polish.

'Bit tired, that's all... Teenagers,' he added, by way of explanation.

Patrick laughed. 'Guess I'll have all this to come. First dirty nappies and sleepless nights, then as they get older, more worry and more sleepless nights.' He placed his foot on his desk and daubed polish onto his black Barker shoe then buffed it to perfection. Patrick liked to make sure he made a good impression.

'I've got a joke for you,' said Simon, tapping his teeth with a pen.

'Okay, shoot!'

'A wealthy young banker pulls up outside his bank, opens the door of his top-of-the-range Porsche, when suddenly another car comes racing past, hits the door and rips it off completely. Luckily, the police aren't too far away and rush to the scene. When they get there, they're confronted with the man shouting and carrying on about the damage to his precious Porsche.

' "Look what some twit's done to my brand new Porsche!" he screeches as soon as they get out of their police car.

' "You bankers make me sick," replies the policeman. "You're so materialistic it's untrue. You're so busy yelling about your stupid Porsche that you didn't even notice that your left arm was ripped off."

' "Oh my god!" replies the banker, finally noticing the bloody left shoulder where his arm once was, "Where's my sodding Rolex?"

'Badum-tish!' said Patrick, mimicking playing the drums. 'Talking of rich blokes, I hear Tony Hedge has bought a new toy.'

'Yeah, I heard it thwacking overhead last night and again this morning. He's taken to flying into work.'

'Thought so. It was parked on a helipad right outside his offices when I passed this morning. It's certainly noticeable – bright orange. He's got the company logo on the side of it. Subtle, eh?'

'You know Tony. "Subtle" isn't his middle name. Well, not since he started making more money than the amalgamated salaries of everyone at the entire Ernest-Deal empire.'

'Did you know he bought two robots to cut the grass at his place?' asked Patrick.

'Go on.'

'They're like large model cars to look at. At night, they attach themselves to a docking station to recharge, then at a fixed time they reappear and whiz about the garden keeping the grass short, so that all Tony has to lift when he gets home each night is a gin and tonic. Anyway, not satisfied with having these little robot cars, he got permission from a Formula 1 team to have them painted in their racing colours so he could entertain his guests with them. Jim Davies went around last week. He told me he and Tony raced them around the garden. He almost crashed one into the lake.'

'No! Tony's incredible. Gosh, I remember when he lived next door to me and was normal. He used to push the mower up and down every weekend like the rest of us, although he preferred leaning over the garden fence and chatting to me. He never liked grass cutting. No wonder he has robots to do it now.'

'Probably has a few robots to do the housework too. Can't see the lovely Selena breaking her nails washing up,' said Patrick with a grin. 'He's mixing in some very important circles. Did you hear about Ascot?'

'No.'

'He took a box for his male guests at Ascot and filled it with supermodels. I don't know how he does it.'

'It must be the money,' said Simon.

'He certainly knows how to attract beautiful women. I expect that's why his wife spent the last month in Switzerland having special anti-ageing treatment Whatever they did to her, it was worth it,' sighed Patrick. 'She came into the showroom yesterday when you were out on a test drive and I swear every guy here stopped working and gawped at her. There was a collective sound of tongues falling out of mouths and much drooling. The floor needed mopping after she'd left. Not me of course, I'm a happily married man with a sprog on the way,' he added, winking at Simon. 'She's definitely one hot lady though and she'd be a serious contender for the "rear of the year" award. Ryan got neck strain staring at her from his desk. Tony has to be the luckiest man in the world. Fancy going home to that babe? I think I'd give up work completely and stay in bed with her every day. You definitely would, wouldn't you?'

Simon ignored Patrick's knowing look.

'First off, I'm married, Patrick. Secondly, I hardly think Selena would be interested in a worn-out old codger like me. The way my hair is falling out I'll soon need to shine my head with Turtle Wax rather than use shampoo. She's well out of our league – yes, even you, my handsome young colleague. I can see why Tony dumped his first wife and married her though. Selena's the perfect trophy wife.'

'She suited his new entrepreneurial image far better than Thelma. Poor cow. I heard she moved back to Australia after the divorce.'

'I heard that too. She stuck by him when times were rough though. I bet Selena wouldn't. I have a sneaking feeling she wasn't attracted to Tony's looks. He's in good shape and not bad looking, but I think the millions helped with her decision to move in with him.'

'I hope we don't have a girl. If she's blessed with my height, her mum's looks and golden hair, I'll be forced to lock her up until she's thirty. I might even invest in a shotgun and sit on the front porch to see off any suitors. Bet you feel like that about Georgie. Talking of Georgie: how's she enjoying China? Lucky girl. We went skiing in Austria with the school when I was her age. I'd have preferred China.'

'She's not back yet. Haven't heard a thing from her. Not even a text, ungrateful little madam. You went to Austria? I went on a day trip to France!'

'Ha! Times change, mate. Travel is educational and all the schools send their children to new places nowadays. Dave's son is off to New York on an Art trip with the college to study paintings and artists… more likely to be piss artists.'

'I sure missed out.'

'It's not too late. Book a trip with Veronica and go exploring.'

Simon winced. 'It might be a while before we manage a holiday. I've got quite a few outgoings at the moment, what with Georgie's trip, Veronica's new car, the usual hefty mortgage repayments, credit cards I'm still paying off, along with medical bills for that private eye operation I had to have last year. And now I have to shell out for a new kitchen for Veronica's mum. She's chosen some fancy one from that bespoke kitchen maker in Birmingham. I wanted to get one from IKEA. Unfortunately, Morag refused. She wants a "posh one". That woman assumes I'm made of money.'

'I'd forgotten about that incident. That was a real shame, mate. Pity the insurance wouldn't pay up. It was an accident, after all.'

'They didn't think so. They thought I'd deliberately set fire to the top. That's the last time I try and help fix electrical stuff. I told Morag I didn't really know what I was doing yet she insisted she didn't want a workman in. Bloody toaster just fizzed and – *poof!* – up it went in flames. If only she'd had a fire extinguisher we might have salvaged the situation. Those damn firemen made me feel like a right twit afterwards. It wasn't that they were rude; it was just the way they looked at me, like I was a halfwit – or a useless old git. I can't believe they thought I was Morag's husband.' Simon looked crestfallen. Patrick checked his reflection in his shoes and put his cloth away in the top drawer of his desk. He stood up and patted his friend on the shoulder.

'Never mind, eh? It'll get better.' He paused and added, 'I've got a buyer coming to look at the SLS AMG GT this morning. If I sell it, I'll treat you to a pint tonight.'

'You lucky sod! I thought I'd sold it last week. That was until the finance deal didn't go through.' He paused. 'I need to pull my socks up. I'm having another rubbish month.'

'Look, if I get any potential customers, I'll send them over to you.'

'Mate, you can't do that. You need the money too. You've got to think about your own family.'

'And you have to hang on to your job. From what you said about your last meeting with Her Highness, the situation is becoming serious. You can't afford to give sales away. Come on. Chin up and woo those punters. Go grab some sales. You're a good salesman. You're just off your game at the moment. I don't want to get too personal, but you and I are friends and, to be honest, you have looked pretty glum recently. I think you need to try to be a little brighter, cheerier and smile a bit more at them. You know what I mean. You've done this for years. You don't really need me to tell you how to sell. You've not been yourself of late. If you need to talk—'

'Nah, I'm okay. You're right. Veronica said something similar this morning. I'm letting it all get on top of me. Veronica complained I'm becoming a grumpy old man. Guess I am. Thanks for the advice. I'll shake myself out of this gloom and grin like a three-year-old who's eaten several bags of Smarties. Good luck with the SLS.'

'This should be a simple sale. One of the Villa players is looking for something tasty for his girlfriend. She likes the gull-wing doors and he isn't bothered by the £190,000 price tag.' Patrick checked his reflection in his shoes again, popped a piece of mint-flavoured chewing gum in his mouth and stood up. Outside a throaty burble announced the arrival of a Ferrari. 'Aha, I think he's just arrived. Catch you later.'

'Jammy git,' said Simon under his breath. He'd been desperate to sell the SLS. He'd spent weeks going through his contact book trying to interest clients yet had drawn blanks every time. Only the day before, he'd finally found someone who indicated he might be interested in the car. The man couldn't get in to test drive it until the weekend and now it seemed that would be too late. Patrick would certainly sell it to the footballer.

Ryan, a 22-year-old from Wigan, breezed over to the sales desks whistling a tune that Simon couldn't recognise.

'You all right, mate?' he asked. Simon bristled. He was most certainly not Ryan's 'mate'. Whatever happened to respect? Once upon a time, a seasoned salesman was regarded highly. Not nowadays. The new blood brought in over the last few years treated him like an old bit of furniture. God, he felt ancient! Not surprising. He would be fifty in another month. That had come around quickly. And what had he got to show for his many years on the planet? A house that would need paying off for another twenty years, a wife who was bored with him, two children who were itching to leave home, an overweight cat and a weak bladder. Next stop, old age and a care home. He caught himself before he was rude to the young man. Patrick's words echoed in his ears. He needed to pull himself together. He was being cranky. Ryan was okay really. Just young.

'Yeah, good thanks. Do you mind, Ryan? Sorry, I have to make my calls or the business manager will be breathing down my neck again.'

'Oh yeah. Sure. Got to get those sales in before the big boss gets hold of our nuts and squeezes them, eh? I hear she can make grown men beg for mercy. I need to go and talk to the workshop about a Golf GTi they're prepping for one of my clients. The customer just phoned to say he wants to collect it earlier than we planned. The workshop's going to love me. Stewart is already going nuts about all the work they've got on. He'll probably have a coronary when I tell him they need to bring the Golf's inspection forward. Laters!'

Simon grimaced at the thought of having his nuts in a vice and called out, 'Oh, before you go, I got one for you. A man walks into a garage and says, "I'd like a petrol cap for my KIA." The owner thinks for a few seconds and replies, "Okay, that seems like a fair trade."'

Ryan laughed. 'Thanks; I'll pass that one on to Stewart. It might make him happier to prep the car.'

'I wouldn't. His wife's got a KIA. She loves it.'

'Really? Better not tell him then.'

'Ha! Only kidding you. She doesn't have a KIA. She's got a Vauxhall.'

Ryan smirked and lifted a hand, middle finger raised. Simon grinned, picked up his phone and punched in numbers. Goodness knows how Ryan found time to sell cars. He was always chatting to someone yet still managed to clock up his quota of sales every month, which was more than Simon had done over the last few months. His stomach lurched. If he didn't watch it he would get an ulcer through worry. He glanced up to see a couple hovering by a Jaguar; the man was peering through the front window. Simon's eyes swept around the showroom as he rose to greet the couple – Barry was on the phone, Peter was talking to an elderly gent and Ryan had disappeared. At last, here was a sales opportunity. He straightened his tie and plastered on his best smile – show time. As he approached them, Kimberly emerged from her office door, blocking his path. She spoke in a quiet yet firm voice. 'Simon, could I have a quick word, please? Shut the door behind you.'

Simon did as bid and shuffled into the office. Kimberly motioned for him to sit down and, peering through her thick-framed glasses, read through some notes while he wriggled uncomfortably in the chair opposite. Everyone in the showroom could see into the glass-fronted office, so it made no difference if the door was open or closed. Most of the staff could read body language well enough to know what was going on inside. Simon caught Barry glancing up at him. Simon gave a small nod towards him. Barry looked away without returning it. The temperature appeared to drop in the office and a pain stabbed through Simon's stomach, making him grimace. He looked at Kimberly, who was still studying her notes.

A petite woman who dressed conservatively in drab-coloured skirts and jackets, Kimberly resembled a librarian more than a general manager. In her case, looks were extremely deceptive. She had enjoyed a meteoric rise through the ranks. Her first job was selling shoes. She got her lucky break when a Mercedes-Benz manager, shopping for some shoes as a gift for his wife, was so impressed by her that he offered her a job within Mercedes-Benz, where she'd fast-tracked to management. Thanks to the lure of a superb salary package and a challenge, she was now at Ernest-Deal. The company had several sites throughout the country all selling prestigious vehicles and if one was struggling, they sent Kimberly in to turn it around. Her previous appointment had been as a trouble-shooter at one of Ernest-Deal's other failing branches in the south. She replaced some staff with eager-to-learn youngsters who were offered incentive packages and intense training. Within eighteen months, the dealership was transformed into the best performing site in the country. Tideswell, now ranking bottom, was in danger of being closed if the team couldn't improve their performance. It would be down to Kimberly to save it. She would be wielding her virtual axe and scything anyone whom she considered to be dead wood.

Kimberly gave a small dry cough. Simon felt his insides turn liquid.

'Right, Simon, I won't beat about the bush here. I have been examining performance figures and I'm somewhat disappointed in what I'm seeing,' she said, steepling her fingers together and looking Simon in the eye …

CHAPTER SEVEN
Polly

The nightclub was hot and when she stood up to dance, the room spun in various directions, yet Polly didn't care. She was going to party until she dropped.

'I think it's time to go, Polly.'

'One more drink.'

'No, it's time to leave. You've had more than enough. You've had too much. The answer doesn't lie in alcohol.'

Polly looked up at the woman leaning over. She focussed her eyes. 'Mum?' she asked.

'Of course I'm your mother. Who do you think I am? Mother Teresa? Now come on. Look at the state of you.'

Polly looked down at her tutu. It was pink. It matched the pink ballet shoes she was wearing. Polly had a feeling her mother had made it for her.

'One more dance, Mum.'

'Polly, I don't think so.' Polly heard soft laughter. Behind her mother stood a line of identical blonde-haired girls aged seven. They giggled in unison.

'Why are they laughing at me, Mum?' slurred Polly.

'They're just being silly, sweetheart. Now, let's find your coat and leave.'

One of the girls pointed a finger at her. 'Fat fairy!' she taunted. The other girls joined in. 'Fat fairy, fat fairy!' they jeered. Polly looked at her pretty pink skirt. It had ripped and beneath it her chubby legs, clad in white tights, looked like tree trunks.

'Mum!' she wailed.

'Ignore them, Polly. Don't let them bother you. You're strong. Names can't hurt you. You're an independent young woman. You're much stronger than you think.'

The girls pirouetted about her, making her dizzy. Her mother walked away into a crowd of faceless people.

'Mum!' she called. 'Where are you? I need you?'

'Polly, you're a grown woman. You don't need anyone,' called a voice.

'Don't leave me,' Polly cried.

'I have to go. I need a life too. I spent too long trapped in a loveless marriage, Polly. I stayed for you and now I need to experience some of the rich offerings before I'm too old. Don't make the same mistake as me. Don't let anyone spoil it for you. Choose wisely. Find someone who makes you laugh – someone who makes you happy.'

Polly observed her mother fading into the distance. The small girls continued to pirouette around and around, taunting her as they spiralled away. 'Fat fairy,' they chanted. Polly's cheeks were wet with tears. She felt desolate. Then, from afar, another voice called to her, 'Polly, come on. Time to get up.'

Kaitlin stood beside her bed, a glass of orange juice in one hand. 'Hi. Thought you could do with some vitamin C to help with any hangover.'

'Oh Lord, I've got a mouth like a fur boot!'

Kaitlin gave her a wan smile. 'I know how you feel. I threw up earlier. Miguel isn't impressed with me.'

Polly tried to sit up. The room swam. 'Yeurgh! That will teach us to go out for sangria.'

'Don't mention that word,' said Kaitlin, turning green.

Polly took the orange juice. 'Thanks, Kaitlin. And thanks for looking after me last night. Was I really bad?'

'You were very well behaved. You didn't take your top off and shake your boobs at anyone like the hens we met at the nightclub. They were really well oiled. Not sure which one was getting married since they were all snogging anything in trousers. You were quite quiet for you. I stopped you phoning Mike: you wanted to apologise to him for the break-up. And I prevented you from texting Gabi – the message made no sense or I might have let you send it. I think you'd tried to say she was a bitch, but it read, "You're a beach of the fine order". We were remarkably good – boring even. Miguel and the band members turned up after their gig and had a quick drink with us.'

'I have a fuzzy recollection of that.'

'Matías insisted on sitting next to you in the van and helping you up the stairs.'

'I sort of remember that. He sat close to me and kept holding my hand.'

'Once a nurse, always a nurse. He told me to make sure you had plenty of fluids and to ensure you couldn't swallow your tongue!'

'Thanks for looking after me. The strain of the last few weeks caught up with me. I didn't plan on being a nuisance.'

'Hey, that's what friends are for, and you weren't a nuisance. Now, as much as it pains me to say so, you have to pack to go back to the UK. Your flight leaves at twelve-thirty and you need to be at the airport by ten-thirty at the latest so chop, chop!'

'Mum used to say that when I was slow getting ready for school – chop, chop!'

'You spoken to her recently?'

'No. They don't like phones there. They're into peace and nature. She sends me postcards almost every other week about what she's up to. She's full of life these days. I saw such a change in her when she visited after Dad's funeral – confident, looking younger and much, much happier with life. I know she loves me. I also know how much she sacrificed to stay and look after me. If it hadn't been for me she'd have left my father years ago. I had no idea how miserable she was until the day she left for the States with Austin.'

Polly shut her eyes for a moment …

Golden leaves blow against her legs as an icy wind hurls needles of cold air, causing her eyes to run. She tugs at the soft cashmere scarf – a gift from her mother. It caresses her neck, reminding her she's loved. Streetlights flicker pale orange as dusk sets. It's only four-thirty, but the bruised skies have kept daylight from cheering the day.

Polly opens the door with the house key her mother gave her when she left home. 'In case you ever need to come back,' she'd said. Polly had no intention of returning. She had a new life with Callum and now they were married. She should hand over her key.

Two suitcases are standing in the hallway.

'Hi, Mum. You didn't tell me you were going on holiday. How did you ever persuade Dad to take time off?' she calls as she shrugs off her coat, hanging it on the wooden stand that has been there forever. She breathes in the smell of polished wood – the scent of a cared-for home. She wanders into the kitchen. One look at her mother's face tells her what she suspected might always happen.

Her mother, Alice, sits by the kitchen table. Her rosy face is pale. Her carefully coiffeured hair, normally secured in a neat French bun, hangs loosely around her face, making her seem years younger. Her soft brown eyes are dewy. 'Polly,' she whispers. 'I'm so sorry.' She stands and folds her arms around her daughter, gripping her tightly.

'You're leaving,' says Polly, finally pulling away.

Alice nods mutely.

'I don't want you to go,' Polly cries.

'I must,' replies Alice. Her usual air of fragility has been replaced with a determination and confidence Polly hasn't seen before.

'Dad?' she asks.

'He knows. He's gone out. He didn't want to be here when Austin comes to fetch me.'

'Austin – your yoga teacher? He's so young.' Disbelief splutters from her lips. Then she says, 'Are you sure?'

'I'm sure. I can't live with your father another day. He drains me – my energy, my enthusiasm for life, my optimism. He doesn't mean to but he does. Austin is the opposite. He makes me happy. He's easy, funny and doesn't imprison my mind. I don't know what will happen in the future. I only know I have to seize this opportunity. You don't need me so much these days. You're grown up and have a life with Callum. I have tried to be everything your father needs, but his needs keep changing and I can no longer be that person.'

Polly understands. Her father has always been difficult to handle – taciturn and withdrawn one minute, bad-tempered and irrational the next. Polly cannot remember the last time he smiled. She looks at her mother and sees hope in her eyes. Polly cannot deny her that.

She blinks. The vision of her mother vanishes. 'I still have trouble getting my head around it,' she says with a sigh. 'One minute, she's at the Women's Institute with all the other respectable housewives, baking cakes for the local annual fête, and the next she's met an American yoga instructor almost half her age, fallen in love, taken up tantric sex – I do not want to even think about that – and headed overseas to join a commune and find herself. It seems best to leave her to enjoy her time. The last postcard she sent contained a picture of a forest and a quote about making the journey alone. Wise words. I should heed them.'

'I disagree. Sometimes we need love and friendship to help us along the way. When you get home, go and see Dignity. You shouldn't be alone. And don't worry too much about all this nonsense with Gabi.'

'I'll be fine.' Polly tried to rise from the bed and let out a groan. 'On second thoughts, maybe I'll stay here and die a death by hangover.'

'I don't want a corpse in my spare room. You have to get up. Besides, Miguel's gone to meet up with the group. They're all coming back here to rehearse. According to Miguel, their act went down so well last night, the hotel want them back next week. They're trying a couple of new songs – "Eagle" and "Does Your Mother Know".'

'That's fantastic. Bet you're chuffed to bits.'

'I'm pleased for him although I can't help but wish the group were a tribute act for the Foo Fighters instead. I'd prefer seeing Miguel dressed up as Dave Grohl rather than Benny. Dave's one of the coolest frontmen around.'

'I wouldn't care if Miguel dressed up as Shirley Bassey and sang "Big Spender". He's a great bloke. He dotes on you. If I found a guy like him, I'd be on cloud nine. And, talking of clouds, I'd better move it. I have a plane to catch.'

An hour later, seated in a taxi, she waved goodbye to her friend. It was hot outside. Nevertheless, an icy chill ran up Polly's spine. She dreaded returning home. She caught the taxi driver studying her face and gave him a small smile. He nodded back then dialled a number on his mobile and spoke *sotto voce*. Even though Polly didn't understand what he was saying, she had a peculiar feeling the conversation was about her.

CHAPTER EIGHT
Simon

When Simon emerged from the office, he headed straight back to his desk, avoiding the salesmen clustered around the coffee machine laughing raucously. He heard guffaws as Barry regaled them about some poor soul named Nick Kevin Richardson who had chosen a personal number plate using his initials and ended up with one that read 'W4NKR'. The lads were on fine form and bandying friendly insults along with suggestions for other rude combinations for their colleagues. Simon wasn't in the mood to join them. His conversation with Kimberly had hit him hard.

He pretended to be engrossed in work, but his mind flipped from one thought to another. He recalled the day Tony Hedge had come in to buy a new Ferrari. He'd wanted a special number plate for it. Simon had helped him choose one. Personal number plates were all the rage in those days and fetched big money …

'What about AH13?'

'Thirteen. That's unlucky, isn't it? That won't do, although I like the initials A for Anthony and H for Hedge. On second thoughts, drop the A. Only my old mum calls me Anthony. Sounds too pretentious,' Tony explains, sitting back in his chair, cup of coffee in one hand.

Simon taps his teeth with his biro and scrolls through some more possibilities:

'*TDH 704?*'

'*That number isn't important enough. I want it to shout Tony Hedge has made it. Look at him! He's now driving a Ferrari.*'

'*928 TH. Pity you haven't bought a Porsche. That'd be a good one for it.*'

'*Maybe I should buy a Porsche 928 as well,*' says Tony.

'*Why not? As long as you buy it from me,*' Simon replies.

Tony laughs, an easy friendly laugh. 'I'll always buy my cars from you, as long as you want my business.'

Simon had wanted his business and, to start with, Tony had bought a few cars: a Bentley Continental, a Porsche and a Maserati. Then he acquired a fabulous Rolls-Royce from a friend who no longer wanted it, and hired a chauffeur to ferry him about. His lust for cars waned. More recently, he'd purchased a helicopter. It seemed Simon was never going to get rich selling cars to Tony.

'*Got it!*' exclaims Simon. '*T9NY.*'

Tony sits forward. 'That's not bad,' he says.

'*Or,*' continues Simon scrawling through the list, '*What about '40 TH?*'

Tony looks bemused. 'I'm too young for that one. I'm not forty for another three years.'

'*It'll probably be worth a lot in a few years if you want to sell it and it'd look fantastic on a large Bentley,*' offers Simon.

'*Now you're talking. I could get both and have that one on the Bentley and keep T9NY for the Ferrari.*'

Simon wondered what had happened to those number plates. Tony had probably sold them and made even more from the sale. He was that type of person. They say money attracts money and

Tony had oodles of the stuff, along with other riches associated with wealth…

'Hi, honey,' says Tony. The stunning woman places her hands on his shoulders and leans in to kiss him. Simon catches a waft of perfume. He doesn't recognise the scent. Veronica usually smells of soap.

'This is my old mate, Simon,' says Tony, enjoying the reaction his woman is having on his friend. Simon pulls at his tie. It's feeling tight. 'We used to be neighbours before I moved to The Manor House.'

'Erm. H-hi,' Simon stutters and extends his hand. The woman laughs – a tinkling sound – and extends her own. He feels the coolness of her flesh pressing into his own sweaty palm and pulls away almost immediately, embarrassed. She looks at him through almond-shaped eyes. Everything about her is perfect, from her glossy mane of hair, lively dark eyes and full sensuous lips to her model-like figure.

'This is Selena,' says Tony. 'She's moving in with me. Aren't you, gorgeous?'

She drops a kiss onto his head. 'I certainly am. Someone needs to keep an eye on you,' she says in a husky voice that makes Simon's knees go weak. He would love to have Selena keep an eye on him.

The day dragged on. Simon spent the afternoon with a couple of tyre-kickers. What was it with people? They spent hours looking inside cars, asked a million questions about the dimensions and spec, nit-picked about whether the cars had a sunroof or a reversing camera and then complained about the colour not being 'quite what they were looking for'. When they finally found something they liked, they insisted on a lengthy test drive before sitting down to thrash out the financial details. Several cups of coffee later and having listened to the customer's entire life story, the poor salesman had to run back and forwards like a blue-arsed fly to talk to the sales manager and negotiate a price the customers were comfortable with, only for them to stand up, shake hands and depart, uttering those words every salesman hates, 'You've given us something to think about.' You either wanted the damn car or you did not. Simon bashed on his keyboard seeking out similar cars in case the couple returned so he could offer alternatives, knowing it was all wasted effort. It was almost six before he lifted his head from the computer. He'd been so engrossed in his work he hadn't heard Patrick return to his desk. Patrick was watching him, a look of concern etched on his face.

'Coming out to celebrate, Simon?' he asked, grabbing his coat. 'Not every day you sell a top Merc. I've got a pass from the wife to go out tonight. The lads and me are going for a few jars at a new pub in Wroxley. Come and join us. You look like you could do with cheering up.'

'No. Thanks all the same. I'd make lousy company. I didn't get much sleep last night and I've got a bit of a headache.'

Patrick put on his coat and wandered over to Simon.

'Did she give you a hard time?' he asked quietly.

Simon laughed. 'No, gosh, no! Just wanted to go over some figures, that's all. And I've got a few things on my mind – Haydon, for one. I've got some paperwork to finish and then I'll head off home and have an early night. Have a good time. Congrats on the sale.'

'Come on, Simon. It'll do you good. You haven't been out in ages. I'll treat you. You could do with time out. It's been a long time since we all had a bit of fun. The pub in Wroxley is supposed to have some great beers.'

'Nah, I'll pass all the same. Don't want to put a dampener on the evening.'

Patrick shrugged. 'Okay, if I can't persuade you then I'll get off. If you change your mind, you know where to find us.'

The showroom emptied until only Simon and Ken remained. Ken collected and delivered cars all over the country. He was currently sorting out his list of destinations and jobs for the next day. He was often seen leaving or arriving with trade plates under his arm. When not delivering cars, he was in charge of cleaning and polishing the vehicles to ensure they maintained their showroom sparkle. It was also his job to lock up at night.

'You going to be long, Simon?' Ken asked. 'I have to take an estate car over to Birmingham before nine. Bloke's waiting for it.'

'Sorry, Ken. I'm leaving now.'

'You okay? You seem a little distracted,' asked Ken, wandering over and dropping into the seat opposite Simon.

'No, I'm fine. Really,' replied Simon. For a moment he almost poured out all his troubles and fears. Ken was a few years older than Simon. He'd worked for an accountancy firm before coming to Tideswell. The strain of completing tax returns for underprepared folk had got to him. Stress helped cause a heart attack that almost killed him. As it was, he recovered and after working hard to regain his health, he ditched his job and went to work at Tideswell.

'Well, look after yourself. I know what it's like to be under pressure and I see you guys getting jittery every month when those targets haven't been met. Remember, there's more to life than work.'

'You're right. Maybe I'll go and join the lads for a drink.'

'That's the idea. Then go home to that lovely missus of yours and those super children. You're a lucky fella. Many would swap places to be in your shoes.'

Simon nodded dumbly.

'See you tomorrow.' Simon shut off his computer and made his way to the staff car park. *What a dreadful day!* His mind replayed the conversation with Kimberly that morning.

'There's no easy way to say this, Simon,' she begins. Simon's heart is thudding so loudly he's sure she can hear it too. The sound fills his ears, almost drowning out Kimberly's words. He hears snippets:

'Huge changes afoot ... sorry ... letter of concern ... performance ... targets.' He wishes his heart would calm down but it doesn't. He tries hard to concentrate on her words, his eyes studying her mouth, trying to lip-read as she speaks.

'Tideswell is going through some major redevelopment,' he reads. This might not be bad news. His pulse slows enough for him to finally take in what is being said.

'We have had to look at every employee here, regardless of age, experience or length of service. You've been an excellent salesman over the years, Simon, and I know your colleagues hold you in high regard, but this is about numbers and making money. Tideswell must trim costs, make changes and, alas, let some of its staff go.'

She pauses as if to emphasize the enormity of what she's about to tell him. He waits, paralysed with concern. *'I have highlighted weak areas and the sales team as a whole is behind target. There are, as you are aware, some who are dragging their feet and unfortunately you have been identified as one of those. I have emailed you in the past about targets and my concerns so this should not come as a huge surprise.'*

Simon's mind tries to recall receiving such an email, then remembers there was something that he glossed over. Kimberly sends out so many emails he doesn't read them all. He is too busy trying to get sales.

Kimberly is still talking. She's explaining how the company is streamlining. He thinks she's referring to salesmen losing weight and thinks of Peter, nicknamed 'Cakey' for good reason. Suddenly his brain wakes up and he understands he's expected to respond.

'We would like your resignation and in return you will receive a decent incentive package. I think you'll be pleased with it. Kim from accounts will go through it all for you when you're ready. We shall be happy to provide references for any position you apply for in the near future. You will be allowed to keep your company car until the end of the month and your position until then. Any commissions you earn will be credited to your salary too. We shall naturally be

very sorry to see you go and wish you every success with your career. Any questions?'

Simon shakes his head. He has many questions but none that can be answered by Kimberly. How will he pay his mortgage? Where will he find another job? Who would want to take on a fifty-year-old who has never even filled in an application form for a position? And, most importantly, how is he going to tell Veronica?

Kimberly offers him a tight smile. 'I'm genuinely sorry,' she says. 'Can I ask one thing of you? Please keep this all to yourself. We have other members of staff we need to let go and I don't want morale to sink. If it gets out too soon people will be all jittery and the dealership will suffer. Please be discreet. I know I can trust you.'

He nods. He won't say anything. Not because he's loyal to the company and doesn't want to cause panic among his colleagues but because he dare not admit to anyone that he's a failure. Kimberly thanks him again and he leaves. His heart is no longer beating fast. It rests in his chest like a solid lump of granite.

Simon still felt numb. He'd worked at Tideswell forever. It was all he knew. Where would he go now? He would have to start applying for jobs. Age would be against him. He didn't even know how to present his CV.

Simon was so preoccupied he didn't notice the motorbike and rider parked on the kerb opposite the showroom. As he pulled off the forecourt, the motorbike slid away too and maintained a steady distance behind him.

It was raining heavily – the perfect end to a perfectly awful day. His windscreen wipers were on full, swishing angrily across the screen, swiping at the never-ending stream of water. Simon could barely see the road ahead. A van came steaming up behind him and overtook, leaving him blinded by the spray. He cursed. A dull throbbing – the beginning of a migraine – started behind his eyes. He glanced at the dashboard and cursed again. This time more loudly. His fuel tank was running close to empty. Some idiot – Ryan – had taken his car out on a test drive and not refuelled it. It was all very well driving about in a demonstrator vehicle, but it meant you had to hand it over when a customer wanted to test drive one. He'd given Ryan the keys earlier in the day. Blast! The nearest petrol station was at Wroxley. He could fill up there. He might even join the lads at the pub.

Simon turned off onto a twisting, narrow road. Gusts of wind blew the trees that lined the route. They bent over the road, almost touching his car, as if trying to peer in at him. Leaves brushed at him whispering warnings and then – *crash*! A branch broke from one of the trees, hitting the windscreen with a loud smack and clattering against the roof. The car swerved across the road and, standing on his brakes, Simon brought it to a halt next to a hedgerow. He dropped his head into his hands. The day couldn't get worse. The car was a company vehicle and it would have to be returned in pristine condition to the showroom when he left. It would need repairing and Simon would have to foot the bill. He thumped the steering wheel with all his might, screaming obscenities into the night.

A motorbike drew up to a halt beside him. The driver lifted his visor and yelled,

'You okay, mate?'

Simon wound down his window. In the rain he could only vaguely make out the man's face. 'I'm all right, thanks. Car's been hit by a branch. Don't think it's serious.'

'Bummer. I can't see too much damage though. You look a bit shaky. There's a pub in the village ahead. Why not pull in and take a moment to check the car?'

'Good idea. Is it far?'

'No, it's only about a mile. Just after the petrol station. If you're sure you're okay, I'll get off.'

'Thanks. I'll stop and check the damage.'

The stranger replaced his visor, beeped his horn and left Simon in the road. As he drove away, the stranger spoke into a microphone, 'We have go. He's headed your way. Get ready.'

Simon gathered himself together and drove on. There were no friendly street lights or orange glows emanating from houses, only menacing dark shadows. His head thudded now. *How much worse could it all get?* The road twisted to the right and he found himself on a street, dimly lit by old-fashioned lamps. Raindrops hurled against his windscreen in a mad frenzy, making visibility impossible. Simon passed a row of small cottages, a church and, to his relief, reached the garage. Pulling onto the forecourt and grabbing his anorak from the back seat, he made ready to do battle with the wind and rain.

Car checked for damage and now refuelled, Simon considered calling it quits and heading home. However his attention was drawn to a chalkboard opposite him, lit by his headlights: 'Bad day? You deserve a beer'. Simon's mouth felt dry. He deserved a very large beer. A luminous arrow pointed towards a building – most certainly a pub. There was an empty car park next to it. This had to be the pub Patrick had mentioned. Seemed like the guys from work had chosen a different venue for their celebration or abandoned plans altogether. He could understand why. The place looked more like a single-storey cottage than a pub. Simon felt rain trickling down the back of his neck. It thudded on the car roof like an incessant drumbeat. He made the decision. He would wait in the pub until the rain eased and then make his way home. It was a decision that would change his life.

CHAPTER NINE
Polly

In spite of feeling tired, sleep evaded Polly on the flight home from Gran Canaria. The nightmare about her mother had succeeded in dragging up memories of both her parents, and now it was her father who filled her thoughts.

He seems to have aged twenty years in just a few months. She doesn't remember the flesh on his jowls hanging so loose. He looks frailer. He smiles when he catches sight of her, a smile that reaches his eyes. He rarely smiles and his reaction touches her. She gives him a peck on the cheek and sits next to him. He pats her knee, an affectionate action that takes her by surprise.

'You look well,' he begins. 'I like your hair in that style. It suits you.'

She absently fingers the tendrils that have escaped her ponytail. 'Are you feeling okay?' she asks, unaccustomed to compliments from him. Immediately she regrets her flippancy. A dark shadow flits across his face and the light in his eyes dims. This is more like the man she knows – moody and unpredictable in his nature. He'll no doubt snap back. She attempts to diffuse the situation.

'Sorry,' she says. 'That was rude of me.'

'No,' he replies quietly. 'It was just too close to the truth.'

She takes in his sunken cheekbones, more prominent than usual and his grey pallor and understands. 'You aren't feeling okay, are you?' she says after a moment. A drumming begins in her chest as it dawns on her that he isn't well at all.

All those wasted years of angst, bitter tears and arguments with her parents. She wondered if it had all been worth it. She'd got her own way in the end, left home and moved in with Callum but at what cost? Life hadn't turned out the way she'd hoped or expected. One by one, the people she'd loved had deserted her or disappeared from her life: her mother, Callum, her father, Kaitlin and Mike. The path she was treading was a lonely one. She wondered idly if anyone chose the right path. Her parents had not. They had drifted apart. The glue in their marriage hadn't been strong either. She thought Kaitlin would be okay. There seemed little chance that she and Miguel wouldn't have anything other than a fairy-tale ending.

She wished she'd been a better daughter – she'd let both her mother and her father down. She should have at least tried to understand that they only wanted the best for her. If only her father were here to listen to her. Towards the end of his life he'd tried hard to patch up their relationship. This time she would have heeded his advice.

'Polly, we haven't talked much,' he says, ignoring her question. 'About you.'

'We talk. I told you about the new business and Kaitlin's new Spanish boyfriend, Miguel and about my colleague Dignity, who's into Reiki and Shiatsu massage.'

He looks at her and sighs. 'I didn't mean that. I mean you.'

'I'm fine. You know me. I bounce along.'

He throws her a meaningful look. 'We never talked after you and Callum split up. You always avoid the subject when I ask you about boyfriends. Is it because you think I disapprove of all your men friends?'

She ponders his words. Her father voiced his opinion about Callum on more than one occasion and his refusal to attend their wedding had upset her at the time. Recently, he seems to have changed and has mellowed a little and although still opinionated, he doesn't attempt to boss her as he might have once done. As a result, she's become more tolerant of his grumbles, complaints and foibles.

'Tell me what's on your mind,' she says.

He studies her face for a while before speaking. 'I didn't like Callum because I saw him for what he was and I didn't want him to drag you down to his level. There's no "I told you so" in that statement. Sometimes we are blinkered and can't see what is evident. I have personal experience of dragging people down. I probably won't be around to see the lucky man who will light up your world, but whoever it is, make sure you're careful. Choose someone who makes you happy. Choose someone who is positive. Don't fall for someone who will drain the light from you. I would hate that for you. And, whoever it is, I give you both my blessing. He'll be a very fortunate man.'

He would have detested Mike, Polly decided. The plane was on the descent. Polly felt the rise in pressure in her ears. The stewardess wandered through the cabin to ensure all seatbelts were buckled. A woman in her fifties, she maintained the glamour associated with her profession. Under her smart, blue uniform, she wore a crisp, white blouse, not yet wrinkled from the day's toil. Her fine silken hair was drawn back from her expertly made-up face and arranged in an elaborate bow of black ribbons at the back of her head. She had the palest of green eyes that scanned every aisle with authority. She reminded Polly of the staff nurse at the hospital when her father had been ill, with her efficient manner and professionalism.

Polly hesitates by the ward door. Through the small, square pane of glass at eye level she can see Anne, one of the staff nurses. Her steel-grey hair is as starched as her uniform. Anne is Polly's favourite nurse. She behaves like a sergeant major, but her dark chocolate eyes are compassionate and she's gentle, especially with her patients, who are terminal, and with those who will watch them slip away forever.

Anne spots Polly and signals for her to enter. The ward smells of disinfectant and apart from the muffled babbling of a television set, is almost silent. Anne approaches and puts a reassuring hand on her arm. Polly wonders if she's married and hopes so. She can imagine Anne bustling about her kitchen looking after a husband and wonders idly what he's like.

'I wanted to prepare you, pet,' she says. Anne is from Durham and calls everyone 'pet'. It's an affectionate term and, spoken in her accent, seems homely. 'He's really not well now. We've made him as comfortable as we can. It's only a matter of time.' She pauses to let her words sink in. 'Call if you want anything, anything at all. We're not far away. Would you like a cup of tea?'

Polly thanks her, but she cannot drink anything. Her stomach is churning and she's having difficulty in controlling her emotions. She heads for her father's bed. Blue curtains have been placed around it to preserve his dignity; the dignity of a dying man.

She steels herself, plasters on a fake smile and dips behind the curtains. His eyes are closed. His breath, aided by an oxygen mask, comes in ragged gasps that tear at her heart. Each one demands huge effort from his ravaged lungs. His wispy thin hair sticks up like the downy feathers on the head of a baby bird. Deep crevasses line his brow. His face is gaunt and he's a mere shadow of the man he once was.

A flicker. His eyes flutter open. There is a moment or two then recognition. He attempts to remove his mask to speak, but she chastises him gently. 'You keep it on. We don't want to make Staff Nurse cross, do we?' With time, their roles have been reversed and now he's like the child, anxious to please. He leaves the mask alone.

'Must speak,' he says, the mask muting his words.

She leans in to hear him.

'Promise. Promise to tell Alice I'm sorry, but I don't want her at my funeral. Promise you will tell her. She must not come.' He stops. The effort is almost too much. She waits, holding his hand as lightly as she can so as to cause no pain.

'She has a life,' he continues. 'Happy now.'

Polly fights the tears that are brimming in her eyes, but they spill silently in rivulets down her cheeks. She caresses the back of his hand – the skin is like thin paper – and nods. She'll do as he asks.

Satisfied, his eyes close again. The morphine bag that provides relief drips liquid into his body. His eyes fly open as if he's remembered something imperative.

'Polly,' he says, a sudden lucidity to his speech. 'You made me happy. You made me very happy.'

The tears tumble now. His use of the past tense cuts through her.

'Callum was no good for you,' he continues. 'He made you unhappy. Like me. I made Alice unhappy.' He stops. The effort has almost been too much. Her father drags on the oxygen. 'You deserve to be happy.' His eyes flutter. 'Be happy.' He drifts out of consciousness. Polly chokes on her tears, an anguished splutter that contrasts with the regular rhythmical wheezing of the machine connected to her father.

'I love you, Dad,' she whispers, planting a soft kiss on his forehead. She fears she's left those words too late.

Now on the final leg of the journey home and slouched in her seat, Polly looked around the almost empty carriage, littered with discarded packaging from sandwiches and coffee grabbed in haste at the station. When she embarked, the train was stuffed with commuters, but now only two fellow passengers remained in her compartment and one was dozing, six seats ahead of her. She detected tinny music emanating from his earphones. She had no idea how he could sleep through it. The other sat opposite her, reading a copy of a newspaper. Dressed in dark jeans and a black jumper, the woman was unremarkable apart from a pair of large multicoloured framed glasses that dominated her face. From time to time, she peered at Polly as if she wished to chat, but Polly wasn't in the mood to strike up a conversation and ignored her.

The train whistled past open fields containing morose cows sheltering under dripping trees. They were fast approaching the next station. Grey houses with slate roofs replaced fields, their occupants no doubt snuggled inside watching television, hiding from the dismal day. Polly gazed sightlessly upon the ever-changing scene, her mind filled with anxieties about what she'd yet to face. Outside, the rain hurled against the window and streaked down the glass leaving slug-like trails. The grey outside ate into her soul and dragged her closer towards the black hole of depression that threatened to swallow her.

The train slowed and the woman stood up, nodded at Polly and disappeared down the corridor. A few moments later, the train arrived at the penultimate stop before her own. She watched those disembarked passengers who dashed by her window, umbrellas up against the driving rain, phones held to their ears as they spoke to invisible people. The engine rattled back into life and slowly wheezed on its way again. Polly spotted the woman in glasses standing under a large burgundy umbrella. She was watching the train depart. Polly was sure the woman was looking at her and almost waved goodbye to her. She turned her head to look at the figure until both the platform and woman faded into the murky distance. Only ten minutes remained of the journey. She needed to distract herself. She thought about Kaitlin and her life in Gran Canaria. It didn't help. Looking down, she saw the woman had abandoned her newspaper. It was neatly folded back at a page revealing a half-page advertisement written in bold cherry-red type. Polly turned the paper to read the advertisement. She read it another time then tore it from the paper and stuffed it into her handbag.

The train wheezed to a halt with a dejected air. The sleeping passenger awoke on cue and, yawning, struggled to his feet and shuffled off in the opposite direction to her. The doors released with a sigh and she stepped out into the rain.

Polly unlocked the door to her home – although how much longer it would be hers was now in question. She stooped to gather up the pile of mail accumulated on the doormat and trudged into her living room. Shrivelled carnations drooped in the crystal vase sat on a dusty pine table. The vase had been a present from her mother, years before she'd upped and moved abroad with a new man.

She threw the mail, along with her bag, onto the sofa and drew back the cinnamon-coloured Laura Ashley curtains that complimented the ochre sofa. Even they looked dull in the grey light that struggled to illuminate the room. She stood before a vivid carnelian red and orange sunset painting and drank in its colours. Polly recalled she'd spent a month's earnings on it in the belief it would be worth something in time to come. To date, it was worth less than she'd paid for it. She'd attempted to sell it to pay for some pricey cufflinks for a boyfriend. She hadn't been offered enough for it, so in the end had decided to put the cufflinks on her credit card and keep the painting. It reminded her of late evenings in Gran Canaria – of warmth, of happiness and of Kaitlin.

Polly turned on a stylish lamp that matched the furnishings to brighten the room and make it more welcoming. Today, it failed her. The room didn't feel like her usual sanctuary. Polly ran her finger through the dust on the oak bookcase and gazed at the collection of CDs, the few DVDs and the snow globe Callum had given her one Christmas. It was a mini world within a glass dome where children and contented couples skated hand in hand on a frozen lake surrounded by tiny houses and alpine trees. Even after the horrible time she went through with Callum towards the end of their relationship, she'd never wanted to part with the snow globe. She couldn't discard it or break it and ruin the lives of the little people inside. Her world may be crushed but she could still protect theirs. She shook it and watched flakes of snow tumble softly onto the tiny houses.

Polly had never felt so alone. She meandered into the kitchen and poured a glass of chilled wine. She returned to the lounge, dropped onto the sofa and began to sort through the pile of mail she'd carried in with her, barely acknowledging the contents of the letters.

She paused, glass in hand, and reflected on her life.

At thirty-two years old she had no family or other friends to call upon in her hour of need. Kaitlin was her closest friend and now she lived hundreds of miles away. Of all the dark times she'd survived, this was the darkest. Her discovery that Callum had been unfaithful and the subsequent divorce had been a breeze by comparison. She'd survived that particular bombshell thanks largely to Kaitlin, who had appeared with three bottles of wine, turning the night into a party that culminated in them both singing 'We Are Family' at full volume while bouncing on the sofa before the police – alerted by a grumpy neighbour – arrived and asked them to keep the noise down. They had shared many laughs and tears together. Polly was always going to be fine with Kaitlin as a friend. Kaitlin had been more of a mum to her than Polly's own mother at times. It had been Kaitlin, not her own mother, who had comforted her when her father finally lost his battle with cancer and Kaitlin who attended the funeral service with her while Alice, her own mother, was in America.

Her father had trodden the planet for over half a century yet only five people attended his funeral at the crematorium, including herself, Kaitlin and three neighbours from the road where he'd lived…

Polly sits at the front of the tiny chapel dressed in a dark blue skirt, dark blouse and a gaily-coloured silk scarf. Her father had given it to her, a gesture at odds with his dour nature. Kaitlin sits beside her on the cold wooden bench.

The vicar speaks platitudes and touches on the life of Douglas MacGregor, but Polly feels he could have been talking about a stranger. His words do not correlate with her memories, nor does she believe her father would be freed in everlasting life, although he would be freed from his own prison.

Her mother had phoned that morning and helped her understand.

'He was an unhappy man. He was trapped in a mind that refused to let him enjoy life,' she'd said. Polly's father had been a victim of a depression that turned him into a surly, uncommunicative individual who declined any chance to seek help.

Her mother had done her best, but as Douglas had aged, so he'd become increasingly withdrawn, and in the end it had drained her of her own energy.

'He loved you, Polly,' she'd said. 'He loved us both. Some people are unable to be happy. They have bursts of happiness, but then they fall into a large hole of misery and can't extract themselves from it. I know he didn't want me at the funeral, but I'll be there with you in thought. Don't be too sad. He wouldn't want that. He always thought you were his ray of sunshine.'

Polly listens to the final words from the vicar and imagines her father's spirit rising from the coffin like a freed bird. Her mother was right. If the cancer hadn't taken him then he would have suffered in other ways.

The coffin moves towards the opening doors and music plays. Douglas MacGregor hasn't chosen a hymn but a song from his homeland that he'd sung as a boy. Over the speakers comes the mournful Scottish folk tune 'The Skye Boat Song' and Kaitlin squeezes her hand. Polly vows she won't allow herself to ever become so unhappy. She'll ensure she remains a ray of sunshine.

Polly wiped away a tear. She was failing. It seemed as if she would never be happy again. Not happy as she once had been. Not as happy as when Kaitlin had encouraged her to attend a Sports Therapy course. Back then life had been filled with optimism.

'I'm not sure,' says Polly. 'It's a huge step. What if I don't pass the course?'

'Don't be daft! You're really bright. You can work out the price of a round of drinks without having to use a calculator,' replies Kaitlin. 'And you're a grafter. You'll work your way through the course.'

Polly grimaces. 'They want to know my age. I'm too old to take a course. Everyone else on it will be a mere child by comparison.'

'Look, you want to do this so stop making excuses. You've got wisdom on your side. You'll breeze it. Besides you got an A grade in Biology at GCSE.'

'That was a lifetime ago. I need not remind you I flunked my A levels.'

'You didn't try. You were besotted with Callum. That's in the past. This is now. You're not likely to get too distracted on this course… unless you suddenly decide you're crazy about one of the other students or the lecturer,' Kaitlin adds and smirks. 'Fill it in now, Polly MacGregor, or I'll complete it for you and I shall make it a rare piece of fiction.'

Polly laughs. 'You win. Goodness knows what fabricated half-truths you'd come up with. What have I got to lose? This could be the fresh start I need.'

'That's my girl. I have a good feeling about this. I want to be your first client when you qualify.'

'You will be and you can have free treatments for life.'

'I'll drink to that. To you, your new start and to free treatments for life!'

Kaitlin had been her good-luck charm. Then, like her mother, Kaitlin had left her and Polly had floundered ever since. There had been more failed relationships, the most recent with Mike, and now this awful mess with Gabi. And there was something else. If only Kaitlin knew how far Polly had really fallen. Polly was in far more debt than she'd disclosed.

The first letter was from her bank. She had a good idea of what it would reveal, so left it unopened. She couldn't face it yet. She chucked it onto the floor along with the electricity bill and the outrageous credit-card bill – she never should have spent so much money on presents for Mike or clothes to impress him; that had all been a waste of time. She skimmed over her mobile-phone bill wishing she hadn't wasted so much money texting and calling Mike at every possible moment.

She tore open a brown envelope. It was from a car-park company declaring she'd parked illegally in the local retail car park. According to the letter, she'd stayed longer than the two hours allocated to customers. She remembered going to the car park. It was the day she'd bought the watch.

'Now this one, madam, is very special. It's a Rolex GMT-Master II. It's an iconic two-time-zone watch with an arrow-tipped twenty-four-hour hand and a graduated rotatable bezel. It's the first Rolex to feature a Cerachrom bezel, impervious to scratches and harder than steel.'

Polly has no idea what the salesman means. All she knows is it's a beautiful black and chrome watch that costs over five thousand pounds. It's too much to spend. She looks at the array of watches that are now laid out in front of her. It's so difficult to choose the right one. Mike loves bling and expensive quality watches. Nothing says quality more than the Rolex now being offered to her to handle.

'Stunning, isn't it?' says the salesman. 'They were originally created for pilots,' he continues. 'Hence the two time zones.'

Polly holds the metal strap against her hand. It's heavy and chunky. The watch face dwarfs her wrist but will look great against Mike's. She envisages his face as he opens the box and sets eyes on it. He'll be overwhelmed. This gift will show that she really cares about him and all their recent spats will be forgotten.

It is pricey, but Polly decides while money alone might not bring happiness, if spent on fabulous watches like this it could bring joy. She makes up her mind, much to the delight of the salesman, who scurries off to package it up for her.

She should have thought about buying it beforehand. That was Polly – impetuous. Her mother had always said so. Polly must have got it from her, since Alice was now the one living in a hippy commune in the States with a man the same age as her daughter. Mike's response to the present wasn't as effusive as Polly would have hoped…

'Oh. Thanks. It's very nice.'
   'Don't you like it?'
   'Yes. I just said so, didn't I?'
   'I thought you'd be more excited about it.'
   'Polly, it's very nice. I've said thank you. It's a lovely watch.'
   'But…'

'But what? What do you expect? Did you want me to shout "Yippee! This is the best present in the world! I'm so over the moon!"?'

'Yes, I think I expected something like that. It's a Rolex. I thought you loved that sort of watch. I thought you'd be more appreciative, enthusiastic, happy…' Polly hates sounding so needy and wishes she'd kept quiet. He gives her a steely look that makes her squirm. She hates that look.

'If you must know, I'm not that keen on Rolex watches. I prefer Tag Heuer. They're more elegant. This is a bit flashy for my taste,' he replies in a cold voice. *'I'm not flashy,'* he adds.

Polly is thunderstruck by his words. Her brain has jammed and she cannot think of a response. This is all going dreadfully wrong. Mike's icy demeanour isn't what she expects. She opens her mouth but closes it again.

'So,' he says, crossing his arms. The watch sits on his wrist. Polly cannot bear to look at it. *'You asked why I wasn't so "enthusiastic" and I'm telling you. You should have found out more before you went out and chose a watch for me. You just assumed I'd like it. Guess what? I don't.'*

'I should have asked,' she agrees, wanting him to be less disagreeable.

'It's a bit of insult, to be honest,' he adds. *'I suppose you thought I couldn't afford a watch like this. It's like showing off. It's a way of you saying "I earn more than you".'*

'That couldn't be further from the truth,' she splutters. *'I wanted to get you something you'd treasure. I wanted to show I care about you.'*

He glowers at the watch.

'We'll change it,' she says. *'I've got the receipt. We can choose a different one.'*

His mood lifts. He manages a thin smile. She's relieved. She doesn't want to argue again.

'If you don't mind, I'd rather do that. You're too busy during working hours, so if you give me the receipt, I'll take it back to the shop and pick a different one.'

Polly acquiesces. Mike seems happier, but Polly's stomach is now churning. She wants to argue, but that would defeat the reason for the present. She wishes she hadn't been so stupid.

Polly blinked. The letter made no sense. They were demanding eighty-five pounds. Looking more closely at the date, she noted that she'd missed the payment date and now owed them one hundred and eighty-five pounds. If she didn't pay in – she checked the calendar on her phone – four days, she would receive a county court judgement. That was all she needed. If she got one of those she would be refused all sorts of credit and mortgages and just about anything else. Where oh where was she going to find the money to pay up?

She refilled her glass and downed the contents. Bugger! She was in the mire. Polly thumbed through the rest of her mail then took another slug of her wine. Her eyes felt heavy. She couldn't bring herself to think about her financial difficulties. She had other pressing issues that she needed to cleanse herself of. She would exorcise the past first.

She looked at a pile of letters and cards she'd placed on the table before going to Gran Canaria. They were from Mike. Mike, who decided she was 'too serious about her work' and 'self-obsessed'. It was untrue. She'd made the effort. My, how she'd tried…

Polly twirls in front of the full-length mirror. The petite Italian lady watches her like a proud mother watches her child perform on stage.

'You look divine,' she offers, her accent giving her words extra gravitas. 'The dress was made for you.'

Polly feels divine. The Roberto Cavalli silk satin gown makes her feel like a celebrity. The striking flame design, embellished with eye-catching crystals, is dramatic as she moves. It enhances her curves and she looks glamorous, almost as good as one of the alluring women she admires in the glossy magazines – Holly Valance, Alexa Chung and Fearne Cotton – all women her age who look amazing and sexy. Wearing this dress, she could stand in the same room as them and not look out of place. This isn't the same ordinary Polly who wears elasticated jeans and baggy jumpers to conceal her body.

'It is the last one in the shop.'

Polly's conscience reminds her that she's already put aside a Maria Grazia Severi black cocktail dress and a pair of Max Mara wool and silk trousers in dove grey with a high waist that flatters. She's also in love with the eye-catching Luisa Cerrano fuchsia jacket and the Marc Cain cashmere sweater. Then she reminds herself they are sale items and therefore are all bargains. She twirls again like a matador swirling his cape and know she has to have it all. She looks so much more confident and assured in these clothes and Mike will be wowed.

'I'll take them all,' she says, before she can change her mind.

The owner of the boutique, who has spent over an hour with her, is delighted with her choices. She claps her hands in small fluttering movements like the wings of a butterfly. She sweeps the clothes from the railing in the dressing room and lays them out on her large glass counter, folding each into sheets of tissue paper with precision and care. Her eyes look at each garment fondly as she packs them into bags emblazoned with the name of the stylish boutique.

She uses paper and pen to tot up Polly's spend. She hands Polly the invoice and asks how she would like to pay. Polly looks at the total. It's £3256. She doesn't have that amount in her bank account. She ought to reject the Roberto Cavalli dress as it's the most expensive item but her heart shouts down the thoughts, reminding her how wonderful she looks in it. The woman is watching and waiting. She must ask clients regularly for sums greater than this. Most of the outfits in the boutique are over £500. Polly hesitates. She should explain she's gone over budget, but somehow she doesn't want to lose face in front of this woman with her graceful air, who has helped transform Polly from an ugly duckling into a swan. She'll use her credit card. It's good for up to £5000.

'I'll pay by card, please,' she says, knowing it will be worthwhile. Mike cannot fail to find her attractive dressed in these outfits.

She no longer owned the beautiful Roberto Cavalli dress. It went to a charity shop. Mike had disliked it…

'That's way too overdressed for the party,' he says, as she glides into the room, face beaming and twirls for him.

'You'll look a right idiot if you wear that. Talk about stand out! You're not going to a Venetian ball. Change into something more suitable – that red skirt you have is fine. You can't go in that dress. Who do you think you are? Claudia Schiffer?' he scoffs. 'We don't live in the South of France, you know. People around here are ordinary folk and I don't want you showing me up in front of my work colleagues in that dress. I'll be a laughing stock.'

Defeated, Polly races out, red-faced. Mike's right. What was she thinking? She'll get rid of the outfits before he sees what else she's bought. Dump them. She can't return them to the shop as they have a no-return policy. They're far too grand for her lifestyle. She's so stupid sometimes.

She thought about her conversation with Kaitlin in Gran Canaria. Kaitlin believed Mike was to blame for the break-up. Polly blamed herself. She'd made a lot of effort to please Mike, but their relationship hadn't been her priority. She'd always put the business first. If she hadn't been so work-driven he might not have started seeing a co-worker for illicit sex sessions in the car park and the staff loos. He had needs and Polly hadn't fulfilled them. She'd been too exhausted every night. Running a business was demanding and giving massages all day was physically draining. However, he'd systematically destroyed her self-confidence.

She stands sideways and breathes in. Her stomach remains obstinately rotund. Even after a week of eating very little and drinking green tea she looks the same. Her stomach protests with a mournful gurgle. 'Shut up,' she growls back. In exasperation she removes the silk, crimson underwear and shimmies into a black lace teddy. It cost her a day's wages but it would be worth it, and if he ripped it while pulling it from her, it wouldn't matter. She slicks on her new hot-pink lipstick, runs trembling fingers through tousled hair and slips manicured feet with matching nail varnish into high-heeled sandals.

She checks her reflection. She looks good. She looks sexy. A frisson of excitement mixed with desire courses through her body. She enters the sitting room. Mike is watching several young men wearing combats who are attempting to evade hunters by lurking waist-deep in a river. Polly decides that's not the best place to hide. She coughs gently and adopts a suggestive pose.

He drags his attention from the television and looks up briefly.

'Well,' she says. There is no whistle of approval or flicker of lust in his coal-black eyes. His regard is completely neutral.

'New shoes?' he asks, returning his gaze to the television set.

'You coming to bed?' she asks after a minute.

'Yeah,' he replies. 'Won't be long. Just want to watch this.'

The anticipation whooshes out of her to be replaced by anger, then almost immediately by defeat. He no longer fancies her. She's fighting a battle that is lost.

Polly picked up the top card and eyed the picture of a teddy bear hugging a kitten. Inside the card, Mike had written about how much he loved her. She gazed at the photo of the woolly teddy bear and with a heavy heart tore the card straight down the middle, then again into smaller strips before throwing them onto the carpet. She picked up a second card. This one bore a heart-shaped pebble on a beach. Inside it was a message about how penguins give their chosen ones a pebble to declare their love. This was his 'pebble' for her. It made a loud ripping noise as she tore it into shreds. She continued through the pile of photos, cards and letters. With each rip, a little tension lifted until finally she sat back with a fresh glass of wine in her hand. She caught sight of her reflection in the television screen and raised her glass in a toast.

'To me,' she declared. 'To another new beginning.' Crossing her legs, she kicked her handbag next to the sofa, sending the contents tumbling over the carpet. The advert she'd removed from the *Metro* fluttered out and landed face upwards. She lurched forward and fumbled for it and read, 'Is Your Life a Living Hell? We can change it for you. Telephone Nick 0800 666 666.'

That summed up her life – a living hell. She studied it once more before placing it on the coffee table. She peered at her watch. It was four o'clock. She would phone the number after one more glass of wine. What harm could it do? That was what she needed – a change.

CHAPTER TEN
Simon

The maniacal face of a devil grinned down at him from the sign for The Devil's Tavern. Illuminated by a bright red light, the raindrops that cascaded in front of it looked like droplets of blood. A shiver went through Simon. He drew his coat over his head and raced to the front door, unaware of two figures observing his arrival. They recoiled from the darkened window of the building, concealing themselves in the shadows of the room.

Simon pushed open the heavy wooden door and stood for a moment, dripping water over the tiled entrance floor. A door on his left was marked 'Private', leaving no option other than the staircase to the right that led downstairs. This was a pub unlike any other he'd visited. He squelched down the steps to emerge blinking into a room empty of life. A bar at the far end was bathed in a deep burgundy glow and afforded the only light other than the flames of a crackling fire. Two black winged chairs were positioned beside the stone fireplace. Simon headed towards them and, removing his sodden anorak, hung it on a stand adjacent to the fire. He looked about the room. Flames from the fire spat and leapt higher, casting dancing shapes on the dark walls. To his right a black leatherette banquette stretched the length of the room, while scattered black tables and chairs punctuated the space between it and the bar. All were empty. A pool table stood on the other side of the room. Two neglected cues were propped against it. He made for the bar. The sudden blaring of a jukebox playing 'Runnin' with the Devil' by Van Halen startled him, stopping him in his tracks. The sensible voice in his head reminded him that he should not be considering drinking and driving. Before he could turn on his heels, a man popped up from behind the bar. At least, Simon assumed he was a man. He sported a black goatee beard and, more peculiar still, appeared to have two short horns sticking out from his head.

'Hi, can I help you?' the man asked. 'Sorry. I was out back. Bitter was off.' Simon tore his eyes away from the horns – they definitely looked like horns. It must be part of the pub's theme – the cave, the flames, the music and this guy, a sort of demon. That was it. It was a themed pub.

'Uhm, just a bottle of Heineken, please,' Simon said. The man turned and rummaged in the fridge for a cold bottle. He pushed it towards Simon. 'Glass?' he asked. Simon shook his head. The man prised the top from the bottle using the open mouth of a demon-shaped bottle opener. Simon raised his eyebrows and handed the barman a five-pound note. It was seriously weird in here. No wonder Patrick and the lads had gone elsewhere to drink.

'Is it always this quiet?' he asked, as the man trotted to the till to punch in numbers and retrieve Simon's change. The clattering sound made Simon peer over the bar. The man was wearing a long red tunic over thick red tights and shoes that resembled goat's hooves. They must be specially made. *Weirder and weirder.* This guy was really taking the whole devil theme seriously.

'Nah, weather's put folk off. It's normally busier than this. It might liven up later. It's always a little quiet early doors.'

The fireplace in the corner of the pub gave a soft roar. Van Halen stopped singing about debauchery and excess. There was a brief pause, during which Simon downed half of his beer, before

Iron Maiden began singing about the number of the beast. Simon sniggered. This was too crass for words. Little wonder there were no customers.

'So what brings you into The Devil's Tavern?' whispered a voice by his ear, making him jump. He turned to see another demon perched on a barstool next to him. This man also had two horns and hairy goat shoes and, Simon blinked in disbelief, a long tail. *Gee, the blokes here really were wacky. Wait until he told the guys at work about this place. Work. Huh! Not for much longer.*

'Bad day at the office,' said Simon by way of explanation and not wishing to appear rude asked, 'You work here?'

'Yeah. How did you guess? It's my local too so I often drop in when I'm not on shift. You never know whom you're going to meet,' said the stranger.

The barman appeared again from nowhere.

'Hi, Nick,' he said. 'You're early. The usual?'

Nick nodded. The barman pulled down bottles and set about mixing a cocktail. Nick turned towards Simon. 'Fancy one?'

'What is it?'

'Virgin's blood,' replied the man with a smile. 'It's very popular in these parts.'

Simon screwed up his face. 'If you don't mind, I'll pass on that. Not in the mood for virgins tonight.'

The man gave a lecherous grin. 'Since I don't know you, I'll refrain from being disgusting. I'm often told to watch my tongue,' he added and winked. 'If you're not in the mood for virgins you must be in a bad way. Same again?' he offered. Simon looked at his empty bottle.

'Yes, okay. Thanks. Why not?'

The barman placed a large glass containing some raspberry-coloured concoction on the bar, along with another bottle of beer.

'Cheers! Thanks,' said Simon and raised his bottle, clinking it against the man's glass.

Nick stirred his red mixture with a long plastic spoon and took a noisy sip of it.

'You live nearby?' he asked. 'Not seen you around these parts before.'

'No, I was on my home and had to stop for fuel,' said Simon. 'It was raining. Saw the sign for the pub. Thought, *why not*? Needed some me time before I went home to the wife.'

The stranger threw him a knowing look.

'What about you? Wife? Kids?'

Nick laughed. 'No chance. I'm young, free and single. Well, free and single anyway.'

The jukebox fell silent. Both men drank. The barman polished some glasses. The fire crackled. Simon began to feel light-headed. He remembered he hadn't eaten all day. He'd better get going before he was too drunk to drive home. At that very moment, his phone rang. It was Veronica. He excused himself and moved away to take the call.

'Where are you? Have you any idea what time it is? Are you at work or are you and all your mates from work in the pub? Are you coming home at all tonight?' Veronica barked. Her questions ricocheted through his head.

'On my way. No, it's not late. No and no. Yes, of course I am. Why?'

'I expected you back ages ago. Mum's here. You were supposed to be here to welcome her and make a good impression for once – especially after burning down her kitchen. I had to make excuses for you again. You're not making this easy for me. I told her you were involved in an important sales meeting. She didn't buy it though. She's not stupid. She thinks you're hiding from her. She thinks you're too cowardly to face her. So what do I tell her now?'

'Oh crap! Sorry, Veronica. I had a bad…'

'I don't want your usual pathetic excuses. This was important, Simon.'

'Veronica, I said I was sorry. I really have had a hellish day…'

'Simon, you can explain later. Don't bother racing home. We're going out to bingo. We've all eaten so you'll have to get your own tea. Honestly, Simon, I thought this time you would have made an effort. I should have known better.'

The call disconnected. Simon stared at the mobile's screen and the small red receiver blinking at him and groaned. He'd completely forgotten about Veronica's mother. She was staying with them while workmen set about renovating her kitchen. How could he have forgotten? He should have at least been at home – pretending to be the family man, breadwinner and considerate husband – trying to suck up to the old dragon.

Simon stuffed his phone into his back pocket and plodded back to the bar. Another bottle of beer was waiting for him. He looked around for Nick. He was nowhere to be seen. The barman was shaking bags of pork scratchings – at least that's what Simon hoped they were – into small ceramic dishes. 'Thought you might need another,' said the barman, concentrating on filling the bowls. 'It's on the house.'

'Thanks, that's very generous of you. Are you sure I can't pay you for it?'

'Nah. You're all right. That's what pubs are for. Help folk forget their woes; warm, friendly watering holes for those in need.'

Simon took a slug of the cold beer. His stomach growled.

'You haven't got any hot food, have you?' he asked.

'Yeah, Nick's out the back heating up some hot 'n' spicy pies. Fancy one?'

'Yes, please. Not eaten since this morning. The day didn't go the way I expected and I lost my appetite for lunch.'

'Nick,' shouted the barman. 'Pie for the gent out here.' He put the bowls out along the bar. 'You look like a man in need of something hot and spicy,' he added and winked.

'For the moment, I'll settle for something cold that cures my headache,' replied Simon, indicating his bottle of beer.

'You have had a bad day, haven't you?'

'You don't know the half of it. It's been the day from hell.'

The barman pointed at the sign above a door that said 'Hell's Kitchen' and said, 'Looks like you're in the right place to tell us all about it then?'

Nick appeared from that very door carrying a plate, on which sat a pile of crispy golden chips next to an equally golden pie.

'Here, you go,' he said, dropping the plate down in front of Simon.

Simon picked up a fork and speared the pie. Steam rose, carrying with it the scent of thyme and fragrant spices that Simon couldn't recognise. He scooped up a large chunk, popped it into his mouth and chewed appreciatively. Nick picked up a couple of bar snacks, nibbled on them and leaned against the bar.

'Your man here has had the day from hell,' said the barman.

'A problem shared,' said Nick.

'I don't like to whinge,' began Simon.

'Nonsense. It's not good to carry about a lot of stress. You'll end up having a heart attack and being whisked off to casualty.'

Simon snorted. 'Suits me. I might get some peace and at least I'd be looked after there.'

Nick shot a glance at the barman, who gave an imperceptible nod. Simon, oblivious to the pair, chomped on the pie.

'This is very good. It has an after burn that is quite pleasant.'

'That'll be the chilli. We like things warm around here,' said the barman. 'So what's happened today to give you a headache and send you scurrying to The Devil's Tavern to hang out with a couple of devils?'

Simon looked at the pair in their outfits. Nick twirled his tail and raised his eyebrows up and down in comedic fashion.

'It is pretty odd in here. I've never been to a hell-themed pub before. Are you always dressed like that?'

Nick nodded. 'It's standard uniform. All the employees have to wear it. The girls look much better in theirs. They manage to make red tights look sexy.' He twirled his pencil moustache and for a moment looked truly demonic as light from the fire reflected in his dark eyes.

'It was an average day to start with,' began Simon. 'The cat tried to murder me, my son deliberately ignored me and treated me like I was a stupid old fool, my wife emasculated me as usual, the mole ruined a bit more of the garden I spent months working on, I lost another sale at work, then lost my job, a branch fell on my car damaging it – the car I have to return at the end of the month that will now cost me to repair – and to cap it all, I wasn't at home to greet my mother-in-law.' He drank some more beer.

'Rough. Don't see why missing your mother-in-law arriving is important though. You'll see her later or tomorrow.'

'You don't know my mother-in-law. She detests me and is always trying to get my wife to see the error of her ways in marrying me. It started way back when we were going out together. Veronica, my wife, was quite something in those days, big brown eyes – and they always had a hint of sparkle,' he added smiling at the memory. 'Long light-golden hair, huge… you know,' he continued indicating ample breasts with his hands.

Nick nodded. 'Many a man has lost his senses when it comes to a comely wench with big bazongas,' he said.

'Yeah, I certainly did. On the third date, I walked Veronica home and what began as an embrace and cuddle intensified into fervent ardour. You don't need all the details except, suffice to say, I'd just wrestled the catch on her lacy bra and released the prize within when her mother flung open the front door. Veronica pushed me away to do up her blouse. I stumbled backwards and landed on the pet pooch, Arnold. In an attempt to drag the squashed animal from under me, Morag – Veronica's mother – almost took out her eye on my straining erection. The flipping dog snapped and bit my calf. I automatically kicked out and caught the animal in the chest. It flew against the wall and made a load of pathetic noises, even though it was uninjured. Anyway, she decided there and then that I was an inconsiderate monster, intent only on ravaging her precious daughter. She hauled Veronica inside and has never liked me since.'

Nick's lips twitched. He fiddled with his moustache, trying to control the smile that wanted to spread across his face.

'She's made it her life's work to turn Veronica against me. She spends hours telling Veronica all about her past boyfriends' successes. There's Jeremy – he's a top lawyer. He's into criminal law, no less. He won some intellectual game show a few years ago and is so successful he has a private yacht moored at Monaco. He holds swanky parties there over the summer and invites clients to join him on it during the Grand Prix.' He paused to stab at a chip. 'Infernal man has called the yacht *Veronica*. Old Morag loves that. She goes on and on about it at every opportunity.' Simon stared absent-mindedly at a sign above the bar. It read, 'Don't get mad – get even.' He blinked and took a swig of beer.

'Then there's Adam. He's a property developer and according to Morag, he owns half of Wales and some huge developments in Dubai on The Palm and The World. He's seriously loaded and even has two town houses in London. He lets them out to wealthy foreigners. They cost about eleven million each! He regularly features in the glossy magazines and is one of the most desirable bachelors in the country. He and Veronica were an item when she was at college. Morag can't understand why Veronica jilted

him. To be honest, neither can I. Veronica never talks about him.'
Simon noticed another sign above the bar. This one was of a small
demon with the words 'Mission Imp-ossible' written above it.

'And there's Toby. He runs a couple of Michelin-starred res-
taurants in Devon,' he continued. 'Toby is every mother-in-law's
dream. He used to take Morag flowers when he was going out
with Veronica and boxes of Belgian chocolates, and – listen to
this – he used to help Morag with the cooking. Little creep. He
set the bar high. No one was ever going to be good enough for
Veronica after him.'

The fire crackled in agreement and Simon speared another
lukewarm chip and shoved it into his mouth.

'Anyway, over the years I've been a continual disappointment
to Morag. I've not been promoted in years. I don't run a business.
I'm not even a manager of one. Our house is average – simply
average. We don't go on flashy holidays or do anything she can
brag about. A couple of weeks ago I cocked up big time. She
needed someone to repair her toaster. She moaned on about it
to Veronica, who volunteered my services. I don't know why she
didn't buy a new toaster. Instead, yours truly was dispatched to
fix it. I'm normally fairly handy about the house, however, on
this occasion, it all went wrong and the toaster caught fire. There
wasn't a fire extinguisher handy, so I chucked a towel over it to
stop the flames. That caught alight too and then the fire spread
to the worktop before I knew what was happening. Next thing,
the fire department tipped up and Morag's kitchen was a stinking
black mess. She moved in with an old school friend who lives by
the coast to get over the shock. I think she outstayed her welcome
there because now she's staying at our house while the builders
renovate her whole kitchen – at my expense. Morag has made
sure she's getting a top-of-the-range kitchen too, so my pathetic
pile of savings will be decimated. I wanted to use it to upgrade the

old television and buy a nice large widescreen one. I'd purchase one on credit except I'm stretched on my cards at the moment. Had to fork out for my daughter's school trip and my missus is always spending on something. Money goes nowhere these days. That was my nest egg. I've been saving it for ages.'

Nick tutted in sympathy.

'Sorry, I sound like a right misery, don't I? The thing is, I used to be able to take all the criticism on the chin. I was young and confident. I had a decent enough job that I enjoyed. I knew Veronica loved me. My kids loved me. The past is the past so it didn't matter who Veronica saw before me. Recently, things have changed. The kids act like I don't exist and she sides with them all the time. We argue more than we ever have in our lives. My opinion doesn't count for anything. She looks down on me, I'm sure of it. I see her looking at me sometimes and I wonder if she's wishing she'd taken a different path and married someone else; someone who earns more than a basic salary of £20,000 and works like crazy to top it up with commissions each month so she can have all the things she wants: a nice home, new clothes – oh, you know what I mean.'

The two men grunted in agreement.

'It's not easy being the breadwinner,' Nick mumbled. Simon wasn't listening. He was staring at the remains of his pie. The alcohol was loosening his tongue.

'There's no sex any more either. There hasn't been any for three and a half months. Imagine that? There's not even a little canoodling. I'm sure if we had a spare bedroom, she'd make me sleep in it. She's always complaining about my snoring. She and I have drifted way apart and I'm not sure I can cope with her damn mother needling me this time. I think I might just snap.' He ran his finger around the top of his bottle for a few moments and sighed.

'Look at me. I'm not really a catch, am I? I'm a short-sighted, balding bloke in specs with a beer belly. I'm just the man who pays the bills. Not even that. As from the end of the month, I'll be the useless, short-sighted, balding bloke on the dole. Morag is going to love that.'

Simon stopped, drained his beer and dropped a twenty-pound note on the bar.

'Thanks for listening to me. It's really good of you both to listen to the ramblings of a depressed stranger. I'd better get off. I've got a way to travel.'

'It's still pouring down. Have a bottle of water and wait for another half an hour. It'll give your system a chance to dilute the alcohol.'

It was warm in the pub. The beer, combined with the heat, was beginning to make Simon feel sleepy.

'Okay, I'll have a coffee and a water. They're not expecting me back now and won't be home until eleven. I'll just nip to the toilet.'

'Over there on the left. Door marked "demons". Don't stray into the "angels" by mistake.'

Simon laughed and wandered through to the toilet where his attention was taken by a poster over the urinal: 'Is Your Life a Living Hell? We can change it for you. Telephone Nick 0800 666 666.' Simon laughed again. *If only,* he thought.

Back at the bar Nick and the barman were setting up the pool table.

'Fancy a game?'

'Nah, I'm rubbish at it. I'll watch.'

The jukebox whirred into life of its own accord. Freddie Mercury began singing about breaking free. 'I wish I could break free,' Simon said.

Nick looked at the barman. The barman nodded again. Nick coughed and twiddled his moustache. 'How much would you like to break free?' he asked.

'Very much. I'd do anything to change my life.'

'You'd happily swap it with someone else's life?'

'Of course I would. If that was possible, I'd do it now.'

Nick smiled, revealing yellow teeth. 'Excellent, then let's see what we can do about that,' he said and rubbed his hands together

CHAPTER ELEVEN
Simon

'You're joking, right?'

'No. We're deadly serious.'

'You expect me to believe you are actually demons who can transform people's lives?'

'Didn't you see the poster in the toilets?'

'That's just a bit of fun, isn't it? Telephone 666 666 – the sign of the beast and all that. It's part of the whole devil theme.'

'Theme? What theme?' asked Nick. 'This is The Devil's Tavern where devils drink, and we are demons. We hide here so people don't get freaked out by us, but we are demons nevertheless. Look, how about we show you some testimonials from our website?'

Simon sat opposite the two of them. He'd just learned that the barman was called Len.

'It's "Leonard" really. Means master of black magic and sorcery,' explained Nick.

Simon was reeling from the whole surreal setup as he stared at a laptop screen. The website header read *Mission Imp-ossible*. The two men opposite him now grinned out wickedly from a photograph under a banner that asked, 'Is your life hell? We can fix it.' Underneath the banner was a poem written in olde-worlde italics:

Come sup with us and tell us your woe,

Then sign a pact before you go.
We'll change it all and swap your life,
Even dispose of a troublesome wife.
We guarantee to make it all swell;
After all, life shouldn't be hell.

Simon shook his head in disbelief. 'Surely this is some sort of joke. It has to be.'

'Pull my tail,' said Nick.

'You what?'

'Go on, give it a tug.' Nick held it out for Simon.

Simon tentatively put out his hand to pull it. As he did so, the tail moved of its own volition and waggled at him. Simon stifled a shriek.

'It's... real!' he gasped.

Nick's grin was evil. 'Indeed it is.'

'No... no... no,' spluttered Simon.

'Come on. Man up. You have more to worry about than Nick's tail and us being a couple of Satan's little helpers. We're on your side. You can't tell your family or friends about us though. Actually, it might be wise not to tell anyone. They'll think you've lost the plot,' Len continued, 'you know, gone a bit potty, gaga, loopy, nuts, loco, mental—'

Nick interrupted his list. 'I think he's got the idea.'

Simon's mouth flapped open. He ran his hand through his hair.

'Okay, let's get down to business. Ever heard of Faustus?'

Simon gulped and nodded. 'He's the bloke who sold his soul to the devil, isn't he?'

'That's him. He was the inspiration for this whole business. Humans are often sick of their lives and want to change them. We saw a gap in the market and decided to fill it. We offer people the opportunity to change their lives. You can change all of it or some of it. It's up to you.'

'How?' asked Simon, beginning to feel light-headed.

Len raised his arms. 'How do you think? We're demons. We can do all sorts of stuff.'

'Like what?' Simon asked. Half of his brain refused to believe these two. He was being set up. He turned towards Nick and screamed. Nick's head had turned 180 degrees and was staring at him in a horrifically demonic way. Simon keeled over and fell off his stool.

'Oh Nick, that was too much,' chastised Len, wafting air at Simon with his bar towel. 'You even gave me a nasty fright then.'

'I couldn't go through the whole *it can't be real* thing. We need to get him signed up. Time's pressing. You heard what the guv told us.'

'Okay, but no more scary tricks. He needs gentle persuasion.'

Simon opened his eyes. A man with horns, black hair, small moustache and a goatee beard looked down on him. No, he wasn't dreaming. He was in a bar with a couple of demons.

'You okay?' asked Nick. 'Sorry about that. I get impatient. Len's always telling me off about it.'

'Erm. I'm fine. I think.'

Len brought him some water. 'Here, drink this. You'll soon feel better.'

Simon struggled from the floor, assisted by Len, and drank the water.

'Before you say anything else, let me ask you this… would you like to have a different life? One in which you still had a job, your kids adored you, your wife wanted to rip your trousers off you every night and jump your bones and your mother-in-law thought you were Mr Perfect?'

'That would be wonderful, but I can't imagine it happening.'

'Oh yes it can. You can have it all. Or you can enjoy something completely different. You can even be, what's-his-name, Veronica's boyfriend with the yacht? You can swap lives with him.'

'Get out of here!' Simon said his eyes wide open. 'Oops, sorry! I'm just surprised.'

'It's okay. We often get that reaction. The last guy told us to fuck off so your response was quite tame by comparison. Yep. It's definitely possible. You can swap with whomever you wish. Well, within reason. You write out a list of folk you'd like to swap with and we do a lucky dip and choose one; then we fix it. Just say the word and sign the contract. We can make you the richest man in the world, the best looking...' Len gave Nick a prod.

'Enough. He's got the idea.'

'I could be the President of the United States or—'

'Whoa! Hold up. There are a few rules. You can't just go straight to world domination. Normally, we prefer you to swap with someone you know or have had contact with. How about you stick to people whose lives you fancy, or whose jobs you'd like? Let's make a list.' He reached over for a biro and grabbed a beermat. 'Okay, shoot,' he said.

'Adam.'

'Adam?'

'The guy who has a yacht that Veronica went out with.'

'I wouldn't swap with him unless you're of the other persuasion.'

'Huh?'

'He – how can I put it? He bats for the other side.'

'He's gay?'

'Yup.'

'I don't think I'd like that. I don't have a problem with men being gay, I just don't fancy other men.'

'Fair enough.'

'I'd like Sebastian Charmer's life,' Simon replied. 'He's one of my best customers. He has a massive collection of classic cars and lives in the middle of nowhere surrounded by fields and sheep. I don't think he's even married. I could tinker about with the cars and go off whenever or wherever I wanted.'

'Really?' said Nick, rolling his eyes.

'Yeah, really?' echoed Len, crossing his arms and tutting.

'Why not? What do you know about Sebastian? He's rich, good looking and loves motorsport. He has everything I could want.'

'Including piles – poor man, that'll teach him to go biking every weekend – a mountain of debt that is threatening to make his empire crash around his ears, a lawsuit for molesting an employee and a nasty cocaine habit. Not the best person to swap with.'

Len nodded in agreement.

Simon's mouth fell open again.

'We know all sorts of things though about these people. You need to be guided, Simon. How about we start with something small? You can swap with someone at work. You could exchange jobs with your manager. We can fix it so when you go to work, you'll be the one in charge and she'll be in the firing line. Shall we start with that?'

Simon's face broke into a smile. 'You can make that happen? I could have Kimberly's job and fire her? Oh God!'

Nick and Len shoved their fingers in their ears and hissed in unison. 'Not in here. Don't mention *that* name,' reprimanded Nick. 'It hurts.'

'Oh, sorry lads. I didn't think. Hang on. What do you want in return? Do I sell my soul like old Faustus and spend eternity in hell?'

The demons cackled loudly in unison. 'That is so old school,' said Nick.

'It's the twenty-first century. We gave up trying to persuade people to hand over their souls. They wised up. It didn't matter what we offered, they didn't fancy the idea of spending any time *down there* being tortured for eternity. Besides, no one liked the

idea of all that infernal heat. We've got a new strategy. You nominate someone else's soul. Nowadays, it's a piece of cake. You hand
over the soul of a living being – one of your household members
or friends, and we give you everything you could wish for.'

Simon's face fell. 'I can't do that. I can't destroy people's lives
by nominating them willy-nilly. And as for my family – I could
never hand over my children and Veronica doesn't deserve to
spend an eternity burning in hell. She's already had to put up
with me for most of her life.'

'Sure you can't come up with someone?' asked Len. 'Think
carefully.'

Simon sipped his water again.

'Life could be wonderful – a top salary that will allow you
to pay your mortgage, pay for driving lessons and a new car for
Haydon, and you could buy that new top-of-the-range kitchen
for Morag. Imagine the praise you'll get – you'll be her favourite
son-in-law. And think of the respect. Your children will look up
to you and your wife will be so thrilled she'll smother you with
attention. You'll feel like a man again and yet if you don't take us
up on our offer, what will happen to your family? Will Veronica
continue to put up with you grumbling on as well as jobless? Will
she and the children leave you? We can prevent all of that from
happening. Once you decide you like the first swap we make on
your behalf, we can go from there.'

Simon bit his thumbnail. It was tempting. Was it possible?
Could these two fix his world?

'Go on, who gets on your nerves the most? There must be
someone you can live without. It's not that bad in hell. We love
it there. We party most nights. There's all sorts of stuff going on –
orgies, drinking fests; we even get to watch television if we want.
Admittedly, there's only one show – *Big Sissy* – on twenty-four
hours a day. Still, who doesn't enjoy watching irritating creatures

stuck in a house together, unable to leave, each doing mindless tasks every day and arguing all the time? It's very entertaining.'

Simon put down his glass.

'Any soul? Any living being?' he asked.

'Yes, yes. Any living creature, although you can't suggest that mole you mentioned. It lives in the garden. You're not friends with it. Don't try and fool us. Doesn't count. It has to be the soul of someone you know personally. You can't nominate a politician – most people try that. You must choose a living being you know, work with, live near or who lives with you.'

Simon scratched his chin absent-mindedly and then blinked twice.

'Okay, I'm in,' declared Simon. 'What do I have to sign?'

Nick walked to the bar, bent down and pulled out a folder marked *Mission Imp-ossible* in large italics. From it he withdrew a piece of aged parchment. The writing on it was the colour of merlot wine.

'This is it. It's a standard contract. It's not very long. I'll read it to you. It's a bit gloomy in here to see it clearly,' said Len, taking it from Nick. '*I "blah, blah, blah" promise to hand over the soul of "whomever", to be removed from this planet and taken to hell, hereafter known as "down there". In return I shall be allowed to exchange my life with someone whose life looks a lot more fun than my own, have my wishes granted (within reason) and may enjoy a life of excess, greed and debauchery should I wish it. If I divulge the whereabouts of The Devil's Tavern, the presence of demonic Nick and Len or discuss this contract with anyone, I shall be immediately taken "down there" where I will spend eternity with devils and fiends who will torture and torment me and make me wish I had never agreed to this.* Okay so far?'

A pale-faced Simon nodded his agreement.

'*On signing the contract we, demonic Nick and Len, shall deliver on our first promise within forty-eight hours. The beneficiary of the demonic services is obliged to name a soul for collection. The soul will be collected on delivery of the first service. Signed, etcetera, etcetera.* That's it. We'll sign it first, then after a little think, you can let us know who you're nominating. There's no rush. Next week will do.'

Simon looked at Len. 'Where do I sign?'

'At the bottom. The signature has to be in your blood.'

'Oh. I wasn't expecting that. What do I have to do, cut my finger or stab it?'

Len burst out laughing. 'Only kidding. That's archaic too. We're modern-day demons. We have red-ink pens. Just sign it with your name. Nick will sign it too and that's that. All official.'

Len held out a pen. Simon took it and scrawled his name at the bottom of the contract. Len signed his name and handed the pen to Nick, who added his signature and a smiley face with horns. Simon looked across at the two eager demons. Their dark eyes sparkled with excitement.

'Okay. That all looks fine. Just need a witness.' He whistled loudly. A six-foot female appeared in the doorway, head lowered like a bull ready to charge. Simon gasped in amazement. She was magnificent. Dressed in a full-length black leather jumpsuit that clung to her lean sculpted body stood a she-devil. Her short funky hair was jet-black. Two small horns rose from her head. Her complexion was pale, her eyelids coloured with shimmering rose-pink eyeshadow. Her scarlet lips pouted seductively as if to blow Simon a kiss. She raised her head and opened her eyes suddenly. The irises were also scarlet. Simon stifled another scream and clamped his mouth shut as the she-devil sashayed towards them. Her velvet-black tail swished from side to side as she walked.

'We require a signature, Mania. Our man here is in need of a change.'

Mania chuckled deeply. 'A change is as good as a rest,' she retorted throatily, her blood-red eyes staring at Simon. He shuddered.

'Mania is top dog *down there*,' said Len.

'Actually, more like top bitch,' added Nick, earning a scowl from Mania. He ignored it. 'And she used to be a lawyer so we like to make sure she witnesses the documents. Management prefer to have one of their own involved in the paperwork. You understand, don't you? Don't want anything slipping through the net, so to speak.' He eyed Mania up and down and blew her a kiss.

'In your dreams,' she purred. He winked at Simon and shrugged. Mania checked the document, added her signature and stood up, towering over Nick and Len.

'Thanks, Mania,' said Len. 'Give our regards to the Big Man. We'll be down in a couple of days with the latest offering,' he added.

Mania ignored him and continued to stare at Simon. 'Delighted to have met you,' she said. 'Hope to get to know you more intimately one day.' She strode back to the kitchen. Nick gazed with open lust at her buttocks as she moved off.

'In your dreams, Nick. I know you're staring at my booty. You always stare. My tush is out of bounds to imps. I'm a top-brass lady only,' she called and disappeared immediately from sight. The fire crackled in the fireplace and the room seemed to get hotter. Simon pulled at his collar. It was mighty hot now.

'She fancies me rotten,' said Nick, grinning again.

'No, she doesn't. You go through this every time. She's out of your league,' Len replied.

'Imps?' Simon said. 'She called you imps? I thought you were devils or demons?'

'Just her joke. Besides, imps are demons.'

'Okay, Simon. If you wouldn't mind, we need details of where you work and live, phone number, email address and so on. If you could fill in this form, that'll help.' Nick pushed another piece of paper towards Simon, who set about completing it.

'Take the day off work tomorrow and go in on Saturday. You'll notice a big change. Mission Imp-ossible is about to begin.'

'Really?'

'Oh yes. We are good at this. Substitutions are our speciality. So come on. Don't keep us in suspense. Who are you nominating? Veronica? Your mother-in-law?'

Simon flicked his tongue across his dry lips. 'I'll let you know when I've decided,' he replied.

CHAPTER TWELVE
Polly

Polly checked the company names by the front entrance to the building. She found M.I. Possible and pushed the buzzer.

'Good morning, Mission Imp-ossible.'

'Oh, hello. I'm Polly MacGregor. I phoned yesterday. I've got an appointment with Mania.'

'Yes. We're expecting you. I'll buzz the door open. We're downstairs. Basement level. See you in a moment.'

The buzzer sounded. Polly pushed against the glass door, which opened with a loud click, and entered the foyer. There were no signs inside the building. It was gloomy and uninviting for business premises, but, given that the receptionist sounded friendly, Polly forced aside her anxieties and made her way downstairs where she found a door marked 'M.I. Poss'. She tapped lightly and the door swung open to reveal an unusual office. It was minimal, to say the least. There were no paintings or diplomas. Red circular patterns of lights swirled across grey walls and over soft black leather chairs that were set out around an empty glass table. It looked more like a nightclub than an office. In the background she could hear Cliff Richard's 'Devil Woman' – a song she knew thanks to her parents, devoted fans of Sir Cliff, who owned all his albums.

She was startled from her thoughts by a young lady, no older than twenty, who stepped out from a back office. She was dressed in a shiny black leather catsuit and high-heeled boots. A bright red headband perched on her head held back equally bright red hair. It was one of those novelty headbands with small horns sticking out of it. Polly was somewhat taken aback at the attire. It wasn't the usual garb of a secretary. It was probably something to do with the company name. This girl was dressed like an imp – that made sense.

'Hi, I'm Lilith. You must be Polly. Can I get you a drink? Mania's on a call at the moment. She won't be long. Take a seat. Tea, coffee, water or something else?'

'Water's fine, thanks.'

'After the morning I've had,' said the girl, 'I'd happily crack open the Pinot Grigio.' She smiled at Polly, who had the strangest feeling they had met before.

'First the computers all went down, then Mania had a fit because I couldn't find a document. Still, it's what keeps life interesting, isn't it?'

Polly nodded. 'Um. How long have you been in this business? It looks very new and modern in here.'

Lilith laughed. 'We've been at this for a very, very long time. Don't be deceived by the looks of this place. We move with the times. The offices have recently been given a makeover by one of those top design agencies. You know the sort: some chap wearing a flowery shirt comes in, waves his arms about, drinks chamomile tea and then goes all silent as he gets into his creative zone. I thought Mania was going to throttle him by the time he'd finished going on about karma and space. He was one of those designers who wants your brand to be "out there" and suggests covering the walls in zebra hide or wants to paint everything in oddly named paints like "Elephant's Breath" which just looks grey to me. Our design team was heavily into minimalism. They insisted we dump all the old furniture and went for what they called "the Zen look". It's so empty in here I can hear my brain whir. At least I no longer fall over filing cabinets.'

Polly relaxed and smiled at Lilith. The girl teetered over to a sleek black cabinet, pressed lightly on the front door and it opened to reveal a fridge. She peered inside.

'Sparkling or still?'

'Sparkling, please.'

Lilith wandered back and placed both bottle and glass in front of Polly. She sat down opposite her. Polly noticed her eyes. They were as black as polished onyx and blacker than her leather outfit.

'Yes, I didn't drink enough water on the flight and rather stupidly had a glass or two of wine last night, and no food,' Polly babbled. She'd never seen eyes such an intense black before. She poured the water into her glass and gulped at it.

'I'm hopeless at drinking water. I forget I ought to consume eight glasses or whatever the amount is. Give me wine any day. Or vodka.' Lilith grinned at Polly, revealing a slight gap in her front teeth. 'Mania asked me to have a chat with you before you go in and see her. I'm her assistant so I usually do all the preliminary stuff. Is that okay with you?'

'Yes, fine.'

'You saw our advert in a newspaper, is that correct?'

'Yes, it was in the *Metro*. I picked it up on a train.'

Lilith nodded in a dismissive manner and continued, 'I spoke to the imp that took your telephone call yesterday evening—'

'Imp?' asked Polly.

'We're all imps here, apart from Mania. She's a demon. That's why we're called Mission Imp-ossible.'

Polly's mouth turned upwards. 'You take your role as imps pretty seriously then?'

'Definitely. We are imps just like bakers are bakers or shoemakers are a bunch of cobblers,' said Lilith, making Polly smile again. 'I had a conversation with Zepar this morning. He said you sounded very upset.'

'Zepar? Was that the person I spoke to last night?'

'That's him. He's not in this morning. He's out assisting Nick and Len, two more of the team – they're on a mission. You'll like Zepar, all the ladies do. He's very charming. Anyway, Zepar brought me up to speed. Been a tough few months for you.'

'Yes, life's not the greatest at the moment.'

'Most of our clients say that. That's what we're here for,' said Lilith, placing a cool hand on Polly's. 'If you want to talk, I'm happy to listen.'

'You've probably heard it all before: broken relationships, debt worries and so on. I'm probably wasting your time and ought to leave—'

Lilith didn't remove her hand; in fact she seemed to tighten her grip on Polly.

'Don't leave. We really can help you. You see, I already know about you, Polly. We did some research. We research all our client's backgrounds in order to give them the best possible service, of course,' she added, seeing the look of concern on Polly's face.

She picked up a small iPad and scrolled onto a page, read through some notes and sat back.

'I can see why you phoned us. If it had been me, I'd have wanted to kill my husband for cheating on me. Mind you, I'm not known for my patience,' she said. Her smile didn't reach her eyes.

Polly drew a deep breath. This was an odd situation. Lilith was looking at her, expecting her to continue. Polly needed to talk. She needed a friend and at that moment, Lilith fitted the bill.

'I was upset and hurt at the time. It was a shock, although in reality I shouldn't have been that surprised. It had been on the cards. There had been a palpable tension in our relationship for some time, yet I chose to ignore it. Callum complained I nagged all the time about money and he wanted a quiet life – pub, gaming sessions and a night out with the boys every week, dinner on the table when he came in – nothing too demanding. The real problem was that he was too complacent. He was happy coasting along. He didn't try to better himself and often didn't seem to want to work at all. His track record for holding down a job hasn't improved even today. When we were short of money, he wasn't too bothered. Me, I was bothered. I hated struggling to find bargains in the reject bin at the supermarket, so I got a second job. I worked the evening shift in a pub and days as a receptionist in a clinic. I got sick of doing two jobs, paying the bills and coming home to discover he was asleep in front of the television, having spent the entire day there. Then he became violent. He slapped me a couple of times. He apologized immediately afterwards and promised he wouldn't hurt me again. He blamed it on the pressures of work and made me feel like I'd deserved it. When I found Gabi in bed with him, I actually felt calm. It was a relief to have an excuse to walk away. I left him in that crummy rented apartment and moved in with Kaitlin. He still rents the apartment. Now he shares it with Gabi. They got married last year.'

Lilith sat forward on the chair, listening to her every word.

'With Kaitlin's help, I started over. I retrained – hours studying at night while working during the day and it paid off. I became my own boss with a decent business that brought in sufficient money for me to raise a mortgage on my house and rent space in town where I was happy practising as a therapist. I worked alone for a while then Dignity hired the room opposite me to do Reiki sessions and other alternative treatments. We get along well and clients pop upstairs from the beauty salon and hairdressers below us.' Lilith nodded. Polly took a sip of water. Music continued to play in the background. She recognised The Rolling Stones singing 'Sympathy for the Devil'. They certainly had eclectic tastes in this office.

'Callum's path and my own don't tend to cross any more, thank goodness,' she said, remembering her last encounter with him.

It's late. Her last client stayed behind after her treatment to discuss various exercises that might be beneficial to her back. Polly hadn't the heart to ask her to leave and spent time demonstrating the correct way to perform the exercises and stretches. Mike will be furious. She told him she would be home early today and would cook dinner. This isn't the first time she's broken her promise. She decides to stop at the Chinese takeaway to treat him to a meal of spring rolls and Peking duck. That should appease him. She's so preoccupied with thoughts of what to order she doesn't see the dark figure coming out of the betting shop. He stumbles into her, knocking her bag from her shoulder. She looks up, her eyes registering surprise.

'Look where you're going, you dozy bint,' he growls.

'Hello, Callum,' she says, shouldering her bag again while taking in his unshaven appearance and scruffy clothes.

'Oh, it's you,' he says.

He no longer looks attractive. His once gleaming hair is lank and dirty. He smells unwashed, but he's as cocky as ever he was.

'Well look at you, Miss Fancy Pants,' he snarls, looking her up and down, eyes alighting on her Ted Baker bag. 'See you've been splashing your cash.'

Polly realises he's been drinking. She doesn't want to row in the street. She has better things to do. She walks away with a 'Goodnight, Callum'.

'You stuck up bitch! Don't you walk off like that,' he yells and pursues her on unsteady feet. 'You don't walk off when I'm talking. Do you suddenly think you're better than me? You're not. You're just a scrubber like most women. Bet you still put it about like you did

when I met you. I was the first though, wasn't I? Bet there's been no one as good as me since. That is if anyone else wants to shag you.'

She carries on walking, blocking out his rant.

'You craggy cunt!' he screams. 'You're nothing but a toffee-nosed minger!' he bellows. He stumbles and swears some more. She turns the corner. He doesn't follow. She's relieved. She hastens to the Chinese takeaway, eager to see its bright lights and get home to Mike. She's glad she's moved on from the part of life that was Callum.

'He's a very different man to the one I loved and married,' she responded.

'You've had other relationships since him, though? What about Mike?'

'Yes,' said Polly taking a nervous sip of water. 'You've done your research. You didn't contact him, did you?'

'Oh no! This is between you and us. We're very skilled at this. No one ever suspects what we're up to. It's very important that we do everything in our power to give our clients the best possible solutions.'

'Mike loved me. I'm certain he loved me until I ruined it all. He accused me of neglecting him and thinking only about work. At the time, I believed I gave him enough. I poured everything I could into the relationship. I was exhausted trying to be someone he wanted me to be. He still dumped me. It was an emotional roller coaster living with him. I can't face any more heartache like that. So first I messed up with Callum, then with Mike. There were a few other disasters between those relationships too. I have a great track record with men, don't I?'

Lilith took Polly's hand in her own. Polly marvelled at its coolness. Lilith's voice dropped to a whisper. 'You're not alone. Many women and men have similar experiences. Sometimes you have to kiss a few frogs before you find your prince.'

Polly breathed in deeply and sighed. 'I guess so. I have too much to worry about though, for now. I'm not sure I have the energy or the confidence to embark on another relationship, even if I stumbled over someone I liked.'

There was a pause then Lilith began again. 'I also know about – er, how should I put it? – the financial problems you've had recently.'

Polly pulled her hand away and buried her head in her hands. 'I'm so ashamed. Up until yesterday afternoon, I'd kept it secret. It must have been the wine that loosened my tongue. One minute I was asking about how Mission Imp-ossible could help me, and the next I'd blurted out everything to Zepar.'

'He has a way of coaxing information from people,' said Lilith.

'No one, but no one, knows about the huge debt I've amassed. I've maxed out on all my credit cards, my overdraft and I'm going to get a County Court Judgement against me if I don't find £185 to pay for a car-park fine.'

'That little issue of the parking fine has been resolved already. Mania dealt with it first thing this morning. She thought it would show you how serious we are about helping you change your life.'

'How did you even find out about the fine?' asked Polly, looking up at Lilith.

Lilith tapped the side of her nose. 'It's what we do. Don't be alarmed. Your secrets are, as I said, safe with us. Now we've aired that dirty secret tell me – how come you got into so much debt?'

Polly looked down at her shoes. They were her best pair – Jimmy Choo. She recalled going to London with Kaitlin and seeing them in the shop window. She'd needed little encouragement to buy them. Kaitlin declared they would look fabulous on her.

'Go on, Polly. Treat yourself. Go on. You know you want them, and besides, they'll look perfect with the Armani dress we got earlier.' And so she'd purchased them.

'I think I've worked out why.' Polly paused, then took a deep breath. 'I… I spend a lot of money. Money I often don't have. I don't mean to spend it yet if I see something – a dress or shoes, or a handbag – and I think it'll make me look better or prettier or more desirable, then I get this… urge. It won't go away. I try to forget about the item I've seen, but a voice in my head keeps telling me to buy it. The feeling of wanting it overwhelms me and I can't think about anything other than the shoes or the dress or whatever it is that I've decided I need. I spent three days unable to think about anything other than a Hermès scarf I'd seen in a magazine. It was a beautiful swirl of greens, splashed with pink. I wanted it so badly that I couldn't eat or concentrate on anything important. I kept looking at the magazine picture and fantasising about wearing it to the Italian restaurant with Mike. I was sure he would like it. Green is his favourite colour. In the end, I ordered it online. It didn't suit me. Mike said it made my eyes look bloodshot and I only wore it the once.'

Polly looked down. Her hands plucked at an invisible thread on her jumper.

Lilith squeezed her hand. 'Trust me, you're not the first woman to have lost her mind over a pair of Louboutin shoes or a Louis Vuitton handbag to make her feel good about herself. I spent all my first month's wages on a Ted Baker outfit and had to go around to my mum's for tea every day because there was no food in my house.'

'It's not always just for me. I'm not completely selfish. I like to buy things for other people; people I care about.'

She thought about the similar pair of Jimmy Choo shoes she'd bought Kaitlin, insisting she could afford them. Kaitlin had been so excited she'd actually kissed Polly in the shop. The look of surprise on the sales assistant's face had made them fall about giggling. Lilith was still holding her hand. Polly had no idea why she was pouring out all her secrets to a stranger. It felt right. The room was relaxing. Soft music was playing. Lilith's eyes were hypnotic. Polly could almost see her own reflection in them.

'Go on,' said Lilith quietly.

'It was when things began to go wrong with Mike. I hit a low point. I could see his interest fading before he could. I was hurt – hurt beyond words. I thought we had found real love; however once we'd had sex a few times, he quickly became disenchanted. I worked so hard to keep him in my life. I raced home every day to cook for him and see him before he went to work. I organised weekends away at expensive hotels, surprise trips abroad and meals out. I don't think he ever intended staying with me for a long time. I was just one of his conquests. He became distant within weeks of us moving in together and that was at my insistence. What a fool I was!' She shook her head in dismay.

'I kept getting it wrong. For instance, I knew Mike had a thing for Abbey Clancy – the television presenter – so I purchased some underwear I'd seen her pictured in and some leggings she looked fabulous wearing. They didn't suit me though. I looked like a carthorse in them. I became obsessed with trying to look glamorous. I bought new lingerie, shoes and designer clothes in an attempt to be attractive. Do you understand?'

Lilith nodded in agreement.

'I bought things for Mike too – presents to show him I cared. I found out that if someone falls out of love with you, you can't buy them back. It didn't stop me trying – clothes, silly gifts, cufflinks, gadgets – I kept spending. I even bought a car for Mike – a nice little classic MG. You should have seen his face when he saw it. He was so nice to me – for about a fortnight, before he became snarky again.' Polly sniffed miserably, took a sip of water and carried on. 'Then, I got a bank statement and saw I'd burned through all my wages and savings,' said Polly, her eyes filling up. 'My credit-card bills came through and I could barely afford to pay off the interest on them. The rest of the bills flowed in after that. I borrowed money from one of those online money-lending sites to pay off some of the debt and that caused more problems. My mortgage payments are behind. I had to sell some of my clothes and belongings on eBay to pay the rent on the treatment room last month. I didn't renew my insurance because I couldn't afford to and now I'm about to go through hell with this ghastly case against me.'

Lilith stood up, walked to the black cabinet again and returned with a box of tissues. Polly took one and blew her nose.

'Thank you. You're being very kind.'

'So you didn't tell Kaitlin about this. Did she not guess you were in trouble? After all, you were very close.'

Tears started to fall down Polly's face. 'I couldn't tell her… I hoped… I don't know what I hoped. I wanted it all to go away and then I saw your advert.'

'You've told me enough for the moment,' said Lilith. 'It's not as bad as you think. You've come to the right place.'

Lilith patted her hand again.

'I don't know. I'm a fairly hopeless case.'

'I doubt it. Theoretically, let's say if it were possible and you could get rid of all your problems by swapping lives with someone else, who would you swap with?'

Polly's preparing the treatment room when her client breezes in, enveloping them both in a cloud of bergamot and orange perfume. Dressed in an understated leather jacket teamed with jeans, grey suede boots and a beautiful Louis Vuitton handbag, this woman looks like any ordinary well-groomed thirty-year-old until she waves her hand, dominated by an enormous emerald cluster ring, and speaks:

'Polly, you are such a sweetie to see me at such short notice. The tension in my neck is driving me insane. The flight from New York was hideous. I don't know why I pay for first-class travel. A ghastly couple dressed from head to toe in Burberry brought their sprog into the cabin and it wailed all night. It shouldn't be allowed. Babies should be banned from flying. I didn't get a wink of sleep and I wanted to look my best for the big celebrity bash tonight. It's going to be quite something; those charity events are the best and I have a Stella McCartney creation especially for it.'

Polly sympathises with her client, eager for her to continue. She loves hearing about Stephanie De Loren's lifestyle. It's like a mixture of gossip magazine combined with fairy tale, for Stephanie lives in an enormous mansion in the country but spends most of her time hobnobbing with celebrities and jetting about the world. Over Easter she'd hung out on Sir Richard Branson's Necker Island and she shared some very interesting tales about her experiences with Polly.

'Bless you. That feels so much better,' Stephanie gushes once Polly begins her massage. 'You have healing hands. I always feel so much better after I've visited you.'

She's quiet for a while. Polly's hands glide over her athletic body. Her muscles are toned. She's in excellent shape. She has it all; looks, connections and money. Polly wishes she could be like Stephanie. She's everything Polly wants to be.

'Did I tell you about the fiasco at the Monaco?' She continues chatting, amusing anecdotes about A-list celebrities who are as familiar to Stephanie as Dignity and Kaitlin are to Polly.

'There is someone. She's everything I would like to be. And even though she's filthy rich, she's actually quite down to earth about many things.'

She was going to continue but a husky voice called, 'Lilith!'

'That's Mania. Excuse me a moment.'

Lilith left Polly lost in thought about Stephanie. How nice it would be to change places with someone. Stephanie has no money troubles. She's a free agent who goes wherever her mood takes her. She's never lonely. Her contact list reads like a who's who list of celebrities. Polly has seen her carrying a leather-bound diary in which she keeps all her appointments and contacts. *'I never trust phones. You can't beat the old-fashioned way. Phones can break.'* And she had a collection of shoes that Polly coveted more than anything else. Polly stared at the water left in the glass and sniffed it. It smelt sweet. Was it some sort of truth serum? It was most unlike her to open up to anyone about her innermost fears or problems. As close as she and Kaitlin had been, Polly had always been careful about what she revealed to her friend. Kaitlin wouldn't have liked this dark side of Polly. She looked about. Maybe this was a bad idea. It was certainly an odd sort of office. She placed her glass on the table and stood up to leave.

'Ah, Polly. So sorry to have kept you.' A tall figure strode in. Polly couldn't speak. The woman, if indeed she was a woman, was also clad in a black leather catsuit. Polly craned her neck backwards to look up at her. The woman sat down beside her and extended a hand. Her fingernails were painted deep red and were so long they curled forwards.

Polly shook the hand. The woman's grip was much firmer than she expected.

'I must apologise for not greeting you. I understand Lilith has had a preliminary chat with you. Thank you for contacting us and let me assure you, your life will be dramatically different after your visit

CHAPTER THIRTEEN
Simon

Simon awoke in a groggy state to find the other side of the bed empty. Veronica had already got up. She'd been asleep, or pretending to be when he'd stumbled up the stairs and dropped into bed, so he'd yet to explain his absence. He yawned. The evening before now seemed unreal. He must have drunk too much and imagined the whole thing. There was no way on this planet he'd met two demons. Yet he had. He sat on the edge of the bed and peered at the clock. It read five past seven. He ought to get ready for work. He was leaving it tight if he didn't want to get stuck in traffic. He would be later than usual. He reached for his glasses. His eyes felt sore. Ever since he'd suffered a detached retina, they had been weaker. He still winced at the thought of the treatment. It was the stuff of nightmares – and costly. Still, his glasses helped ease the strain. He stood up, scratched his backside, yawned, drew the curtains and looked out upon his driveway then gave a shriek and jumped away, startled. The dark grey S 63 AMG Coupé currently parked on his drive belonged to Kimberly. It was most definitely hers. It had cream leather seats – 'porcelain' to those in the know. He remembered the car arriving at the dealership and how all the sales team had been envious of it. It was the latest model from Mercedes-Benz and had incredible specifications – Swarovski crystal headlights, a Magic Sky Controlled panoramic roof that gave the impression of open-top motoring even when closed, a diamond front grill and a clever suspension system called Magic Body Control, which read the road ahead and actively pulled the wheels up and down to absorb each bump as the car rolled over it. It was the epitome of luxury and one of most prestigious cars money could buy.

He shook himself out of his stupor and checked the number plate. It was her car's registration. What the hell was she doing here? His heart began to batter against his chest as he flapped about the room, grabbing at clothing strewn on the floor. If Kimberly had come here to talk about his imminent resignation, he was in big trouble. He pulled on his boxers from the day before. No time to look for a clean pair. He needed to intercept Kimberly before she spilled the beans to Veronica or, worse still, to Morag.

Simon hopped about the bedroom struggling into trousers and socks, crashing into the set of drawers and stubbing his toe on the bed. He pulled on a shirt thrown over the back of a chair, fumbled with the buttons and, ramming it into his trousers, flung open the bedroom door and hurtled downstairs. He charged into the living room. No sign of her. Voices came from the kitchen. Simon smoothed down his hair with a shaking hand, checked his reflection in the hall mirror and headed for the kitchen.

'Look what the cat's dragged in,' growled Morag, cigarette in hand. Smoke curled above her head. She was perched on one of the kitchen stools, cup of coffee in front of her. 'Nice to see you up and keen to get to work, Simon,' she continued. 'What? Lost your tongue? You did remember I was staying here, didn't you?'

Simon recovered quickly. Kimberly wasn't here. Veronica stood by the kitchen sink, spooning cereal into her mouth.

'Morning, ladies,' Simon said, looking around to spot Kimberly. 'Just you two here?'

'Of course. Who else did you expect to be here? Joanna Lumley? President Putin?' Morag chortled.

Baffled, Simon looked out of the window to check no one was waiting at the door.

'Are you feeling ill?' asked Veronica. 'You seem a bit strange.'

Simon stared at the Coupé. His mind flashed back to the night before and the pact that had been made. Gradually, it dawned on him that his own C-Class company car wasn't in the driveway. Could they? Had they? Had Nick and Len begun to change his life? He looked at Veronica. She waved her spoon at him.

'You look awfully peaky. I think you might be overdoing it at work.'

'Yes, that's it. I am overdoing it. I think I might take some time off today and spend it with you and Morag. By way of apology for missing your arrival,' he added, looking at Morag.

'Oh, you're forgiven,' said Morag airily. 'You should have said you were late because you had to collect your new company car. We'd have understood, wouldn't we, Veronica?'

Veronica smiled. 'Yes, you kept that quiet, didn't you? I expect you wanted to surprise us about it. Got any more surprises for us?' she asked.

Simon rubbed his chin. He needed to think. 'Oh crikey, forgot to shave in my excitement to see you, Morag. Better go and tidy up. In fact, I'll grab a shower, get changed, let work know I won't be in and later we'll go out to town in the new car – it's one of the first in the country. Treat you to a bit of luxury, eh Morag?'

Morag cocked her head to one side and gave him a piercing look. 'Yes,' she said after a moment. 'That would be nice. It will make a change. I won't be cramped in the back as usual.'

'Great,' replied Simon through gritted teeth.

He dashed upstairs, peeled off his clothes and stood under a hot shower to reflect on the day before. His brain whirred in confusion yet a small part of it managed to process events and attempt to explain what was happening. By the time he'd towelled off, he was convinced that demons or imps were in the process of transforming his life. He sat on the edge of the bed, a towel wrapped around his waist and rummaged through the pockets of his trousers. He extracted a crumpled piece of paper. It was his copy of the contract. He smoothed it out and read it over. It seemed he'd signed over a soul for a life of luxury. He checked it again. At the bottom of the contract was some small print so tiny he couldn't read it however much he squinted. He needed a magnifying glass. He would have to purchase one later and see what it said.

By now, it was coming up to eight o'clock. The showroom would be opening. Ken would be there and a couple of the receptionists. The after-sales team would be in getting ready for the delivery of vehicles requiring servicing and maybe one or two of the sales team. He decided to phone up and let them know he wouldn't be in.

The phone was answered on the fifth ring. 'Good morning, Ernest-Deal, Tideswell Dealership, can I help you? You're speaking to Jackie.'

'Hi, Jackie,' said Simon. 'I don't suppose Kimberly is in yet, is she?'

'Actually, she is. She was here when I arrived, which is most unusual. She's in the back office with three men in suits.'

Jackie had just turned sixty, lived alone – following the death of her husband – and knew every person at Tideswell, along with members of their families. She was Eric's sister-in-law and Georgie's godmother. She was the face and heart of Tideswell. Whenever someone celebrated a birthday, Jackie brought a home-made cake in for them and whatever the occasion, she ensured a collection was made and a present purchased. In brief, she was a surrogate mother to them all. She was also the warm, welcoming face for the customers. Often an angry, frustrated or grouchy customer would be softened by her calm voice and cheerful demeanour. The place wouldn't be the same if she left. It would lose its heart and soul. *Soul*: that reminded him of the reason for the phone call.

'Jackie, I need a favour,' he asked.

'Name it,' she replied.

'Could you please tell Kimberly I'm not feeling too well and I'm taking the day off? I have a feeling she won't mind.'

'Well, that's not really a favour. Of course I shall. You take care of yourself. You've been looking run-down all month. It gets silly here sometimes with all these new targets to be reached. It's little wonder you're not well. Look what happened to Alan. He's still off and taking the antidepressants. You could do with a holiday.'

'No, I'm okay. Just under the weather. That's not the favour. I need you to look in the car park and see if Kimberly is in her car today. It'll be in the usual bay.'

'Hang on.'

Simon waited a few minutes. He heard muffled clattering as Jackie put her headset back on. 'Hi, Simon. You still there? No. She's not in the flash Coupé. That space is empty and I looked around the staff car park and I can't see it. Has she had an accident in it?'

'No, nothing to worry about. I thought I saw it drive by. Maybe her husband is using it today, that's all.'

'I'm not sure that's allowed. Still, when you're the boss you can do what you like, eh? One rule for them…'

'Another for us,' Simon finished her sentence. 'Thanks, Jackie. You're the best. See you tomorrow.'

'Hope you feel better. Oh, and tell Veronica I've finished sewing that dress for Georgie. I hope she likes it.'

'Bless you. Thanks, Jackie. You're a star.'

'I'll sit here and twinkle then. Take care, Simon.'

Simon disconnected the call. Poor Jackie. If she were next for the chop, her life would change too and not for the better. He scratched his ear and tried to think what to do next. He reached for his trousers again and dragged out the business card he'd been given. It was black. In oxblood coloured italics it read *Mission Imp-ossible* with the phone number 0800 666 666. He dialled the number.

'Morning, Simon,' said a voice he recognised. 'Enjoying your new car?'

'It was you then?'

'Who else? We told you we deliver on our promises. We're pretty busy at the moment. Got lots to arrange for other dissatisfied people. We'll sort out when to meet you next – same place as last night – to bring us your nominated soul. We're looking forward to meeting him or her. Is he your ex-neighbour?'

Simon gulped. Maybe he ought to 'fess up before things got out of hand. Then he looked outside at his beautiful new vehicle and decided he would leave it as it was. What was the worst that could happen?

'No, it's one of the family.'

'Excellent. See you soon.'

CHAPTER FOURTEEN
Polly

'I think you took off your specs too soon,' said Lilith in a hushed tone. 'Those scarlet eyes are pretty damn scary.'

'She'll be fine,' replied Mania. 'See, she's coming round already.'

Polly let out a soft groan.

'It's okay, Polly. You just fainted.'

Polly opened her eyes and looked up at Lilith. For several seconds various emotions crossed her face as she wrestled with the truth of her situation.

'I'm not dreaming, am I?'

'No. Sorry I frightened you, Polly,' said Mania.

Polly attempted to shunt herself away from Mania, who was squatting on the floor beside her.

'It's okay. No one's going to hurt you. We're here to help, remember? We've got rid of your parking fine and we were just discussing whose life you would like to live instead of your own.'

Polly sat up then struggled to her feet.

'You're a real imp,' she said, pointing at Lilith. Lilith nodded. Polly recalled trying to pull off a horn only to discover it wouldn't detach from Lilith's head. She shook her head in disbelief. 'And Mania is… a demon?' she continued, as she slowly gathered her wits once more.'

'I am,' replied Mania. 'I didn't intend to scare you senseless. That's why I keep my eyes covered and hide my tail.'

Polly shuddered. The tail had shocked her, but the scarlet eyes had frozen her in fear. However, now she felt less scared. Lilith and Mania had been very gentle with her. So what if they were demonic; they were offering her a solution to all her problems.

'You feeling okay now?' asked Lilith, handing Polly a glass of water.

'I'm all right. Really. It was just the shock. That and the fact I didn't eat yesterday. I'm absolutely okay. Let me go through this one last time. You'll arrange it for me to swap lives with Stephanie de Loren, pampered, stinking-rich, single girl if I nominate someone I know to spend eternity in hell?'

'That pretty much covers it. Looking at the list of people you would like to swap with, you've made a good choice.'

'It was more by luck since it was her name I pulled out of the hat. I suppose swapping lives with Angelina Jolie or Kate Middleton was too ambitious.'

'It's against the rules. If you had personally known Kate and her name had been pulled out of the hat, you'd have been headed off to join William. Unfortunately, rules are rules and you can only choose people you know. You happy with your decision to swap with Stephanie?'

'Well, she certainly has more fun in life than I do. She visits from time to time for a massage – apparently she prefers my massages to those from her personal trainer. She often gets her nails done at the salon downstairs and always seems to be going out to lunch or other events. I could live that life. I'd love to lounge in bed until I wanted to get up, and then zoom off to the salon to be made-up before I strutted my stuff at the latest red-carpet show or charity gig. I could put up with wealth, freedom to enjoy it and endless fun. Last time I saw her, she told me all about a celebrity bash she was attending in Paris – a ball being held at the president's palace of all places. Can you imagine that? It'd be incredible. I wonder what I'd wear to an event like that? I'd have to go to a top French designer and get fitted for something. I wouldn't want to look shabby and I'd need a dress that could hide my short waist – make it look leaner.' Polly sat lost for a moment in a reverie. 'And I believe she's friends with David Candy. I think I could thoroughly enjoy a life of parties with company like that.'

'I think you mean Gandy. David Gandy the model.'

'Oh dear, I think I need to swot up on my celebs. It'll be fun – champagne, parties, designer clothes, beautiful people – what's not to like?'

Lilith took care not to smile at Polly's comment.

'Well, in light of what you said about loving designer clothes, you've probably made a good choice. Stephanie is certainly well off and also has a penchant for all things glamorous. I'm sure we can arrange a swap for you. Of course, you won't get her body, only her life, and she'll have yours. Now we need to seal the deal. Happy to sign?'

'You bet I am. This is all surreal. I'm having a huge problem understanding that you ladies are not ladies at all.'

Mania twirled her tail.

'It takes some getting used to, but I think you've seen how convincing we are.'

CHAPTER FIFTEEN
Simon

For Simon, the day passed in a fog. He drove his wife and mother-in-law to town, treated them to lunch, behaved like the perfect husband and then sat in front of the television with them both watching programmes that in ordinary circumstances would make him grumble and complain. He preferred documentaries or films. These talent and game shows got on his nerves. The adverts came up and Veronica headed off to prepare dinner, leaving him sat opposite Morag, who began muttering about how uncomfortable she was.

'You should buy a better sofa now you've finally got promoted,' she announced. 'The springs have gone in this one.'

More likely your springs have gone, thought Simon, studying his mother-in-law's spreading backside, which filled the cushion. He mumbled in agreement and focussed on an advert for the new Jaguar XE. It was followed by a cryptic message: *'Can You Keep a Secret? Coming Soon'*. He huffed. There seemed to be a glut of Danish or Scandinavian dramas appearing on screen. This was undoubtedly a trailer for another. Some of them were quite good – dark and moody – the only problem was you had to keep one eye on the subtitles all the time to understand what was being said. At least they were better than the crap Morag and Veronica enjoyed. Dancing dogs and shows with hopefuls trying to make it into the big time, or so-called celebrities hanging on to what little fame they had, were not his bag. The programme started up again. Morag perked up as a man with a monkey puppet came on stage and faced four judges. Simon fantasised about his new role as manager and ignored Morag's commentary.

'Thanks, Simon,' said Veronica in a hushed tone, when he went through to the kitchen to get Morag a small sherry before dinner. 'You pulled out all the stops today. The new Mercedes was a real surprise. You should have told me. I was horrible to you last night. It's just that she's difficult to handle at the best of times and you promised you'd be home. Still, I should have given you a chance to explain. I suppose the car means you are finally getting the break you deserve.'

Simon uncorked the sherry and tried to avoid his wife's gaze. 'Yes, it's the start of a new Simon Green,' he said.

'Not before time,' said his wife. 'I was getting frustrated with the old one. He needed a makeover.'

He scurried out of the kitchen, leaving Veronica to chop up vegetables for dinner. He almost collided with Haydon.

'Hi, how's the studying?' he asked.

'Yeah, fine. Cool motor. Is it yours?'

'Yes. New company car.'

'So if you've got a new car, it must mean you've got a pay rise,' Haydon continued. 'And, if you've got a pay rise, maybe you could sort me out some lessons and a car then?'

'Let's not jump the gun, Haydon. It hasn't been settled yet,' he added, then, seeing the look of disappointment registering on his son's face, he clapped him on the back. 'I'm sure we can come to some arrangement though.'

Haydon's face lit up. 'Great. Oh thanks, Dad.'

Simon was almost crushed by the bear-like hug his son gave him. It had been a very long time since they had had any contact. Simon recognised the feeling inside as warmth and pride. Although it was early days, he was on the path to winning his son over. He owed those demons.

Ivan was curled up on Simon's chair. Simon handed the sherry to his mother-in-law and attempted to shove the cat from the chair. The animal refused to budge.

'Oh, leave him be. He's happy there,' said Morag in a peevish tone. 'It's probably more comfortable than this sofa.'

Simon put out a hand to remove the cat then decided against it. Ivan might just accidentally claw the old boot when he next sat on her lap.

It was an optimistic Simon that dressed for work the following morning. He put on his best suit and shone his shoes. If all went to plan, he would have a new job and no further money worries. He headed to the showroom in his gleaming, luxurious vehicle feeling every inch the manager. He arrived at the dealership and parked the car in its usual bay, then took a deep breath and marched inside.

He walked towards his desk and stopped short. His computer was missing, along with the large framed photograph of his children and Veronica taken on a family day out to Animal World. It had been replaced by one of a good-looking man in a sweatshirt and jeans posing with a large Rottweiler. Both looked confidently at the camera. Simon's nameplate had gone too. In its place was one that read *Kimberly Clarke – Car Sales*. His heart fluttered. The imps or whatever they were had pulled it off. Kimberly was now positioned at his desk and had his old job. He turned towards the manager's office.

'Morning, Patrick,' he called, seeing his colleague scurry in.

'Morning, boss,' replied Patrick. Simon beamed. It had happened. He didn't know or understand how, but he was now the manager of Ernest-Deal.

'Got one for you,' he said to Patrick. Patrick looked blankly at him. 'Joke of the day,' continued Simon, with a wry grin. 'A man was browsing through the classifieds when he noticed an advert: "Brand new Ferrari for sale for £200." He checked the price again. It was definitely £200. He decided it was a printing error or a joke until curiosity got the better of him. Off he went to the address stated to see the car. A woman answered the door and led him to the garage, where there was indeed a brand new Ferrari. "Wow!" said the man. "Can I take it for a test drive?" The woman agreed and off he went for a fifteen-minute drive. It was perfect. Drove like a dream. He had to have it. He returned to the house and asked why the lady was selling it for only £200. The woman laughed and said, "My husband ran off with his secretary. He told me I could keep the house and furniture but to sell his Ferrari and send him the money." '

Patrick gave a weak smile. Simon shifted uncomfortably from leg to leg. 'When's your footballer collecting his SLS?' Simon asked, changing the subject.

'He changed his mind. He phoned me just after I left the office. He's going for an Audi R8 from Supercars. I've come in on my day off to try and find another client.'

Simon wanted to commiserate with his friend, yet he sensed a shift in their relationship. The camaraderie that normally existed between them had vanished. In its place hung an awkward silence. Patrick avoided Simon's eyes, staring at his polished shoes instead.

'Never mind. I'm sure you'll sell it. You're a good salesman,' Simon replied. Patrick mumbled something and shuffled off towards the area where all the sales staff congregated. Simon heard laughs. Barry and Ryan slapped Patrick on the back and no doubt were cheering him up with lewd jokes or perhaps some rude comments about Simon.

Simon shrugged it off although his heart felt heavy. He should have guessed there would be a change in his relationships once he was in charge. It wasn't how he'd envisaged his promotion. He had always assumed he would remain one of the boys as well as being a respected member of staff who could steer the company to new heights. He would have to work on that. He wasn't keen on being ostracised. He made his way to the manager's office. On top of the desk was a small pewter plaque – *Simon Green, Manager*. He dropped onto the leather swivel chair and spun a full circle then opened the top drawer. His chewy mints, stress ball and best fountain pen were laid out as they had been in his old desk drawer. He circled again in the chair, looking out at the showroom as he did. He was master of all he surveyed.

The other employees were arriving now. Ken sprinted in, grabbed some number plates and hared off to the workshop, hardly glancing at Simon's office. Jackie came in carrying a large canvas bag, unpacked a Tupperware container and placed it on a shelf under the reception desk. She looked over at the office and Simon waved at her. She nodded curtly then turned her back to him, fixed her headset ready to take calls and got into position to greet the first customers of the day. Almost immediately, a tall girl in her early twenties wandered in. Jackie buzzed through to Simon.

'Miss Chance to see you.'

'Thank you, Jackie. Oh by the way, whose birthday is it today?'

'Mine,' replied Jackie.

'Gosh! I'd forgotten the date. I've been – erm – otherwise preoccupied. Many happy returns. Did you like the present Georgie sent?' he continued, recalling the porcelain mug in the shape of a cupcake sitting in the kitchen waiting to be wrapped. He'd complained about the price of a silver bracelet Veronica insisted on getting for their friend and now winced in embarrassment at the recollection.

'I don't know why you're being so nice to me today. You made it clear when you got this job that you no longer wanted to *associate* with us employees, so if this is your idea of a joke, then it's not one of your best ones. Now if you'll excuse me, I have work to do. I'll send Miss Chance in.'

Simon scratched his ear and puzzled over the conversation. Did this mean he and Jackie had fallen out? Surely not. They had been friends for too long for that to happen. A polite knock interrupted his thoughts. A scantily clad young lady stood by the door.

'Come in, Miss Chance,' he said, standing up and holding out his hand to greet her.

'Thank you, Mr Green.'

'Simon, everyone calls me Simon,' he said then reminded himself that might no longer be the case.

'I've brought my qualifications as you requested,' said the girl as she sat down. Her tight skirt rode up, revealing long shapely legs.

'Ahem, yes,' said Simon, tearing his eyes away from her thighs. He leaned forward to take the folder she was handing him and found he was face to face with a size forty-inch bust straining to escape a snug-fitting cashmere sweater. His face flushed a similar shade of pink to the sweater, and with burning cheeks he opened the folder. Jennifer Chance had worked as a receptionist in a dealership in Birmingham for three years.

'Ah, this all seems in order. Now Jennifer, could you please remind me where we are with this?' he asked, trying to make sense of the situation.

The girl arched perfectly groomed eyebrows in surprise. 'I thought this was a formality, Mr Green. You assured me the job would be mine if I turned up today with my qualifications and a CV. I hope you're not going to go back on that.'

'Yes, yes, of course. I just wanted to clarify it and make sure you're happy with that and if I recall we agreed a salary package, didn't we?'

The girl pouted, her indecently full lips shimmered and for one crazy second Simon had an urge to lick the pink gloss from them and kiss them.

'Of course we did. You offered me double the amount my last employers were paying me.'

Simon loosened his tie. All of a sudden it felt rather tight. 'And I was due to start today. You're not going to go back on the arrangement are you? I handed in my notice as soon as you offered me this job and they weren't happy with me walking out. I've been a huge asset to them and, as they said, I'm irreplaceable.'

'Gosh, no. I wouldn't dream of it,' replied Simon, wondering why on earth anyone at Ernest-Deal would pay a ridiculous high salary to a receptionist when they were already struggling as a dealership.

'Good. I'll get started then.'

'Erm, okay. I just need a few minutes with Jackie. If you wouldn't mind waiting here, Jennifer.'

He scurried out of the office. Jackie was reading a magazine at the desk, a cup of coffee in one hand.

'Jackie, ah, we have a new employee starting today. Would you mind showing Miss Chance the ropes please?'

Jackie placed her cup on the reception desk with a clatter.

'Is that cheap tart working on reception?'

'Jackie, keep your voice down. That's no way to talk about a fellow colleague.'

'Colleague? She's a – and I don't like using this word – a slut,' she hissed. 'Ask the lads here. She's well known in this area. She works in Birmingham, doesn't she? I know the folk at her dealership. She does the best part of bugger all there. She's always filing her nails or screwing one of the workshop juniors. It's no secret,' she continued as Simon's face screwed up in disgust. 'She's got a reputation for being lazy, sluttish and I bet they couldn't wait to get rid of her at her last job. So which idiot has employed her? Oh,' she said as Simon went pink once more.

'I'm not working with her.'

'Now, Jackie. Be reasonable. Give the girl a break.'

'No. You ask her about last Christmas.'

'What happened last Christmas?'

'She was caught in the manager's office giving him – let's call it a special Christmas present. Word has it that's her speciality. It must be those Botoxed lips that help. Or maybe you already knew about it,' she added and sniffed in disgust.

Simon gulped. 'No, of course not. I would never… I couldn't… no! An emphatic no.'

'I'm surprised you hadn't heard about it. We all knew. The video of it went viral on YouTube.'

'It was videoed?'

'Yes, and she tweeted about it, along with her other sexual exploits. She's got thousands of followers. Little surprise. All her tweets are about sex.'

'Honestly, I didn't know. You don't think I employed her because I wanted her to—'

Jackie folded her arms and stared at him. 'I'm not working with her and that is that. She's poisonous. She ruined a friend of mine's marriage by sleeping with her husband. Dorothy and Brian had been married almost forty years. Fancy a young thing like that jumping into bed with a sixty-year-old. She has no morals. She also spreads catty gossip and flirts with all the customers. I think too much of the people here to let her come and ruin our family. And ruin it she will.'

Simon glanced at his office. Jennifer was administering more shiny gloss to her lips.

'Look, give it a few days and I'll see how she fits in and if it doesn't work out, I'll fire her.'

Jackie picked up her magazine, folded it neatly and, picking up her bag and coat, she turned to Simon. 'I'm not working with her. If you want her that badly you'll have to get her to learn the ropes by herself. I resign.'

With that, Jackie marched out of the showroom, head held high. Simon started to run after her and was halted in his tracks by a cry from Barry, 'Mr Green!'

'Not now, Barry!' yelled Simon as he resumed his race after Jackie.

'It's serious, Mr Green. It's Patrick!'

'Patrick?'

'He had a large pot of pills. Ryan saw him with them and now he's locked himself in the toilet and won't come out. He took losing that last sale badly.'

Simon watched Jackie unlock the door of her car. He'd phone her later and sort it out. She couldn't walk out. The place would crumble without her matronly influence.

'Hang on, I'm coming,' he said and followed Barry to the toilets.

'Patrick!' he shouted. 'Can you hear me?'

No sound.

'Patrick, if this is about losing that sale, it's really not important. Come out and we'll chat about it.'

There was still no sound. Barry wrung his hands together.

'Patrick!' called Simon, banging on the door. 'For God's sake don't do anything stupid. You've got your family to think about. What about the new baby? Come out, please.

'Patrick, say something. Just talk to me! For crying out loud! Patrick!'

'Did you call me?'

Simon spun around. Patrick was looking at the pair of them as if they were circus clowns.

'Oh Patrick, thank goodness,' said Barry and kissed him on the forehead.

'Get off, you big poof,' said Patrick and pushed him away playfully.

'Ryan saw you with some pills and he assumed—' Barry looked relieved.

'They're vitamin pills, you knob,' replied Patrick. 'They're for my wife. She's run-down. She needs to look after herself with this baby on the way. I had to nip home and give them to her. You didn't think I was trying to top myself, did you?'

'The thought might have crossed our minds,' replied Simon, trying to discover the correct balance between manager and friend.

'I'm fine, Mr Green,' said Patrick, automatically raising the invisible barrier between them. 'Apologies for inconveniencing you. I'm sure you have more important things to deal with. Come on, Barry. Let's go sell cars.'

Simon rubbed his head. His bald patch seemed even bigger. He checked it in the mirror. He ought to ask the imps for a hair transplant. If he had any more stress today, it would all drop out entirely. He returned to the office to find Ryan sitting on his desk chatting to Jennifer. He leapt up when Simon walked in. 'Sorry, guv. I was keeping Miss Chance company. Want me to introduce her to the team?'

Jennifer looked like she wanted to rip Ryan's trousers off with her teeth. Simon wiped invisible sweat from his brow and wished it wasn't turning into one of those days. He needed to talk to Jackie and sort out this mess. In the meantime, there was no one manning reception so he needed Jennifer.

'Thanks, Ryan, could you settle her in at reception. Sorry to throw you in at the deep end, Jennifer. Jackie was feeling ill and I let her take the day off, especially as it's her birthday.'

Ryan gave him a quizzical look. 'She okay? She didn't say anything when she came in.'

'No, woman's troubles,' replied Simon, then wished he hadn't. Jackie was well beyond all that. Ryan didn't question it, probably because he was too busy throwing surreptitious looks at Jennifer's breasts. 'I'll sort out someone to sit with you in a while.'

'No probs. I'm quite capable of working reception,' she replied and stood up, pulled her top down so it almost covered her midriff and, shaking her dangling earrings, she swanned out of the office with Ryan in hot pursuit.

Simon regarded the pile of papers on his desk with a sigh and wondered what he was supposed to do next. So far he'd achieved nothing. There was another knock at the door. Dave stuck his head around.

'Got a minute, Mr Green?' Simon was getting sick of being called 'Mr Green', especially by people he'd known for years.

'Yes, Dave, what is it?'

'I've got a problem with an E-Type Jaguar.'

'What sort of problem?'

'I took it as part exchange for a new XF and the workshop team has just told me it's been bodged. It appears someone did some poor repair work on it. Entire panels need to be replaced and it'll cost a fair bit to rectify the damage. It'll eat up all the profit I made on the sale. Dave said he's never seen such a terrible job. It's an absolute cock-up.'

'Okay.'

'That's it? Okay?'

'For the moment. I need to think about it and decide what to do. Leave it with me.'

'Righty-ho!'

Simon gazed out of his window. The way things were going there would be no Ernest-Deal left in a month. He would have to work out how to swallow the loss the car had cost the dealership and fathom out how to dispose of Jennifer and get Jackie back. The phone on his desk rang.

'Hi, Simon. Some bloke from head office wants to talk to you,' announced Jennifer.

'Thanks, Jennifer. Put it through.'

'Putting it through. Which knob do I press?'

Simon groaned and wondered if the morning could get any worse. He was about to discover it could.

CHAPTER SIXTEEN
Simon

'Morning, Simon,' boomed a male voice. 'Tom Sanders here. Just wanted to confirm what we were discussing yesterday – the overhaul. We looked at the shortlist of salespeople you submitted and we agree with you. We need to dispose of Patrick Johnson. He's underperformed for the last quarter. To recap, you've chosen: Trevor Allbright from servicing; Jackie Turnbull from reception; Patrick Johnson and Kimberly Clarke from sales; and Ken Close, the chap who delivers cars and cleans them. We can't stand still as a company and, as we agreed yesterday, these changes are necessary.'

Simon squeezed his eyes shut and rubbed the bridge of his nose. Tom continued to bark instructions at speed. 'Talking of changes, I hope you've installed that new girl – Jennifer. Charming young lady.' Simon could hear the lust in Tom's voice. 'It'll be nice for customers to be greeted by a pretty young face. Right – could you inform those chosen for dismissal and ask them to collect their P45s? Obviously, they'll get the package we talked about and references. Talk to you next week. You're still on for the corporate golfing weekend, aren't you?'

'Yes, oh yes. Wouldn't miss it. See you next weekend.'

Simon replaced the receiver and wiped his forehead. Tom Sanders was a middle-aged jerk with a spreading girth thanks to too much corporate entertainment. He had a fat ruddy face and dreadful halitosis. No one could understand why he was in senior management, although rumour had it that he'd been best buddies at school with the current director. Simon surmised from the phone call that his first job as manager would be to fire his colleagues and friends. He wasn't doing that. He pulled out his mobile and phoned Mission Imp-ossible.

'Welcome to Mission Imp-ossible. Is your life a living hell? We can change it forever. Please leave a message after the growl and we'll get back to you. Thank you.'

'Len? Nick? I know you're there. Pick up. Okay, here's the thing. I've arrived at work and I've been told to fire my friends. Now that wasn't part of the bargain. I wanted a nice cushy job as a manager. I do not want to fire the only people who have been civil to me over the years. Phone me back as soon as you get this.'

He slammed down his phone and chewed on a hangnail. This wasn't what he'd expected. He read through some of the papers on his desk. They were general missives about the running of the place and documents about turnover and expected growth for the dealership, along with a whole load of other information that only made his head hurt. He opened the drawers to his desk and found a document marked 'private'. He opened it. It contained notes about the plan to streamline the dealership. They must have been made at the meeting the day before because they confirmed what Tom Sanders had told him. Five people had to leave the dealership – three from the sales team and two from elsewhere. He would have to start somewhere. He had to fire someone. He would fire Kimberly. That would teach her a lesson. She shouldn't have asked for his resignation. This was all her fault. If he began with getting rid of Kimberly there was a possibility that the imps would get back to him in time to rectify this whole situation.

He had no idea what he should say. He could try the same speech she'd given him. What if she cried? She might cry. He could handle that. He would hand over his handkerchief, let her wipe her tears and place a comforting hand on her shoulder to let her know he cared. On second thoughts, maybe not the comforting hand. She might think he was trying to harass her. He tapped his teeth with a pencil and tried to work out how best to handle the situation.

'I'm so sorry, Kimberly: management has decided to let you go.' Yes, he liked that. It didn't sound as if he'd been directly involved. He jotted it down on a notepad before he forgot. Now how should he look? Sad. Not sad. Disappointed… as if management hadn't listened to him. She must not discover he'd suggested her name. He looked out of the window. Kimberly was walking to the water fountain. He tapped on the window and beckoned her in.

'Yes, Simon?' said Kimberly.

'Ah, sit down, please.'

Kimberly straightened her slate-grey pleated skirt and sat down. She adjusted her glasses and looked up at him. Her eyes, the colour of young leaves flecked with nutmeg, sparkled with a merriment that Simon hadn't noticed before. Sat in front of him she looked much younger than he recalled. Her unblemished skin glowed a soft pink. Clearly, losing the pressures associated with being a manager suited her. She no longer looked hassled and frayed. He coughed.

'Kimberly, you're an excellent salesperson,' he began.

'Thank you. I love selling cars. It must be in my blood. I get excited every day at the thought of making a sale.'

'Er, yes. Well, I, er, I've been looking at the last few months figures and you haven't been reaching the targets we agreed.'

Kimberly looked down at the desk. 'It's been tougher recently. The targets are pretty high and everyone is so competitive.'

'Yes. Yes, it's difficult at the moment. It hasn't helped having a new Audi salesroom open down the road and the government's austerity measures are affecting people's general spending. Er, there's no easy way to say this.' Simon tugged at his tie. It felt like it was strangling him. 'Kimberly. You're an excellent sales-woman and if we were in different economic times I wouldn't even have to talk to you about this, but my hands are tied.' He shot a glance at her. She was sitting on the edge of her seat, her mouth slightly ajar.

'I've had a missive from head office and cuts have to be made across the board, including a significant number from our sales department. Kimberly, I'm very sorry to tell you that I shall have to let you go.'

'Sack me? You're going to sack me,' Kimberly said, her voice barely above a whisper. 'No. You can't!'

'Well, I don't like the word "sack". I'm afraid I have to ask you to leave Tideswell, I mean Ernest-Deal. It's not all bad news. I can offer you a special redundancy package – it's pretty gener-ous. And you can keep your company car until the end of next month and, of course, I'll…we'll write you a glowing reference. Kimberly? Are you okay?'

Kimberly had her head in her hands and was rocking on her chair. 'No. No. No,' she repeated.

Simon pushed a box of tissues towards her side of the desk and adopted what he considered a fatherly, concerned look.

'Kimberly, you'll be fine. You're a great salesperson…'

'You said that already!' she retorted, raising her face to glower at Simon. She no longer looked young and fresh-faced. She looked defiant and tough and ready to give him a very hard time indeed. He was correct. She erupted suddenly. 'If I'm so great, why are you firing me? Why aren't you getting rid of Patrick or Barry or Ryan? Ryan's sales are way below par. Mine are only a little off target. It's because I'm a woman, isn't it? You've never liked me. I bet you can't stand having a woman selling cars in this macho environment.'

Simon shook his head furiously. 'Not at all. It's only that you were last in and so should be first out,' he blurted, trying desperately to regain control of the situation. He hated confrontation.

'What rot! You're a sexist pig and I bet it's you who wants me out. Well, I shan't go quietly. I'm going to contest it. It's sexual discrimination, that's what it is. It's unfair dismissal!' she shouted.

'Kimberly, calm down,' Simon said, standing up and checking to make sure no one was gawping at them. Too late. Everyone in the showroom – including three customers – was watching the drama unfolding behind the glass window. Simon stood with his back to them all, attempting to block their view. Kimberly was now banging on the desk with a curled up fist demanding to talk to someone in head office. Simon had expected tears, mild hysteria even and maybe some pleading but not this.

'I'm not leaving this office until you get head office to explain exactly why I'm being victimised here,' she screeched. 'My sales haven't been as weak as some others I could name.'

'Kimberly, can we please lower our voices?' he urged. 'We don't want everyone to know what we're discussing.'

'Don't we? I do!' She pushed back her chair. It screeched on the polished floor. In three steps she was at the door to the office and before Simon could stop her, she'd thrown it open and was yelling, 'Someone call the press, I'm going to make a statement about how Ernest-Deal treat their female staff.'

Simon stood in front of her. 'Ignore that. Kimberly is just joking.'

'No, I'm not.'

'Kimberly, come back into the office. We'll sort something out,' pleaded Simon, rubbing his hand frantically through his hair.

'You'll tell head office to change their mind?'

'Yes, um, I'll phone them if you come back and sit down.'

Kimberly moved back to the desk. 'Back to work, please, everyone,' he stated in what he hoped was a suitable managerial tone and shut the door again.

'It is no reflection on your sales ability. You were the last person employed and so it's right you're first to leave,' he insisted, wishing he'd thought of a better response.

'I thought you were going to phone head office,' replied Kimberly, crossing her arms and giving him an icy stare. 'If not, I'm going to call the local paper and give my version of events. I'll start by saying how unprofessional you've been in this matter.'

'Me?'

'You should have given me written warning about my performance so I was prepared for this rather than just dumping it on me. You ought to have explained the situation the company is facing and outlined any redundancy package to me before asking if I wished to take it up. You can't just tell someone they're out. This isn't the 1940s. There are procedures to go through and you need to be clear of your facts before making someone redundant. You ought to have checked to see who was closest to retirement age and asked for voluntary redundancies before selecting someone. Did you?'

Simon slumped in his chair. This was intolerable. Kimberly hadn't given him a written warning before she told him he was out. On reflection, he had received a letter of concern and there was an email from her saying something about sales targets. He'd deleted it without reading it. He assumed it was a general email and everyone had received it. He rarely bothered with all that in-house stuff. It was time-wasting drivel. Voluntary redundancies? Had anyone else left in the last month? He racked his brains and remembered that one of the senior technicians,

Chris, a 58-year-old had left three weeks prior to the meeting with Kimberly. Jackie had organised a leaving collection. Had he taken voluntary redundancy?

At that moment, Jennifer rang through.

'Simon,' she said in a breathy voice, 'There are two police officers here.'

'What, already? Have they come about the little upset with Kimberly? We're just sorting it. It was nothing – just a difference of opinion. Tell them that. Who called them?'

'I don't know. They said you have an urgent appointment with them. Shall I tell them to wait in reception until you've finished?'

Simon glanced up. He recognised the goatee beard belonging to the taller one of the two – it was Len. He breathed a sigh of relief.

'Take them to the greeting area. I'll be right out. Thanks, Jackie. I mean Jennifer. Thanks, Jennifer,' he added.

'Kimberly, leave it with me. I'll have another meeting with head office and we'll include you in it. Let's see if we can come to some amicable agreement and alternative.'

Kimberly regarded him coolly. 'All right. However, you had better sort it out today. And I want a full apology in writing about the way I've been treated. It's highly irregular.'

Without further discussion she rose from her seat and, head held high, walked back to her desk to the sound of applause from her colleagues. Simon removed his glasses and pinched the bridge of his nose tightly. This was dreadful. He'd made a complete mess of the whole affair. He really wasn't cut out to be management. If he was unable to sack someone he didn't much care for, how could he possibly fire his friends?

He left the sanctuary of his office and made a dash for the greeting area; an area given over to customers while they waited for their cars or for appointments. It was a private room with brochures, magazines and newspapers. There was a large television screen that showed Sky News all day and a coffee machine offering all sorts of beverages.

Len was slurping a large cappuccino noisily and watching television while Nick had his nose in a *Top Gear* magazine.

'I can't do this,' hissed Simon. 'You have to change it all. I'm not enjoying it one bit. Kimberly is going to expose me to the press.'

'Ooh, Matron!' said Nick and giggled.

'It isn't funny,' continued Simon. 'I'm in trouble here. I'm supposed to dismiss three people who are my good friends and who will never forgive me. Jackie is my daughter's godmother... sorry, I forgot,' he added, as both demons stuck their fingers in their ears and winced. 'She's... important to my daughter and my wife, and me. I'll have all sorts of problems once they discover I've fired her.'

'Looks like she's saved you the bother by walking out,' mumbled Len.

'I'm getting her back,' hissed Simon. 'Well, you are. You're going to sort this out.'

'No, we're not. We swap lives, but if you manage to cock up another one, there's not a lot we can do about that,' said Len. 'All we can do is swap you again.'

'I thought you could give me a life of debauchery and all my wildest wishes?'

'We can, if you swap with the right person. You'd need to aim higher than this though. Can't see Kimberly getting up to anything mildly frisky, let alone debauched. For mega wealth, you'd have to swap with someone like Donald Trump. Mind you, the last person who did that didn't last a day. He couldn't wait to get his old life as a gas-meter reader back. Far too much pressure.'

Simon rubbed his head again.

'You should stop doing that. It'll make you bald,' said Nick, looking up from his magazine. 'It's a pity you don't know Lewis

Hamilton. It'd be fun to swap lives with him. You'd get to drive loads of top cars instead of selling them and travel the world earning stacks of money.'

'So you can make some terrific swaps for some people yet you can't find a way out of the pickle I'm currently in. You're rubbish demons. I thought your motto was Mission Imp-ossible. At the moment you're Mission Imp-Partly-Possible. I want a refund. I want out!'

'Ouch. Harsh,' said Nick, placing the magazine on the table. 'We went to a lot of trouble to give you what you asked for. Anyway, you can't get out of it. You signed a contract and, if I'm not mistaken, in the small print it states—' Nick pulled a copy of the contract out from under the magazine '—*break this contract and you will be obliged to pay a forfeit of your own soul and those belonging to those closest to you.* So you and your family will get to spend eternity "down there". Won't that be fun?'

'So if I try to go back to my old life, I can't?'

'I suppose we could try to swap you back. You'll be in the same mess you were in when we spoke to you – debt, unwanted, nagging mother-in-law – she'll be ten times worse when she finds out you've not only lost your promotion, you've lost your job. I wouldn't want to be in your shoes. Isn't there anyone else you'd like to swap with? We could arrange to transfer you later today.'

Simon tapped his fingers together nervously. 'Okay, I have it. How about you swap me with Tony Hedge? I've always fancied his life. He spends most of the time on the golf course or sunning himself abroad. He has a hot wife, pots of money and I don't think he does much work. He's a financial advisor. Financial advisors just look after other mugs' money don't they? Should be a breeze.'

'You sure?'

'No, but I can't think of who else to exchange lives with and I need to get out of here before there's a mutiny.'

'Righty-ho. Go home for now while we clean up. We'll fix this mess here. When we're ready, we'll arrange for the new transfer. This time, make it work. We can't keep chopping and changing. We're busy demons.'

CHAPTER SEVENTEEN
Polly

Polly ogled out of the window as the limousine turned from the lane and pinched herself. No, it wasn't a dream. She was indeed sitting on a plump, cream leather seat, with a crystal glass of champagne in her hand, being driven to her new abode. The phone call she'd received two hours ago telling her to pack essentials and get ready to live her new life had been real.

The car drew up to a large gate that opened automatically when the driver pointed a control at it and crunched onto a lengthy gravelled driveway. The house – The Old Rectory – was a delightful three-storey building surrounded by nothing except for gardens and woods, and it was all hers. She hugged herself and squealed with excitement.

'Is there anything wrong, madam?' asked the chauffeur.

'Oh sorry. I'm fine, thank you. Glad to be home.' She let the word 'home' roll around her mouth a little. It felt good.

The man pulled up in front of the house, came around to her side of the car and opened the door for her. He took the empty glass from her.

'Will you be needing me again today, madam?'

'No, thank you.'

'Will you be needing me tomorrow, madam?'

Polly had trouble keeping the broad smile from her face as she recalled Lilith's last words.

'No, no need, thank you. I'm having a new car delivered tomorrow. I'll be driving myself about.'

'Very good, madam. Just call the agency should you require me.'

He handed her a business card. She took it and thrust it into her handbag. The boot of the limousine opened silently and the man brought out her overnight bag. He carried it to the front door and put it down for her. She followed behind in a trance.

'Good day, madam.'

He tipped his cap in a gentlemanly fashion. Unsure if she should shake his hand, Polly decided to bow her head in a sort of dismissive gesture. He returned to the car. It purred quietly up the drive, leaving Polly standing before her new front door. She ran her hands over the wooden nameplate. It was real. It was all real. The keys jangled as she extracted them from her pocket. They had been in her tight grasp ever since the chauffeur had arrived outside her former house and handed them to her in exchange for her old keys. That episode already seemed a lifetime away. She tried the first key and it fitted the lock. She opened the door, stepped into the wood-panelled hallway and screamed loudly as two hairy missiles hurtled towards her.

'Get off!' she yelled as the small animals jumped up at her. They were sturdy creatures, each weighing about ten kilos. Together they succeeded in overbalancing her so that she dropped on her backside onto the marble floor, where the animals snuffled and snorted at her. One bounded from her side and went to examine her stuffed overnight bag. The zip, which was worn, pulled apart on inspection and various items fell out. The dog came away with a pair of her best knickers and ran about the hall with them. The other continued snuffling at her, its meaty breath coming in hot puffs. She pushed the dog off and got to her feet. 'Get out of there!' she shouted at the one who was racing about, underwear in its mouth. A game of chase ensued, dog and woman skidding about the hall. The second dog joined in and grabbed the knickers. There was then a tug of war, with both sides eager to win the prize. Polly crept up on them, snatched at the garment and yelled at them. One dog abandoned his end and watched the scenario as Polly grappled the knickers away from the other creature. 'Leave! Drop! Sit!' she shouted. Her words only served to stir them both into an even greater frenzy and they raced around her in circles. She scrabbled about in her bag, extracted her emergency bar of chocolate and held it aloft. The two dogs sat immediately, as if an invisible puppet master were working them, tongues out. 'Ah, that's sorted you pair,' she said, tearing the wrapper open and pulling off a small piece of milk chocolate.

'You shouldn't feed chocolate to dogs,' said a low voice. Polly turned to discover a young girl leaning against a door, smoking a cigarette, arms folded. She wore multicoloured leggings and a ripped grey top. Her feet were bare, revealing manicured nails painted in black nail varnish.

'Who are you?'

'I could ask you the same thing. I assume you're the replacement for my mother – Stephanie. I've been expecting you. She's gone. Best thing. We had, as she put it, *a few issues.*'

'Hang on, how do you know about this? I was supposed to move in and live the glam life of a single woman. No children were mentioned. They weren't part of the deal.'

'And I asked for a new mother. You're not quite what I expected either,' she said. 'You're not any good at the whole pet pampering thing, are you? My mother – my ex-mother – would have scooped that pair up by now and been showering them with kisses while giving me a filthy look for having my nose pierced.'

Polly noticed the subtle stud in the girl's nostril.

'Then she'd have ordered me to get it removed. I'd have told her to *eff off* and that would be that. Hope you're better at cooking than she was.'

'You? You asked for a replacement mother?'

'And is that strange?'

'I'm a bit confused. Who did you ask?'

The girl rolled her eyes. 'Duh, demons, of course. Probably the same ones who said you could live in luxury. They promised they'd get me a replacement if I gave up a soul to them.'

'They told me the same thing. Is that legal? I mean, can they offer the same thing to two people? I'm not sure…'

She looked at the dogs sat in front of her. They were both gazing intently at her, listening to her every word.

'No chocolate?' Polly said.

'No, it can kill them. Go ahead if you hate dogs though. I won't care. They're Stephanie's dogs. I don't have much to do with them. Pity she couldn't take them with her. They're her "babies".'

'What breed are they?'

'French bulldogs.'

'They're quiet for dogs. They don't seem to bark.'

'No. They don't bark much: only if you wave biscuits at them or if the doorbell rings. I wanted a Labrador. Stephanie chose these two instead. That's Dolce,' she said, pointing at the browner of the two dogs. 'You can probably guess what the other is called. Stupid names!'

Polly returned the chocolate to her bag. The dogs gave her an accusatory look.

'Dolce. Gabbana,' said the girl in a firm yet quiet voice. 'Bed. Now!' The dogs look pained and scuttled off, their claws clattering on the marble floor.

'So what am I supposed to do now?' asked Polly.

'I don't know. Mum stuff, I suppose. You can start by telling my boarding school I'm not going back next term.'

'School? How old are you?'

'Almost sixteen. Why? You got a problem with me not going back?'

'You're only fifteen? You look... older.'

The girl toked on her cigarette and glared at Polly.

'Hey, it's not really my business but ought you to be smoking?'

The girl looked her up and down; a tight smile made its way across her face. 'Yes, that's it. Start with the nagging. You're a natural at being a mother.'

'This isn't about being bossy or nagging. My father died of cancer thanks to cigarettes. He smoked from the age of thirteen. He had a cough for ages, then it turned out it was lung cancer and it took a year for him to finally pass away. It wasn't gentle. It wasn't slow and peaceful. He didn't die quietly. It was a horrific thing to watch happening to someone you love. I sat beside him and watched this disgusting illness rob him of his health and his life. I now tell anyone I see smoking – especially younger people – that it isn't worth it. It's definitely not worth the heartache it causes for those left behind.' The girl shifted position. 'Your mother will never forgive me if I didn't try to explain why it's so bad for you.'

'She didn't seem bothered. She knew about it. Anyway, you're my mother now.'

'In that case, I don't want you getting ill through smoking, so put that cancer stick out immediately or... or... you'll be grounded.'

The girl snorted. 'LMAO! You're well funny. Okay. I'll stub this one out. Only because you made me laugh,' she added.

Polly looked about the long entrance hall. Several doors led off to the left.

'I'm not convinced about doing this. I'm sure you're a nice girl and all that, but I can't suddenly become your mother. I have no experience. I can barely look after myself. That's why I'm here. I've made a hash of my own life. I've let down people and I've got a lousy track record with relationships. I haven't even got a boyfriend.'

'Neither had Stephanie. She preferred her own company. I'm almost sixteen. I can look after myself. Give me my allowance each month and I'll stay out of your hair. I need to have a parent around until I'm eighteen when I collect my trust fund, then I'm out of here and you can do whatever you like. It's a win-win.'

Polly fiddled with her hair. The situation was peculiar and her gut instinct was to walk away from it. If she phoned Lilith to swap with someone else, who would then keep an eye on this girl? Beneath the make-up, nose ring and bravado was a vulnerable child. Polly saw a younger version of herself, full of hormones and confusion.

'You don't have a father you can stay with?'

A dark shadow crossed the girl's face. 'Never met him. He got my mother pregnant when she was young and didn't want anything to do with me. Anyway, I don't talk about it. I'm fine.'

Polly heard the hurt in the girl's voice. It struck a chord.

'Okay, well, I'm here now. Let's see how it goes for a day or two. If it doesn't work out, we'll sort it with Mission Imp-ossible. I bet there's some loophole we can exploit. In the meantime, I don't think I can get my head around being your mother. Can I just be a friend for the moment?'

The girl gave a curt nod. 'Anything that makes life easier. I expect you'd like to settle in. Help yourself. It's yours now. I'm going out later,' she added. 'I'm staying with a friend. And there's no point in telling me I can't.'

Polly didn't know how to respond. She couldn't stop the girl from going out.

'That's a shame. I was going to order in pizza. I've got a bottle of wine. We could have shared it and found out about each other. I don't even know your name.'

'You're weird. You tell me off for smoking and then ask if I want a drink. Talk about mixed messages.'

'You have a point. I'm anti-smoking. I'm not against the odd glass of wine. If you're anything like I was at your age, you'll be drinking all sorts of alcoholic concoctions with your friends.'

'You think drinking alcohol is perfectly acceptable at my age?'

'You're right. I shouldn't be encouraging you. Forget it. I'm not very good at this whole mother thing.'

The girl grinned. 'No. You're rubbish. Stephanie hated alcohol. She never touched a drop herself. Said it addled the brain and ruined the complexion.'

Polly squirmed under the girl's cool gaze.

'Didn't stop me though,' she said. 'The girls at school smuggled in alcohol every Saturday. We've got loads of hiding places in our dorms. Matron never suspected a thing. I prefer Red Bull and vodka to wine. Wine's okay when the vodka's run out. I'll pass though. I've made plans.'

The girl stared at Polly, her amber eyes searching Polly's.

'Chelsea – my name's Chelsea.'

'Nice name. Okay, Chelsea, I'll look about the place and see you in a moment.'

'Whatever,' replied the girl and drifted back inside the room, shutting the door behind her.

Polly scratched her head. This was a setback. However, the house was incredible. She collected the clothes strewn on the floor and rammed them back into her bag. She pulled it over her shoulder and went exploring. The first door led into an impressive room with a wooden-beamed ceiling, wooden flooring and large windows. Plush leather settees sat adjacent to a fireplace. The room was dominated by the baby grand piano set at an angle in the centre. Without any carpet, the space felt cool and bare. The artwork on the walls was clinical – large paintings of geometrical shapes in bright colours. If the room was for entertaining, then it lacked warmth and homeliness. There were no photographs, ornaments or furnishings to indicate that it was used. There wasn't even a television set. Polly would change that.

A second reception room housed inset bookcases filled with murder/mystery and chick-lit novels, along with several self-help books and a vast CD collection. Polly recognised the names of several of her favourite authors included in the collection. There were a few books she fancied reading, although the books on macrobiotic diets and how to discover yourself through meditation held little appeal. Further investigation revealed a sound system secreted in a modern cabinet that opened with a gentle push of a finger. This was clearly a room for reading in peace and Polly loved reading. Now she would have time to enjoy it.

She wandered out in the opposite direction to discover the hub of the house – the kitchen. The dogs jumped up from their beds next to the dark Aga and bounded towards her as if she were a long-lost friend. With their serious flat faces and bat ears they were comical to look at. She bent down and patted them. They licked her hand and gazed at her with gratitude.

'You're a pair of softies, aren't you? I don't know why you were given Italian names when you're French. You,' she said to the first, 'look like a Hugo rather than a Dolce and you, with your doleful face and big eyes definitely have an air of Serge Gainsbourg about you.' They soaked up her words, almost nodding in agreement before accompanying her while she searched through chic cream kitchen cupboards. It seemed Stephanie wasn't into food or drink any more than she was into television sets. Polly unearthed bottles of spring water, packets of rice cakes, lentils, tofu and organic coconut oil. If this was all she ate it was little wonder Stephanie remained so slim. Polly unearthed a bag of dog biscuits and pulled out a couple for her new friends, who wolfed them down. The fridge was empty apart from some organic soya milk and two eggs. A bowl of fruit stood on the marble-topped breakfast bar. Polly took an apple and chomped on it while she absent-mindedly tried out the two taps in the Belfast sink. Her heart lifted when she found a wine cooler then sank when she discovered it was full of bottles of vegetable and fruit juice. They would have to go. She rummaged in her bag and extracted a wine bottle. She shoved it in the cooler, glad she had insisted on stopping at a supermarket en route to the house to buy some essentials.

The kitchen opened out into an orangery housing a wood burner and seating area. It was cosier here than in the first room. It would be a comfortable place to hang out with friends. She paused for a moment and thought about Kaitlin. The imps had told her to leave her telephone behind as her past life was now erased. She hadn't. There was no way she was going to lose her connection with Kaitlin. Wait until she told her about this place. Kaitlin would be on the first plane over to see for herself. She opened the double doors to a paved terrace with a decked area and gasped again. There was a hot tub. She had to phone Kaitlin.

She removed her phone from her pocket and without a moment's hesitation, dialled her friend's number, grinning in anticipation of sharing her news. It rang out. With a small sigh she palmed the phone. She would try again later. The dogs gave her a look of sympathy. She broke the apple core into two pieces and tossed it to them. It disappeared instantly. Hopeful of more titbits they accompanied her upstairs, their claws silent upon the lush plum-coloured carpet. Polly thought it was like walking on a giant sponge.

She opened the first door on the left. This was definitely her room. She dropped her bag on the floor and stood in wonder. A four-poster bed sat in the middle of the room. It was quite simply the largest bed she'd ever seen. The two dogs hurled themselves onto it, scuffing at the covers and settling down to watch Polly as she walked about the room admiring the antique dressing table, the period fireplace and the view of the gardens from the window. Three oak doors led off the room, the first into a walk-in wardrobe the size of the kitchen back in her old house. Two rows of designer dresses hung from rails, while shoes of every colour imaginable were neatly laid out in rows below the rails. It appeared that Stephanie took the same sized shoes as Polly. She tried a pair of Gucci sandals and strutted in front of a full-length mirror. She ferreted through the racks, mouth agape. There were shoes by Christian Louboutin, Manolo Blahnik, Louis Vuitton, Miu Miu, Jimmy Choo and *ohmigosh* – a pair of Alexander McQueen shoes in outrageous green. Polly was in shoe heaven. She grasped the green shoes and held them to her chest. These were hers! Dolce joined her and sat by the door, approving her choice of footwear.

The clothes, Polly soon discovered, were far too small for her. That didn't prevent her from looking through the hangers, grabbing them and holding them up to her. She would lose weight and fit into them... or buy more. She could afford to buy anything she fancied now. She wondered how rich she was. Maybe she could afford to go to Paris or New York and buy an entire collection of clothes.

Time stood still as Polly wafted her way through the clothes in the wardrobe, admiring each and every one of the outfits. Eventually, she headed through the second door and almost collapsed in ecstasy. It was kitted out in beige and brown marble with a double-sink unit on one side of the room, shelves along the opposite side and marble steps opposite her, leading to a sunken bath. Checking the various bath oils on the side of the bath and marvelling at the golden waterfall tap, Polly decided she could spend an entire week soaking in this tub. If she didn't fancy a bath then the adjacent wet room would provide her with endless entertainment. It appeared to have several massage settings and a rainfall head.

'I'm going out,' shouted a voice from the bedroom.

'Whoa! Wait a minute. Don't go yet.' Polly walked into the bedroom to discover Chelsea now wearing a very tight black dress that left little to the imagination and purple Doc Marten boots.

'Look, I know I've only been here five minutes—'

'Forty-three actually,' replied the girl, looking bored.

'I haven't! Surely not? Gosh. No. Never mind how long I've been here. I can't let you go out.'

'Looking like this?' the girl added. 'I'm nearly sixteen and quite able to decide what I want to do and where I want to go.'

Polly felt herself going back in time and remembered a different girl, wearing shorts, patterned tights and platform shoes shouting at her mother. That girl had gone out regardless of her mother's pleas or tears. And look what had happened after that!

'No, you look fine. In fact, you look very stylish. I love the boots. I wish I could carry that look off. I'm more of a baggy jumper and elasticated-waist jeans lady at the moment. No, what I mean is we need to sit down, get to know each other and talk about important stuff like school.'

'I'm not going back so we don't need to talk about it. And I already know about you. The demons told me.'

'What do you know?'

'You're Polly MacGregor. You're in your thirties. You're – you *were* – a sports therapist. You like clothes and shoes – even if you hang about in baggy jumpers and rather garish socks,' she added, pointing at Polly's fluorescent yellow socks with smiley faces on them. 'You're not in a relationship and you like watching films and having a laugh.'

'And you chose me based on that summary?'

'You were better than the others I was offered. Besides, I figured you'd be too busy shopping to bother about what I got up to.'

'Hang on a minute. That's a mighty big assumption. I might bother a lot. Let's start by getting to know each other.'

'We've got loads of time to talk if you want to. I'm not that interesting. I like teenage stuff, Vine, Snapchat, that sort of thing.'

Polly nodded, having no idea what Chelsea was talking about.

'I'm sick of the stuck-up bitches at my school who make snide remarks about the way I dress and the stuffy teachers who keep picking on me. I loathe being incarcerated there term after term, studying subjects that hold no interest for me. It's pointless. I don't want to take my exams. And I don't actually need to take them because in two years' time I'll have enough money to do what I like. I won't need a job.'

'You're refusing to take exams? That might not be the wisest decision, you know.'

'If you're going to be a pain about it,' said Chelsea, lips curling, 'I shall get the demons to send you back to your old crappy life.'

'Fine,' replied Polly, folding her arms. 'Do that. See if they can find some irresponsible person who doesn't give a damn. You're about to make a mistake. I'd rather not be here anyway. A massive house, a few pairs of shoes and a great big bath are not worth it if I have to deal with a stubborn girl who thinks she knows best. Education is important, regardless of money. You will need it at some point in your life. I wish I'd been given the chance to go to a private school instead of the school I attended. I spent most of my time avoiding the bullies and drug-dealing kids.'

'And what good did education do you? You're here, aren't you? You couldn't stand your life the way it was.'

Polly felt the air rush out of her. 'I made a few mistakes, that's all. Working hard, getting my diplomas and setting up my business was the best thing I ever did. I was genuinely proud of myself once and it was thanks to studying. I couldn't have done it otherwise. Don't throw away your chances. You don't get many,' she said and sat on the bed. Gabbana put his head in her lap and she stroked him. His earnest face made her want to cry. 'I'll phone the office and get my old life back. You can do what you like.'

The girl pulled a face and shrugged. 'No,' she said, after some hesitation. 'I'll think about what you said. Don't go yet.'

On cue, Dolce appeared and launched himself onto Polly's legs. He licked her knees before settling down. Chelsea's lips quivered slightly.

'They seem to approve of you. You must be okay if they like you.'

Polly nodded. 'We'll talk tomorrow.'

'Cool. See you.'

Chelsea strode off, leaving Polly wondering what she'd let herself in for and why she'd agreed to stay.

CHAPTER EIGHTEEN
Simon

Simon was skulking in his shed. It was the only place he could get any peace from his wife and mother-in-law. Morag's shrill voice had given him a headache. The novelty of having a successful son-in-law was wearing off and she was back to her usual sniping ways. At least he would get some calm if he swapped lives with Tony Hedge. He doubted Selena would give him a hard time – *only in one department.* He wasn't sure how he felt about the sex side of things. As much as he wanted to make passionate love to Selena, it would feel strange. He'd been faithful to Veronica all their married life. Even though he wanted to escape his life, it was all a bit weird. He would have to see how it worked out. Those imps had better get it right this time. He thought about Selena, her smoky black eyes and, of course, her magnificent breasts. He imagined what it would feel like to nestle his head between them. They would be white, unblemished and so soft and—

A sharp rapping on the side of the shed interrupted his reverie. He jumped to his feet, grabbing the closest object to him.

'Hello, dear,' he said, as Veronica stuck her head around the door. 'I'm just looking for something to fix the wardrobe in Georgina's room.'

Veronica looked at the barbecue tongs in his hand. Simon thrust them to one side and picked up a screwdriver.

'I've been looking all over for you. You promised to have Georgie's wardrobe door repaired before she got back. By my calculations, you have twenty minutes.'

'I'll get it done now.'

'Good. It almost fell on my mother when she went to hang up some of Georgie's clothes.'

Simon wished it had fallen on the old bat. It might have shut her up for a while. She always found ways to make him look inadequate. He grabbed his tools and marched back to the house, entering via the kitchen in the hope of avoiding his mother-in-law, who would most certainly be watching television.

'Oh there you are, Simon,' came a shrill voice from behind the breakfast bar. Simon cringed inwardly. 'Veronica is looking for you. The—'

'I was in the shed looking for a screwdriver to repair Georgie's wardrobe.'

'About time, too. Veronica told me it's been broken for over a month. Hope you're better at DIY than electrical repair,' she added.

Simon rolled his eyes. He was about to defend himself when the doorbell rang.

'I'll get it!' called Veronica. Morag shuffled off to the living room.

A chubby-faced girl wearing an Asian conical hat came racing into the kitchen. A taller, sulky-faced one carrying a large backpack followed her and plonked the backpack onto the floor by the fridge. Georgina was back.

'Where's Ivan?' she asked.

'He's on your bed, asleep. He's missed you a lot,' replied her mother. 'Almost as much as us,' she added and gave her daughter a hug. The girl squirmed away but not before Veronica had planted a wet kiss on her cheek.

'Hi, Faith. Have a good time? Nice to have you back home, Georgie,' said Simon as his wife's head bobbed up and down at him, signalling that he should make conversation with his daughter. 'How was it in China? Bet you had a blast,' he said.

'Hi, Mr Green. We had such a fantastic time, didn't we, Georgie? We saw a ginormous army made of clay, temples and the Great Wall of China. It took ages to walk up to it. Georgie puked when we reached the top.'

'I did not,' said Georgie, turning pink.

'She did,' continued the small girl, oblivious to Georgie's discomfort.

Veronica cast an eye over her daughter, who was busying herself with her rucksack and trying to ignore her friend. 'Glad you enjoyed it. Love your hat.'

'Georgie's got one too. Hers is purple and black.'

A weary-looking dark-haired woman came in behind the girls. She was carrying a couple of holdalls that she deposited onto the floor.

'There, that's your kit, Georgie. Just got to sort out ours now.'

'Hi, Karen, thanks so much. Simon was on his way out to get the bags,' said Veronica, staring at Simon.

'Sorry, Karen. You should have left them in the car. I'd have got them.'

'No trouble at all. They were under a pile of mess. I'm used to carrying them. I've been carrying kids' bags all week. I have to say that although it was the trip of a lifetime, I'm glad it's over. It was gruelling looking after an entire year of kids who have enough energy to power a small country. However, it was definitely educational and very enjoyable, wasn't it, girls?'

Faith's head bobbed up and down. She pulled out a mobile. 'Want to see some photos of the Great Wall of China? We took selfies there.'

'I'm sure Georgie will want to show them her own photos, Faith. Besides, we need to get home. I have a stack of washing to do and your dad and Charlie will be eager to hear all about our adventures. So say cheerio for now. You okay to have Faith on a play date next Friday, Veronica? I have a staff meeting and Adam is away in London. Should be finished by seven.'

'Of course. It's always a pleasure to have Faith come and play.' Georgie scowled at the word 'play'.

'I'll bring my *High School Musical* DVD. We can watch that, Georgie.'

'Great,' mumbled Georgie. Her mother gave her a sharp look that she ignored.

'I'll see you at school on Monday, Georgie,' said Karen. 'Have a good weekend – what's left of it. By the way, that's a very nice car on the drive, Simon. Is it yours?'

'Yes,' said Veronica proudly. 'It's beautiful, isn't it? Simon's going up in the world.'

'Well done you,' said Karen. 'After visiting China, I've decided I'd like to do more than just teach geography. Still, it pays the bills. Come on, little miss, let's get going and leave everyone here to catch up. Bye!'

'Bye and thanks for dropping Georgie off. Georgina, say thank you to Mrs Benton.'

'Thanks,' mumbled Georgina.

'See you Monday, Georgie,' shouted Faith, skipping off like an excited puppy. Karen waved and, shooing her offspring in front of her, headed back to her car.

'So did you have a good time, then?' asked Veronica.

'Yeah, it was okay,' replied Georgie. 'I'm going to unpack and see Ivan.'

'Hey, wait a minute. Aren't you going to show us your photos and tell us all about your adventures?' asked Simon. Veronica shot him a look.

Georgie fumbled about with her backpack. 'Later. I'm a bit tired. I'm going to my room.'

'Gran's here,' said Veronica. 'She'd love to hear about your trip. Want to come and see her? She's in the living room.'

'Later,' Georgie repeated, heaving her bag onto her shoulders and heading off.

'What's that all about?' began Simon.

'Leave her,' warned Veronica. 'She's had a long journey and Faith probably cheesed her off. Faith can be quite immature for twelve at times – and tiring. Georgie will come round in time. Something's happened to upset her. She'll tell me what it is in her own good time.'

'I spent a fortune on her going across the globe to a country I myself would love to visit, and she can't even manage one ounce of enthusiasm. Why are you letting her behave like this? She's out of order. She needs telling off,' he said, his voice rising.

'No, Simon,' hissed back his wife. 'Leave it for now. I'll sort it later. Go and take Mum her glass of sherry. She's forgotten it.'

Simon snatched the glass from the top of the counter and stomped into the living room where Morag was sitting watching a talent show with Ivan purring in contentment on her lap. Neither acknowledged Simon.

'You're welcome,' he muttered, as he placed the sherry in front of her.

'Simon,' called Veronica. 'You've got a call. It's Ernest-Deal. You have to go in.'

Simon groaned. He couldn't face another day of falling out with people. He picked up the phone in the hall.

'Simon speaking.'

'It's me, Len. Pack a bag. You're swapping with Tony. We've fixed it. I told your wife you were needed at work. We'll sort that end out when you've gone. Off you go. Have fun.'

'What? Just like that?'

'It's what you wanted.'

'Yes, I did,' replied a somewhat-flustered Simon. He chewed his lip and thought briefly about the implications of changing lives with Tony. 'Georgie returned from China a short while ago. I haven't even had the chance to chat to her about her exciting trip. And Haydon will be home soon for dinner. I can't do it. I'll be missed here.'

Len chortled. 'You won't be missed, my man. Have you ever seen the film *Men in Black*?'

'I watched it years ago with the children. We went to the cinema to see it. Haydon wanted to be a man in black for years afterwards,' Simon replied.

'They had those zappers that eliminated memories, didn't they?' said Len.

'That's how you'll do it! You'll erase me from their memories. That's incredible.'

'We zap everyone associated with the swap. Now off you go and start your new life. Leave everything to Mission Imp-ossible.'

'I'm not sure. Can't I stay another day? I ought to be here for the weekend. I have to cut the grass and I'd like the chance to have a last meal with them.'

'I wouldn't. Jackie just found out you've lost your job and is on her way to commiserate with you. That means Veronica and Morag will soon also learn about your situation. Meanwhile Haydon has bragged to all his friends you're going to buy him a car so imagine how that will go down when you suddenly can't fund it?'

'Okay, okay. I get it. I'm going.'

'We'll be over in a jiffy to zap everyone. Oh, nearly forgot to tell you. The key to the house is under the mat. Selena is out at the moment. She won't be back until tomorrow so make yourself at home.'

'Righto.'

The line went dead. Simon's heart raced. This was it. The new start he'd requested. No more hassle, nagging, sulks, misery or moles. It was fast cars, helicopters and passion for him. He hesitated. *This wasn't right, was it?* He had a family here – family who cared about him. He couldn't up and leave them. A vision of watching his robot lawnmowers at work while he drank a cold beer and Selena massaged his back popped into his head.

Simon headed for the lounge and said, 'Sorry. I've got to go to work.' Veronica sat beside her mother on the sofa. Simon noticed they were starting to look alike. Once her hair turned grey, Veronica would morph into her mother. Again, he was ignored.

'I've got to go and deal with some problems at work,' he said more loudly. Only Ivan looked up and meowed. Simon waited for a moment. The women were engrossed in the television programme. No, he wouldn't be missed. Even if they weren't zapped to remove their memories of him, they still wouldn't miss him.

He stood by the front door, coat in hand. A noise above reminded him of his daughter. He hung his coat on the banister, climbed the stairs and tapped on the door. 'Georgie, it's Dad.' No answer. 'Ivan's downstairs if you want to come down and see him. Georgie, are you okay?'

'Go away. I'm busy,' came the reply. Deflated, he descended the stairs. He wouldn't be missed at all. He picked up his coat once more, opened the door and left behind his life.

CHAPTER NINETEEN
Polly

The dogs woke Polly. Her body seemed welded to the bed and she was loath to move any of her heavy limbs. The dogs snuffled and fidgeted, then jumped off the bed and landed with thumps on the floor. A visitor, determined to raise the household, was holding down the doorbell so it rang incessantly. She sat up with a jolt, unsure of where she was until she saw the two sturdy sentinels who had slept beside her. She was in her new home. The dogs looked up at her and then bounded off when she opened the bedroom door. She padded to the landing and down the stairs.

The dogs were now huffing excitedly under the front door. The doorbell continued to peal.

'At last,' said the visitor as Polly opened the door. 'I thought I was going to have to climb up the wall and drag you out of the bedroom. Morning, sweetie,' he said, leaping towards her and kissing her on both cheeks. Before she could react, he'd pushed past Polly. The dogs jumped up at him, vying for his attention. He put a hand into his tracksuit pocket, pulled out a couple of dog treats and dropped them in front of the animals. They were gobbled up immediately. 'You're very good guard doggies. Are you being good for Polly? I bet you are. You're lovely boys, aren't you? Give Uncle Calvin your paw, Dolce.'

The little bulldog sat gazing in adoration at the man and handed him a paw. The man fussed over the small dog and then gave it another biscuit. 'Good boy. Now you, Gabbana.' Polly wondered if this man was a dog whisperer, as both dogs were spellbound. Before she could ask, he'd cuddled both dogs again and stood up.

'So, sweetie, are you ready?'

'Ready for what?'

'Our regular morning session. I suspect, judging by your attire, you aren't. Never mind. I'll wait in the kitchen and you can slip into your kit and we'll get started.'

'You're going to have to explain this to me. I have no idea what you're on about.'

'Oh dear. You obviously didn't get the brief. Chelsea was supposed to explain your itinerary for the week to you. The little minx, I bet she deliberately didn't tell you. I'm Calvin – your personal trainer. I used to be Stephanie's trainer. Now you and she have changed places – which is amazeballs – I'm all yours.' He gave a high-pitched giggle. 'We usually work out every day except Sunday. We train for three hours, starting with a five-mile run. We then nip into the gym for a weight session and finish with a nice stretch. Have you seen the gym yet? I helped design it.'

Polly shook her head in disbelief. 'No. I haven't seen it. I don't do gyms anyway. That whole exercise thing isn't going to happen. Do I look like I can run down a supermarket aisle, let alone five miles?'

Calvin crossed his arms and pursed his lips. He cocked his head to one side. 'I've seen worse,' he said. 'There's hope. Now stop chattering, get into your training kit and we'll get off.'

'I don't have any kit.'

'Of course you do. Come on, I'll show you,' he said, striding down the hall as if it were his own. Polly scurried after him as he took the stairs two at a time. Dolce and Gabbana raced after them, almost tripping Polly up as she attempted to reach her bedroom first. Calvin marched straight through the bedroom and into the wardrobe where he pulled out a drawer. It was full of Lycra. He grabbed a pair of bright yellow running shoes and handed them to her.

'There you are. I'll meet you downstairs. I'll get you a glass of water before we begin.'

'Hang on a minute,' said Polly, puffing already thanks to racing upstairs. 'I really don't want to train. I hate exercise of all sorts. It hates me. I'm not an exercise sort of person. I'm built for comfort and I'm quite happy to be this way.'

'Of course you're not,' said Calvin. 'If you were, you wouldn't have swapped lives with Stephanie. You wanted to be like her and the only way for that to happen is to make some effort. Come on, sugar. You'll thank me in the end. Downstairs. Hop to it.'

Polly snorted in disgust. She wasn't going to go running with anyone. She was going back to bed. She caught sight of her flushed face and flabby legs in the mirror and paused. It would be nice to be trim and look good in outfits like those in the wardrobe. One session. She would try one session with Calvin, since he was here, and if it was too much to bear, she would tell him not to return. She struggled into the stretchy Lycra bottoms and luminous yellow T-shirt, surprised at the fact they fitted her. The trainers weren't a problem either. She swept her hair up in a scrunchie, decided she looked like a neon banana and set off to join Calvin.

She found him in the hallway doing lunges and stretches. He looked up and nodded.

'There – you look the part. You look fitter already. Let's start with a little warm-up. We'll jog from here to the end of the lane and take it from there.'

The dogs sat down by the door.

'Don't they want to come with us?'

'You're joking! They're pedigree French bulldogs. They don't do exercise. You'll be lucky to drag them out for a walk down the drive. Bye bye, boys,' he called and took off like a gazelle being chased by a lion, leaving Polly to race after him and wonder why she'd decided to swap places with an exercise freak.

CHAPTER TWENTY
Simon

Simon sat in the lounge staring at a blank television screen. He thumbed the keys on the control unit. Nothing. He turned the set on and off again – still nothing. It had been the same with the television in the kitchen. Maybe there was a problem with the satellite dish. He sat on the edge of the large embroidered chair. He couldn't relax here. He felt like an intruder. He wandered about staring at various art objects. The place looked like something out of an interiors magazine.

He headed for the kitchen and stared into the fridge. There was nothing he fancied in there other than a can of beer. He pulled the ring and slugged half of it. Back home his family would be sitting down to one of Veronica's meals. She was a good cook. It was shepherd's pie tonight. He liked shepherd's pie.

A noise from the back door made him jump. A small, energetic man with neatly cut black hair and a clean-shaven face, dressed in black trousers and a striped shirt hurried into the kitchen, stopping only to drop several plastic bags onto the worktop.

'So sorry, sir. I got held up on the M42. I can only apologise. I'll get everything ready in no time at all. I collected the trays of canapés – they're in the back of my car. The arrangements have been made as you requested and your guests all had invitations sent to them as per your instructions. Everything will be ready for eight-thirty. I'll run you a bath, put your outfit out on the bed and then ensure everything is as it should be.'

Simon sat in a state of confusion. The man must be a butler or manservant or equivalent. It came as a surprise. He had no idea Tony had servants. He felt uncomfortable about it. No one had ever run him a bath before, only Veronica on the odd occasion – when he'd been ill. How did one speak to servants? The man returned and began emptying the contents of his carrier bags into the fridge. Simon wondered what he should say. Fortunately he was saved by the telephone. The man picked up the receiver and spoke. 'Good evening, Paul speaking. No, I'm afraid Selena is out tonight. She'll be back tomorrow afternoon. Can I take a message for you? You'd like to talk to Simon? Certainly. I'll pass you over.'

He handed the phone to Simon and left him to his conversation.

'Hello,' said Simon.

'Hello, rich boy,' said Len. 'Forgot to warn you Paul would be there tonight. He's an agency worker – a butler. You hire him from time to time when you have an event. He's been working for you for a while, although he's actually based in London. He deals with all those things you can't be bothered to deal with. Normally, Selena arranges for him to come up. She maybe thought you'd need some company tonight. Anyway, that's it. Got to go. Got some awkward humans to deal with.' With that the line went dead.

'Your bath is ready, sir, and I laid out your usual outfit,' said Paul.

'Right, thank you, Paul. Eight-thirty, you said. The guests?'

'Yes, sir. They'll be here at eight-thirty. You have plenty of time. Would you like another beer?'

'Thank you, no. I'm okay for the moment. I'll go and have a soak. It's been a strange day.'

'Yes, sir. Indeed. I'll be in the kitchen if you need anything.'

Simon climbed the stairs to the large bathroom that was
obviously his. Earlier he'd discovered the master bedroom and en
suite. That bathroom was obviously Selena's. Elaborately designed
bottles containing make-up and perfumes were laid out on shelves
over the scallop-shaped sink and a pair of sheer stockings hung
over the side of a large claw-foot bath. This bathroom was more
masculine in design, with a nautical theme – blue-and-white-
striped wallpaper with small embossed silver anchors adorned the
walls, an enormous painting of a fish hung above the bath, and
propped on the side of a distressed blue-painted dresser stood a
large wooden-rigged boat. He sank into the warm tub of water
and languished there. It soothed his mind for a while and he
wished he could stay hidden in the bathroom. He wasn't a fan
of parties and he didn't know any of the guests. Had the imps
zapped everyone who was coming? What happened if they had
missed someone out?

The smell of fresh pine rose from the water. He breathed in
the aroma and imagined himself in a forest. So far, everything
had worked out. Paul was there. He would handle the guests.
Simon would have to wing it. He was good at that.

Feeling a little calmer and slightly woozy from the beer drunk
earlier on an empty stomach, Simon made his way to the bedroom.
Paul had put a large rabbit costume on the bed. It was much like
a large onesie only more authentic in design. The head, indeed,
resembled a giant rabbit's head, with holes for him to eat and
drink. It had been some time since he last wore a costume. He
and Veronica had dressed up as Fred and Wilma Flintstone for
a friend's fortieth birthday party. He'd enjoyed waving his club
about but had got into trouble with Veronica when he tried to
throw her over his shoulder and carry her home. He'd looked
okay in a caveman's outfit. He wouldn't dare wear a costume like
that nowadays. The more a costume covered the better, as far as

he was concerned. The Fred episode was back in the days before he let himself go. The rabbit costume wasn't his first choice, however it was a good disguise. No one would know who was in the large furry suit.

The first of his guests arrived just as he was squeezing into the costume. It was warmer than he expected inside. He must have ripped it as it had a hole in the rear end, under the tail. After some speculation he'd deduced it was an *Alice in Wonderland*-themed party he was hosting and that he was the White Rabbit – although he was positive the white rabbit in the book had sported a waistcoat and a pocket watch. He waited a few minutes. The later he was, the more chance there would be that he could mingle unnoticed. The doorbell rang and raised voices reached his ears. Paul was dealing with them. He gave it another ten minutes then slipped downstairs.

As he entered the lounge, he found to his surprise that several people had gathered, each dressed as a furry animal. Paul had been around with trays of drinks, so furry paws clutched glasses as mice and weasels chatted to wolves, and rabbits engaged in conversations with cats, tigers and lions. Several guests were dancing, their ears sticking up as they jigged about to The Black Eyed Peas. A badger was stroking a tiger's fur, comparing the softness to its own. Simon found it all strange. He wondered if, in fact, the theme was 'Woodland Creatures', or perhaps it was an event in aid of an animal charity?

A black rabbit with an American accent came up to him, complimented Simon on his costume and asked if he'd attended the fur con in Baltimore the year before and if he knew any fursuiters in the vicinity. He had no idea how to respond so he just nodded and patted the rabbit on the back. The rabbit snuggled closer. In fact, the rabbit seemed to be stroking Simon's furry tummy. Simon felt uncomfortably warm in his heavy suit.

The last thing he needed was a frisky rabbit coming on to him. He made excuses about food and drink and left the fellow furry standing in the middle of the room.

A large fox grabbed hold of his arm as he tried to leave. 'Evening, Simon. It is you, isn't it? Thought I recognised you. After last time, eh? One never forgets a cute cotton tail.' The man inside the fox's costume laughed heartily. Simon imagined he was a large man with a rubicund face and a handlebar moustache. 'I must say I think you're being very brave holding this little fur con soirée at your home. It wouldn't do for this to get out, would it? If anyone found out what we got up to it could be the end of our careers and life as we know it. Imagine if the papers got hold of it? Still, Selena isn't here and I understand your man, Paul, is very discreet.'

Simon nodded. 'Yes, he's a good chap,' he said, somewhat puzzled by the comment. The fox gave a sharp dog-like bark that surprised Simon. 'Look forward to seeing you later,' he growled. 'I think we can make Thumper shake more than his foot, what?'

Simon laughed a nervous laugh, turned and bumped into a lion. '*Rwoar!*' it said.

'*Rwoar* to you, too.'

'You can't *rwoar*. You're a rabbit.'

'I'm an angry rabbit,' replied Simon. 'I can *rwoar* if I want to.'

'Get you. You're all worked up. You probably overdosed on lettuce. Want me to stroke your ears to make you feel better?'

'No. Go stalk someone else.'

These people are bonkers, Simon decided and went off to seek out Paul.

He was in the kitchen putting carrot sticks on plates. He jumped when he saw Simon. 'Sorry, sir. I didn't expect you to come in here. Everything okay? How are you getting along?'

'It's very odd in there. Everyone seems to be dressed as animals. I've seen four foxes and three rabbits, two cats, two wolves, a weasel, a badger and a load of other strange creatures.'

'What do you expect at a yiffing party?' said Paul.

'Yiffing? What's yiffing?'

'Ha ha! Of course. I get it. Don't worry. I won't tell a soul. I promise. Not even Selena. Your secret is safe with me. I'll put these nibbles out and depart. All the drink is in the large fridge in the utility room and, of course, in the cellar. You'll be able to… well, do whatever you need to do in peace.'

Paul scurried off to serve the canapés, leaving Simon feeling confused.

'Hello, Bunnykins,' said a soft voice. 'I've been looking for you. Fancy a carrot?' The small weasel shoved a long carrot into Simon's mouth and stroked his head. 'There's a good rabbit. You like carrots, don't you?'

Simon felt his heartbeat quicken. The weasel was putting its arms around him and rubbing itself up and down his leg.

'Er, I-I don't think we've met,' he stammered.

'Oh we've met, Bunnykins. We've met several times. And of course, we know each other online. You were my first. No other rabbit went at it like you did. The last time, I couldn't stand up for days.'

'I think you've got me mixed up with another rabbit,' said Simon, backing off.

'Oh, I see. Too much choice for you at this gathering, is there? Well, see if I care. Plenty more rabbits out there.'

The weasel left, its head held high. Simon groaned. This was awful. People with an unhealthy obsession for furry animals were quite probably going to do unspeakable things in this house – his house. He had to get out. Or get them out.

Paul came back with an empty tray. Simon cornered him.

'Paul. I need to get these people out.'

'You do?'

'Yes. I thought this was a fancy-dress party. I now suspect it might be more than that.'

Paul's eyes widened. 'Of course it's more than that. Have you been drinking? It's a yiffing party – it's the first time it's been held at your house and I thought it was a risk deciding to have it here. It's better outside in the woods where no one can see you. I only do as I'm asked. You pay the wages, sir.'

'That's right. I do,' said Simon, his mind working overtime. *What had that fox said?* 'Round everyone up and say you've heard that a reporter has been alerted and is on his way here. That'll get rid of them.'

'Are you sure?'

'Never been more sure. Get those furry monsters out of this house and then you can go home too. Thank you, Paul.'

'If you insist. Do you want me to clear up before I go? I'm staying with a friend in the village tonight, so I don't have far to travel.'

'No, I'll do it. I'm used to washing-up. It'll take my mind off things. By the way, the television doesn't work.'

'You must have satellite problems. I'll ring someone in the morning and have it fixed. If you want to watch a film there's always the home cinema in the basement.'

'Good idea. I'll be down there. Let me know when the coast is clear.'

Three hours later, Simon tumbled into bed. He'd drunk several cans of beer, eaten a pile of carrot sticks and tried to watch *The Usual Suspects* in the home cinema but lost concentration halfway through the film. This whole swap business was becoming too complicated for him and he was beginning to lose his grip on reality.

He wondered if Veronica was asleep. He couldn't bring himself to think about Tony. Then another thought struck him. He always slept on the right-hand side of the bed, but what if Selena slept on the right? He would have to change sides.

He fumbled for a light switch and swore as he struggled to locate it. In the end, he smacked the base of the lamp in frustration and it illuminated. It produced sufficient light for him to open the bedside drawer and peer inside. It was definitely Selena's side of the bed. He whistled loudly in surprise as he pulled out an enormous luminous pink vibrator. He pressed the switch on it and the head rotated. Further investigation of the drawer produced some Cool Tingle lube, then some Heat Wave lube. He extracted a weird gold device that he suspected might be a vibrating cock ring. One of the guys at work had received something like it as a birthday present one year. This wasn't an area of expertise for him. Veronica had never been into any sex toys. Their relationship had been healthy enough without. Certainly, in the early years, just ripping off each other's clothes had been enough of a turn-on for both of them.

He tipped the remaining contents of the drawer onto the bed, wondering how or where he was supposed to use them on Selena. He held up a string of light blue beads of varying sizes and puzzled over it until he gave up ruminating, went downstairs, fired up the laptop in the office and Googled 'sex toys'. Half an hour later he was familiar with Thai anal beads, jiggle beads and anal finger-toys. He wiped his glasses with the sleeve of his paisley pyjama jacket and considered purchasing a large box of Viagra online.

He returned to the bedroom, swept all the toys, lubricants and pastes into the drawer and rolled over to the other side of the bed to see what was in his bedside drawer. It was empty apart from three asthma inhalers. It appeared Selena was going to be a difficult woman to satisfy. He was completely out of his league. He was going to need more than a huge box of Viagra and several inhalers.

He finally dozed off in the early hours of the morning.

CHAPTER TWENTY-ONE
Simon

Simon was in heaven. The reclining electric seat was set at the optimum comfort level, allowing him to relax with his legs raised. The mood lighting was now adjusted so his eyes were comfortable and he had everything he needed – a beer by his side and a large bag of popcorn in his lap. He was engrossed in one of his all-time favourite films and marvelled at how much better it was played on a 126-inch screen. This was a far cry from the 38-inch television screen he was used to. Even though the film was often on the television, he never got to watch it in peace. Every time he tried to settle down to enjoy *The Bridge on the River Kwai*, one of the kids would disturb him or Veronica would come in and change the channel to some damn soap or romantic comedy. This was bliss – his own private cinema. All that was missing was the ice-cream lady during the interval. Who wouldn't want a home cinema room like this? It consisted of two rows of eight seats each with a small table for drinks. Tony Hedge thought of everything. There was even a bar in the corner of the room so you didn't have to find your way back to the kitchen – genius!

He'd spent the entire day in the games room playing a few holes of golf on one of St Andrew's courses, albeit virtually. He'd always enjoyed the chance to play in spite of having no handicap.

Such opportunities had been few and far between. The last was on a family day out to Blackpool where he'd won the pitch and putt against Haydon. He sighed. That had been a good day. Still, now he could play whenever he wanted and no doubt, judging by the golfing paraphernalia in the wardrobe and the clubs in the games cupboard, Tony spent many an afternoon on the green. Simon could hack that.

He loafed about the house in the early evening, trying not to think about the drawer in the bedroom. Poring through the vast collection of Blu-ray discs in the cinema room had provided adequate distraction. Discovering a DVD of Lee Evans, he'd suffered a crisis of conscience and phoned his house. Haydon had answered the phone. It had been the weirdest conversation of his life.

'Hello?'

'Hello, is that Haydon?'

'Yes, who's this?'

'Uhm, it's your father.'

'Yeah, right. It's not April Fool's Day, you know?'

'It is your dad.'

'Is that you, Adam? It is, isn't it? Buzz off and stop being a prat. My dad's here. He's playing Scrabble with my mum and gran and I don't want to piss him off. Gran's been winding him up all day. Georgina is sulking in her room about some boy and won't come downstairs. Mum is looking like she's going to murder Dad because the wardrobe door he should have fixed is still broken, and the cat has just been sick over his chair. Best go. I'll see you soon. Bye.'

It appeared Len and Nick had worked their magic and replaced him with Tony. He was now not sure how he felt about that, although the more he thought about Tony playing Scrabble with Morag, the more appealing the whole episode became. Tony was now living his wretched life and he was sat in Tony's house – no, his house. He was master of all he surveyed. It was surreal. A soft rustling indicated that Selena had returned home. Light beads of sweat gathered on his forehead. He turned to face her. She wore cream jeans and a red top. The diamante love heart on it glittered as light from the screen flickered onto it.

'Hello, Simon. I thought you might be here, or in the billiard room.'

'Oh… er… hi, Selena.'

'Do you want another beer?'

'No, thanks. I'm okay, thanks. I have one.'

'*The Bridge on the River Kwai.* Now that's a terrific film. Do you mind if I watch it with you?'

Simon felt awkward then remembered this was his house now. Selena was his woman. As far as his old world was concerned, he no longer existed. He guessed Len and Nick had subjected Selena to some laser trickery too. She seemed quite comfortable with him there.

'Please do. It's more than halfway through, though. Want me to start it over for you?'

'You're okay. I'll pick up from here.' Selena walked to the bar, her stilettos silent on the plush carpet, and poured herself a drink then, returning to the chair next to his, she slid off her shoes and curled her feet under her.

By the time the film ended, Simon was convinced Selena had been zapped too. Why else would she have kept him plied with beers and now be in the kitchen preparing their dinner? She was cooking his favourite meal – rib-eye steak, onion rings and chips. Simon rubbed his hands together with glee. Who would believe it possible? He strolled from the cinema room to the kitchen. Selena was humming as she cooked. The kitchen table was set.

'Hope you don't mind, I thought we'd eat in here tonight. It's easier than carting it through to the dining room and after the last time we ate there, I thought it better to stay here, although if you feel like it—'

Simon smiled at her. *What was she on about?* 'Yeah, sure. Here's fine tonight. Whatever you want.'

'Can you pour me a glass of wine, please? I don't want to leave the steak. It's almost ready. There's an open bottle of Châteauneuf-du-Pape over there. I opened it earlier to let it breathe. I thought it would go well with the steak.' She gestured in the direction of the bottle with her elbow.

Simon poured the wine into two sparkling crystal glasses, admired its colour, swirled the glass and sniffed the bouquet – a rich raspberry with an intense aroma of violets. Breathing in, he was transported to Provence, to perpetually windy slopes and rocky terrain redolent of garlic, lavender and thyme. It was a far cry from the usual plonk he drank. He handed Selena a glass. She kissed him tenderly on his cheek. 'Thanks, lover,' she murmured. Simon felt a rush of blood to his head and another rush below his belt. He clinked glasses with her, took a large gulp of wine and scurried off to the table. Selena arrived almost immediately, elegant china plates in her hands. She stooped to place one in front of Simon, brushing him with her breasts.

'Hope it's okay,' she said, slipping onto the seat opposite and gazing through sultry eyes.

'It'll be delicious,' he answered, although suddenly his appetite had changed and food was no longer a priority.

Selena speared a tiny piece of steak. Simon watched the portion of meat lift towards her parted crimson lips and into her mouth where it was momentarily caressed by her pink tongue before disappearing. He gulped and dragged his attention back to his own meal.

'I booked the South American trip we discussed,' she said. Her mouth now empty.

'Super. When do we go?' replied Simon.

'Sixteenth of next month.'

Simon stopped chewing mid-mouthful, his appetite evaporating as he digested the news. The sixteenth was his daughter's birthday. He'd never missed one of her birthdays, regardless of how busy he'd been at work. He always made time to see her, watch her open her presents and blow out the candles on the birthday cake Veronica made each year. It was a tradition that he sang to her first thing in the morning at breakfast when he handed her his own home-made card. He always gave her a funny card. He recalled the one he'd prepared for her earlier in the month while the family was out. It was in the kitchen drawer – a card with a silly drawing he'd sketched of a grumpy teenager dressed like a superhero and the message, 'It takes years to perfect the bad teenage attitude. You have a new superpower.' In that instant everything changed for Simon. Images of his family swam before his eyes: memories of birthdays past, trips to the zoo, themed parties and dressing up as a clown to entertain Georgie's friends, taking Haydon to a petting zoo for his fifth birthday, their smiles when Haydon wanted to take the smelly goat home as his birthday present followed by his pure delight when he discovered he had a bicycle instead and hugged Simon, his small arms barely circling Simon's waist. He recalled the rush of pride he experienced whenever he looked at his children and realized they were miracles he and Veronica had created. This exchange was definitely wrong. He needed to go back to his old life.

Before he could articulate either words or thoughts he felt hands caressing his neck. Selena had moved from her seat and was now behind him. He could feel her fingers running through his hair. She moved in front of him, bent her head and breathed onto his spectacles, steaming them up. She released a low, seductive laugh then blew gently into his ear, sending tiny electric shocks through his scalp into his hair. He let out a sigh.

'Husbands who treat their wives are in for a special treat of their own,' she whispered. 'Would you like your favourite treat?'

Simon wanted to protest. He truly wanted to pull away from Selena, however part of him was straining excitedly in anticipation and that part of him was going to lead him astray. He was about to be unfaithful to his wife. What wife? She was zapped. He had Selena. Selena was his and he should savour this moment.

Selena put her arms around him. He could feel her full breasts pushing against him. How he wanted her. Led by an invisible force, his mouth moved closer to hers. He could feel the heat from her lips when his conscience screamed at him. He pulled away.

'No, I can't—' he began to say.

'Come on, lover,' she urged, holding out her hand. He didn't move. She grabbed his hand. Her own was soft and elegant, with manicured nails. It fitted in his so well. His conscience was muffled by the throbbing sound of blood pulsating in his brain. Mutely, he allowed himself to be led to the bedroom by this seductive woman he barely knew. He moved a pace towards the bed, paused and turned towards Selena, words of rejection forming on his lips.

'Not there,' she purred. 'In here.'

She pressed a switch and the door at the back of the room swung open. Simon felt his erection shrivel as he gawped at a large cage hanging from the ceiling, a collection of whips and nipple clamps in a case on the wall next to a gimp mask, and a video camera on a stand. Selena turned towards him, a whip of frightening proportions in her hand. 'So which very naughty boy needs a good thrashing?' she asked in a tone that suggested she would stand for no nonsense.

CHAPTER TWENTY-TWO
Polly

'I… can't… no…' gasped Polly.

'Okay, sweets. We'll call it a day for the running. Now, you must do the stretches or you'll be unable to walk for the next few days.'

Polly muttered something unintelligible.

'I've been called much worse than that,' replied Calvin cheerfully. 'For that remark, I'm going to make you do another five push-ups.'

'I'm on strike.'

'If you don't do them, I'll get your life swap revoked and you'll have to go back to your old life.'

'How come everyone knows about the swap?'

'It's not everyone – only those of us who have requested our own life swaps. I wanted to help you get accustomed to your new life before I'll receive my very own swap. I want to change places with a pop star I used to train. He is totally delish,' he said, rolling his eyes. 'And he lives in Beverly Hills. I can't wait. So on your knees, lady, and give me five.'

'Calvin.'

'Yes, sweets.'

'I hate you.'

'I know you do. Everyone hates me at first. However, you'll love me in a couple of weeks. In fact, you will adore me. I know you will.'

Polly puffed with trembling arms as she completed the extra five push-ups and twenty minutes of stretching exercises that left her feeling weak.

'Okay, sweets. I have to dash. I'll be here tomorrow at the same time. I bet Chelsea also forgot to tell you about your appointment at the spa, too. She's such a handful. There's a card with their details on your office desk. They're expecting you at midday. Get a sauna and a massage while you're there. It'll help you feel less stiff tomorrow.'

'Midday? What time is it now?'

Calvin checked his personal monitor. 'It's almost eight-thirty.'

'Eight-thirty! What time did we start this workout?'

'The usual: six o'clock. Of course, we had to finish early today because you're new to it all.'

'You got me up at six o'clock to run about, do star jumps, make all my muscles burn and feel horribly sick?'

'Looking good doesn't come naturally. You have to work at it. Stephanie knew that. See you tomorrow,' he called, as he jogged towards his car.

Polly struggled up to her bedroom. The dogs were asleep on her bed. Dolce was making small whimpering noises as he slept, no doubt dreaming about biscuits or running about the house like a mad thing. She wondered if they were missing their mistress. They looked quite cute when they were sleeping. Gabbana was curled up close to his friend with only the tip of his small black nose visible. There was a flash of orange under one of his paws. It was one of the fluorescent yellow socks she'd worn the day before. The little perisher had obviously rooted through the dirty clothes she'd left abandoned on the bathroom floor and seized it. She wasn't cross. The socks were wearing out anyway. Dolce could keep it. It seemed a poor substitute for his real mistress.

She ran a bath, peeled off her exercise clothes and eased herself into the warm water. No sooner had she relaxed into the bath than the doorbell rang and the dogs plonked onto the floor and scurried downstairs. There was no peace in this place. So much for having a laid-back life.

Polly clambered out of the bath, quickly dried herself and grabbed a silk dressing gown from the back of the bathroom door. It clung to her damp body. The doorbell rang again. She descended the stairs, grimacing with each footstep. The dogs looked up expectantly.

'Don't you two ever bark?'

She checked that her dressing gown wasn't gaping wide and answered the bell. The man on the doorstep was wearing an anorak with a Mercedes-Benz logo on it. The dogs rushed outside to investigate the stranger, who stepped back in surprise as the canines launched themselves at him.

'They don't bite. They're just excited.'

'With good reason,' he replied, sidestepping away from Gabbana, who was intent on investigating his footwear. 'I have a delivery for you – your new car. I understand you were expecting it.'

'Oh gosh, yes. I'd forgotten. One moment, please. I need to change. I can't come out like this. Do you mind waiting outside? I don't want the dogs savaging you.'

'No problem. I have to offload the car anyway. It's arriving in a minute or two on a trailer.'

'Great. Back in a flash. You two, in!'

Polly struggled back upstairs, dogs in tow, picked up her jeans and tugged them on. She shrugged on her jumper, picked up the trainers from earlier and, tossing the other balled-up yellow sock to the dogs to chase, shut the bedroom door and headed back downstairs to view her new car. Stephanie had ordered a Mercedes. How flash! Polly's last car had been a five-year-old Nissan with 105,000 miles on the clock. It had served her well. She'd been forced to sell it to pay for her airfare to Gran Canaria. She wondered what Stephanie had ordered: a cabriolet? That would be perfect for cruising about in. She pulled on the trainers and flung open the front door. The trailer had arrived and her new car was being offloaded. It wasn't a flashy Mercedes. It was a tiny two-seater pink smart car.

'This isn't a Mercedes,' she complained to the man, who laughed.

'Smart is owned by Mercedes. This is definitely your order. I have it here. You were quite clear on the colour and style. You wanted one identical to Katy Perry's car.'

'It's pink!'

'Yes, it's pink. As you requested.'

'It's tiny!'

'Smart cars are much bigger inside than they look. They're like a TARDIS once you get in them and very popular, especially with the celebs. Justin Bieber has a black one with blacked-out windows.'

'It's not very me though.'

'I'm sure you'll look great in it. They're very trendy. And practical. You'll be able to park in the smallest of spaces. Now if you would like to jump inside, I'll go through the controls with you.'

'It's even got my name on the side of it,' she cried. 'In yellow writing. That's awful. Everyone will know who's driving it.'

'I think that was the point. If you have it, flaunt it,' replied the salesman.

'Can you take it back?'

'No, I'm afraid not. It's a bespoke one, just for you. We wouldn't be able to sell it on easily.'

'I'm surprised you sold it in the first place,' she grumbled, clambering into the driver's seat. It was, as the man had said, larger than she thought. He insisted on showing her every dial and explaining every control. Polly's muscles began to seize up as she feigned interest in the car. Some twenty minutes later, the salesman bid her farewell. She sat in a daze, staring into space, wondering if the life swap had been a good idea. She had two dotty dogs, a teenage daughter and now a minuscule pink car. Life had been less complicated when she was a sports therapist. Still, at least now she didn't have any debts and she owned a beautiful house. She also had an appointment at a spa in a couple of hours. It would all get better. With that thought, she forced her reluctant legs out of the car and headed back inside.

The dogs greeted her like a long-lost friend. 'How did you get out of the bedroom?' she asked. 'Did Chelsea let you out?' Gabbana licked her trainers. Dolce cocked his head to one side and gave her a soulful look. 'Come on. I need some breakfast.'

The dogs scuttled into the kitchen and dropped onto their dog beds, where they watched her every move. There was no food. The first cupboard yielded only an infinite range of herbal teas and one jar of decaffeinated coffee. Latching onto the latter, she filled the kettle and let it boil. There was no food to be found. Thank goodness she'd bought eggs and bread at the shop the day before. She could at least have boiled eggs and coffee. She hunted around for a pan and came across a cupboard rammed full of bags of Royal Canine French Bulldog food. It looked like Dolce and Gabbana ate better than their mistress. She filled two bowls stationed by the sink and watched as the dogs wolfed it down. Dolce snuffled about for any pieces that might have escaped while Gabbana sat and stared at Polly, his bat ears pricked up.

'What do you want now?'

'Biscuits,' came the reply. Chelsea entered the kitchen.

'Morning,'

'Hi,' replied the girl.

'Want some breakfast? I found some eggs.'

'Nah, you're okay. I'm going out.' She stooped to pat Dolce, who licked her hand.

'I need to get some shopping. Do you like pastries?'

'They're okay,' said Chelsea.

'I'll get us some for tomorrow. I'll cook us crêpes. I can make a mean crêpe. They're scrummy with chocolate spread... or Nutella.'

'Nah, you're okay. I don't do breakfast.'

'Most important meal of the—' Polly didn't finish the sentence. She sounded like her own mother, who always hassled Polly to eat breakfast. Polly never wanted to eat first thing in the morning. Nowadays, of course, she wouldn't go out to work without her bowl of cereal or full English. It was different when you were younger. You didn't seem to need food in the same way.

'Fair enough. Are you going into town?'

'Might be. Might hang.'

'With friends?'

'Well, I can't hang on my own, can I?'

'I guess not. I wanted to talk to you about your exams.'

Chelsea's left eyebrow rose, yet she didn't walk off.

'It seems a waste not to at least take them. You've spent years sitting in class and learning facts and information so why waste your knowledge?'

'What makes you think I'd pass them?'

'I can't believe you've spent five years staring into space and ignoring every teacher who has taught you, for one thing. For another, I noticed you were reading *To Kill a Mockingbird*. I'm surmising it's a set text and you enjoyed reading it. You ought to take the English exam, at least.'

'You went into my sitting room, didn't you?'

'You didn't say it was yours. I was exploring, not snooping. If you leave books lying about on the table, then they are likely to be noticed, especially by others who enjoy reading and studied the very same text for their own GCSE exam years ago.'

Chelsea huffed and examined her nails.

'Well, do you like English?'

'It's okay, I suppose.'

'I also found these in the waste-paper bin.' Polly pulled open a drawer and drew out several sheets of A4 paper. Chelsea scowled at her.

'You had no right. They're private.'

'I don't see how discarded rubbish is private. Don't get on your high horse. These show real talent. The person who wrote these poems should definitely take her English exams.'

Chelsea bit her bottom lip and stared into the distance.

'Chelsea, you can write well. You must enjoy writing to even sit down and compose these.'

'I was experimenting, that's all. They're rubbish.'

'Poetry is personal and often explores feelings and emotions. To you they might not be what you were aiming for. To someone who reads them, they are powerful.'

'Whatever. Can I have them back?'

Polly handed her the crumpled sheets of paper. 'What have you got to lose? You sit a few exams. Worst-case scenario you don't do that well and you can at least say "told you so". At best, you'll have a handful of good results and a few options. You can consider a job or higher education.'

Chelsea shrugged again. 'I don't want to go back to school. That's all.'

'How about if I called the school and you only went in to take exams? I'll take you and drop you off after each exam.'

'I'll think about it.'

'Fine. Do that.'

'See you later.'

'Okay. Have a good time.'

'And you. Oh. I forgot. I was supposed to tell you about the diary in the office. All your appointments and phone numbers are in it. It's in the top desk drawer. Sorry.'

'That's okay. Thanks. I'll check to see what Stephanie had lined up.'

Chelsea left the kitchen. Polly heard a motorbike rumble up the drive. She didn't look out of the window. She'd won a slight victory. Time would tell if she was right.

Watched by the dogs she'd nicknamed the Dynamic Duo, she headed upstairs for the bath she'd promised herself. Her bat-eared bodyguards settled on a towel beside the bath and snoozed while she soaked in the orange-scented water. She was musing about what to buy for dinner, when her thoughts were interrupted by The Killers song 'Human' coming from the next room. It played for a minute then stopped abruptly. After drying off, Polly hunted about for a radio in the bedroom. It puzzled her when she could find nothing that suggested where the music might have come from. Finally, she gave up and decided it must have been a blip on the fancy music system.

The doorbell rang again. This time the dogs barked. Dolce made it to the door first and snuffled under it. Gabbana waddled up with Polly. A young man in his early twenties wearing a parka and torn jeans stood on the step. His hair was dirty and unkempt. His sour body odour made Polly's nose wrinkle. The dogs, however, fawned over him as if he were their best friend.

'Hi,' he said. Polly drew her eyes away from the enormous ring in his earlobe. It stretched his lower lobe and looked like a mini Frisbee.

'Hi.'

'Chelsea in?'

'No. She's out.'

'I'll wait then.'

'I'd rather you didn't. I don't know you and I can't let someone I don't know inside.'

'They know me,' he said pointing at the dogs. Dolce sat obediently at his feet.

'They're like that with everyone,' replied Polly crossing her arms.

'I'm Zed.'

'Hello, Zed.'

'Now you know me, why not let me in so I can wait for Chelsea in her room?'

'I'm going out.'

'That's okay. I'll be no trouble.'

The young man picked up a battered guitar case and stood expectantly, waiting to gain entry. Polly continued to stare at him. In the end it was she who broke eye contact.

'Look, let's get this clear. You're not coming in. If you want to waste time out here waiting for Chelsea then do so. I don't think she'll be home for some time. She's gone into town to hang with friends.'

The man gave her a smug look. 'That's me,' he replied. 'I'm one of the people she was supposed to be hanging with. I'm her boyfriend. She was supposed to come and meet me at the bus station. I hitched a lift with some mates instead of catching the bus and came here to surprise her. I hoped to catch her before she left. She'll come back once she sees I'm not at the station. My phone ran out of charge and it's difficult to find a socket in the middle of a field. Don't suppose I could borrow your phone to text her that I'm here?'

'No. And I'm still not going to let you in. I don't know you're telling me the truth.'

'Fair enough. Chelsea told me her mum was a difficult cow. She wasn't wrong. I'll chill here until she gets back.' With that he sat on the doorstep and extracted a tatty Rizla packet from his parka. Polly glared at him, trying to decide what to do next. He ferreted about in another pocket and pulled out a stick of something that he proceeded to break off and add to the papers.

'Is that what I think it is?'

'Depends what you think it is,' he replied, licking the paper and rolling the shape into a long thin cigarette. He searched his pockets for a box of matches.

'I don't want you smoking that on my doorstep.'

'Where do you suggest I smoke it? In that disgusting, lurid pink car?' he asked, pointing at the smart car.

'Funny boy. Look, just sling your hook for a while. Get off the doorstep, please. I don't want to be rude, but you have to understand you could be anyone; a vagrant, someone who wants to rob this place—'

'A Jehovah's Witness,' he added, taking a lengthy toke and letting the smoke stay inside his lungs for a while before exhaling again. It curled upwards into Polly's face. Polly was irritated by the young man's brazen attitude. However, she wasn't going to get into an argument with him.

'Please yourself. You're not coming in and that is that. Chelsea won't be returning any time soon. She was going to stay at a friend's house so you'll be there all night.'

'Whatever,' drawled Zed, continuing to smoke his reefer, his eyes half-closed. 'You really are a miserable old boot.' Leaving the joint hanging out of his mouth, he opened the case and pulled out his guitar, strummed a few chords and began to sing the first few lines of 'American Pie'. A fuming Polly gave up, called the dogs in and slammed the door on the youth, who continued to sprawl on the step. If this was Chelsea's boyfriend it was yet another problem she would have to deal with. It was quickly becoming a difficult life here. Dolce sat on his bed, his grumpy face glued to her movements as she wandered around the kitchen. She wanted to go to the spa, but she didn't want to vacate the house while Zed was hanging about. In the end, she grabbed her car keys and her handbag and set off. She would tell Zed to get off the property or she would call the police. She opened the front door. The step was empty. Zed had disappeared. Dolce and Gabbana padded out with her. Given that Zed smelled as if he hadn't washed for a month and neither dog seemed inclined to seek him out, she assumed he had departed.

'Back in the house. On your beds.'

The dogs sat down as one.

'House,' she commanded.

Both dogs remained on the step, eyes downcast. She strode off in the direction of the car, muttering as she went. The wretched animals could stay outside too. She unlocked the car, grimacing at it as she did so. *Who could possibly want a bright pink car?* She opened the passenger's door to throw in her handbag when she noticed a movement in the bushes.

'Is that you, Zed?' she shouted.

There was no reply.

Leaving the door ajar, she moved towards the bushes. 'Zed, come out of there. There's no point in lurking about. If you don't come out immediately, I'm going to call the police,' she shouted.

The bush rustled and a tiny wide-eyed rabbit scarpered across the grass and into the woods. Polly laughed out loud, walked back to the car and slammed the door, one eye still on the bushes. There was no further movement. She clambered into the driver's side and came face to face with both dogs squashed into the passenger's seat. Dolce licked her nose. Gabbana stared out of the front window.

'Out!' she shouted. Again, neither dog moved. She tugged at Dolce's collar. The animal remained glued to the seat. Gabbana was equally immovable. Polly let out another sigh.

'Okay, Dynamic Duo. It appears we are all going to the spa then. Hope you like steam rooms.' She wound the window down part way to allow both animals to hang their heads outside. The breeze flattened back their bat ears so they looked like they were flying. There was no way of knowing if they were happy or not, but Polly had to admit she was glad of their company.

CHAPTER TWENTY-THREE
Polly

It was after six when Polly drew back up to the house. The dogs were asleep on the seat. They had managed to snooze all afternoon in the treatment room while she'd enjoyed an afternoon of being pummelled back to health. She felt heaps better and was almost prepared to face another session with Calvin. She opened the car door. 'Come on, you two. Home.' Eyes opened and the dogs descended with reluctance. 'You really are the laziest pair of dogs I have ever met. Fancy not even running after a rabbit.' Dolce threw her an apologetic look while Gabbana relieved himself against the car's back tyre.

A light was visible under the door to Chelsea's sitting room. Dolce snuffled at the door. Polly listened for the sound of a television or music. There was no noise. Chelsea might be reading or even writing some poetry. If that were the case, Polly would try and convince her to stay at school and take her exams. She tapped on the door. 'Chelsea?' No reply. She sniffed. There was a distinct sweet smell coming from the room – the same smell that had come from Zed's joint. Had Zed broken in or, worse still, had he got his own key? She didn't want that cocky loudmouth in her house. She knocked more loudly. 'Chelsea, can I come in? Are you alone?'

Again there was no reply. Polly put her ear against the door. She could hear struggling and muffled noises. Her imagination went into overdrive. She'd read about drug addicts becoming unhinged. Zed already looked off-the-wall with his straggly hair and unfocused eyes. What if he didn't actually know Chelsea, or had been casing the place intending to rob it and been interrupted by the girl? Or what if his intention had been to kidnap Chelsea and demand a ransom? The house oozed wealth. Anyone could work out that the family that lived here was well off. She hadn't liked that Zed from the start. He was supremely overconfident and he had disappeared rather mysteriously. Would he steal things and sell them for drug money? He looked the sort. Polly's heartbeat increased. There was someone in the room. In fact, she was sure there were two people and judging by the muffled grunts, one of them was in trouble. She took the decision to face up to the danger. With a deep breath she flung open the door and burst into the room then, with a stifled shriek, retreated just as quickly, though not before she'd been subjected to the sight of Chelsea's legs wrapped around Zed's waist and his spotty backside pumping up and down. Chelsea called out, 'Harder, harder! That is amazing!'

Zed heard Polly gasp, turned his head towards her retreating form and yelled, 'Get out of here, you pervert!'

'Sorry!' Polly backed into the hall, almost falling over Dolce, who, excited to see Zed, charged into the room and jumped up and down at the couple, who both screamed at him to go away. Polly scurried to the kitchen where, with trembling hands, she made a cup of tea. It wasn't long before an angry Chelsea stormed in, pursued by Dolce, who persisted in jumping up and down at her bare legs.

'Who do you think you are, barging into my private space like that?' Chelsea demanded.

'Firstly, it doesn't have the word *private* written on the door. Secondly, I was worried that someone had broken into the house and was harming you and thirdly, I'm your temporary mother so I'm allowed to be concerned.'

'You are not my mother! At least Stephanie knew when to stay out of the way. She respected my privacy and didn't treat me like a ten-year-old. Do you know how embarrassing that was for Zed and me?'

'It was a tad uncomfortable for me too,' added Polly, determined not to be undermined by a teenager. 'And for the record, you should not be having sexual relations. You're underage.'

Chelsea snorted. 'What utter shit. I've been with Zed for three months. He isn't the first boyfriend I've slept with. I learned all about the birds and the bees when I was little. I've been wearing a bra since I was twelve, started my periods soon after and I take precautions, so back off!'

'No, Chelsea. I don't approve of either your choice of boyfriend or the fact that you're in a sexual relationship with him. Accidents happen. No contraceptive device is one hundred per cent guaranteed and you're too young to be in a serious relationship.'

'Bollocks!'

'Mind your language.'

'Fuck off!'

'You've got a right potty mouth. Calm down, Chelsea. Let's discuss this in a grown-up manner.'

'Yes, let's. If you acted like an adult you wouldn't be hanging about here drooling over dresses like you were some sort of princess in a fantasy world. You are so out of touch with the real world. I bet you can't remember what it's like to be young. You're just bitter because you haven't got a boyfriend. I love Zed. He loves me. He asked me to go travelling with him to Thailand and all around the Far East. It'll be far more interesting than school and I'll learn a lot more than I will studying *To Kill a Mockingbird*. You've helped me make my mind up. I think I'll go with him. How about that for adult? So because I shan't be living here, I don't need you as my mother. I'll travel the world and collect my inheritance when I'm old enough. Until then, Zed and I can busk or get temporary work wherever we go. See how adult I'm being? So bugger off upstairs, stay out of my life and tomorrow I'll get the demons to send you back to wherever you came from.'

'No, Chelsea. You don't get to tell me what to do. It was my decision to swap with Stephanie and I'm not going to return to my old life just because you can't cope with what I say. You're going to have to put up with me here in this house. You're angry with me and I can understand why. Don't make hasty decisions because you're annoyed. Let's sleep on it and tomorrow maybe we can talk again when things are less heated.'

Polly leant against the worktop and tried to calm her heart rate. She had no idea if she'd said the wrong thing. Still, at least Chelsea wasn't shouting and screaming any longer.

'Tell Zed I'm sorry I burst in. I won't do it again.'

Chelsea turned. 'You'd better not,' she growled. The sitting-room door slammed and Polly breathed out. She pitied Stephanie having to deal with Chelsea. Handling emotional, hormonal girls was no mean feat. After all, she had been one once.

'Why, Polly?' asks her mother. Her face is white. Her hands tear at a tissue, picking at its edges. Small white fragments flutter to the floor where they rest unnoticed. Polly is exasperated by this overt show of concern.

'It's no big deal,' she answers, shoving her hands under her armpits, her head held high. 'I missed a couple of lessons, that's all.'

'But your English teacher said you also failed to hand in two important assignments. She's most concerned. As are we,' she continued, fixing her eyes onto her daughter's. Polly averts her eyes.

'Mrs Guildford is an old busybody,' she says, although she feels a wave of guilt wash over her as she speaks. Mrs Guildford has been very patient with Polly, who has come up with endless excuses for missing deadlines. She ignores the feeling. Callum is right. Her teachers are always on her back and treating her like she's a little kid. They're probably cheesed off that she's not conforming to their norm and bunks off at lunchtimes or library periods to be with Callum. The teachers never liked Callum. That's why he dropped out of school before he took any examinations. Polly can't look at her mother. She heard the awful row between her parents after the sixth-form parents' evening.

'She needs telling,' her father shouted. 'She's been a different person since him!' He spat the last word. 'And have you seen how she dresses these days? She looks like a tart.'

'You have to understand she's being led by her hormones. It's a phase. She thinks she loves Callum. One way to ensure she goes off the rails completely is to tell her she can't see him anymore.'

'Rubbish. You know as well as I do, he's a no-hoper. He works on a building site carrying hods of bricks, for goodness sake.'

'It's a trade.'

'Are you mad? It's a job – a job for people who have little brains, unlike Polly, who appears to want to give up any future potential she has.'

'You're being too hard—'

'I most certainly am not. If you don't sort it out, I shall. She needs to buckle down to work. I'm not having her messing about.'

Polly heard no more but was aware of her mother crying well into the early hours. Her father had left the house early, slamming the door as he went. Now her mother stands in front of her, face pinched, eyes bloodshot, yet Polly feels nothing but irritation. Callum says he loves her and she knows she loves him. She can feel it from her heart to her toes. They are now lovers. She's committed her love to him and on the back seat of his aged Fiesta, as he drew himself into her for *the first time, he called her name and whispered that he loved her, making every nerve in her body tingle. What did her parents know of such passion? Her father was a cold fish and her mother merely his obedient sidekick.*

'I'm going to leave sixth form,' she announces.

'You can't throw your education away. It's important, Polly,' wails her mother. 'You need qualifications for a good job out there and what about university? We both thought you were clever enough to go on to higher education. Polly, think about this.'

Polly glowers. 'I have thought about it. I hate sixth form. I can't keep up with the work and I don't need A levels to work at Tomkins. They're recruiting for cashiers. I'd have my own money and a life. I have neither at the moment.'

Her mother rips at the tissue and her eyes fill with tears again. 'Polly, please,' she says. 'Hang on until the exams. I know it's difficult, but give it a chance. I just ask you stick it out and then see what your options are.'

Polly considers her mother's words. She's never seen her so upset. If she's honest, she doesn't really fancy working in the supermarket. She'll stick out college to appease her folks even though she'll probably fail her exams. There are only a few more months of school left and then she'll get a job and be with Callum all the time. She fantasises about her future, a future of happy days together, buying a house, then having children. Maybe Callum could start up his own building firm. That would show her father. She's seventeen. Callum is twenty-two. They know what they want.

Polly sighed. She hadn't made life easy for her parents either. No wonder Stephanie preferred to mollycoddle the dogs. At least they were less volatile. Dolce snuffled about her feet. 'Stay away from these socks. They're Snoopy ones and Kaitlin gave them to me. You can't have them.'

In the corner of the kitchen Gabbana, flat out on his back, snored loudly. Fast asleep, he was unaware of the drama that had unfolded. Polly mused she should possibly have asked to swap places with one of the dogs. It would have been far easier.

CHAPTER TWENTY-FOUR
Simon

'Come to bed, lover,' said Selena, stroking Simon's head. 'Mummy will make you feel better. You can have cuddles. You love it when Mummy cuddles her little bub. Mummy will let you suck on her boobies.'

Simon gulped then groaned loudly. 'Sorry, Selena. I feel dreadful,' he said clamping his arms around his stomach and rolling from side to side. 'I don't know where these horrible cramps came from. I daren't come to bed. I'm better here, on the sofa.' He glanced up and winced. Selena was standing holding a large terry-towelling nappy in one hand and a dummy in her other hand. Tony Hedge was a nutter – no, worse still, he was a sexual deviant. Who in their right mind would have sex with people dressed as furry animals one day, want to be thrashed the next day, and then dress in baby clothes to suckle on the same woman who had whipped him senseless?

'What a pity. I was so worried about you when you shot off. You looked like a frightened kitten. It wasn't like you at all. You love the naughty boy's room. I was worried you'd been playing away again and weren't in the mood.'

'No, no, no, no... no. Just these cramps,' he winced again, hoping Selena was falling for his act. 'I have to go,' he said. 'Lover,' he added, spotting her look of irritation. 'Toilet.' He raced to the downstairs toilet, charged inside and locked the door.

He dropped the seat, sat on it and pulled out his mobile. He couldn't stay in this nuthouse. Tony was as mad as a box of frogs and Selena was even crazier. He liked to think he was a healthy male and he certainly had his private fantasies, but having his nipples clamped by anyone – even Selena – had never featured in them, nor had wearing a nappy and pretending he was a baby. He wiped perspiration from his brow and dialled the number. It went to answerphone. 'You have reached Mission Imp-ossible. All our agents are currently occupied with other miserable people. If you leave your name and number after the tone, someone will get back to you as soon as they can.' Three gruesome cackles followed the message.

'Len, Nick, it's Simon. Look guys, this might be your idea of the perfect life, but I have to get out of here. I don't care what it takes, I want out… now! Give me back my old life. Call me as soon as you get this.' Call ended, Simon sat on the toilet wondering what to do next. A light tapping on the door jogged him from his thoughts. He groaned and flushed the toilet a couple of times.

'Simon,' called Selena. 'I'm going upstairs. If you feel better, come and join me. I've put out some stomach settlers on the kitchen counter.'

'Thanks,' Simon said. 'Sorry to disappoint you.'

'You can make it up to me another time,' said Selena. 'Take the tablets then maybe we can have some serious make-up sex. I'll get your toys ready.'

Simon remembered the Thai anal beads and shuddered. 'Okay. I'll see if they help and maybe see you in a while.'

He sat for a further fifteen minutes, occasionally flushing the toilet, to make sure she'd gone. Each time he tried phoning the imps, his call was redirected to the answerphone message. He eased the door open, inch by inch, before tiptoeing into the lounge, where he settled on the sofa. There was no way he was going upstairs to have Selena pounce on him and shove a dummy in his mouth and a ring on his private parts. The ticking of a grandfather clock lulled him to sleep in the early hours of the morning, where he dreamt he was dressed in a pink tutu and being chased by a gorilla wielding a tube of extra strong glue and yelling, 'Come on, Simon. It'll be fine. I've got stacks of lubricating gel.'

The sound of heavy throbbing stirred him from his slumber. It came closer and closer, resonating through his very bones. The noise became deafening as the helicopter landed outside on the grass. Simon shuffled off the sofa, back aching, as he attempted to stretch and look outside. The blades on the helicopter continued to rotate. He peered out of the window. The pilot spied him and beckoned to him. Simon checked the time. It was almost seven. Considering he'd slept in them, his jeans looked passable and uncreased. He sniffed his armpits. *Yeah, okay-ish.* He didn't dare go upstairs to get fresh clothes. He would have to go to work as he was. He raced to the toilet, threw water over his face, dampened the towel and rubbed it under his armpits, raked his fingers through his hair and left.

The pilot saw him approaching and wound up the rotor blades. Simon checked out the name on the shiny sleek orange chopper – Simon Green and Associates – and clambered into the cockpit next to the pilot. He shrugged on the harness and sat back in the seat.

'Morning! You have a busy night again?'

Simon smiled. The pilot was wearing a nametag that read 'Charles'. 'Ha! You know me, Charles,' replied Simon.

'Yes, and so does Madame Whiplash and all her girls! Inti-mately. They wondered why you weren't with me yesterday. I told them you had to go home and service the little woman.'

Simon nodded and forced his mouth to smile. Charles must have been blasted with rays too.

'Headphones,' said Charles and grinned. 'Tiring night?'

Simon nodded, looked about, retrieved the headset and put it on. He could now hear Charles clearly. He pulled the microphone down in front of his mouth. 'All set,' he said.

'Let's go, then,' replied Charles. He flicked a switch and spoke, 'Sierra Golf preparing for take-off from Hills End flying south towards Hillsdon, over.' The engine noise increased as the blades rotated faster. Simon could feel the power surge through the machine. He clenched his buttocks as they lifted from the ground and Charles taxied the helicopter forwards, its nose down, allowing it to gather momentum. Just as it appeared they would collide with the enormous Leylandii surrounding the garden, the helicopter swooped upwards and over the boundary, leaving Simon's new home behind. Simon saw the entire village below him as they soared, and he made out his old house with its scrubby lawn covered in molehills. He stared at it, a pang in his chest. He was sure Ivan was sitting outside on the patio looking up at him. Charles broke his chain of thought. 'Want to take control?'

'Not today,' Simon replied. 'Had too much to drink last night. Got the shakes.'

'Doesn't normally stop you,' said Charles with a wink. 'Go on: take it for a second. I need to check the map.'

Simon yelped. 'I'd rather not. Got sweaty palms.'

'It's only for a moment.'

'Best not.'

'If you're sure.'

'Yes.'

Simon stared out of the window again, hoping Charles would say no more about him piloting the helicopter. He would need some lessons pretty quickly if he were to start flying himself. He wondered if he could enrol at a different flying school from the one Tony used.

'These Robinson 44s are wonderful to pilot,' said Charles after a few minutes. 'Good choice. I saw Jay Kay's R44 yesterday – at least I think it's his, or maybe he leases it. It's registration's G-JKAY – the one he pilots in the music video to the song "White Knuckle Ride".'

Simon feigned interest even though he hadn't heard of the song. The motion of the helicopter swooping over fields and banking left then right was beginning to make him feel queasy.

'Did you know Prince Philippe of Belgium has had one of these little beauties since 2002? It's red. I think he's still got it. He flies it himself – for leisure. Sure is a great way to relax.' Charles banked the helicopter to the right.

'Oh,' was all Simon could manage, acutely aware of his meal the night before. He tried not to think about the fried onion rings and red wine. The helicopter banked again. Peering into the distance he saw the large office block owned by Tony Hedge. It stood next to a busy dual carriageway yet behind it lay open fields.

'Fancy an autorotation into the car park?' asked Charles.

Not wishing to appear ignorant, Simon nodded again. He wished he had not. Charles slowed the helicopter engine and lowered the collective lever between them to the floor, allowing the helicopter to fall downwards at speed. It appeared they would crash into the office block. Before they hit the ground and before Simon could let out a scream, Charles flared the helicopter's nose, landing the machine perfectly onto the helipad. 'Spot on. Your turn tomorrow,' he said, a broad smile plastered on his face. 'Okay, I'll pick you up again at about four.'

'Righto,' Simon said, steadying his hands and unbuckling his safety harness. He yanked off his headset, replaced it on the seat and ducked out of the helicopter. He raised a hand to Charles, who took off into the grey sky. Simon stood for a few minutes longer before staggering to some bushes near the field, where he brought up semi-digested steak and onion rings.

He removed his glasses and rubbed the bridge of his nose. Seeing his old home had affected him more than he had imagined. This was folly. He could no more live Tony Hedge's life than he could fly to the moon in a microlight. This nonsense had to stop. He pulled out his mobile to call the imps, but before he could dial the number, a woman came running from the office block.

'Thank goodness you're here. Have you seen the news this morning? It's chaos on the stock markets and we've had clients calling since we arrived, all wanting to pull out of funds. Hurry, Lord Carson is on the line and he wants to speak to you urgently. He's frantic about his pension money.' She scuttled back towards the building, Simon at her side, puzzling over what he should tell his supposed client.

'Hold the lift, Gavin,' yelled the woman as they charged through the entrance.

Simon noted the burly man with the broken nose who was dressed completely in black and wearing an earpiece. His jacket appeared to bulge under his left armpit as if a gun might be concealed there. Simon began to feel the by-now-familiar uncomfortable feeling of sweat trickling down his back. The man gave him the barest of nods.

'Thanks, Gavin,' replied the woman as she bounded into the lift. Gavin pressed the sixth-floor button and the lift shot upwards.

'You've not heard about the chaos on the Hong Kong markets overnight?'

'No. I was too busy,' said Simon.

'There was some poor economic data out of Asia and the Hang Seng crashed, losing 10.41 per cent of its value. It's rattled European markets and there's speculation that the Dow Jones will drop heavily. The FTSE is currently nosediving. We've been telling clients it's a knee-jerk reaction and markets will bounce back, but the blasted media is having a field day and their sensationalist take on it is making investors, even seasoned ones, wary. The phone has been off the hook all morning. Terry and Dominic have been trying to pacify clients since they walked through the door. We've got significant problems with some of the larger companies – Bunton Holdings want to close their account with us and pull out all savings.'

Simon nodded sagely. He had no idea what the woman was talking about.

'Given they invested 20 million with us, that would seriously dent our finances. Rory has headed off to meet with their financial director to try and persuade them this is only a blip.'

The lift doors eased open into a large penthouse office. The area was divided into sections stationed by various men and women, all on telephones and staring at computer screens. The full-fronted windows gave a superb view of the countryside at the back of the office block.

'He's just walked in, Lord Carson. I'll transfer you immediately,' said a young man dressed in grey trousers and a pink-and-grey-striped shirt open at the neck.

'Lord Carson,' he hissed, handing over the phone. 'Do you want to take it here or at your desk? He's in a filthy mood.'

A quick glance around revealed an unmanned section. Simon assumed it was his.

'I'll take it there.'

'There? At Rory's desk?'

'Yes,' replied Simon, attempting to carry off an air of authority yet feeling he'd just made a mistake.

'Transferring you now, Lord Carson.'

The phone on the desk lit up. Simon picked up the receiver. 'Good morning, Lord Carson. How can I help you?'

'By jumping out of the nearest window,' came the gruff reply. 'Have you seen what's happening or have you been too busy screwing those girls at Madame Whiplash's place to have taken note of the chaos that has occurred?'

Simon laughed – a high-pitched, nervous laugh.

'I've been in a meeting with colleagues about it,' he answered, thinking that this was pretty close to the truth.

'So what's my portfolio currently worth?'

Simon looked about him, panic rising in his chest. He spotted the girl who had accompanied him in the lift and signalled her over. 'Can you get me details of Lord Carson's investments and tell me what it's currently worth?' he whispered. 'One moment. I'm just getting that information for you,' he continued, feeling pleased he was handling the situation so well.

'I can tell you what it's worth,' said Lord Carson with a growl. 'It's worth less than half of what it was worth yesterday. You promised me you would look after my money. You assured me that you had your finger on the pulse. You're nothing more than a charlatan!'

'Steady on. You can't predict what markets are going to do.'

'Poppycock! You have all the technology and expertise there to ensure you choose funds and shares wisely. You convinced me to invest 10 million in Hong Kong funds. You gave me your assurance it was as safe as investing in bricks and mortar and told me swings and prevarications in the market wouldn't affect it. Well, you were wrong. The bloody fund is on its knees. I'd never have invested with you if we hadn't been friends. I should have listened to those who told me you were a con man. I want my money back. I don't care if you have to find it out of your own pocket. I want it this week or I shall be forced to take matters into my own hands. Not only am I a dab hand with a shotgun, I have incriminating photographs of you that I'll happily send to the press. They're very entertaining. There's one of you at a certain yiffing party. You appear to be disguised as a bunny rabbit and, my goodness, you know how to shake that cottontail, don't you? Even though your face is obscured, the girl feeding you carrots in the photo is more than happy to kiss and tell to the press. You might remember Celia? Dressed as a weasel? She says you're a very disgusting rabbit indeed and that you do far more with carrots than nibble at them.' With that he rang off. Simon looked about the office. Several faces were watching him.

'What?' he asked.

'It might have been better if you hadn't put the call on speakerphone,' said the man in the striped shirt.

Simon scraped back his chair and headed for the lift, head bowed to hide his flaming cheeks. Behind him someone said, 'What's up, Doc?' causing sniggers. Simon stabbed the call button and threw himself into the lift the moment the doors opened. Doors closed, he thumped his head against the cool walls then pulled out his telephone and rang Mission Imp-ossible.

CHAPTER TWENTY-FIVE
Polly

The morning had gone badly. After a night of tossing and turn-ing, Polly had drifted off to sleep in the early hours only to be woken almost immediately by the doorbell

'Morning, sweetie. Oh, you're not ready,' said Calvin, his lips pressed together in disapproval as he surveyed her wild hair and smudged eyes.

'It's silly o'clock. I had a lousy night. I ache from yesterday and I don't want to train,' grumbled Polly.

Calvin put his fingers in his ears. 'La, la, la. I can't hear you. Now off you pop. Go get ready. Busy, busy day, sweets. We've got to go through your martial-arts training as well as a run. Come on, leap to it.'

'I don't know any martial arts.'

'Exactly. That's why we need to work on your skills – or rather lack of them. Now hurry up or I'll make that phone call and have you sent back to poverty land.'

'Calvin.'

'Yes, sweets.'

'I deplore you.'

'Excellent. That's the way I like it. Especially when we're doing this sort of training. Hurry up or I'll make you run an extra two miles.'

Polly stomped back to her room to get changed. She was going to have to put a stop to all this training. She would have to talk to Lilith.

Calvin put her through a gruelling three-mile run, warm-up exercises, press-ups and sit-ups before marching her into the gym. The gym was well equipped with various weight machines and cardio-training devices, yet he walked her past those and into the corner where a large punching bag hung from a hook in the ceiling. He handed her a pair of boxing gloves.

'Okay, this is the fun part. Put those on and hit the bag with all your might. It'll help if you give it the name of someone you don't like… ha ha! You wouldn't be the first to call it Calvin,' he added, noting the sudden gleam in Polly's eyes. 'Right, thump it!' he shouted. Polly gave the bag a pounding with both fists for all of two minutes before she slowed as lactic acid built in her muscles, making her arms feel like leaden weights. Beads of perspiration trickled down her face and onto her lips. She licked the salty liquid away and threw another punch. She was only able to make feeble contact with the bag. It barely moved.

'Is that it?' asked Calvin, one eyebrow raised and a wry smile playing on his lips. 'You need to build up some strength in those arms of yours. Oh dear. I thought you were tougher than that.'

Polly grimaced. 'That bag is ridiculously heavy. What's in it? Concrete?'

'Let's try resting those muscles and work on your legs. Ever see *The Matrix*? Watch me and copy.'

Calvin dipped slightly to one side and kicked out with the opposite leg, flicking his leg and foot around until it almost made contact with Polly's midriff. She had no time to react – such was his speed. He chuckled. 'That's a round kick. Useful for taking out bad guys who try to attack you.'

'Like I meet guys who want to attack me every day,' scoffed Polly.

Calvin gave her a steely look. 'Take this seriously, Polly. Trust me, you'll need to know these moves if you're to follow in Stephanie's footsteps.'

'Really? She gets attacked often?'

Calvin refused to comment, instead taking her through various kicks until she was able to try them herself without falling over.

'Right, now I want you to aim a kick at the bag,' he announced. Polly gave it her all and felt it resist before swinging away from her.

'And again. Harder this time.'

She kicked again and again until she could barely stand. Her legs shook uncontrollably. Calvin allowed her to stretch the ache away, after which she launched a final volley at the bag until sweat streamed down her face and she begged to stop. There followed a twenty-minute stretching and cooling-down session, after which Polly felt she could sleep for a fortnight.

Calvin departed at last, leaving Polly to face the day. She flopped into a warm bath that did little to help her cramped, sore muscles. They had well and truly stiffened up. Each time she picked up the hairdryer, her arm trembled so badly she had to put it down again. In the end, she gave up and left her hair wet, frizzy and unmanageable.

She was in the kitchen struggling to lift a spoon of cereal into her mouth when Zed drifted in, clad only in scruffy boxer shorts. His pale torso and scrawny legs put Polly off the cereal. She dropped the spoon in the bowl and glowered at him. He sauntered to the fridge, dragged out a carton of orange juice and headed back out.

'What about some manners? You could try saying good morning.'

'I'm not a morning sort of person,' he replied.

'And where are you going with that?' asked Polly.

'Duh, to the bedroom.'

'You drink orange juice here in the kitchen, not in bed.'

'God, you're a crabby cow in the mornings, aren't you?' was his reply as he walked off, orange-juice carton in hand. Polly slammed her bowl into the sink. She was sick of the blasted youth. It was clear they would never get along. She just wished he would go away. No doubt he hung about Chelsea in the hope that eventually he would get some of her inheritance, or trust, or whatever it was she was waiting for. Zed was just like Callum – a drifter and loser. Chelsea should not be with someone like that. She was intelligent and, of course, she was far too young to be in a serious relationship. Polly gnawed on her nails and paced the floor waiting for signs that Chelsea was up. The girl didn't appear for another hour and by then Polly was so tightly wound her jaw ached. The second she spotted Chelsea she pounced on her.

'Chelsea, I need to talk to you. Alone. Now. I don't want to nag and I'm very sorry about last night, but you and I really need a chat.'

Chelsea gave her a chilly look. 'I don't have much to say to you, as it happens. Zed told me you were rude to him when he came to get some orange juice for me.'

'I wasn't rude! He was the one who was rude.'

Chelsea tutted. 'Have you heard yourself? You sound like the stupid girls in my class at school. *I wasn't rude. He was the one who was rude,*' she mimicked in a high-pitched voice.

'Listen, Chelsea, I know I didn't hit it off with Zed. He and I have a clash of personalities. However, trust me when I say he's no good for you. I have good reason not to trust him. You only see one side of him. I see another. He's arrogant and flippant but worse still, he lies. I think he's lying to you and I believe he's manipulating you.'

'Really? And how is he doing that?'

'He wants to take you away from home and school and keep you in his sight until you come into your money. Then I have a feeling he'll spend it or make off with some of it. I've known people like him,' Polly said, rolling her eyes.

'Just because your life didn't work out, doesn't mean you can mess about with mine. As it happens, Zed isn't at all bothered by money. He told me so. He's not into capitalism.'

'Huh!' said Polly and wished she'd kept quiet as a stony look spread across Chelsea's face.

'Sorry. I'm out of order because I don't know him like you do, however, I have a gut feeling about him.'

'I don't know why you're so concerned. It's not like you and I are related or anything.'

'I like you. It's as simple as that. And I wouldn't want to see you make a mistake. You are only fifteen, after all. I'm the only adult in your life and I have a responsibility towards you.'

'Yeah, I kind of get it. You're wrong about him though. You don't know Zed. If you did, you'd understand that he loves me.'

Zed chose that moment to stroll back into the kitchen.

'Hi, baby,' he said to Chelsea and planted a lingering kiss on her lips. Polly wanted to rip the couple apart. Instead she took a deep breath, choosing to bide her time.

'Morning, Zed,' she said in as cheerful a voice as she could muster. 'Would you like any breakfast?'

Zed scowled. 'I'm okay, ta.'

'Juice?'

'Nah. We're going out to get a proper breakfast, aren't we, baby?'

'Could I finish my conversation with Chelsea before you go, please?'

Zed scowled again and dropped onto a kitchen stool.

'In private?'

'I don't mind him being here,' said Chelsea, holding onto his hand and giving him a shy smile.

Great, thought Polly.

'I'd like to propose that you go to school to take your examinations. I understand you don't want to return full-time, but I'm sure the school will let you go in to take the exams.'

'Exams are a waste of time,' muttered Zed darkly. 'Even if you get top grades, do A levels and go to university, waste another three years getting qualified in some subject you thought would secure you a decent position, you'll still find yourself fighting it out with thousands of other equally well-qualified students, and end up in the dole queue when you leave. You'll also have to deal with the humungous student debts you'll accrue. They'll be around your neck for years afterwards.'

'That's not true,' said Polly, perplexed by his negativity.

''Tis.'

'You're talking rubbish. Education is the only way forward. Your work prospects are limited if you don't have basic qualifications.'

'Crap!'

'Zed, butt out of this conversation. This is a decision for Chelsea to make, not you. You drift about living some sort of hippy life with no responsibilities, playing your guitar and living hand to mouth. However, you shouldn't try and force Chelsea to do the same.'

'Bollocks! Degrees and all qualifications are a complete waste of time. Students are hoodwinked into going onto university by schools who want to shine in league tables. It's all about league tables, especially at those private schools. No one cares what you actually learn as long as they can say that 95 per cent of that year got top grades in GCSE or A-level subjects.'

Polly's mouth flapped open and shut again. She had a nasty feeling that Zed was about to trump her argument and he did, in the next breath.

'I've got a first-class honours degree in sociology and after sending out 150 job applications, can you guess what job I was offered? One in a call centre for the minimum wage!'

He threw a triumphant look at Polly, who banged the mug she was holding onto the draining board.

'You were unlucky, that's all,' she said. 'I'm sure if you had persevered—'

'We both know that education is *not* the only way to advance in this world. Travel and experience counts as much, if not more. Chelsea is a bright girl. She'll be better off leaving that poncey school and seeing something of the world. There's more to life than big houses, dumb pink cars and having loads of dough.'

'I bet you'd change your tune if you suddenly came into money,' Polly fired back at him, annoyed that Zed was winning this argument.'

Zed's look said it all. Polly's stomach lurched. 'I know all about money. My folk are filthy rich. My father's a judge and my mother has her own company that turns over several million a year. I was brought up surrounded by an obscene amount of wealth. We had servants, stables, horses, and an enormous pile in the country and another on Barbados. Money doesn't mean a thing to me. What counts are people. Materialism is a disease. That's why I think Chelsea should travel with me and see something of the world before she comes into her own money. It would do her good to see how other people in less well-off countries survive and it'll teach her to appreciate the greater picture and, of course, be with me,' he added.

Polly gritted her teeth. In spite of his words there was something about Zed that didn't ring true. It was as if he were acting. She had, however, lost this particular round.

Chelsea's eyes sparkled. 'See?' she said. 'I told you you didn't know him.'

The pair left shortly afterwards without saying a further word to her. Now she was rooting through the drawers in her office in search of the elusive diary. The discovery that Zed had a degree and no interest in money had made her even more irritable. She rummaged through the second drawer throwing out paper clips, scissors and a pile of blank sheets of A4 onto the top. She snorted in annoyance. The phone on the desk rang.

'Hello, Polly, how are you enjoying your new life?'

'Hello, Lilith. I'm glad you phoned. It's not going quite as I imagined. I hate all the early-morning training.'

'I'll ask Calvin to come in the afternoon, if you prefer,' replied Lilith cheerfully.

'What I'd prefer is that he doesn't come at all. I need my beauty sleep and I don't need to try and cripple myself every day with lengthy runs and stupid workouts. I want Calvin removed.'

'No, not sure we can do that. You swapped lives with Stephanie and that's how Stephanie lived her life. She was obsessed with training. You'll soon get into it.'

Polly groaned. 'And there's the little matter of me suddenly having an argumentative daughter who hangs out with a smug, know-it-all boyfriend.'

'Chelsea is such fun though, isn't she? We thought you two would get on like a house on fire.'

'That's debatable. She and I are struggling. Why didn't you tell me about her?'

'You'd have chickened out and passed up a fantastic opportunity. You have a lot in common. I'm sure you'll work things out. She'll only be there for a couple of years and then you can get back to being all alone, if that's what you want.'

'I'm yet to be convinced about this,' said Polly with a heavy sigh. 'It's not going as well as I hoped it might. If it doesn't work out, I want a get-out-of-hell-free card and a replacement swap.'

'I'm sure we can come to some arrangement,' said Lilith smoothly.

'On another matter, I've found Stephanie's bank statements and she appears to have less than £200 in her account. That's no way near enough to run this place, buy clothes or even feed the two of us. How am I supposed to live a life of luxury on that amount?'

'That's one of the things I wanted to talk to you about. Stephanie didn't keep her money in a bank. She didn't trust banks. Look behind the Picasso in the office. There's a small knob behind the bottom right-hand corner. Press it.'

'*The* Picasso? Is it real?'

'Of course it's real. You didn't think it was fake, did you?'

Polly's eyebrows raised into her forehead. That was exactly what she'd thought. 'If it's real, it's worth a fortune.'

'Correct. Now go and look behind it.'

Polly felt behind the painting and pressed on the knob. The painting swung to the left, revealing a metal door.

'I've found a safe,' whispered Polly into the phone.

'If you look under the top drawer of the desk, there's a key for it. You'll find what you need in there. Any problems, give us a call back. Don't spend it all at once,' continued Lilith. The phone went dead before Polly could respond. She shook her head. This was madness. However, she was curious to know what was in the safe.

An inspection of the top drawer revealed a key attached with Sellotape. Polly fumbled to release it, her fingers quivering with excitement. The key slotted into the safe, which sprung open with a noisy click. On the bottom shelf were various velvet-covered boxes containing sparkling diamond necklaces, bracelets and rings. She gasped. The stones in them were enormous. In the centre of the safe was a very large box. Polly extracted it with some difficulty and placed it on the desk. It too was locked. *Where was the darn key?* She ransacked the drawers in search of it, then in a moment of clarity she remembered her own key ring. There were two keys on it, both smaller than door keys. She left the office, almost tumbling over two figures lying prostrate in front of the office door.

'Why aren't you on your bed?' she asked. Dolce looked up. He had one of her Snoopy socks in his mouth. 'Oh for goodness sake. How did you get that?' He dropped it and waited for her to grab it before snatching it away gleefully and racing off with it.

'I haven't got time for this. Keep the sock. Don't chew it though.' She staggered up the stairs as quickly as she could, urging her stiff muscles to move, pursued by the two dogs who both scurried into the wardrobe, no doubt to see what else they could pilfer. She found the key ring and headed back to the office, where she shut the door and tried the lock on the box. Eureka! She lifted the lid and peered inside. The room swam in front of her. She clung to the desk and breathed deeply. The box was stuffed full of bundles of fifty-pound notes. She grabbed at bundle after bundle. Each one contained a thousand pounds. She piled them onto the desk. She lost count. She was rich. Rich beyond her wildest dreams.

She checked the safe for any documents or anything else of value, running her hand along the bottom. She touched upon an object, seized it and brought it out into the light. It was a gun. According to the make etched on it, it was a Taurus Judge .410 revolver. The discovery didn't shock Polly. If you had this much money hidden in your house you would want some form of protection. Like jigsaw pieces fitting together, Polly now understood why Stephanie was so keen on keeping fit and practising martial arts. She would be anxious about having huge amounts of money in the house. Polly suddenly decided that training with Calvin wasn't a bad idea. She tested the gun for weight and held it, finger off the trigger in case it was loaded. It didn't feel comfortable. There was no way she would be able to use it. It would have to stay out of harm's way. She returned it to the safe. She thumbed through a bundle of notes, speculating how much she would need for a Mulberry handbag and a top designer outfit, then, pulling out three more bundles, she placed them on the desk, locked the remaining money in the box and returned it to its hidey-hole.

Polly glided up the stairs, oblivious to her stiff limbs. First, she would head to town for some serious retail therapy and lunch at a smart bistro. Then it struck her that she had no one to share in her happiness. Her thoughts went straight to Kaitlin. Years and years of friendship couldn't be forgotten or ignored, no matter what the demons had demanded of her. She dialled Kaitlin's number: it rang and rang. Finally, Kaitlin picked up.

'Kaitlin! Hello, lovely. Have I got some news for you? You're not going to believe what has happened.'

'Sorry, who is this?' asked Kaitlin.

'Me. Polly.'

'Polly?'

'Ha ha! Yes, Polly.'

Polly was met with silence.

'Stop messing about. Something incredible has happened.'

'I'm sorry. I don't know anyone called Polly,' said Kaitlin.

'Kaitlin! Of course you do. Are you winding me up for some reason?'

'I don't know who you are. How do you know my name? And how did you get this number?'

'I know I haven't phoned for a few days, that's why I'm phoning now, so stop playing jokes. I've got something incredible to tell you.'

'You have the wrong number.'

'Kaitlin, please, stop it!'

'How do you know my name? Are you some weird stalker?'

'Of course not. Kaitlin, this isn't funny any more. Pack it in. I need to talk to you, so stop pratting about. I've solved all my problems. This is going to sound bonkers – I've swapped my life with someone else's.' Even to her own ears Polly sounded idiotic.

There was murmuring at the other end of the line as Kaitlin spoke to someone, then Miguel came on the line.

'You have the wrong number. Please don't phone again,' he said.

'Miguel—' The line went dead. She redialled the number. This time no one picked up. What had happened? Why did Kaitlin not want to talk to her? Why did she refuse to recognise Polly? A small voice in her head chirped up. Of course, Polly had changed lives and along with that she'd lost those she cared about, including Dignity and her mother. Polly slumped onto the bed. The reality of not having her friends in her life hit home. Dolce licked her hand and looked up at her. Gabbana hauled himself onto the bed and plopped down onto her lap.

'Looks like you're my only friends now,' said Polly, stroking his silky fur. Tears welled in her eyes and spilled down her cheeks, dripping onto his head. Dolce licked her hand again. The money lay discarded on the bed.

CHAPTER TWENTY-SIX
Simon

Simon couldn't get a signal in the lift. He stomped past reception and the man in the dark suit.

'Everything okay, Mr Green?' he called.

'No, it isn't,' he snapped back. He thundered out of the building. Outside, he could hear the traffic on the dual carriageway. Was it only last week he was in one of those vehicles that chugged past? Last week he had a family, a job and his sanity. He wasn't a sex freak who dressed up as a baby or a rabbit and got his rocks off by being tormented. He wasn't a businessman whose profession seemed to consist of investing other people's money in complicated schemes that carried huge risks. How he wished he were back in his company car heading off to Ernest-Deal. He kicked at a stone. As if it sensed his annoyance, his mobile rang; the mocking ringtone 'Money, Money, Money' by ABBA served to infuriate Simon even further. He stabbed the 'accept' key.

'Morning, Simon. How's it all going?'

'I want out.'

'You can't mean that. Look at what you'd give up! You're rich beyond imagination. You have a babe of a wife who isn't afraid to experiment, not to mention a life many people only dream of. The house is worth a cool £8 million. Did you not see the spa area in it? There's an Olympic-sized pool in the outside barn and a collection of vintage cars that are worth megabucks.'

'I don't care. I want my old life back.'

'Your old life with middle-aged Veronica, sulking, unapprecia-tive teenagers and an awkward mother-in-law who thinks you're a waste of space – not forgetting unemployment?'

'Yes. All of that. I'm done with this swap-a-life arrangement.'

Len continued in a more sinister tone: 'I'd like to remind you that you signed a legally binding contract. Regardless of what you want, you now owe us a soul. If you don't hand it over, we'll be forced to take a handful of souls of our choosing. So it's up to you.'

Simon rubbed his face. The stubble on his chin was coarse. He felt grimy and old, so very old.

'One soul and then we're quits. I'll go back to the life I left before all this madness.'

'Excellent! I knew you'd be reasonable. We'll send a car to pick you up tomorrow.'

'No! I can't go back into the office and I certainly don't want to go back to Tony's house.'

'What, you don't want to go back to that fabulous mansion and that stunning woman? Are you mad?'

'I think I might go mental if I carry on like this. I want to go home.'

'My name isn't Derren Brown. We can't magically undo all this effort. You'll have to stick it out today to give us time to rearrange stuff. You've become our most difficult client to date,' said Len sounding rather annoyed.

'I can't carry on existing in Tony's world. I'm going to make a right balls-up of work. Markets have crashed and I haven't the foggiest what to advise people.'

'Act like the top man you're supposed to be. Tell the staff to sort it out, get the office junior to make you a coffee and chill in the office until it's time to go home. Do some paper shuffling to make it look like you're working – don't tell me you've never done that before. Tell your secretary you're too busy to answer calls and that should cover it.'

Simon sighed and rubbed his chin. There was something on it. He picked it off and shuddered. It was dried vomit.

'Tomorrow morning, I want a car and I want to go back to my old life.'

'Sure you don't want one last exchange with someone else?'

'No. I'm done with this swapping lark. I want to go home.'

Simon heard a sucking of teeth. 'I should warn you that you might have problems when you return,' said Len eventually. 'Because you altered your swap we were forced to employ some unorthodox methods for that to happen as quickly as it did.'

'Len, make it happen. I'll give you the soul you want. I want my family back.'

'They won't be happy if they discover what's been going on.'

'Can't you blitz them again with that *Men in Black* laser?'

'Could cause irreparable damage if we overdose them on that. We'll try. You might have a few problems with them all when you get home, especially if we can't reverse the effects. Veronica seems quite content at the moment and Tony is getting on famously with Morag. She's decided at last that she likes her son-in-law and they're all going out for a meal tonight to celebrate Haydon finishing his exams.'

Simon felt sick. More than ever he wanted to return to his previous life, even if it meant arguing with Veronica and being detested by Morag. He would man up. He would fight to get their respect. He would confess to Veronica that he no longer had a job and sign on the dole, then search for a new position – a better job with prospects. He wouldn't give up. He would look after *his* family.

'Len, make it happen and send someone to collect me. I want out… as of now.' He terminated the call and looked at the busy road. Less than a week had passed since he'd been the real Simon Green and yet it felt a lifetime. One thing was for certain: he'd learned that no matter how bad the situation became, or how monotonous life was, his family was paramount. They helped make him whole. He would make it up to them.

With a look of determination on his face, he returned to the offices. Gavin was staring at an evacuation notice with feigned concentration. He'd clearly heard about Simon's phone call in the office and was wrestling with a grin that threatened to erupt on his otherwise stern face.

'Gavin,' he said. 'I have to meet a client urgently. I haven't time to wait for the helicopter. I need to get there quickly. You drove here today, didn't you?'

Gavin nodded.

'Give me your car keys. I'll use your transport.'

Gavin shuffled from side to side. 'I'm not sure that's a good idea, Mr Green.'

'Come on, Gavin. Hand them over. I'll look after the vehicle. I haven't time to argue about it. I'll give you a small bonus at the end of the month as a thank you.'

Gavin reluctantly pulled out his keys. 'A bonus?'

'Yes, and don't worry, it'll come back safe and sound. Now which one is it?' he asked, scouring the car park filled with BMWs and Audis.

'That one,' replied Gavin, pointing at a purple Vespa parked in the corner of the car park. 'The helmet is in the carrier. Look after Betsy bike, Mr Green. She means a lot to me.' He turned away to suppress a laugh. Simon snatched the keys from him and strode away, refusing to look back. He marched over to the scooter, removed the helmet from the carrier and strapped it onto his own head, thanking his lucky stars he'd driven one of these scooters in the eighties when he'd briefly flirted with a phase as a mod. A vision of him in a parka singing to The Jam's 'The Eton Rifles' sprung to mind. He twisted the key and the Vespa putted into life. Weaving slightly, he took off at speed. Out of the corner of his eye he could see Gavin watching, mouth open and other faces pressed up at the window observing his departure. Let them stare. He wouldn't be coming back.

Parked outside Ernest-Deal, Simon fumbled about in his pocket and extracted his black book of contacts. It had been in his pocket when he left home and he'd hung onto the last scrap of his past life, regardless of the rules. He flicked through it, fond memories of happier times flooding back. He looked over at the dealership. On the forecourt Patrick and Ryan were moving cars into the showroom. Patrick was waving Ryan back into a space, ensuring he didn't clip the wing mirrors of the Aston Martin Vantage. Ryan clambered out of the car and said something to Patrick, who laughed and clapped him on the back. Simon felt a pang of sorrow. He'd forgotten how much fun they all had in the dealership. Even when the chips were down and targets had to be met, the workforce had stuck together and morale was often boosted by jokes or chats. He missed his friends – even Ryan. Dave came rushing outside to join the men. They huddled together, heads almost touching before Patrick pulled out his mobile and called someone. Ryan twisted about, looking for something or someone. His eyes alighted on Simon sitting opposite for a second before he turned back to the men.

Simon pulled away before they spotted him although the likelihood of being recognised was minimal. No doubt they had all been blasted with rays too. A few minutes later, he pulled up outside Eric's bungalow. The grass had just been cut and Eric was standing outside, propped up by his Zimmer frame, taking in some sunshine. Simon was surprised. Eric rarely left his living room. He raised his hand in a friendly hello, hoping Eric hadn't been subjected to the laser treatment. He dismounted the Vespa.

'Nice day,' he called to Eric.

'Beautiful,' replied Eric. 'You have to make the most of these, especially at my age.'

'At any age,' said Simon.

'Can I help you?' asked Eric.

Simon's heart sank again. Eric had been exposed to the same treatment as his family and colleagues. He had no idea who Simon was.

'Just a bit lost. Looking for Ernest-Deal.'

'Oh, you're not far. It's up the road. Turn left at the crossroads and right at the T-junction. It's on the left. You might even have passed it if you came from that direction.'

'You know it?'

'Used to work there. Great place. It used to be called Tideswell in those days. My sister-in-law still works on reception there. They've got some very nice motors. Wish I could still drive. I'd buy one.'

'Salesmen okay? Sometimes you hear about pushy ones. I don't want to be fleeced.'

'Oh you'll be fine there. They really take an interest in their customers. You go in as a customer and come out as a friend.'

Simon cocked his head. That was one of his lines. Eric carried on:

'Ask for Patrick. He's pretty good, or Tony. He's a terrific salesman. Been there years. My Jackie is godmother to his daughter.'

Simon removed his glasses and rubbed his nose to ease the pressure.

'Tony?'

'Nice guy. They don't make salesmen like him anymore. Nothing is too much trouble. Ask for him. You'll be glad you did.'

Simon couldn't listen to any more. He thanked Eric and climbed back onto the Vespa. If he'd looked up he would have seen Eric flapping his hand at someone hidden inside the house, but he did not. Instead, with teeth gritted, he headed for town, where he drew up and parked directly outside the offices of Champington Insurance. He was going to sort out the mess he'd created once and for all.

CHAPTER TWENTY-SEVEN
Polly

Polly had been sitting on the bed for over an hour. Dolce and Gabbana lay flat out beside her. Her misery was interrupted by the sound of the doorbell. All three jumped up. The dogs raced off to greet the visitor, leaving Polly to amble downstairs. She shooed the animals away, opened the door and stared directly at a muscular torso. She tore her gaze away reluctantly. The dogs vied for his attention. He ignored them and focussed on her, holding out a large hand. She took it. He had a strong, confident grip.

'Hi, I'm Matt. You must be Polly.'

Looking up, Polly's insides turned to liquid and she was overcome with the desire to launch herself into his strong arms and be held. His eyes were blue. Not ordinary sky blue or the colour of forget-me-not flowers springing up in an open field. His eyes were blue like a crystal-clear blue sea, shimmering and crashing and churning. Looking into his eyes she could hear the waves falling against the shore, see the foam flying into the air.

'Yes. H-hello,' she stammered.

Matt looked her up and down. The cool air against her legs reminded her she hadn't finished dressing. She pulled at the long cardigan, hoping the shirt underneath was long enough to hide her knickers. Matt's eyes travelled the length of her body, appraising her. He raised his eyebrows and smiled. *He has the sexiest smile*, she thought then flushed pink as she understood why he was smiling.

'Nice,' he said, folding his arms.

'Ah! I have no excuses. I happen to have a thing about novelty socks.'

'Minions. Cute. I take it you've seen the films.'

'Of course. Not the last one though. I missed that. I really ought to get it on DVD.'

Matt nodded. 'Yes, definitely worth watching. It's about a supervillain called Scarlett Overkill and Bob, Stuart and Kevin who are my favourite minions. Talking of supervillains and dastardly deeds, I'm here to teach you to shoot.'

'Really? I need to learn to shoot?'

'You most certainly do. Well, according to the person from some strange outfit called Mission Imp-ossible you do.'

Polly remembered the pistol in the box with the money. 'No offence, I'm just not a gun sort of girl.'

'Aha,' he replied. 'What sort of girl are you? An "I'll scream if I see a burglar" sort of girl or an "I'll run like the wind if someone tries to attack me" sort of girl?'

'I'm a "Oh crap, now what?" sort of girl,' she replied, earning another heart-fluttering smile from Matt.

'Fair enough. I can't force you and I don't blame you. Guns aren't for everyone. Shame though. I'd have liked an excuse to stand behind you and guide your aim.'

Polly floundered for a moment. 'It would need a lot of guiding. I have slight astigmatism and no doubt would end up shooting out telegraph poles and innocent bystanders.'

'Ach, you'd be fine. I was only going to suggest a couple of clay pigeons to start with. To my knowledge they don't feel a thing when you blast them.'

'Clays? They're not real pigeons, right?'

'Definitely not real. It's quite good fun if you fancy a go.'

Polly furrowed her brow in thought. She could do with a distraction. She was fed up being alone and what harm would come from shooting clays?

'So tell me again who you are?'

'Good afternoon, miss. My name is Matthew Thomas, Matt to everyone. I run my own company, "Safe and Sound". I train men and women to use firearms, run clay-pigeon-shooting courses and I'm also the director of a large paintballing site near London. Here's my card.' He presented her with a business card. She smiled and looked it over thoroughly.

'I'm thirty-six years old, ex-military and enjoy reading, paint-ing, making daisy chains and swimming with dolphins.' Polly sniggered. Matt raised his eyebrows and continued. 'I was hired to teach you to shoot, yet I can tell you have no need to learn such a sport. You are a fair maiden, more suited to the genteel art of needlework or playing the harpsichord. Forgive my intrusion and have a nice day.' He tipped an invisible hat.

'Right. Okay. You've sold it. It could be amusing. I'll get some trousers on and join you.'

'You don't have to dress on my account,' he said. 'You've got great legs.'

Polly was speechless.

'Really.'

'I'm not used to compliments, especially about my legs. They're a little chunky for most people.'

'I have a thing about comfortable legs,' he said with a wink.

For a moment she was flustered. Matt was flirting with her. Her mood lifted. A little boost in her self-esteem wouldn't go amiss. Besides, he was nice to look at – his face was tanned and healthy, his hair a light brown streaked by the sun and he oozed masculinity. She noticed a small star-shaped scar on his forehead – the result of some injury. It was partly hidden by a fringe, brushed to one side. She forced herself to stop staring and turned to get changed.

'I'll get the guns and wait for you here,' he said, dropping down to pat the dogs. 'Best to keep these little chaps inside too. Don't want to scare them,' he added.

Matt waited for her beside his Land Rover. He carried a case and two shotguns over his shoulder. He handed her a pair of ear defenders.

'You'll need those or you'll be deaf for ages.'

'Is it that noisy then?' she asked.

'Pardon?' he replied, lifting his hand to his ear. 'What did you say?'

She giggled. And resisted the urge to punch him on the arm.

They walked towards the wooded area behind the house. Matt turned towards her.

'Okay, this looks like the spot the woman told me about. Now, you don't know me and I'm about to take you into a wood with some guns and ammunition. I am, however, 100 per cent professional and I don't want you to be worried about going into the training area with me. Do you want to phone anyone to let them know I'm here? You can use my phone.' He handed it out to her. 'I won't be offended.'

She started to smile then checked herself. He was completely serious. There was a definite aura of masculinity about this man that appealed to her. She wasn't sure she would object if he did force himself on her. 'No, I reckon you're okay.'

'You are an excellent judge of character,' he replied and winked at her.

'Historically that's not always been the case. Maybe I should phone someone,' she said. He passed her the phone. She laughed. 'Only kidding. I'm sure you're someone I can trust.'

'And on what do you base that statement?'

'The dogs like you. Dolce gave you the same "I'm in love" look he gives Calvin, my personal trainer, who dotes on him. Also, when I went to change, I looked out of the window and saw you feeding them biscuits from your lunchbox. That proves you're a softie.'

'Busted!' he said. 'They're endearing little chaps. I don't normally like little dogs but they're different.'

'I know what you mean. They have a way of winning you over without trying. Come on – better show me how to fire these guns. I might need that extra protection – woman on her own in a big house and all that. I hardly think the dogs would save me. That pair would lead any thieves to the safe in exchange for a cuddle and a dog treat.'

'I'm not sure a shotgun would be my weapon of choice against a burglar. I'd invest in a good alarm system instead. Or buy a larger dog – preferably one with big teeth. Anyway, let's go and set up.'

A few feet into the woods stood a clearing. Matt strode to a wooden stand.

'You can only shoot when you're inside the stand,' he said, 'or we might accidentally hit a nosey neighbour or the vicar.'

'That would be dreadful. I'd be thrown out of the choir,' said Polly, keeping a straight face. Matt threw her a cautious look then noticed the corners of her mouth twitching. 'Yeah, right. I can see you in a cassock and a little frilly collar.'

'I've been an angel in a different life,' she answered.

'I bet you made an excellent angel – blonde ringlets and big innocent eyes – you'd have made a sinner weep.'

Polly was about to continue until a sharp pang inside stopped the banter. She had to focus on the present to forget those memories of Kaitlin and her life before this one.

Luckily, Matt was dealing with the shotguns and setting up. He ran through the drill of how to behave within the shooting zone. The emphasis was on safety and sticking to the rules. He told her how to achieve a successful shot. He explained that she had plenty of time to seek, aim and fire and not to shoot too quickly. He showed her the mechanism of the gun and told her what to expect when she fired it. Finally, he passed her one of the shotguns.

'Here, take this one,' he said. 'It's lighter.'

'It feels heavy enough,' Polly replied. 'What do I do now?'

'Are you right-handed or left-handed?'

'Right.'

'Press the butt against your shoulder and peer down the sight here.'

Polly snickered. 'Sorry, that's me being childish. I misunderstood when you said "butt". I ought to act more grown-up. Sorry.'

'Don't apologise. Some folk take things too seriously,' Matt added. 'You're more fun.'

'What make you say that?'

'Minion socks, sparkling eyes and a couple of dimples that make you look mischievous when you smile. I would bet you enjoy life.'

'Seems you're quite good at sussing people too. Yes, I like having fun. I've been guilty of being too serious in the past. Sometimes life makes you serious.'

'That's a truth. A few years in the army taught me that lesson.'

'Did you see any action?'

Matt nodded; the light in his eyes dimmed a little. 'Too much. It's not something I like talking about. Maybe another time. Not now. Now we need to teach you to shoot a clay.'

Polly looked down the sight, her left eye shut. She could see clearly. 'Pull!' she yelled and followed the circular clay as it was propelled through the air with her gun. There was little time to get it fully in view. She spotted it, thought it was in shot and pressed quickly. The clay sailed away into the distance.

'Ah, the one that got away,' she said. 'It happened so quickly. I hardly worked out where it was before it disappeared.'

Matt removed his ear defenders and plugs. 'Take your time,' he said. 'Look, it's like this.' He held the gun with her and together they moved it in a gentle trajectory from right to left, making a swinging arc. He did it again a little faster. All she could concentrate on was Matt's warm breath on the back of her neck and the proximity of his body to hers. His arms were strong, his hands powerful. She would love to feel them on her body. She wanted this man to run his hands down her spine to the small of her back and pull her against him. The attraction was powerful – almost tangible. He let go of her arm and moved towards the firing device. She breathed out and concentrated on the sight.

'Pull!'

The clay was catapulted into the air by the trap. Polly followed it as it sped across her vision, pressed lightly on the trigger and stood back. The clay broke into four pieces.

'Well done. You're a natural. Second shot!' shouted Matt.

Polly glowed. It was another boost to her confidence and just what she needed.

Polly felt like a new woman. A few hours in confinement with Matt was the tonic she needed. She could now aim and fire a shotgun. He had guided her arm on several more occasions as they attempted to hit clay pigeons, holding onto the rifle with her and ensuring the backfire didn't ricochet her backwards. There had been two instances when she wondered if she'd spun around whether he would have held onto her and fastened his lips on hers. As it was, Polly could now point, aim and shoot at a target and was looking forward to another lesson.

'Fancy a cold drink before you go?' she asked, as Matt packed his case back into the Land Rover. The dogs, now out of the house, were snuffling around Matt's feet.

'I'd love to, but I have to get to Shugborough for an event. Next time?'

Polly nodded, disappointed that he couldn't stay, and hoped he wasn't making excuses.

'When are you coming next?'

He climbed into his car. 'If I tell you what time I'm coming will you greet me again in novelty socks and black silk knickers?'

Heat rose up her throat and made her cheeks burn. She began to mutter a response.

'You looked great,' he added. 'Not many clients come to lessons dressed like that. Made my afternoon. I can be here the same time tomorrow if you like.'

'Let me think. I might have lots of appointments lined up already,' she said. She looked away for a fleeting moment. 'No, it's okay. I happen to be free. Oh by the way, Dolce says can you bring him some more of those biscuits?'

Matt looked down at the dog. It was sitting by the open door looking dolefully at him.

'I'll bring biscuits for the poor half-starved animal. See you then.'

Polly called Dolce, who waddled over for a pat. Matt shut the car door and with a beep of the horn, he left her. She laughed. She hadn't felt so light-hearted in ages. Things were improving at last.

She drifted back into the house and wondered what to do with her time. Stephanie's diary and address book lay on the worktop. She hadn't noticed them before. Chelsea must have dropped them there before she went out. She rifled through the diary only to find blank page after blank page. She searched the address book for celebrity contacts. There were none. In fact, Stephanie seemed to have no friends at all. The book was blank apart from the names of tradesmen. What a strange woman she was. Polly tried to piece together Stephanie's life. So far she only had an image of a fit, active woman who spent all her time exercising and going to spas or hanging out with two dogs. She liked reading. There were no televisions in the house, indicating she either hated every programme ever made, or she was anxious about rays seeping into her brain. Polly decided it would be the latter. The woman was odd. She had a wardrobe stuffed full of fabulous clothes and not one appointment in her diary where she might wear them. Polly sat on a stool in the kitchen and pondered some more.

The door opened and Chelsea wandered into the kitchen.

'Hi. Zed not with you?'

'He's gone to see a friend about some stuff.'

'Stuff?'

'I don't know what. It's not my business. Thought I'd come back and catch up on some sleep.'

'Is that how you plan on spending your days now you're not at school? Sleeping and loafing about?'

'What else is there to do?'

'Go out to cinemas, bowling alleys, galleries, theatres, concerts, shops, theme parks, roller skating, try a new hobby, learn a language, take up kung fu or any number of things.'

'S'pose I could go to the cinema. Not much on though. What do you do to fill in time?'

'Exercise. Read. Shop—' said Polly.

'Not much either then, it seems.'

'I'm not used to having free time. I worked all day every day. When I had the odd day spare there was housework to do, accounts to sort out and promotion for the business to arrange.

If there was any time left over, I watched television or sometimes went out with friends.'

'See, it's hard to think of things to do if you don't work, isn't it?'

'Want to go shopping?'

'I'm not sure,' said Chelsea.

'Come on. Let's have a girly afternoon. You can tell me what looks good on me. I only have socks and jeans here. I need something else to wear.'

'Okay. Guess so.'

Polly picked up her bag and hustled Chelsea out to the car, shutting the door on the dogs. 'Sorry, you two. Girls only.'

They headed into the nearest town – a shopping centre some five miles away. Chelsea remained silent throughout the journey, gazing out of the window. Polly started by chatting about her old life and soon clammed up. It was, after all, her old life. Being the mother of a teenager was jolly difficult. She had nothing in common with the girl.

'So where shall we go first? There's an Armani Exchange shop or we could head for the big department store and have a spend-up.'

Chelsea shrugged. 'Whatever,' she replied.

'Department store then. You can look for something for yourself too.'

'I don't need any clothes.'

'All girls need new clothes.'

'Why?'

'To look good.'

'I don't need any new clothes. I like the ones I've got. I look good in them.'

'Please yourself. Come and help me choose a new outfit then.'

Chelsea shuffled along beside Polly, stopping to stare at her mobile every few minutes. Polly pulled a pair of Stella McCartney jogging bottoms from a rail and grabbed a soft leather Saint Laurent biker jacket. Matt would surely fancy her in this outfit.

'What do you think?' she asked Chelsea.

'Okay.'

'That all? This is Saint Laurent. Feel it. It's beautiful.'

'It's a leather jacket. It's nice. Do you think it suits you though? I prefer you in your jeans and silly socks. That's too fussy. It looks like you're trying too hard.'

Dejected, Polly pulled out a copper-coloured Max Mara ostrich-leather pencil skirt and held it up. Chelsea shook her head.

'Why not? It's sleek and sexy.'

'That's why not! You should choose things that suit you. For someone who likes clothes you really do have poor taste in them. Come on. You need to get away from these and find something cheerful.'

Chelsea headed down the escalator into a trendy area.

'I can't shop here. This is for youngsters.'

'Nonsense. You're not old and you should wear younger clothes. Apart from your socks you wear drab colours. It's very ageing. It's proven that women who dress in more trendy, brighter outfits look younger. You'd look great in some of these tops. Look,' she said as she picked up a multicoloured blouse and a denim skirt. 'See, much better. Makes you look brighter, younger... happier.'

'Have you thought about being a stylist? You're good at this.'

'I had lots of practice. Stephanie insisted I went shopping with her when I was younger. I spent hours sitting about while she tried on clothes. That's why I don't really like shopping now. It's boring. I only buy stuff if I need it.'

'I suppose Stephanie needed designer clothes and outfits for all those parties she went to. She needed to fit in with all the celebrities.'

Chelsea pursed her lips and blew. 'Celebrities? Stephanie? You're kidding! The only celebrities she ever saw were in magazines. She was a complete loner. Imagine what it's like living with someone like that. You come home and your mother is sitting about listening to music and acting as if it's quite normal to serve bulgur-wheat salad in a Vivienne Westwood dress.'

'I thought she was a bit of a jet setter. She often spoke about going off to galas.'

'In her dreams. She didn't even go to Gala Bingo. As I said before, she had issues. Anyway, I don't want to talk about her.'

'Okay. I'll try this on and if I like it on me, I'll buy it and then we'll go and get a Coke or whatever you want,' said Polly.

Chelsea looked up. A scruffy figure was headed in their direction. Polly groaned. *Just as things were going well,* she thought.

'Hi, baby,' said Zed, stooping to kiss Chelsea and put a protective arm around her. 'Wasting some of *your* wealth?' he asked Polly with a sneer.

'Just looking at a few things.'

'You ought to be careful what you buy. Some of these fancy labels are produced in sweatshops by little kids who earn next to nothing.'

'Look, why don't you—' began Polly. She closed her mouth. Even though she didn't like what he said, there was some truth in his words. She had heard about the sweatshops. 'Why don't you two go to the cinema?' she ended lamely.

'I'm taking Chelsea on an alternative art tour in London. We're going to check out some street art. Might even add to some of it.'

'Street art? Do you mean graffiti?'

'You say graffiti and I say street art,' he said, shrugging. 'I think Banksy would definitely say "art".'

Polly twisted the blouse in her hands, wishing that it was Zed's neck.

'Don't let me hold you up,' she said in as light a tone as she could muster.

'You going to buy that?' asked Zed, nodding at the garment in her hands.

'I was thinking about it.'

'Yeah, of course.'

'What do you mean "of course"?'

'Just, it'd be logical, wouldn't it? You in a clothes shop with clothes in your hands,' he replied, a sly grin on his face.

Polly knew that wasn't what he meant at all.

'Come on, Chelsea. Got to go. We've got a train to catch.'

They left her. Polly returned the skirt and top to the rail. She didn't have the heart to shop for a few outfits. It had lost its appeal. She went down to the hosiery department and bought three pairs of new socks – one pair for her and one each for the dogs – then headed back to her car.

CHAPTER TWENTY-EIGHT
Polly

'Quick, pinch me! You're not only up, you're dressed and outside waiting for me. It's a miracle!' joked Calvin.

'Oh look, my sides have just split apart with laughter. Cut the funny-man routine, Calvin. I'm warmed up. Let's go. We've got some serious training to do.'

'I've never managed to transform someone's attitude in three days before,' he quipped as he ran beside Polly, who, already red-faced, was running with grim determination. 'It's totes amazeballs.'

'Can't talk. Just run,' she answered. Calvin grinned to himself and sped beside her, shouting now and then to encourage her as she struggled on. After a while, she began to lose momentum and slowed to a trot. She continued nevertheless, swiping at the sweat as it ran down her face and into her eyes, making them smart. She didn't rest until they reached the finish point by a bench near the house, where she stopped, hands on thighs, and wheezed before stretching her hamstrings.

'Phew! What happened to you? Did you take energy pills or have the demons swapped you for Paula Radcliffe?' Calvin asked.

'I needed to get something out of my system,' replied Polly, moving her damp hair from her neck and rubbing the sweat away with the palm of her hand. 'I think I can understand why Stephanie liked exercising. It's therapeutic and you feel much better after you've done some.'

'Endorphins,' said Calvin. 'Feel-good hormones are released when you exercise. It gives you a high. Careful though. You can get addicted to that feeling. I know someone who couldn't go a day without exercising – even on Christmas Day they ran twelve miles and spent all afternoon in the gym. Missed all the fun of the present opening and everything.'

'I know all about addictions,' Polly replied. 'At least this one does you good as well. Okay, I'm ready. Want to put me through my paces, or shall we go thump the bag?'

'Calvin the bag?' he asked cheerfully.

'I changed its name. It's called Zed,' she replied.

Chelsea had still not returned by lunchtime. Polly checked her bedroom. For a girl of fifteen there was little to suggest a teenager lived in the room, and it was surprisingly neat and tidy. One toy bear sat on the bed, books were arranged on a shelf, CDs arranged alphabetically and an iPad was propped up on her desk. A make-up bag was open by her bed and a long T-shirt thrown onto the duvet. Polly checked the wardrobes. They revealed a few items of clothing and several pairs of shoes. Polly could find no evidence of Stephanie at all. Chelsea hadn't even kept a photograph of her mother. She puzzled over it all. What girl would happily swap her mother for a stranger and dispose of anything to do with her past? It wasn't natural. No wonder she wanted to be with Zed. There was no one else in her life.

Her musings were interrupted by the arrival of Matt. Her heart lifted as she answered the door.

'Afternoon, miss. Is your mum at home?' he asked.

'Very funny.'

'It is a bit over-the-top cheesy, isn't it? I need to work on my chat-up lines,' he replied. 'How about "Good afternoon, Polly, you look radiant today"?'

'Better. Keep working on them though.'

'Okay. What about "I'm very sad you're not showing off your sexy legs today"? I spent all night thinking about them.'

Polly laughed. 'Much better.'

'I'll try harder for next time. So what socks are we wearing today?'

Polly raised the leg on her jeans to reveal shocking-pink animal-print socks along with the words *Born to be Wild*. Matt chuckled. 'Okay, wild thing: you up for some shooting practice?'

'Yes, I think I am. I'm not going to have to hit any animals or anything though, am I? I'm fine with clays. You don't plan on taking me out deer stalking or shooting at cute little fluffy bunnies, do you? I couldn't face that. Besides, I lost my Elmer Fudd deerstalker. Shame, it suited me.'

Matt gave a chuckle. 'Not at all. Funnily enough, for someone who does this for a living, I actually don't approve of violence, or hunting. I prefer the paintballing side of the business. That's where the money lies and it's the most fun. Nothing like a group of friends getting popped at with paint and having a laugh. It brings out the little boy in me. I used to be more grown-up, then I regressed – a reaction to the horrors of real life, I suppose. Paintballing is a game. It's escapism. I'm only doing this with you because I couldn't refuse the fat pay cheque that came with the job. It's funny how a person can change. I used to be besotted with shooting before—' A melancholic look crossed his face, making Polly want to reach out to him. Before she could, it disappeared and Matt smiled at her. 'You're not what I expected. I thought you'd be one of those serious sorts. You know what I mean – all moody and aggressive.'

'I am after too many tequilas. You wouldn't like to see me then.'

Matt thought for a moment. 'Yes, I think I would.'

Polly felt a warm tingle rising up from within. She pointed to the ground. 'Look, wabbit twacks,' she said in her best Elmer Fudd voice. 'Let's go find the scwewy wabbit.'

'You're scwewy!'

Polly raised her eyebrows. 'Only a little.'

'Scwewy is good. Want to try and hit a wicked wascal wabbit clay?'

'Bwing it on,' replied Polly.

Polly sang as she washed her hair. She and Matt had made a real connection. She knew it. She was not, however, going to push it. She still bore the scars of her last relationship. This one would only be for amusement. That was if she allowed it to be. So far, she'd rebuffed his compliments and refused an offer of a drink with him. She'd wanted to go to the pub. Goodness, how she'd wanted to say yes to his request, yet that nagging voice in her head reminded her that being keen wasn't the way. Matt had left with a disappointed look on his face. If he liked her enough, he would ask again. For some reason, Polly felt more confident – whether this was the result of an exercise regime that was already producing a leaner look or making headway with a truculent teenager, either way she felt renewed, as if she'd been on holiday and would now go home refreshed. She stopped singing. That's what she would really like to do. Go back home. Return to her old life and resolve all those problems. She felt strong enough to handle all the difficulties that were drowning her before she moved to Stephanie's home. Now she was both mentally and physically prepared to manage her debts, take on Gabi and win the case.

It had been interesting living here, but it still didn't feel like it was her home. She liked Calvin, Chelsea, the dogs and, indeed,

Matt, but they didn't make up for Kaitlin or Dignity. This remained alien to her. It was some fantasy world. She wanted to phone Kaitlin and have a giggle about some of the antics in the treatment room, such as when snobby Elaine Potter had farted non-stop during a massage and tried to blame it on her pooch, Foxy – an ageing poodle who had slept through its mistress's treatment. She wanted to go and share a tea with Dignity at the end of a busy yet satisfying day. Most of all she wanted to feel she belonged somewhere and in spite of all the luxury in this house, she didn't feel comfortable.

Stephanie's life wasn't even as good as her own. She was a lonely lady in a large soulless house with too much money. What an odd person. Whatever did she do all day apart from exercising and beauty treatments and shopping? Entering her bedroom, Polly heard soft music. It was The Killers singing 'Human' – the same song she'd heard before. She scoured the room. It seemed to be coming from a drawer in the wardrobe. She hauled it open. Dolce grabbed at a sock.

'Hey, get off! It's not a game this time,' she said. Pulling the sock from him she became aware it contained the source of the music – a mobile phone.

The music stopped. The screen stated that 'T' had phoned. T had in fact phoned eight times. Curiosity got the better of her. She pressed 'dial'.

'Finally,' said a deep voice. 'New mark. I'm sending details through. The client wants this one terminated immediately. He's a nasty piece of work. You have forty-eight hours. One million will be paid as usual after the job.' The line went dead. Polly stared at the screen. Had she just been asked to kill someone for money? It had to be a prank. Stephanie's life was turning out to be seriously bizarre.

Gabbana was tugging at another sock in the drawer. She moved him away and shut the drawer with a bang. The vibration caused the full-length mirror next to the drawer to swing slightly to one side, revealing an aperture. Dolce pushed behind the mirror and disappeared, followed by a snuffling Gabbana. Polly pursued the pair. At the rear of the mirror was a dark room. She fumbled for a light switch, first on the left, then right, her fingers finally locating one. A dazzling light came on and Polly stumbled forward in a daze. Although the area was similar in size to the wardrobe, this room didn't contain clothes. Neatly laid out on a table was an assortment of weapons: hand grenades, knuckledusters, knives and other deadly weapons. A cupboard housed two sniper rifles with telescopic lenses and several smaller handguns. Photographs of men and one woman were pinned to a large corkboard next to the cupboard and in neat red writing someone had written 'terminated' on each of them. Polly blinked. Her mouth had dried out. The phone beeped, announcing the arrival of a photo message. It would be of the next person to be 'terminated'. She opened the message and cried out. The phone clattered to the floor. A face looked up at her. It was her ex-husband, Callum.

CHAPTER TWENTY-NINE
Mission Imp-ossible Headquarters

Lilith was reclining on the office sofa, filing her cherry-red nails. 'Shouldn't be long,' she announced. 'Mania, you'll wear a hole in that carpet if you keep pounding backwards and forwards.'

Mania checked her watch and tutted. 'She lasted longer than I thought. I expected her to want out on the first day. She's going to crack, isn't she?'

'Of course she will. There's no way she'll stay there after her latest discovery. You worry too much.'

'We've got so much riding on this and there are a lot of people involved now.'

The phone rang.

'See, told you,' said Lilith, putting away her nail file and grinning at Mania. 'Want it on loudspeaker?'

'Yes, go on. I'm dying to hear what she says.'

Lilith pressed a key on the phone pad. 'Good afternoon, Mission Imp-ossible.'

'Lilith! I have to get out of here now!' yelled Polly. 'Stephanie is an assassin. You didn't tell me she killed people for a living. I can't do that. I can't kill folk. And someone's put out a contract on my ex-husband. I'm supposed to bump off Callum!'

'Seems ideal. Here's your chance to sort that problem out,' purred Lilith.

'You're bonkers. I dealt with Callum years ago. He and I split up. I don't have much to do with him. I certainly don't need to kill him. Besides, he has a new wife – Gabi. She'll be distraught.'

'I don't think so. Who do you think put out the contract?'

'No! She wouldn't. Surely not? It wasn't her, was it? Oh my gosh! Hang on a minute, how did you know about the contract? This is seriously nuts. I can't cope with this any more. I can't do this. I don't want to be a mother to a teenager who wants to run off with a pot-smoking drifter who has no idea what soap is. I don't want to be a gun-toting woman anxious about someone stealing a Picasso from her study. And I'm not going to take up a new profession murdering people.'

'No kill, no money. No money, no lifestyle,' said Lilith and winked at Mania.

'I'd rather be poor. This is lunacy. You have to get me out of here and return me to my old life immediately. I can make my old life work now. I've done some serious thinking and I'll go bankrupt if I have to and start again. I don't need flash clothes and bright pink cars or jewellery or anything. I am who I want to be. I shouldn't be ashamed of that.'

'What, you've suddenly gone off clothes?'

'I spent ages in front of that mirror holding up outfits and imagining me in them and do you know what? None of them made any difference. I'm still me. I'm still plump Polly, however, I can see beyond the exterior, the imperfections and the average looks. I know who I can be or, more importantly, who I want to be. And as far as money is concerned – sometimes it causes more problems than it solves. If you have too much, what can you spend it on if you have no one to share it with?'

'I understand what you're saying. What about Chelsea? You can't walk out on her.'

'I'm going to write her a long letter. I'll advise her to have a proper heart-to-heart talk with Stephanie when she returns. Stephanie needs her daughter more than she appreciates. I'll also advise her to take her exams and then go around the world with Zed. I don't like him, but he seems to be sensible enough. She'll probably learn a lot by visiting countries where people have little or nothing. It'll prepare her for her inheritance when she gets it. At least that's what I hope. I was wrong to want to run away and change lives with someone else. It doesn't solve anything. I want my mother and my friends Kaitlin and Dignity back in my life, and I want this craziness ended. Zed had a point – although I'm loathe to admit it – when he said there was more to life than material possessions.'

'You want your old life returned to you even with the threat of going to court?' continued Lilith. 'You will probably end up going to prison. It'll be lonely in there.'

'It can't be any more lonely than being stuck in a huge house. At least my pride would be intact and I'd have done the right thing. I can come to terms with that. I'll go to prison if I have to. First, I'll fight to stay out of jail. I've been falsely accused and I'll try to prove that. There must be some way. I'll get another job or start another business too if I have to. I'm not a quitter. For a while I forgot who I really am.'

'Okay, if you're sure.'

'I'm sure.'

'The chauffeur will come and get you in half an hour. You'll be taken to a holding area while we rearrange for your life to be given back to you. Pity. Stephanie was enjoying being a masseuse. She's not keen to go back to her old life. Oh, by the way. You still owe us a soul. We'll be collecting it now you've experienced your life swap.'

'But I didn't like my swap.'

'Contracts are contracts. We have to collect. It's in the small print. See you later.'

Lilith turned towards Mania who high-fived her.

'That couldn't have gone better, could it?'

'The timing was perfect. According to Nick's email, Simon is ready to throw in the towel and we have Polly en route. I'll let the bosses know it's time to get hell ready. This is going to be the coolest show ever!'

CHAPTER THIRTY
Simon

Simon sat quaking in what they called 'the red room'. He was unsure why it was called the red room because there was nothing red in it unless you counted the burgundy wine and the pale pink strawberries on the table.

'You can help yourself to anything here,' the man-mountain with pointed yellow teeth had said as he directed him to the room. 'You have to wait here until they're ready to present you to some of hell's inhabitants. You'll like them,' he continued. 'Hell is where the really interesting people end up.'

Simon rubbed frantically at his glasses and tried to remember how he'd got here; it was all a haze. After his meeting in town, he'd travelled to a motel where he got a decent room, a full minibar and free access to all the porn channels on the television. He'd settled for a documentary about Australia, glugged the contents of the minibar, scoffed the bag of complimentary nuts and fallen asleep. The phone woke him from a dream in which he was wearing a pink fluffy dressing gown, furry slippers and little else. For some bizarre reason he was singing '…Baby One More Time' in a falsetto while being whipped by Mania. It took a few minutes to figure out that he was in the dimly lit bedroom at a motel and his mobile was ringing. The call came from a woman who called herself Lily, or similar. She worked for Mission Imp-ossible and said they were sending a car for him. It was time to face his fate.

That had been four hours ago. He hadn't taken much note of the journey. The blacked-out windows in the limousine had prevented him from seeing outside and the complimentary bar inside had meant he'd spent most of the trip drowning his sorrows and wondering what awaited him. It had all been most peculiar. It had got even odder when the chauffeur had handed him a blindfold and requested he wear it. Given that the man looked like he used to be a prize cage fighter before he took up driving folk, Simon had agreed and put it on. After what felt like hours, even though it was probably only fifteen minutes, the car had come to a halt. Simon had been hauled out of the back seat by the chauffeur and guided up some steps, stumbling as he went. He felt like a kidnap victim.

'Any clues as to where I am?' he asked the chauffeur.

'I could tell you, but I'd have to kill you afterwards,' the man replied.

Simon wasn't too sure if the man was being serious, so he shut up and allowed himself to be guided along corridors where his feet echoed eerily as he walked down a flight of stairs and finally into this room, where his blindfold was removed. There were no windows in the room, only chairs placed against the wall as if it were a doctor's waiting room. He commented on this to the chauffeur. The man merely nodded at him and told him to wait there. A sign reading 'Welcome to the red room. Help yourself to food and beverages' hung above a table filled with plates of meat, cheese, salad and smoked salmon. A basket of rolls sat alongside with a collection of biscuits, chocolate bars and cakes. Crockery and cutlery was stacked neatly next to the food. A fridge next to the table was crammed with beer, while bottles of spirits and wine stood on a shelf behind. He pulled out a beer, opened it and took a slug, then spluttered as the door opened and Nick strode in carrying a cat basket.

'So,' he said, wagging his finger at Simon. '*This* is Ivan.'

Simon nodded dumbly.

'He's not what we expected. I think you were being devious, weren't you, Simon?'

Ivan meowed at Simon, his eyes wide with fear. Simon put his hand out to calm the frightened animal. Ivan recoiled.

'He doesn't like cages. Can you let him out for a minute?'

Nick huffed in irritation.

'Please. He's terrified. Look at him.'

Nick opened the door. Simon coaxed the animal out. 'Come on, big boy, out you come. Don't be frightened. No one is going to hurt you.' Little by little, Ivan edged nearer to Simon until he was close enough for Simon to haul him out. He trembled as Simon stroked his coat. 'It's okay,' he repeated in soothing tones. The cat snuggled against Simon and purred – it was a deep, grateful, resonant sound. Simon felt a pang of guilt.

'You're not going to take his soul, are you? I panicked and thought of him first. I really don't want to nominate him. It was a mistake. I shouldn't have chosen him,' Simon pleaded.

'That was the deal. The big boss is pretty annoyed about this turn of events and we're sending you in front of an audience to decide if we should accept this pathetic offering or take your soul and the soul of each member of your family as punishment.'

'No, don't do that. Take mine. Don't involve my family. I'll do anything I have to in hell, but please don't take them.'

'Anything? That could be most entertaining. I'll pass that on to the big boss. I hear he's looking for a new stooge. His last one actually wore out after ten thousand years.'

'If it saves my family, I'll do it. I got myself into this mess and the more I thought about it, the more I decided hell can't be much worse than the life I'll get if I go home. It's not fair to hand over Ivan. He's a pet. My little girl will miss him. She'll miss him more than me,' he added miserably. Ivan meowed in agreement.

'The big boss has decided you have to face the consequences. You can plead your case to the audience. You'll have to wait here until we're assembled and then someone will come and get you. We'll do our best to give you a decent trial. I'll get somebody to come and give you a touch of blusher. You look awfully pale.'

With that, Nick detached an unenthusiastic Ivan from Simon's arms, forced the animal back into the cage and left the room. Simon moaned out loud. It couldn't get any worse than this. The door opened once more and a female imp in a short skirt and high heels came in, carrying a box. She threw him a beaming smile.

'Hi. Nick said you needed my magic box of tricks. Been sent to make you look more presentable,' she said in a chirpy manner. 'Don't want that mob booing you because you look pasty and ill, do we?'

'Mob?'

'Oh yes. This event's been ever so popular. I've never seen so many imps and demons. They've been queuing all morning to get in. It's not just you. There's another contestant – a woman. They're going to decide which one of you will be dropped *down there*. Stay still. I need to put some eyeliner on you to make you look more... devilish,' she tittered.

'I don't understand. What's happening exactly?'

'Sorry, can't talk and do make-up. I'll shove the mascara wand into your eye if I don't concentrate.'

She worked on Simon's face while he fretted about the forthcoming proceedings.

'There,' she said, as a beep came from her belt. She looked at the device. 'You look heaps better. See you out there. The other contestant needs my services now. It was nice meeting you. Break a leg!' With that, she grabbed her kit and left before Simon could say a word. He rubbed his head and reflected on his life. He thought of Ivan sitting on his head while he slept. Somehow that now seemed charming. Ivan wouldn't want to suffocate him. He was a cat – a cat that bore no malice. Simon thought of the frightened creature in his cage-prison and felt heavy-hearted. What an idiot he'd been to nominate the animal. Still it was too late now.

The door opened once more and a thin, male imp wearing leather-bibbed shorts over a red shirt trotted in, his goat hooves clattering on the wooden floor. He held a large pitchfork in one hand and a clipboard in the other. He grinned, revealing a wide gap in his front teeth.

'Ready, Simon?' he asked, waving the pitchfork at him. 'It's show time!'

CHAPTER THIRTY-ONE
Polly

'You okay?' asked Lilith.

'Sort of. I guess I'm in shock. I can't believe Gabi would put out a contract on Callum. That sort of thing doesn't happen in real life, only in films. I would never have imagined her doing that. I thought she was besotted with Callum.'

'All sorts of strange things happen in this world. People are often not who you think they are.'

'I thought I was being mean nominating her to spend eternity in hell for making up all that rubbish about me hurting her and destroying my business, but that's decided it for sure. I don't feel guilty about choosing her now.'

Lilith looked up from the furry beanbag where she was seated, legs crossed, a notepad on her lap. She waved her ruby-red pencil at Polly.

'So I need to confirm, you are definitely nominating Gabrielle Dawson to spend eternity in hell?'

'Yes, Gabi it is.'

'As I explained on our way here, we must wait and see if the judges will accept your nomination or decide to choose you instead. You broke the agreement and in so doing forfeited the right to nominate someone to stand in for you. Mania and I fully support you and will explain that the person you stood in for was an assassin for hire. It's plausible the audience will accept that being asked to kill an ex-husband is grounds for breaking the contract although, knowing that lot, they'll be wondering why you didn't leap at the chance to bump him off.'

'I'm sure they'll see reason and hurl that spiteful bitch down there,' Polly replied, tucking her hair behind her ears and wishing she felt as confident as she sounded. 'Why all the cloak-and-dagger stuff?' she asked, looking around the windowless room. Her eyes rested on a plate of cream cakes.

'Got to be careful. It isn't wise for you to know the exact location of the entrance to hell, is it?'

'It was a good thing you were in the car with me. I'd never have put that blindfold on if I'd been alone.'

'Oh, I think I might have. It's not every day a hunky guy asks you to wear a silk blindfold,' said Lilith with a tight smile. 'Are you clear on the proceedings then?'

'I wait here in the red room, get my make-up done then someone will fetch me, attach a microphone to me so I can be heard and take me to the stage arena where I face baying masses, plead my case and go home.'

'That's pretty much it. You'll be fine.'

A knock at the door interrupted them. It was the make-up girl.

'Hi, Kakshasi,' called Lilith as the pretty imp came in. She had the longest eyelashes Polly had ever seen. If it weren't for the horns sticking out of her long auburn hair she could have passed for a model. 'I'd better go and get ready too,' continued Lilith. 'See you out there. You'll knock 'em dead!' She put her hand up to her mouth and giggled.

'Hi,' said Kakshasi, dropping her bag onto a table. 'I'm here to do your make-up. Now let's see. Oh yes, you have great bone structure. I think we can make you look amazing.'

Polly sat in the chair clutching her hands to prevent them from shaking. Whatever was she going to face now?

CHAPTER THIRTY-TWO
Hell

The buzz of excitement was palpable. An enormous crowd of imps, demons, devils and sprites were seated in a semicircle facing a huge round stage. The crowd was in good humour, having just been entertained by a warm-up demon that had been telling rude jokes.

An imp scampered to the centre of the stage, tapped the microphone and spoke. 'Imps, demons, devils and other unworldly creatures,' he began. The audience chortled. 'Tonight, you are in for a humongous treat.' The crowd cheered. 'So without further ado, let me introduce you to our hosts for tonight – that comic duo from *up there* – Grant and Dick!'

The crowd erupted as the two presenters walked on stage, bowing and raising their arms to the welcome. Grant, the taller of the two, with curvy black eyebrows, long lashes like a cow and a quiff of dark hair swept back, turned towards the camera and the audience. 'Good evening and welcome to—'

'*Mission Imp-ossible,* the brand new show that tests people to the limit,' continued Dick, the smaller, chubbier presenter. Both were attired in sparkly sequinned evening suits.

Grant waggled his eyebrows, earning laughter from the audience.

'Just like you,' continued Dick, a cheeky grin spreading across his boyish face.

'What do you mean?' asked Grant.

'Well, Grant, you test me every day.'

'How's that?'

'Well, yesterday, you asked me what the capital of Australia was.' The audience laughed as one.

'No, Dick. Not that sort of testing.' The presenter waggled his eyebrows again and looked suitably perplexed, while Dick scratched his head. 'I mean, we find out just how far someone will go to change their lives.'

'Oh. I wouldn't change mine,' said Dick.

'No, Dick. Why would you? You earn loads of money presenting shows and… you work with me.' Grant paused. There were a few guffaws from the audience.

'We have the ideal life – parties, fun and each other. Some people don't have such a good deal as us. Let's be sensible for a moment,' continued Dick.

Grant feigned a serious face, earning him more cackles from the audience.

'As you know,' he said, 'our two contestants were both nominated because life has been a bit difficult for them recently. At the moment, they're waiting in two separate rooms and they have absolutely no idea they've been duped.'

'No idea at all,' added Dick.

A split screen lit up behind the stage. It revealed Polly eating a cream cake and Simon chewing his fingernails.

'There they are, poor things. They're convinced they're in hell.'

'Aye, it must have been a *hell* of a week for them!'

'They must have been nervous as *hell*.'

'Pity there was no one to *hel*p them!'

The audience laughed loudly again as Dick shrugged his shoulders and Grant's eyebrows rose up and down as if attached to marionette strings.

'It's been really tricky to convince them and this is how it happened. I know most of you have been glued to the programme every night, however here are some of the highlights from last week, along with some behind-the-scenes footage. Sit back and enjoy as we watch our first contestant, Simon Green. He thought he was going to have an ordinary week at work, although that's not how it went,' said Grant.

'Didn't it?' asked Dick innocently.

'No, Dick. Things went from bad to worse. Roll the footage!'

The lights dimmed and the screen behind the stage flashed to a video of Simon at work. The audience watched Simon, a huge smile on his face, attempt to greet some customers. Intercepted by Kimberly, he's instructed to go to her office where he's told he's to be laid off. Unbeknown to Simon, a television crew stationed outside in the service area is watching and monitoring the conversation. The audience tittered as Simon staggered from the office and back to his desk, oblivious to the group of salesmen hiding behind a large cardboard cut-out of a Mercedes-Benz ML Class, nudging each other and stifling laughs. Kimberly is shown doubled over with laughter before giving a thumbs up to the hidden camera in her office.

This is followed by footage of Ryan and Patrick draining the fuel out of Simon's company car and conversing with a man on a motorbike. Next, a road chase as the man on the motorbike follows Simon, filming the journey with a camera attached to his helmet. Another camera secreted in the car captures the vehicle taking fast bends, the rain hitting the windscreen barely drowning the grumbling monologue from Simon. There are laughs as a frustrated Simon pounds on his steering wheel before heading to The Devil's Tavern. Grant and Dick's commentary accompanied the scenes.

The film cut to Nick and Len trying out their costumes. 'How am I supposed to walk in these goat shoes?' grumbles Len.

'You'll manage. Think like Pan and trot a bit,' suggests Nick.

'Pan as in Pan's People, the dancers?'

'No, numbnuts. Pan from mythology – half goat, half man. Just got trouble guessing which half is goat with you.'

'Ha ha. Is my tail working?'

Len presses a tiny control inside his pocket and his tail swishes authentically.

'It's a go-er.'

'Mania!'

'What?' shouts a woman.

'Come out and let's take a look at you.'

'No. I'm trying to get my horrific contact lenses in. You'll have to wait for the big reveal.'

A radio crackles. 'He's five minutes away. Places everyone.'

'Okay, this is it. Let's reel him in,' says Nick.

Tittering turned to howls of laughter at the antics in the pub especially when Len's tail falls off while Simon is in the toilet. The audience, in hysterics, hooted with laughter at the montage of scenes revealing how Simon struggled to be a manager. One row of demons in particular roared at his efforts to sack Kimberly.

Each piece of the set-up was revealed, and the audience tickled by Simon's angst and dismay as he struggled to prevent anarchy at Ernest-Deal. The video ended.

Grant and Dick took over again.

'Not satisfied with tormenting Simon at work, our team allowed him to think he could change places with his friend and old neighbour, Tony Hedge.'

'Not that he's old or anything,' interrupted Dick. Grant smiled like a weary mother might at an exuberant toddler.

'No, he's not old. He *used to* be Simon's neighbour. Tony told our researchers he missed living next door to Simon. They enjoyed good times together and he wished they saw a bit more of each other. The camera showed a handsome suntanned man, his arm draped around a stunning woman. He spoke into the camera:

'I've known Simon for years. I used to live next door to him. After I moved away, we seemed to drift apart. I had lots of new clients to deal with and he was always snowed under with work so we never found time to go golfing or out for a pint like we used to. Life got in the way and it shouldn't have. It's about time we made more of an effort. None of us are getting younger so I hope this little gag helps re-cement our relationship. It'll be nice to see more of Simon and Veronica. Selena deserves an Oscar for her part in this. Well done, sweetheart,' he said, pecking her on the cheek. Grant and Dick bounced to the front of the stage.

'He wasn't wrong, was he?' said Dick.

'No, you're right, Dick. Selena definitely deserves an award. She used to be an actress before she met Tony and her talent shines through in this incredible piece of acting. Check this out. Roll the footage.'

In the audience Selena, in full devil headdress, smiled at her performance. Tony squeezed her knee and chortled when she emerged on screen with her whip. She whispered in his ear, 'The film crew let me keep some of the kit. You want to try it out later?' Tony's eyebrows shot up and he nodded enthusiastically.

Gales of laughter rang out during the mock seduction scene. When the hidden camera showed a panicked Simon pretending he had the trots, the mob was in stitches. It took some time for them to calm down.

'Just when Simon thought things couldn't get any worse—' said Grant.

'They did!' said Dick.

'Indeed they did. We sent a professional helicopter pilot to collect him and take him to his office at "Simon Green and Associates",' he said, marking the quotation marks in the air with two fingers.

'Was it not really "Simon Green and Associates"?' asked Dick.

'Course it wasn't, although it was filmed at Tony's premises. We changed the signs over the building, replaced all of Tony's staff with actors, and even had fake lettering stencilled onto the side of the helicopter.'

'Aye, he wasn't too keen on that chopper though,' said Dick and held his stomach, a pained look on his face.

'Nah, bit too *choppy* for him,' replied Grant. 'Let's take it up with Simon now in the helicopter, where he was in for a rough ride.'

The screen burst to life revealing Simon in the passenger seat of the helicopter, eyes screwed tightly shut and grimacing as the pilot manoeuvred through a series of stomach-churning twists and turns. Next came a shot of Simon dismounting and walking unsteadily away from the helicopter, before leaning forward and throwing up in the bushes by the car park. A woman came running out to greet him and he trotted beside her into the building, where he was ushered into a lift.

When he emerged, he had the look of a deer caught in head-lights. His eyes flitted from person to person in the office. A stain of something yellow was stuck to the front of his shirt. His face was ashen. The audience listened to the supposed conversation with Lord Carson and roared with laughter as Simon squirmed in his seat at the accusations thrown at him. The clip ended. Grant and Dick took over.

'We lost Simon after that. It took several calls to track him down. We tried the dealership and fortunately, one of the sales team spotted him outside. He'd done a runner on a Vespa – a purple one at that! Anyway, our crack team was one step ahead of him and, having worked out he was travelling to his friend Eric's house, we got our people there just in the nick of time. Luckily, Eric was able to play along too.'

On the screen, Eric was being briefed by a man dressed in motorbike kit who then helped him to his feet and, together with a cameraman, walked him outside. No sooner had they got Eric in position and the cameraman hidden behind the fence, than Simon pulled up on a lurid purple Vespa. Eric played his part and, as Simon left, pulled a face at the camera.

'Well done, Eric. He bought it.'

'Poor bloke. He looks dreadful. I hope you give him the good news soon. I almost told him the truth.'

'Don't worry, Eric. It'll be worth it. Think of all the practical jokes he played on you. This is the daddy of them all.'

'Yes, he'll laugh when he sees this,' said Eric. 'He loves a good joke.'

The film finished and the presenters addressed the excited audience.

'Well, I think it's fair to say Simon has lived through his own personal hell. However, it's not over for him yet. Who wants to meet Simon Green?'

'We do!' yelled the audience.

'Patience, my fiendish friends. Before that, we must introduce you to the next contestant – Polly MacGregor. We'll see what she's been up to, thanks to the devilish antics of our mischievous team here at *Mission Imp-ossible*. First, let's welcome our wonderful tribe of dancers – Troupe De-Ville with their own special interpretative version of that Rolling Stones classic "Sympathy For The Devil"!'

A group of sprites leapt on stage and began dancing, miming the lyrics to the song. Dick nudged Grant. 'Going well. I don't know who'll win this. It's going to be a tough one.'

bag on the step. On cue the dogs hurtled at her, knocking her backwards and, as one of them dashed about the courtyard, a pair of lacy knickers in its mouth, being chased by an exasperated Polly, cackling could be heard throughout the theatre.

The scene changed to show Zed and Calvin hidden in the attic, watching the action that was taking place in the kitchen on a television monitor and eating crisps. The pair collapsed with fits of giggles as Sophie, now in character as Chelsea, attempted to drag on a cigarette and look cool. While Polly was attempting to push away dogs, Chelsea signalled that her cigarette wasn't alight and a member of the team had to sneak downstairs and give her a lit one. Polly had no idea she was being set up. Her reactions made the team and the audience chuckle. Oblivious to the chaos going on behind the scenes and focussing on discovering she was mother to a troubled girl, Polly missed the fact that the dogs had sneaked off set to see their real owner and had to be shooed back on again.

Calvin stole the next scene. His camp performance as a personal trainer went down very well. Little did Polly suspect he was taking selfies while sitting on a bench the whole time she was struggling with press-ups.

Of course, the most popular scene was the one in which Polly walked into the sitting room interrupting Chelsea and Zed having sex. The film showed how difficult it had been to get right. It depended on perfect timing. Zed played about with artificial legs, created to look like Chelsea's, while Polly stood outside the door, ear pressed to it. He had them hanging around his neck and was making Chelsea snigger. Upstairs, Calvin watched on the monitor waiting to give them the cue. Chelsea groaned and banged a chair about to encourage Polly to enter the room. What Polly saw wasn't in fact the reality. Chelsea was hidden behind the sofa moaning and calling out, while Zed was pretending to hump her. After Polly rushed out he turned to face the camera, waved the legs about and revealed a large codpiece, which he happily shimmied in for the camera before giving a toothy grin.

Gales of laughter filled the room when Polly made her phone call to Kaitlin who, in on the whole scam, pretended she'd no idea who Polly was. She had to pass the telephone to Miguel as she couldn't keep a straight face and collapsed into his arms after he hung up, unable to speak for giggles.

Polly's startled expression at discovering her ex-husband was to be murdered caused much merriment and a few cheers as she backed out of the secret room, anxiety etched on her face, only to trip over Dolce who was chewing a dog chew his owner had given him to tempt him into the secret room. In her confusion she thought it was a sock, wrestled it from him and threw it into the drawer. When she left, the dog trainer retrieved the chew and returned it to a confused Dolce who immediately scurried off with it under the bed in case it was taken away once more. It then took a lot of coaxing to drag him out. His owner eventually pulled on his collar and hauled him out, his sad face earning more chuckles from the onlookers. The footage of Polly's disastrous week came to an end and the presenters stepped forward again.

'Okay, that's it folks... or should I say... demons. It's time to meet the contestants! Now remember they believe they are actually at the entrance to hell and you're all demons.'

'You certainly all look frighteningly demonic,' added Dick and shivered. 'It's time for you to play your part. Grant and I have got to hide for the moment because the contestants might recognise us.'

'They might not,' said Grant.

'Nah, of course they will.'

'Yes, of course they will,' agreed Grant, his eyebrows dancing up and down. 'So let's bring in our fabulous head demon, Mania, and let's play part two of *Mission Imp-ossible – The Drop*!'

Mania glided into view in impossibly high stilettos; a red sequinned evening dress split up one side emphasised her shapely figure. She strode onto the set brandishing a whip to resounding applause. Some of the male members whistled.

'Thank you. Thank you,' she purred. 'Behave yourselves, boys, or I might have to come down there and use this on you,' she said and gave her whip a crack. The audience lapped it all up, winking and grinning at each other.

'As far as the contestants know, I'm an important female demon. So, for now, that's what I am,' she continued and flicked her long tail in the direction of the front row. 'Bring on the contestants,' she called.

Simon was escorted onto the stage by two fiends playfully prodding him with pitchforks. Polly appeared from another direction, chaperoned by two female sprites in red leotards that swished tails and danced on stage in maniacal fashion to 'Bat Out of Hell'. Blinking and ogling at the bright lights and spectators, both contestants were ushered to seats on opposite sides of the stage. They sat down and observed the demons now prancing about together twirling pitchforks and tails and spinning like whirling dervishes. The music continued to play, the creatures danced and the onlookers wolf-whistled and cheered. Finally, the music stopped. The demons bowed and left the stage to raucous applause. Mania moved forward, held up a hand and silence fell. She sauntered over to Simon who shrank back in his chair from her scarlet-eyed stare.

'So, Simon,' she purred into the microphone. 'Welcome to the upper chambers of hell. We need you to clarify a few things for our audience before they decide whether to drop you *down there*.'

There was a rumbling from below and the stage floor turned red. 'Are you happy to talk?'

'Yes, in fact, I have something I need to—'

'There's plenty of time for you to have your say,' interrupted Mania. 'For now, we need to stick to the questions. Please explain to us why you wanted to change your life.'

'Technically, I only changed part of it to start with. I wanted to have a better job, promotion and kudos. It's been tough trying to make ends meet. The kids are growing up and need all sorts of help financially – trips, clothes, you know the sort of thing – and recently I've struggled to stay on top of repayments on my credit cards and paying household bills. I might have managed if I hadn't lost faith in my selling ability. I had a lousy few months and the bills kept mounting up. On top of the usual repayments, I had to pay to sort out a kitchen and quite frankly it all got a bit much. There were a few arguments at home too and I felt – pointless. I no longer mattered. All I did was go to work, come home, sleep, go to work. There was no more fun.'

Mania shifted the microphone into her other hand.

'Okay, so life was boring.'

'No, it was more than that. I've given it a lot of thought over the last few days. It wasn't just that things were difficult or dull. That's life, isn't it? It was more. When I looked into the mirror every morning, I no longer saw a man with hope. I saw my old man – beaten and worn out by life. There was no bright future, and worse still, I hadn't really done a lot with the time I'd already had. Yes, I had a lovely family, two bright children and a wife who cared about me. I don't regret a moment of my family life. I love my kids to bits and Veronica is my soulmate. I couldn't have had a better family. It's just that I've never done anything amazing or exciting. I've never had the money or time to travel somewhere exotic or take up an exciting pursuit. I've been on this planet almost fifty years and I've seen nothing of it.'

Mania waited as Simon licked his lips before continuing, 'You see, I'm ageing and I know I can't halt nature but there's a sense of frustration too. Ask any man who has to get up every night to have a pee, or who sees his hair receding, or whose six-pack has turned into a giant keg, or who actually looks at nasal hair trimmers and thinks *I'd really like one of those.* Talk to any man who no longer attracts women and who can't walk into a wine bar without worrying that the young folk there will think you're some sort of pervert.' The audience tittered. Simon ignored them.

'You become invisible when you get older. You lose your sense of purpose and that's what happened to me. It's bad enough when you feel like a granddad at work, but when your daughter no longer laughs at your jokes, or your wife is too occupied with her own friends, hobbies and life to have time for you, and your son would rather cross the street than bother with his old man, you start to wonder if there's any hope. I began to feel lost, insignificant and old.'

There was no sound from the audience. Simon continued, 'It was all so silly really. I don't know what got into me that particular day. I was having a really bad time. I learned I was going to lose my job. I was feeling the lowest I'd felt for a long time and when the chance to change all that came up. I… I grabbed it. In hindsight, I should have thought it through. I should have spoken to my wife… to someone before… before all this.' He looked into the darkness in front of him. He could make out demons watching his every move and listening intently to his every word. Mania moved the microphone away from him.

'So, Simon, who did you nominate in exchange for this reward of changing your life?'

Simon gulped. 'Look, I'm not proud of myself. I couldn't nominate a member of my family. Not someone who means the world to me – a real person, for heaven's sake.'

'Shh! Not here,' hissed Mania. 'Don't mention *that* word.' Someone in the audience snorted. Mania glowered, her red eyes boring into the auditorium.

'Sorry. I couldn't nominate someone I loved, even if they had stopped loving me.'

'Demons, imps and sprites, would you like to meet Simon's nomination?'

'Yes,' roared the audience.

A sprite entered from behind a curtain carrying a cage that he sat on the floor. Inside, a miserable Ivan looked out at his master and meowed. The audience gasped.

'Simon nominated this poor, helpless creature.'

'Look, I was stressed. I didn't know who to choose.'

'You didn't think about nominating your mother-in-law? I heard there was no love lost between you.'

'Hard as it is to believe, I didn't. She loves the kids and the kids love her and Veronica is very close to her. Ivan seemed the only choice. I thought it was a way out without hurting anyone. I regretted it almost immediately and I changed my mind. That's what I wanted to say earlier. I can't send a poor cat to spend eternity in hell. He's a family pet. More importantly, he's my daughter's cat. She'll be devastated if he disappears. At her age she needs love and a friend, even if it's a furry four-legged one. I'm volunteering to go to hell myself. Send me. It's what I deserve.'

The audience inhaled as one, then a few cheers erupted. Mania strode about the stage cracking her whip and looking ferocious.

'You're willing to face an eternity in hell?' she asked at last once the excited audience had quietened.

'Yes. I can't go back to my old life. I've proved I'm a failure. I have no job, I can't provide for my family and even if I returned to them, I'll soon lose any remaining respect they might have for me. Best I go and they can claim on my life-insurance policy. If anything happens to me, they'll get a tremendous payout. I've seen to that. Do what you will to me. I'll meet any horrible end.'

Mania nodded in approval. 'We shall have to put it to a vote in a minute, but now we need to talk to our other contestant – Polly MacGregor.' The audience applauded.

Polly had been listening to the poor man opposite her and was only now aware of the faces looking at her. She could make out horns and demonic grins. A shiver ran through her in spite of the warm lights shining down on her.

'Polly, you too agreed to a life swap?'

'I did. My life was also plagued with money woes and someone decided to wreck my career. I have a succession of failed relationships and my business was all I had to keep me afloat. Like Simon, I was also at an all-time low when I saw an advert suggesting my life could be changed. To be fair, I was given the life I requested, but it didn't work out and now I have to pay the consequences.'

'You don't seem too worried about the consequences, Polly.'

'I'm not as worried as I was. I've discovered that the person who was intent on wrecking my life also hired a hit man to kill her husband. That man was my ex-husband. I don't have any compunction in sending her to spend an eternity in hell.'

'And this person is?'

'Gabi Dawson. The woman who ran off with my husband when he was married to me, spread vicious rumours about me, brought my business to its knees and is suing me for money I don't have.'

'This is all fascinating stuff, Polly. Isn't it everyone? Shall we bring in Gabi and hear her side of the story?'

The audience cheered. 'Gabi! Gabi! Gabi!' they chanted.

Gabi, wearing a surgical neck collar, was led in sandwiched between two demons. A third danced behind, carrying a chair that was settled next to Polly's. Gabi avoided Polly's glare and sat head lowered, lip trembling. Mania marched up to Gabi, microphone in her hand.

'You've heard what Polly has to say, Gabi. We'd like to give you a chance to defend yourself.'

The pale woman wiped away a strand of hair and coughed. She looked directly at Polly.

'Polly, I'm so sorry. It wasn't meant to happen like that. It was Callum. He made up the stories about you breaking my back. It wasn't me. You know what he can be like when he's had a few drinks.'

Polly sat up straight. Gabi dissolved into tears. Mania stuck the microphone under Gabi's nose.

'Speak up, Gabi. We all want to hear what you have to say.'

'This isn't easy for me. I never wanted to hurt Polly. In fact, I admire her for standing up to Callum and starting a whole new career.'

There were boos from the crowd. Someone yelled, 'Liar!' Gabi sobbed some more.

'Polly, it was a silly fib that got out of hand. I hurt myself, which is why I came to see you. I hoped you'd be able to help me before Callum found out I was injured. I went home after the massage. Callum had been drinking and felt frisky. I wasn't in the mood, but he wouldn't take no for an answer. He pushed me onto the table and I screamed out because it really hurt. That didn't stop him, though. He pulled down my trousers and forced himself onto me. I started crying because he was hurting me, and that made him madder. He told me to shut up. Afterwards, he noticed the bruising on my lower back and around my hips. He went mental. He thought I'd been 'putting it about'. He said that this explained why I didn't want to have sex with him. He started throwing things about the room. I was terrified. I couldn't tell him the truth. He was insane with jealousy.' Gabi shook her head at the memory.

'He shook me and kept on and on asking if I was sleeping with someone else. He smacked me hard and my head hit the wall. I hurt my neck. I wanted him to stop, so I told him the first thing that came into my head – that I must have got the bruises when you gave me a massage. Of course, as soon as I said it I knew I'd said the wrong thing. He went ballistic. He punched me and told me I was a stupid cow to go near you. He's never got over you being so successful. Called you all sorts of names and stormed off.' Gabi paused. Her make-up had run down her face, streaking it grey-black. She made no attempt to wipe it off.

'I was frightened he was going to hurt you and phoned you to warn you. You must have been out because you didn't pick up. Turned out he went to the pub and when he returned he seemed calmer. Said he'd sorted it out and you'd be paying for leaving him and for injuring me. He told me to go to the doctor and get fixed up. I have whiplash. The doctor gave me this collar, but I couldn't tell anyone how I got the injury, could I? I've been indoors since then, hiding. I'm so, so sorry, Polly. I had no idea what Callum had done until a few days ago. When Mission Imp-ossible contacted me and told me they had evidence that I was suing you for thousands of pounds, I couldn't believe it. I found out it was Callum. He was trying to con you out of your money. The official letter you received was from a bogus solicitor – one of Callum's friends. Callum wanted you to be so frightened about losing your business you'd agree to pay up rather than face charges. I would never do such a thing. I confess I fell in love with your husband and stole him from you, but I've paid for that sin. He's transformed into a mean-spirited, aggressive individual. He's not even a shadow of the man I loved. This whole episode has been a turning point for me. I've finally found the courage to leave him.'

Gabi looked ahead at the audience. 'If you think I deserve to go to hell for that, then punish me. For the last few years I've been living in purgatory. Hell doesn't frighten me.'

The audience applauded and cheered. 'Gabi! Gabi!' they chorused.

'That's right, people. Gabi didn't slander Polly,' shouted Mania. 'Nor did she start court procedures to ruin Polly.'

'How did you get the bruises? How did you hurt yourself?' asked Polly. The audience fell silent. Gabi fidgeted in her seat.

'I tumbled off a pole at pole-dancing classes.'

The audience erupted in laughter. Gabi looked affronted. 'It's not funny. I was taking classes to lose weight. It's much harder to do than it looks. If I'd told Callum I'd injured myself while pole dancing he'd have throttled me. He'd have assumed I was working at a lap-dancing club. I didn't dare tell him. I wish I had though.'

Polly gazed thoughtfully at Gabi, who was no longer crying.

'What about you hiring the assassin to kill him?' she said quietly.

'I-I didn't hire any assassin,' stammered Gabi. 'I wouldn't know how to hire one.'

Mania interrupted the conversation. She marched centre stage and spoke to the audience.

'So, you demonic lot, you've seen what the contestants got up to and you've seen who they want to nominate. It's up to you, the audience, to decide who should be dropped *down there*. Someone must be chosen.'

A buzz of excitement went around the audience.

'Will it be contestant number one, Simon Green, employee at Ernest-Deal, father of two, fed up with lack of promotion; or will it be Ivan, his chosen soul? Ivan, the cat who detests Simon and is out to kill him?' Loud sniggers echoed around the room.

'Will you vote for Polly McGregor, who wants no more than to get on with her life and be a success but who has chosen an innocent woman as her soul?'

Polly opened her mouth to protest then shut it again as Mania continued: 'The choice, my fiendish friends, is up to you.'

There was collective scrabbling as demons extracted control pads from their armrests.

'Use your controls in the arms of your chairs and vote A for Simon, B for Ivan, C for Polly or D for Gabi.'

The screen behind the stage lit up again. This time, a bar graph with each contestant's name in large red lettering appeared. Polly had been watching the sobbing Gabi. She put a hand on the woman's knee.

'I believe you, Gabi,' she said. She stood up. 'Mania, tell them to drop me, not Gabi!' she yelled over a shrieking siren that signalled a drop into hell was imminent.

'Let the voting begin,' shouted Mania, ignoring Polly's pleas.

There was a flurry of activity. Demons stabbed at keys on the control panels and watched the screen eagerly. As the votes were counted, the bars began to climb. Ivan's green bar didn't move. Gabi's yellow bar increased slightly then stopped. It was between Polly's blue bar and Simon's red bar. Both bars climbed to the beat of several drums whose frantic rhythm rose to a crescendo as the final votes came in. The stage rumbled. The floor became transparent and revealed a pit below. The pit glowed orange, coral and then deep crimson. The drums beat louder and faster. The crowd cheered as the screen revealed the result. Ivan meowed. His cry was drowned out as a klaxon sounded. The floor above the pit slid back and several demons carrying pitchforks appeared from offstage. Gabi screamed 'No!' as demons flanked the chair next to hers and hands grabbed Polly. She was lifted from her chair. Simon rose and raced to Polly's side to protect her as she was dragged to her feet and propelled towards the pit, but he was caught by demons and restrained. Polly was hauled to the edge of the pit. Weeping and wailing came from below. The demons on stage chanted in a strange language and the spectators clapped in time to the drums that had slowed to a heartbeat.

'Take me instead,' yelled Simon. 'I don't deserve to stay here. I've hurt too many people.'

'It's okay,' said Polly. 'I'm not afraid. My life was pretty much hell anyway. I'm not frightened. Take care, Simon. I hope you have a happier life.'

'Polly McGregor, you've been chosen for the big drop *down there*. Any last words?'

'Gabi, stay strong and keep away from Callum. He's bad news. I wish we could have been friends. I think we could have been good together. Move into my house and try to make a go of things without him. Please wish Dignity well with the business. She's welcome to my client list and… tell Kaitlin I love her. I don't know why I thought I'd be better off without her as my friend. She's the best and worth so much more than any amount of money or possessions.'

Polly stood tall and proud as the drumbeat accelerated once more. A whirring noise filled the auditorium and, with a loud clunk, a trapdoor opened below Polly's feet, dropping her into the flames.

The crowd cheered wildly. Simon looked on in horror. Mania bowed to the audience and from the shadows of the stage emerged the two presenters, Grant and Dick.

CHAPTER THIRTY-FOUR
Simon

'So, Simon, how does it feel to avoid the big drop?' asked Grant, shoving a microphone under Simon's chin. Simon sat, dazed. 'Don't I know you?' he asked.

'Mebbe. That depends on how much telly you watch.'

A silence fell over the audience.

'Aren't you both on that talent-show programme?'

Grant smiled as if Simon had suddenly discovered a new planet in the solar system.

'Correct. That's us.'

'What are you doing down here? Did you sell your souls?'

The audience exploded with laughter.

Dick put his hand on Simon's shoulder. 'Sorry, Simon, we're not in hell, or even at hell's entrance. None of us are. You've been part of an elaborate and complicated piece of mischief and you're on television.'

Sweat ran down Simon's face, making his make-up run. He shook his head to clear it.

'I don't understand,' he said.

'Let's help you out. Look into the audience and check the front row. Is there anyone you recognise?'

Simon peered into the gloom. Several demons were waving at him. Two held a banner that read 'Vote Simon'. Simon squinted. It was Ken and Jackie. They were wearing red tunics and black caps with horns. Simon panned along the row and spotted Kimberly dressed in a sexy ruby-coloured basque top. He squinted again into the gloom and made out his wife, Morag and both of his children all waving and smiling. Even in their demonic attire he recognised them. Veronica blew him a kiss.

Grant walked to the other side of Simon. 'It was a set-up. You've got your work colleagues and family to thank, or blame, for it. They sent in your application to be part of this new show. Patrick, where's Patrick?' An arm flew up in the audience. 'Can we get a microphone over to Patrick please?' asked Grant. The runner appeared and passed a handheld microphone to Patrick who was disguised with a goatee beard and huge black eyebrows.

'Tell us a bit about Simon,' asked Dick.

'I've known Simon now for over ten years. He is an absolute brick. He often covers for me if I have to nip off early – oops, sorry boss,' he added, covering his mouth with his hand. Kimberly wagged a finger at him. He continued, 'And he's even handed over his own sales to me to help me reach targets. He really deserves a break. He's had a run of bad luck over the last few months. He set fire to his mother-in-law's kitchen and he could do with a helping hand. No one wants to have problems with their mother-in-law, do they?'

Chuckles filled the studio.

Patrick passed the microphone to Ryan. 'He's a top bloke. He took me under his wing when I started at Ernest-Deal. I had no idea how to sell cars and, to be honest, if it wasn't for him I'd have been chucked out years ago and gone back to plumbing. He put up with all my daft questions, taught me how to talk and listen to customers. He sorted me out loads of times when I got stuff wrong so I didn't get into trouble with the bosses. He's my role model. No one is a better salesman than him. He's terrific.

All his customers like him. The boys in the workshop like him and they don't like many of us salesmen. He's usually the joker at work – always telling jokes or kidding people. One day, he phoned up Patrick and claimed to be a policeman who had evidence of Patrick speeding in one of the cars. Patrick was cacking himself and was almost on his way down to the station to look at footage of the offence when he saw Simon peeping around the screens on his mobile phone, wearing a toy police helmet. He's been off his game a bit recently so maybe this'll cheer him up. I think he'll find this all a huge laugh. In time,' he added, earning more laughs from the audience.

Next up was Kimberly. 'Simon is loyal, trustworthy and hard-working. He's usually the first in through the door each day and the last to leave. He gives up valuable free time to come in and clear paperwork or deal with customers who have queries. Cars are his life, his passion, and he's one of those valued members of staff who rarely gets flustered or has an off day. I hope he forgives us for setting him up. We wanted to do something special to mark his forthcoming birthday and the fact he's been with Ernest-Deal for twenty-five years this year. I'd like to blame the sales team for setting him up, however, I really enjoyed my part in the duplicity and so I have to take my share of the blame. Sorry, Simon.'

Grant nudged Simon in the ribs. 'See. You are loved. You're a lucky man. Jackie, pet, could you please read out the letter you sent us?'

Jackie stood up and pulled out a sheet of paper from a pocket in her tunic.

'Dear Grant and Dick,' she read.

'The advert for the show asks "*can you keep a secret?*" We are all able to keep a secret and we'd like to nominate our friend and work colleague, Simon Green, to take part in the new show *Mission Imp-ossible.* He is admired and highly regarded among all of his colleagues and has a tremendous sense of humour. Simon has worked for Ernest-Deal for twenty-five years this year and we would like to mark it in some special way for him; something he'll remember and appreciate more than just a watch or glass ornament. He is always there for a colleague in need and lately has been through bad luck himself. Please consider him for your new show. One thing's for certain – he'll be a most entertaining participant.'

Jackie folded the paper, blew Simon a kiss and sat down.

'A set-up?' Simon repeated, having digested the information at last.

'Yes, the biggest practical joke ever,' replied Grant. 'Before you get mad at them all, there's a plus side.'

'What's that?'

'You've won your wish list!'

'I don't have a wish list.'

'Oh yes, you do! Your lovely wife gave us your list. Veronica, where are you?'

Veronica, looking rather fetching in a tight black top and leggings, smiled shyly and waved at the camera.

'We asked Veronica and all your family to choose what they thought you would like most in the world and this is what they came up with.'

The screen lit up again. The audience oohed and ahhed as Grant and Dick described the prizes being shown.

'You have won… a family holiday to Madagascar!' The crowd whistled. 'And membership to a local golf club along with a new set of golf clubs and golf lessons.' He paused, while applause rang out again.

'You have also won a romantic weekend for two at a top spa hotel. Ooh! Now then, I wonder if you'll get to use the spa… or maybe you'll be too busy being romantic!' He waited for the whistles to die down. 'You've also got a superb Bang & Olufsen BeoLab 14 sound system suitable for any home-cinema system and finally... I bet you know where it will be going... a top of the range bespoke kitchen!'

The audience whistled, stamped feet and applauded.

Grant slapped Simon on the back. 'Anything to say?'

Simon's mouth flapped open several times. 'This was a wind-up? Everything?'

'Everything from the pretend sacking to Selena trying to whip you! You'll get a chance to ask them all about it at the after-show party. Some of your friends have some explaining to do.'

'I still have a job? A family?'

''Fraid so. I bet you'll be wanting to pay some of them back.'

Simon looked at his friends, colleagues and his family. 'Nah, wouldn't swap them!' he said. The crowd roared.

'Hang on. What about Polly?' asked Simon.

'Ah, Polly. Shall we all see what happened when she dropped into the pit?'

The screen came alive once more.

The trapdoor opened and Polly tumbled into the wailing pit. She shut her eyes tightly, images of flashing lights imprinted on her retinas as she hurtled towards the ground. She landed bottom first onto a bouncy surface where she was gently tossed up and down until she came to a comfortable rest, flat on her back. The horrific wailing ceased, replaced by applause. Her eyes flew open. She was lying on what looked like a bouncy castle without sides. People were standing around it forming a human barrier ready to catch her should she tumble forward. Whoops of delight made her turn in the direction of the sound and she gasped. Kaitlin, Miguel and Dignity were smiling widely at her.

'What are you doing here? I didn't nominate any of you!'

The inflatable mattress deflated gently, allowing Polly to sit up. Three people came to assist her off it. Kaitlin broke from the group and scrambled over the sinking surface to help too. Polly could now make out other people, wearing jeans and T-shirts inscribed with *Mission Imp-ossible*. Hauling Polly to her feet, Kaitlin embraced her friend. A cameraman filmed them.

'No, you didn't nominate us, but we nominated you. And now we have such a lot of explaining to do,' she said. 'I'm sorry. You're not in hell, nor have you ever exchanged places with Stephanie. She's upstairs in the audience along with some of our clients. The whole thing was a tremendous prank. Before you go ballistic, there was one very good reason we put you through it. Come into the room and we'll explain everything.'

Dignity and Miguel helped the women down from the inflatable. Lilith was waiting by the door. She had removed her horns and flashed a grin at Polly.

'Congratulations,' she said. 'You were brilliant. I really enjoyed working with you. I'll be back in a few minutes when your friends have revealed what happened and how we hoodwinked you. You need to catch your breath and come on stage for the presentation.'

Kaitlin turned towards Polly. 'We knew you'd win. We've been watching every episode. You were so funny when you went running with the trainer. I think that scored you extra votes. As for taking the dogs out in that pink car! That was hilarious!'

'You've been watching me?'

'Oh yes: *Mission Imp-ossible* has been on every night this week. The whole nation has been glued to it. People have been phoning in and voting for their favourite contestant to win the big prize. The newspapers got hold of the story yesterday and there was piece about both of you: *Mission Imp-ossible – Can You Keep a Secret?* It's amazing how they managed to keep it from you and Simon. You must be the only two people in the country who didn't know about the show. Well, you and the other contestants who are currently being filmed. None of you have been allowed access to televisions. There are more shows over the next three weeks. They choose a winner at the end of every week. This final is going out later tonight. I think they have to edit it first. It's a two-hour special. Bet you'll be on all the big television shows tomorrow now the winner has been decided. You'll be famous.'

Miguel handed Polly a glass of wine. She drained it in one. Kaitlin was buzzing with excitement and continued gabbling at full speed.

'So you've been a contestant on a show all week. Isn't it amazing? It was Dignity's idea.'

Dignity's cheeks flushed pink. 'I hope you're not angry. I saw an advert for the show online. They were looking for fun, outgoing and entertaining people to be nominated. I thought of you immediately. I thought it would be a way to cheer you up. I phoned Kaitlin to see what she thought and we decided you were ideal for the show. You're smart, funny and deserved some good luck. Of course, at the time, we didn't know about Gabi or how unhappy you were. Once we heard about Gabi, we asked the production team to track her down and discover why she was suing you. Of course, she wasn't guilty of that. She became part of the whole set-up too. Poor woman thinks you're in hell now. Someone should be explaining it all to her. We wanted you to have some fun.'

Kaitlin's head bobbed up and down in agreement. Dignity continued, 'We spent ages with researchers working out how best to fool you. They were going to convince you at work, and then that turned out to be too difficult, so they set you up on the train you caught when you came back from Gran Canaria. Kaitlin gave them your travel details and they had various people positioned all along the route. You missed the advert in the taxi from Kaitlin's to the airport – the driver told them you hadn't picked up any of the cards he'd set up in the pocket behind his seat – and you didn't see the large poster in the toilet at the airport so they made it more obvious and left the advert for *Mission Imp-ossible* in full view so you would see it. The woman with the newspaper on the train played Lilith too. Her real name is Sandra and she's an actress.'

'I thought I'd seen her somewhere before when she met me at the Mission Imp-ossible offices,' said Polly. Miguel passed her another glass of wine.

'Anyway, we don't have time to tell you everything now. You have to collect your prize. You won hands down,' interrupted Kaitlin.

Polly shrugged. 'What have I won? What's worth me making an idiot of myself on national television?'

Dignity and Kaitlin exchanged a look. Kaitlin nodded.

'The person who gets dropped wins £250,000,' said Dignity.

Silence fell in the small room. Dignity licked her lips nervously. Kaitlin's eyebrows furrowed as Polly digested the information and gave them a penetrating stare.

'I've been tricked, been made to look a complete idiot, worried myself senseless for no good reason about daughters, dogs and assassins all for £250,000?'

Kaitlin's brow knotted itself further. Dignity took to biting a hangnail. Miguel threw an anxious look at his girlfriend and was about to interject when Polly continued, 'My *friends* set me up for £250,000?'

Kaitlin bowed her head. Dignity shuffled from side to side.

Polly spoke quietly, 'I have only one thing to say to you all.'

Kaitlin raised her jaw, tears gathering in her eyes.

'Woohoo! Thank you!' squealed Polly and, leaping from her chair, grabbed each of them in turn and embraced them.

'Oh, you wretch!' said Kaitlin when she caught her breath again. 'You had me going. We were already concerned you'd be angry with us.'

'Angry because I can now pay off debts, buy premises for me and Dignity to set up a proper pain clinic together and, thanks to this show, probably get more clients? You're amazing – all three of you. I'm the luckiest person in the world!'

A knocking alerted them to the arrival of Lilith, now in a black satin dress and long diamond-drop earrings.

'Sorted?'

'Oh yes,' replied Polly. 'Well and truly.'

CHAPTER THIRTY-FIVE
Mission Imp-ossible Headquarters

Nick and Len sat in front of the big boss. The tension was palpable. Nick's left leg bounced up and down as silence hung and the boss studied the sheet of paper in front of him. At last, he looked up at the pair. His grey eyebrows were furrowed; his craggy, lined face set in a grim expression. He grunted then spoke in a voice that betrayed he was a sixty-cigarettes-a-day man. 'Over 30 million people tuned in to watch the Den and Angie divorce episode of *EastEnders* on 25 December 1986. On 22 November 1980 just over 21 million watched *Dallas* to discover who shot JR. *The X Factor* results show in 2010 attracted viewing figures of 17.7 million.' He pressed his fingertips to his lips and looked around at those assembled before him.

'We took a chance with this suggestion. It was a wacky idea and we took a massive gamble commissioning it. It depended on so many factors: a committed team, tremendous acting, secrecy and top presenters.' He nodded over at Grant and Dick, who sat next to Louise Handson, the actress who had taken on the role of Mania.

'In the past, both of you have managed to get excellent viewing figures of 16 million per show,' he continued, staring directly at Grant and Dick. They gave charming synchronised smiles. 'As you know, we weren't aiming for 20 or 30 million. That was never going to be viable but ten would have been excellent. However,' he continued. Everyone stopped breathing as they waited to hear the verdict. 'Nothing prepared me for these latest viewing figures. It appears 14 million people tuned in to watch the results show. We smashed the record held by *Can't Bake Anyway!*'

Nick breathed out. Len raised his arms in victory. The boss, Tom Dickinson, head of the television channel, shook hands with each member of the team.

'I have to admit, although I was very concerned about how the show would be received, I can't deny the success – everyone is talking about it; clips of the show have gone viral on YouTube and *#MissionImp-ossible* is trending on Twitter again. The media adores the show, which is just as well since we have all these other contestants throughout the country being duped as we speak. A second series has been commissioned. Obviously we'll change the format – now everyone in the country knows about the demon thing we have to go with the other options we discussed to trick people into changing lives. We've already been inundated with people nominating friends and relations for future series so, if the show maintains this level of popularity, there will be many more series. And, finally, this morning I received interest from television companies in the United States and Japan who are interested in copying the format. Congratulations, guys, you picked a winner!'

CHAPTER THIRTY-SIX
Simon

SIX MONTHS LATER

Simon Green was driving a Maserati around the racetrack at Le Mans. He was savouring the throaty burble of the exhaust as he flew past the chequered flag. The engine noise rose in him, making his very core vibrate to the sound. He woke, aware that he could still hear the noise, and turned to face a content Ivan purring deeply as he slept on Veronica's head. Simon smiled and stroked the animal, who opened one eye. A mumble from beneath the cat caused him to grin further and he lay back, waiting for Veronica to thrash about and knock Ivan off.

'Blasted cat!' she spluttered after she heaved him off. An unconcerned Ivan lifted his head towards Simon. His fur had flattened around his mouth, giving the impression he was smirking.

'He's only protecting you. That's what Georgie told us. He does it all the time. He loves you. It's his way of proving it.'

'He can stay in Georgie's room tonight,' said Veronica, extracting a long ginger hair from her mouth.

'I wonder if she enjoyed the party,' said Simon.

'You can bet she did. She spent all yesterday afternoon in a right state because she was going to it with Travis. All I heard all afternoon was, "He's so lush, Mum."'

'She's growing up, Vee. Can't believe the transformation. No more little girl. She'll soon be like Haydon – all grown up and heading off to university, or out into the big bad world.'

'We've got a few years yet. Although she's thirteen going on twenty-three at the moment.'

'At least she's not such a mardy mare these days.

'You've Travis to thank for that. She's in the throes of first love. We'll have to deal with more moods when they split up.'

'She'll survive. We're all survivors in this family. Fancy a cup of tea?'

'No.'

Simon looked across. Her tone of voice had changed. 'I don't fancy a cup of tea. I fancy you!' she said and reached over towards him.

'Whoa! I've got to get to the office and I'm in charge of all those salespeople now. We've got a meeting on how to improve sales targets and I'm doing a training session with the new intake of salesmen at Solihull later today.'

Veronica kissed his neck, making the hairs on it stand up, and blew gently into his ear. Her right hand caressed his stomach muscles and travelled lower. She moved his face towards hers with her other hand and kissed him long and deeply. After a few moments, Simon pulled away.

'Okay. Just one thing. No voyeurs,' he said. He scooped up Ivan, leapt out of the bed and carried him to the door.

'Sorry, old chap. What happens in the bedroom stays in the bedroom. Go find next door's Persian to play with.'

He placed the cat on the floor and pushed the door to. He was sure Ivan winked at him.

Polly

Dignity drew up outside the quaint stone cottage. A cascade of late-blooming roses tumbled from an archway above the front door, which opened as soon as she emerged from her car. A small animal with a bright green sock in its mouth raced outside, leaping up at her. She bent down to stroke it.

'Hello, Alfred. How are you?'

The dog rested its paws on her knees and considered her with doleful eyes.

'Do you want to play tug-of-war?'

The dog dropped down and checked to see if she was going to attempt to take the sock. She obliged, leaning forward to steal it from him. He lowered his head, backed away, then hurtled towards the house where he turned to check that Dignity was in pursuit. Seeing she was, he changed direction and raced around the garden, Dignity chasing him.

Matt observed the scene leaning against the door. He wore a light fawn jacket over a cream pullover. A smile pulled at the corner of his mouth as Alfred raced past him.

'Alfred, if that's one of Polly's Shrek socks, you're in trouble. She's been looking for it. Hi, Dignity,' said Matt. The dog raced outside again, almost tripping her up. 'Come on, Alfred. I know you adore Dignity, but let her come inside.'

Dignity entered the house, Alfred by her side. Matt leaned over and brushed her cheek with a kiss. 'What a beautiful morning. Seems we're getting our Indian summer the weathermen predicted after all. Sorry, I've got to rush. I still haven't shaved. I have to take a group of businessmen on one of those bonding courses. Goodness knows how learning to shoot is going to help them get along with each other. Still, it pays the bills. Ah, here she is. At last!' He whistled. 'It was worth the wait,' he added and stopped to smack Polly on the bottom before disappearing upstairs, leaving Polly looking flushed.

'Still madly in love then?' asked Dignity with a smile.

Polly grinned. 'It's difficult not to love him. He's... delicious,' she said, after some thought. 'And dependable and a lot of fun. We're taking it steadily. It's early days and, if it all goes wrong, I have this little fellow to keep me sane.'

She picked up Alfred and gave him a kiss. The animal looked suitably unimpressed and licked his mistress's nose.

'Is that my sock, you little horror?' she asked, spotting the discarded item on the floor. 'Alfred, you are a monster. And I love you.' She hugged the dog and placed him down on the floor.

'I love that blouse, Polly. It's so pretty.'

'Thank you. Have to make an impression today. I was worried it was a bit too casual.'

'Not at all. It's bright, cheerful and suits you perfectly.'

Polly looked pleased. 'One thing I've learned, Dignity, is that clothes do not make the woman. The woman makes the clothes.'

'You certainly rock that outfit.'

'Thanks. It's from H&M and under thirty quid! Goes to show you don't need to shell out on very pricey clothes to look glam. Mind you, I think it's mostly about feeling good about yourself rather than what you wear. So are you ready for the big opening?'

'As I'll ever be. It's all arranged – champagne, VIP guests and the press. Should be an afternoon to remember. I can't believe we've come so far – celebrity clients and more therapists on board.'

'Hard work, lots of luck and good friends like you. Did Gabi manage to get hold of that photographer?'

'Oh yes, she's so excited about it. I think we'll all get on fine. She's very organised. We really couldn't have a better receptionist.'

'Yes, she came good, didn't she?'

'Lilith – I mean Sandra – phoned before I left home. Some of the team from *Mission Imp-ossible* are coming. Nick and Len are working though and can't make it. Mania, Lilith and that nice guy, Edward, who plays Zepar are coming in costume for the press.'

Polly raised an eyebrow. 'Edward?'

Dignity gave a small smile. 'Very early days,' she said. 'But looking promising.'

'You dark horse. No wonder you're all dressed up!'

Dignity changed the subject. 'Sophie's coming too. She's got this week off before she starts filming in Australia.'

'That girl! How she made me believe she was my new daughter, I'll never know. What an actress! She'll go far. I had lunch with Stephanie last week. She thinks it's hilarious that I thought she was an assassin. She said she's told all her friends, including David Gandy! Right then – time to collect Kaitlin from the airport. I have to drop off this letter to Mum en route. She was so excited about the new clinic she wanted to jump on the next flight over, but I managed to persuade her to wait until the dust has settled and come for Christmas, with Austin, of course. Come on, Alfred. Can't leave you here. You'll pine away. Matt! We're off. See you tonight.'

Matt appeared at the top of the stairs. 'Good luck. Don't forget, dinner is booked for seven-thirty. I'll be ready in my best suit so don't you lot come home drunk as skunks. I can't cope with an entire house filled with sozzled women! I'm a timid little thing really.'

They laughed. Polly blew him a kiss and tucked her arm into Dignity's. 'Come on – let's go open our new clinic. I feel on top of the world at the moment. I can't believe how lucky I am.'

'So you wouldn't swap your life then?' asked Dignity smirking.

'Are you kidding? No way!'

CHAPTER THIRTY-SEVEN
Mission Imp-ossible

Len was in the Gents toilets in a bar, struggling to get into his demon's outfit.

'Bloody hell, I think it's shrunk,' he grumbled.

'More likely you've been eating too many Key lime pies,' Nick scoffed.

'The crew did a good job finding this place. The people are very friendly… and gullible,' he added and chuckled. 'I like Florida.'

'Obviously,' retorted Nick, prodding his friend's belly.

'Ha ha! You're too funny some days. Could you just check my tail for me? Is it working?'

He fumbled with a switch hidden in a small pocket and the tail flicked up at the end.

'Yes, that should do it. That'll convince Ben Younger you're a real demon.'

'Is Ben en route, yet?'

'Yes, the producer called through to say he should be here in about ten minutes. That new bloke, Karl, is tailing him. They gave him a Harley-Davidson to ride. I think he's in love. He keeps asking if anyone wants to check out his big black hog. Reckon he'll be heartbroken when he has to part with it and return to the UK.'

'It's all good fun. I'm looking forward to this. Having done it before, it shouldn't be too difficult this time around. Ben sounds like he could do with a break. Hope we can convince him to swap his life. Fancy him losing his house and all his money in a game of poker. No wonder his wife wants to divorce him. Poor chap. I bet he won't need much persuading. Might not need all our technical wizardry and devices this time. Talking of which,' he continued, making his tail swish about some more and perfecting a demonic grin, 'there was something that puzzled me about the episode in the pub at Wroxley when we were attempting to convince Simon Green we were demons. How did you manage to turn your head three hundred and sixty degrees? That was really clever. You kept that device secret. The techies didn't even tell me about it. Scared the shit out me, I can tell you. It was like something out of *The Exorcist*. If you're going to do it this time, I want to be forewarned. Come on and spill the beans. It was a really clever trick. I thought about it afterwards and I can't fathom it out. It can't be magic or hocus-pocus after all; we're not real demons. Can't understand how you did it. It's impossible.'

Nick peered into the distance. A chuckle rose from the back of his throat, rising louder and louder until the room filled with the chorus of demonic laughter. A vermillion flicker lit his eyes for a brief moment. The temperature in the room dropped several degrees and in a voice Len didn't recognise he growled, 'You really don't want to understand how I did it, Len. Let's just say I'm devilishly good at the impossible.'

LETTER FROM CAROL

Dear everyone,

Thank you so much for reading *Life Swap*. I thoroughly enjoyed writing it and I hope it made you chuckle in quite a few places.

Like Simon Green, I love making people giggle and believe laughter is indeed a great medicine, although I draw the line at playing pranks on folk. I once was victim to one that ended up with me holding a large eyeball!

I try to practise what I preach and indeed do thorough research for my books. *Life Swap* took me abroad to try being a living statue in Gran Canaria (I was rubbish at it) and saw me hanging around car showrooms, chatting to salesmen – much to my husband's anxiety. He went hot under the collar every trip, worrying I would come away with a new motor.

I would like to say a heartfelt 'thank you' to everyone that has been involved in this project, especially my publisher Bookouture and my wonderful online family of bloggers, readers and friends. You are the reason I write and you keep me going on those long nights when I'm alone tapping away in my garret – you and many bags of chewy sweets.

If you enjoyed reading *Life Swap* please would you take a few minutes to write a review, no matter how short it is. I would really be most grateful. Your recommendations are most important.

To find out what I'm up to next and to get a good dose of daily humour why not sign up using the link below?

www.bookouture.com/carol-wyer

Join in the madness on Facebook or Twitter too and please get in touch with me. I love receiving emails and messages (and your jokes).

Warmest wishes,

Carol x

www.facebook.com/AuthorCarolEWyer
www.twitter.com/carolewyer

Lightning Source UK Ltd.
Milton Keynes UK
UKOW06f0146180516

274433UK00009B/188/P

'I think the show will be the biggest winner,' replied Grant, looking at the faces of the audience, contorted with laughter, as the sprites continued their comic dance routine. 'I reckon we've beaten *Can't Bake Anyway* in the ratings this time. Another success and hopefully another television award.' Dick high fived Grant and, with arms folded and smiles plastered on their faces, they watched the antics of the dance troupe.

CHAPTER THIRTY-THREE
Hell

The audience settled back to enjoy viewing Polly's week.

'Hello, my name is Sophie and I'll be playing Polly's new daughter, a troubled fifteen-year-old called Chelsea. This is Andrew. He's my boyfriend in this setup – Zed. The man waved at the camera. And these little chaps are Max and Claude, aka Dolce and Gabbana. They're trained by Christine Mondieu and will be playing Stephanie's cute little doggies. Over here, we have Calvin the trainer who isn't a personal trainer and is definitely not called Calvin. Calvin smiled at the camera.

'Hi. I'm Sebastian and you might have seen me as an extra in the BBC's production of *Poldark*. I was hidden behind several bales of hay so, if you missed me, not to worry. You can see me playing Hamlet at the Brighton Hippodrome next month. Tickets priced from £10. Oh! Naughty me. Shouldn't advertise.' He winked at the camera.

'Okay,' said Sophie. 'Action stations. The hidden cameras are set up and we've heard that Polly is on her way here to what she believes is Stephanie's house. It isn't though. It's one we prepared especially for this event and it's full of surprises. Enjoy!'

The camera panned to the chauffeur-driven car coming up the drive and showed Polly exiting then bowing her head and waving her hand like Her Royal Highness as the driver put her